Journeys of the Heart

Denise Dietz
Linda Colwell
Colleen Gleason
Sally Painter
Kelley Pounds

Avid Press, LLC   Brighton Michigan USA

Published by
Avid Press, LLC
5470 Red Fox Drive
Brighton MI 48114-9079 USA
http://www.avidpress.com
1-888-AVIDBKS

Journeys of the Heart
ISBN 1-929613-92-X

Dear Reader:

Journeys of the Heart was a special project for Avid Press. We took four of our most popular authors—and a fifth new one—and asked them each to write a novella that would preview their next book from Avid Press....and then we put them together to create an anthology of adventurous love stories.

Each story features a map that is instrumental to the plot—hence the title *Journeys of the Heart*—and each story acts as a prelude to a full=length novel that will be released by Avid Press in the next six months.

We hope you enjoy the stories included here, and notice the wide range of talents and imagination brought to you by Avid Press.

Check the back of the book for information about how to win a $100 Gift Certificate to your favorite bookstore!

Enjoy...and welcome to Avid Press.

Warmest regards,
Kate Gleason
Editor
Avid Press, LLC

Dream Angel

by Denise Dietz

ONE

Paris, 1850

"The lady's about to fall, Mum," gasped the little girl, her pigtails swaying, her chin tilted like the prow of a miniature ship—assuming the ship crested a wave.

Without looking up, Hortense Downing-Cox Kelley said, "That's part of her performance, Charlotte. She *pretends* she's about to fall. It's all right to pretend."

Hortense heaved a deep sigh, then slanted an angry glance toward her stepson, Sean. He was the reason why she and her five-year-old daughter Charlotte were stuffed like sausages into this small compartment, this ridiculous red box, surrounded by other spectators, all of whom were shouting and applauding—in French! He was the reason why every time she took a breath, she smelled sawdust and horse manure. He was the reason why she spent the afternoon at a circus when any sensible woman would be sipping tea in the comfort of her own parlour.

But then any *sensible* woman wouldn't have married Timothy Kelley.

Hortense had succumbed to Tim's devilish charms, enhanced by the Irish brogue—and to be honest, the Irish tongue—that tickled her ears. Twenty-nine years old and plain as a pudding, she had ignored every warning issued by her proper British parents; had even ignored their threat to disinherit her.

Prudently, she hadn't told Tim about her parents' caveat.

Which, as it turned out, had been her biggest mistake. When her new husband discovered the truth, he had carted her across the sea to an obscure French relative who owned a café and always smelled of onions. Tim had the good grace to wait for the birth of his daughter before he'd set sail for America, but that had been five years ago and Hortense had not heard from him since. Furthermore, if she had tricked him into marrying her, his duplicity was far more profound. For he had neglected to tell her that he'd buried the first Mrs. Timothy Kelley in Ireland, and that the issue from his previous marriage, a twenty-year-old son named Sean, lived above the onion-woman's café.

Sean had been cordial enough during their introduction, but Hortense had been astute enough to read the unspoken words he'd directed toward Tim: *Did ye wed yourself an elderly lass with an inheritance, Da?*

Of course he had, or thought he had. A pity Hortense had been too busy vomiting in the loo—or whatever the blasted French called it—to hear Tim's reply. Carrying a child was a bloody nuisance. Truth be told, Sean had been of more assistance than Tim. As Hortense's belly expanded into an unbelievable girth, reminiscent of an elephant, it was Sean who finished her chores, helped her rise from chairs, and fetched the midwife when her labour pains began.

As far as Hortense could tell, the only advantage to birthing a child was that one's figure tended to change. Before Charlotte, she had been thin and angular. Now her breasts were globes, her hips bounteous. Even her hair could be considered more mahogany than brown. A pity Tim hadn't stayed long enough to savor his wife's new, enticingly abundant body.

Sean hadn't left with his father, and Hortense knew why. The lad, now twenty-six, had an Irishman's fondness for children. He adored Charlotte, and while one half of Hortense deplored what she considered a lamentable, if not downright disgraceful weakness in a man, the other half was eternally grateful. In Hortense's opinion, a baby was just as bothersome as a damnfool pregnancy. Especially since Charlotte was a sickly child with none of Tim's robust qualities.

Nor Sean's, for that matter.

Which was the fly in the bloody ointment, Hortense reminded herself daily. Sean looked too much like Tim. The same thick ebony hair, the same merry green eyes, the same broad shoulders, narrow waist, and muscular legs. And if that wasn't enough, her stepson possessed his father's charm. Hortense has seen young ladies pretend to swoon so that Sean could catch them. Not necessarily *fille de joie,* either. Well-bred girls swooned.

If honest, and Hortense was always honest with herself, she had seriously considered the same ploy. Yet she feared rejection. Not because she was Tim's wife and older than Sean, but because she knew full well that he wanted to woo an heiress. To that end, Hortense had re-established contact with her parents. It had taken five years, but the Downing-Cox's desire to see their only grandchild had helped a great deal. Finally, Hortense swallowed her pride, begged for mercy, vowed she'd never stray from the fold again, and was anxiously awaiting a reply.

She fibbed, of course. About straying. Despite Sean's many attributes, he possessed one fatal flaw. He could be bought.

"Look, Mum! Look, Sean!"

Charlotte's strident voice pierced Hortense's haze, and she allowed her gaze to follow her daughter's plump finger, gesturing toward the building's apogee.

The chit atop the rope was taking dainty, tentative steps, as if she wanted to tease the prudent people who were safely rooted below. She didn't use a balancing pole, nor even an umbrella. And what on earth was she wearing? Hortense darted a quick glance toward Sean. His mouth had become unhinged, his attention riveted on the rope. No. His entire focus was on the piece of baggage who'd just finished performing a series of dazzling back-flip somersaults.

Hortense's heart sank to the bottom of her shoes. The

young girl who now *danced* across the rope was certainly no
heiress, yet Sean's expression clearly revealed that he didn't
give a fig. Hortense's corset felt too tight. The candied apple
she'd eaten earlier rose in her throat, whole.

Even while she lost what remained of her breath, her mind
raced. She wanted Sean to play the part of her devoted companion. An obstacle to that scheme danced above her head.
Surely there was some clever way to get rid of that damned
ropewalker—that damned Petit Ange.

Along with the rest of the audience, Sean was clapping and
yelling. "*C'est magnifique! C'est la plus bell—*"

"Ohhhh." The world whirled and the applause dimmed.
Shutting her eyes, Hortense keeled over.

Sean Kelley wondered if his stepmother's convenient faint
yesterday had been a ruse to leave the Nouveau Cirque.
Reluctantly, he'd carried her out, Charlotte walking in his
shadow. Once they'd reached their hired carriage and drawn
its curtains, he had loosened Hortense's corset stays, where-
upon her eyes had fluttered open, and God knows what
might have happened had Charlotte not been present.

Sean had no illusions. He had no guilt, either. He wasn't
related by blood to Hortense, and his father had spent the
last five years in America. Furthermore, he suspected
Hortense was about to regain her inheritance, and he had no
qualms about playing the part of her amorist.

At least, not until he'd seen Petit Ange.

His first glimpse of the "Small Angel"—whom he now
though of as *his* small angel—had not been during her performance. On the rope, she'd been too high up for anyone
to appreciate her flashing gray-green eyes; too high up for
anyone to admire the pure golden hair that framed her
blush-stained cheeks. Her lower limbs and hips, although
they seemed in perfect proportion, were really small for her
robustly developed breasts and shoulders.

She was, in a word, perfection. And it was this perfection

that had brought him back to the Cirque, despite Hortense's wrath, despite the fact that today's post had included a generous draft from her father.

Upon cashing the draft, her anger had swiftly become a list of promises. Sean could have a dozen new suits, a new horse, a townhouse in London.

Except that wasn't his dream. No one knew his dream. He wanted to own a traveling circus, the finest in the world. He wanted to work for P.T. Barnum's Museum in New York City, America. Someday, when Sean had learned all he could about showmanship, he wanted to establish The Sean Kelley Circus.

And he wanted Petite Ange for his circus.

In truth, he wanted Petit Ange for his wife.

The Nouveau Cirque was housed in an octagonal building, with seats facing three sides of a single ring. Along the ringbank were plush red boxes. Behind the boxes were arena seats, then a gallery that extended to the roof. There was no menagerie or Congress of Freaks, but the audience could descend to the basement and inspect the horses. A forty-piece string and woodwind orchestra occupied a platform above the performers' entrance. The Cirque changed its bill monthly, holding over the most popular acts, and regardless of this afternoon's enthusiastic applause, Angelique Aumont feared she might not be held over.

"You silly peagoose." London-born Gartrude Starling, the Cirque's pretty trapeze artist, gave Angelique the budge. "Even if your rope act wasn't spot-on, half the fellows would pay dear for your maidenhead."

Since Angelique usually thought in French, it took her a moment to translate Gartrude's remarks. Then, cheeks ablaze, she reached out to caress a dray horse's velvet muzzle.

"That cannot be true," she replied in her heavily accented English.

"Wot cannot be true? That they'd pay, dear, or that you

have a maidenhead?"

"Do hush, Gartrude, *s'il vous plait.*"

"God-a-mercy, Petit Ange, my brother Tom says he'd marry you!"

"*Mon Dieu*, I shall never wed a *cirque* performer," she exclaimed, then smiled to take the sting out of her words.

As if summoned, Tom Starling appeared, and the only English word Angelique could summon up was "dolt."

At twenty-three, five years older than Angelique, Tom was a tall, blunt-faced man. He wanted to wed her in order to bed her, but Angelique knew that marriage was out of the question. Her parents had died within two weeks of each other, Papa first. On her deathbed, Maman had confessed that she had a sister, to whom she'd written a letter. The sisters had been close once, and Maman had no reason to believe that Bernadine wouldn't welcome Angelique with open arms. The *dilemme* was that those open arms would have to extend across an ocean, for Tante Bernadine lived in Connecticut, America.

"Petit Ange," Tom cried. "*C'est magnifique! C'est un triomphe!*"

"She twigs English, you great booby," Gartrude said dryly.

"*Merci,* Tom." Angelique smiled again. "However, I was just—how you say?—deliberating a new act, something more daring. Perhaps even…" she paused, trying to keep the excitement from her voice "…the forward somersault."

"No girl can do the forward," Tom said. "It's impossible."

"God-a-mercy, no *man* can do a forward somersault on the rope. And what could be more daring than your costume?" Gartrude wrinkled her nose. "If there wasn't beads sewed at your bosom and between your legs, gillys would think you was in the nuddy."

"Mon *doo*, who cares what *they* think?" Tom waved his arms expansively.

A third smile tugged at the corners of Angelique's lips. The flesh-coloured tights and leotard, beaded for propriety's sake, had been an inspiration. She'd heard the indignant, astonished, and admiring gasps from the audience, and a few gallery faces were beginning to look very, very familiar. From her rope, she couldn't see the ringbox gillys, but...

Speaking of familiar faces, the young man from yesterday was here, visiting the horses again. Only this time he had waited until *after* her performance.

Angelique knew that her parents had fallen deeply, irrevocably in love during their first meeting. Papa's traveling *cirque* had been performing in England. Maman's papa, a prosperous shopkeeper, had been occupied when Papa entered the shop, so Papa asked Maman for some white satin braces, embroidered with forget-me-nots. Maman melted at Papa's smile, but she didn't understand French and became confused, until an elderly gent said: "Galluses, Miss, the things to hold your breeks up by." The second time Maman and Papa met, Papa had learned English, Maman French. Almost immediately, Maman accepted Papa's bouquet of forget-me-nots and his marriage proposal.

Maman's parents had disapproved; had, if fact, locked Maman in her small attic bedroom until Papa's *cirque* left London. However, Maman then made what she called "a journey of the heart." With only one gown, one pair of shoes, one pair of gloves, and one bonnet, she had followed Papa to Paris.

Angelique had never quite believed the romantic tale. Now she did. Briefly, she stood, unmoving. Then, as if pulled by a puppeteer, she gravitated toward the dark-haired stranger.

In his green eyes was a kind of lazy amusement, which made Angelique feel speechless and a little angry. For how was she to impress him if she couldn't think of anything to say? In fact, she had a peculiar sense of inadequacy, a fear that whatever she said or did would seem foolish to him.

His absorbing gaze seemed to undress her, as he stared at the blue silk robe that concealed her costume. In truth, she could almost swear that his eyes were *discarding* her costume.

Angelique found herself studying the face around those

eyes, noting his expressive brows, bold nose, compelling mouth, and deeply cleft chin. Handsome but not handsome, she thought illogically, wondering how he would look with a mustache and beard. He possessed a pirate's arrogance, and she imagined him bare-chested, wielding a cutlass, lithe as a panther.

And probably just as dangerous!

"Do ye comprehend English?" he asked.

His voice was as mesmerizing as his eyes, and she felt a shudder build at the base of her spine.

"I guess you do not, mademoiselle," he said. "So perhaps you won't take offense when I say you're the prettiest lass I've seen in the divil's own time, and I've got a mind to lay with you."

Angelique's bones turned to water, and she cursed herself for her tongue-tied inertia. She usually had a pert remark for any man, no matter what his age, and this young man deserved nothing less than a slap across his smug face.

"I would imagine ye did not sleep well last night," he continued, his voice a croon. "Nor did I. To tell the God's honest truth, I did not sleep at all. But I've a perfect cure for that, mademoiselle. A carriage awaits my return, and the parson lives but a short ride away."

Parson? Still dazed, Angelique allowed him to lead her outside the building.

He halted, gently caressed her face, then smoothed the wind-tousled hair away from her forehead. "Sean Kelley is me given name, lass."

She finally found her voice. "I am Angelique Marie Danielle Aumont, Monsieur, and you are a rude, insufferable—"

"Connoisseur of beauty," he finished, in perfect French.

They stood there, staring at each other, and Angelique understood that he had been teasing her all along. She didn't know if she should slap him, sputter indignantly, or laugh, so she followed her only other impulse and swayed toward him, her eyes shut. His hands closed about her waist, drawing her closer, and she felt his powerful leg muscles. Without conscious thought, her mouth parted to receive his kiss.

It was several moments before he released her, but when he finally did, it seemed too soon and she felt cheated. Opening her eyes, she saw that he was gazing at her tenderly.

"Ye must go back now, me precious darlin'," he said. "Your family would be troubled to have ye disappear with no word of warning. And I would not be troublin' your family, for I might have need of their blessing."

Impulsive words sprang to her lips. *I have no family. I do not care if I never return to the Nouveau Cirque. I do not care about the forward somersault. I do not care about anything except you.*

Instead, she said, "Blessing? Do you intend to wed me, Monsieur?"

"Aye, lass." He thunked his forehead with the heel of his hand. "'Tis a swell-headed mooncalf I am, niver bidding your consent. We shall talk more tomorrow, if that pleases ye."

Talk more? His Irish-green eyes had done most of the talking.

"Does that please ye?" he pressed.

She nodded, thinking about her maman and papa.

As he walked away, she could still smell the masculine sweat on his clothes and the scent of leather from his boots, and she felt both dizzy and lonely.

He halted and made an about-face. With a glance that took her in from head to foot, Monsieur Kelley smiled. His thumbs snapped the galluses that held his breeks up, and Angelique fell deeply, irrevocably in love.

Hortense knew exactly what she must do. Her faint two days ago had been far more beneficial than a mere loss of consciousness, for upon awakening her mind had been crystal clear and her scheme had been conceived as quickly and easily as Charlotte.

Impatiently, she served the cafe's customers. Soon, very soon, she needn't perform the hateful chores that secured her lodgings above the cafe ... if one could call them lodgings. The room she shared with Charlotte boasted a feather mattress, a chiffonier, a wooden tub, and a tiny parlour. Hortense yearned for the spacious interior of her parents' home, where she wouldn't have to elbow her daughter or the onion woman or Sean every time she walked down the hallway toward the loo.

Her usual mode of transportation, a carriage, would have been more comfortable, but a hackney was more prudent. Dressed in a severe black gown, a heavy black veil fell from the top of her head to the tips of her toes. Now all she had to do was enter the bloody building and find Petit Ange.

This morning, while preparing the cafe's daily fare, Sean had told a delighted Charlotte all about his propitious meeting with the Cirque's *danseur de corde,* but Hortense had no way of knowing if his puffery had been truth or fantasy..

The orchestra had been playing a song called *Susannah* by American composer Stephen Foster, Sean had said, and forever more that would be his favourite ballad. Petit Ange, whose real name was Angelique Aumont, had been in the basement with the horses. Surrounded by a mob of admirers, all of whom toted bouquets of flowers and boxes of candy, she'd left her suitors to stroll with Sean.

"Did she swoon and did you catch her?" Charlotte had asked perceptively.

"No one can catch a falling star," he had replied. "But sometimes, if you're very good, ye can capture a dream."

In Hortense's opinion, Sean was neither good nor virtuous, but perhaps God did not consider Sean's weaknesses imperfections. After all, God was a man.

The smell hit Hortense as soon as she spied her first horse. Withdrawing a handkerchief from her beaded reticule, she pressed the small square of linen against the piece of veil that hid her long, sharp nose. In doing so, she dropped her reticule.

"You've lost your *porte-monaie,* Madame."

The voice was young, musical, heavily accented. The hand that held out the reticule looked young and strong, with fingernails buffed to a soft sheen. Hortense felt resentment build anew. After years of washing and chopping vegetables, her own hands had become rough and chapped, her nails ragged.

Snatching the reticule, she silently thanked God for gloves.

"Are you in mourning, Madame?"

"What? Oh. Yes. My … father recently expired." Hortense directed her handkerchief toward her eyes. Meanwhile, she gave what she hoped was a convincing sniffle. "But one must take the good with the bad, mademoiselle, for I inherited a small fortune."

"I have suffered a recent loss as well, Madame. My papa never earned a fortune, but he died happy."

"How did he die?"

"He fell from a rope," the girl replied. "Maman followed him."

"Your mum fell from a rope, too?"

"No, Madame. She died of a broken heart. You see, she was part Irish, and the Irish can only love once."

Totally nonplused, Hortense stared into the girl's gray-green eyes, now shiny with unshed tears.

"You are Angelique Aumont, are you not?" Hortense finally managed.

"*Oui,* Madame. And you are…?"

"Hortense Downing-Cox Kelley," she said, then took a deep breath. "My husband told our daughter all about how he met you yesterday, after your performance. He sang your praises, mademoiselle."

"Your husband? Your daughter?"

"My husband, Sean. Our daughter, Charlotte, is five years old. We saw your rope act the day before yesterday, and I have to admit my husband was smitten, one might even say thoroughly infatuated."

With satisfaction, Hortense saw the tart's face turn white

as a ghost. Even though it hurt her pride, Hortense continued with the words she had rehearsed inside her parlour. "Only last month my husband became infatuated with a young girl who appeared in a production of Mr. William Shakespeare's *A Midsummer Night's Dream*. Sean has a … fondness … for performers. I myself once considered the stage, but a well-bred lady…" She shrugged.

Had she gone too far? The chit's eyes were now more green than gray, jade rather than slate.

"As a *well-bred* Englishwoman, Madame, I am astonished that you endure your husband's indiscretions."

"I remain loyal to my husband, mademoiselle, because deep down, he loves me. As you say, the Irish only love once."

Hortense felt her heart pound. She knew that beneath her veil, her face was red and splotchy. Mentally reaching into her bag of tricks, she withdrew her last weapon. "Sean will never leave me, mademoiselle, for I am once again with child. We hope and pray that this time I shall birth a healthy son."

"A healthy son," the girl echoed.

Hortense nodded and patted her belly. The onion woman's food, not pregnancy, had caused its roundness, for she and Sean had never slept together. Momentarily, she felt shame at her fib. Then she remembered what she had told Charlotte: *It's all right to pretend.*

"Perhaps you should sit down, Madame. I did not know he was married, I swear! You look unwell. Please sit down. There is a bench—"

"No. No, thank you." Hortense did indeed feel shaky as relief washed over her. Still, she had one more piece of business to negotiate. At five feet, five inches tall, she topped Petit Ange by a good two inches. And although she desired nothing more than to sit, once seated she'd be at a disadvantage. "Sean will return to you, mademoiselle. He will tell you lies, just as he did with his actress. He will say he is not married. He might even swear that Charlotte is not his daughter." Yanking off her left glove, Hortense flaunted her wedding band. "Charlotte is a Kelley, and so am I, and may God strike me dead if that isn't the truth."

"Madame, you are upsetting yourself for nothing. I will not see your husband again, I promise."

"I appreciate your sincerity, Angelique, but unfortunately that's one promise you'll never be able to keep. So here's what I propose." Hortense reached inside her reticule. "I'll give you a share of my inheritance, more than enough to settle someplace far away from your Nouveau Cirque. You could find yourself a husband, or set sail for America, where, I've heard, the streets are paved with gold."

"Truly, that is not necessary. Only today I received a letter from my Tante Ber—"

"No, please, I insist. Perhaps you might leave right away, tonight. Should my husband discover that I have paid you this visit, he'll beat me. He has a violent temper and I could lose my baby." Shamed anew by the monstrosity of her lies, Hortense saw a tall, toad-faced man race toward them.

"Petit Ange!" he shouted. "Here you are! Everyone is celebrating Gartrude's birthday. There's cake and *vin rouge* and—"

"A moment, Tom. I am conducting an important business transaction."

"Thank you." Hortense realized that her face was not only red and splotchy, but slippery with perspiration. If she really was with child, she had no doubt she'd miscarry. "*Merci,* Angelique."

"*Bonne chance,* Madame Kelley."

"Good luck to you, too."

Sometimes luck had nothing to do with anything, Hortense thought. Neither, for that matter, did good behaviour. Catching a dream was easy. Holding onto it required assiduity, duplicity, pretense and sweat.

Charlotte possessed a lisp that would probably be consid-

ered an asset one day. For now, it made her words too large
for her tongue, and more often than not her attempts to
converse—especially in French—were misunderstood.

Desperate, she switched to English. "Sean, you must listen.
Mum made Petit Ange leave the Cirque. I do not know what
Mum toldher, but I do know that she gave Petit Ange some
of Grandfather's money. Mum showed me the leftover ban-
knotes, bundled inside her beaded reticule."

Sean hunkered down and stared into the child's owl-round
eyes. "I understand what you're sayin', little darlin'. What I
cannot understand is why Petit Ange would accept a bribe
… would accept your mum's money."

"I do not think it was the money, Sean, but what Mum
told Petit Ange."

"And why do ye tell *me* all this, knowin' I shall be leavin'
ye? For I could niver stay after hearin' 'bout your mum's fid-
dle-tinkerin'."

"You'll leave anyway, once we return to England,"
Charlotte mumbled, "and you must find Mademoiselle
Cinderella."

Heartsick, his hopes for the future dashed, Sean still managed to give his stepsister a lopsided grin. "And when I find
Mademoiselle Cinderella, what must I do?"

"You must kiss her awake."

"'Tis the Sleeping Beauty who was kissed awake."

"*Oui*, but Mum … benumbed Petit Ange."

"Where did you learn that word, sweetheart? Benumbed."

"From Mum. She looked and sounded like a crow, all brag-
gy."

"And did your mum happen to mention where Petit Ange
would be goin'?"

"She said something about America," Charlotte lisped.

Sean could feel his face settle into new lines of despair.
"'Tis a podgy place, America."

"As big as London?" Charlotte's eyes grew even rounder.
"Mum says London is bigger than Montparnasse, and
Montparnasse is lolloping big."

"I've niver visited London, darlin', but I've heard America is a wee bit bigger."

"Perhaps that is why my papa is lost."

"Perhaps." Sean tried to keep the anger from his voice. "If I should happen to trip over Timothy Kelley, do ye want me to kiss him awake too?"

Charlotte giggled. "In the fairy tales you have read to me, no man kisses another man awake. And I do not believe my papa is asleep … just lost. Please, Sean, you must promise to look for Petit Ange and kiss her awake."

"I promise to try."

"You said if you are very good, you can capture a dream."

"Then I shall try and be very good. But first, I must find the means to reach America. It takes money and … why do ye stare at me like that? Have ye another secret?"

"*Mais oui.* I have been naughty."

"You? Naughty?"

"I have been very naughty." She sighed. "Close your eyes."

Perhaps *he* should be kissed awake, Sean thought, as he suddenly realized that his stepsister's hands had been behind her back ever since they'd begun their conversation.

"Do you have a going-away present for me, sweetheart?" he asked, squinting through his dark scrim of lashes and wondering if she planned to present him with her favourite toy, a floppy-eared rabbit she'd named Fromage.

"Yes," she replied. "My gift is heavy, for it is filled with America."

Withdrawing her hands from behind her back, Charlotte thrust forth her mother's beaded reticule.

TWO

Thanks to Hortense, Sean Kelley knew more about Tom Thumb than he did his own father. Timothy Kelley had blown in and out of Sean's life like a black squall while Tom Thumb remained a constant source of discussion.

General Tom Thumb stood less than two feet tall, weighed fifteen pounds, and had visited England in 1844. Tom's popularity had been so extensive that his likeness was reproduced on plates, mugs, and fans. Tom Thumb dolls were sold in the shops, a song was composed in his honour, and there was even a children's dance called the Tom Thumb Polka.

The American Dwarf had been accompanied by his guardian, P.T. Barnum.

Over the years, Sean had only half listened to Hortense's excited chatter about how she'd seen Tom Thumb sing, dance, recite poetry, and perform his clever impression of Napoleon Bonaparte. Sean had no doubts about that; after all, Barnum had exhibited his star attraction in a public hall. But when Hortense lapsed into tales about Tom Thumb's visits to Queen Victoria at Buckingham Palace, Sean stopped up his ears. Hortense could not have been in attendance when the Queen's pet poodle charged Tom and the boy brandished a tiny cane and began fencing with the dog. Yet Hortense made it sound as if she'd been among the Queen's guests, and her frequent brags would have made Timothy Kelley—a windbag of the highest order—flush a vivid crimson.

Finally, one fact penetrated Sean's fog-drenched brain. During his London visit, P.T. Barnum had earned a bloody fortune. Tom Thumb's appearances at Buckingham Palace had been rewarded with expensive gifts and gold coins. His public performances brought in hundreds of dollars a day, and Barnum had collected the proceeds from the Tom Thumb booklets and souvenirs that sold by the thousands.

Furthermore, Barnum didn't even have to perform!

Not that Sean was against performing. While attending the Nouveau Cirque, he had recognized his own dormant desire to strut before an audience, the focus of everyone's attention, a manipulator of emotions … not unlike Napoleon.

And wasn't Napoleon's campaign merely one hell of an immense circus?

Still, in Sean's admittedly biased opinion, Barnum had bested Napoleon. Why commission armies and structure expensive wars when you could hire the talent that would eventually stud your life with legendary superlatives? In years to come, the public would no doubt remember Tom Thumb, but they'd also speak—with awe and admiration— about the man who had turned a child with a defective growth gland into a vast, universal luminary.

The object of Sean's musings came into view. P.T. was clothed in black. The hair that framed his balding forehead was in its usual disarray, but the deep nose-to-mouth lines that dominated his bulldog-like face revealed a smug smile.

"She agreed to the tour," Sean guessed, greeting his bene-factor.

"She did, indeed." Barnum darted a glance toward one of his most popular attractions, The Happy Family, a large cage filled with animals considered natural enemies—cats and dogs, owls and mice, hawks and sparrows—all living togeth-er in harmony. "But the girl drives a hard bargain, lad. Aside from her fee, one hundred and fifty thousand dollars, *payable in advance,* I'll be responsible for the salaries of two servants, her musical director, and a male singer to accompany her in duets. Needless to say, I agreed to pay all travel and hotel expenses for the entire entourage."

"Ye take a huge gamble, sir, bringing Jenny Lind to America. She's a serious concert singer, not a music hall singer, and there's no evidence that she'll appeal to a widespread populace."

"When I want your opinion, I'll ask for it!" Almost immediately, Barnum's face relaxed into a second wreath of a smile. "We must whet the public's appetite, lad, and I would guess you have some tricks up your sleeve."

"Yes, sir. I've been thinkin' ye could use the average punter's adherence to religion and morality since the lass herself regards her voice as a gift from God."

"Splendid!"

Encouraged, Sean continued. "I've also been thinkin' we could auction the very first ticket."

Barnum's brow furrowed. "Please explain that scheme."

"First, ye must convince your chums that high bids will be good for their own businesses. Then we inform the press."

Barnum snapped his fingers. "If my friend John makes the outstanding bid, he'll sell more hats."

"'Tis that very notion I had in mind," Sean replied, relieved that his benefactor required no further explanation. "I needn't state the obvious. Dishes, fans, flasks, trivets, and—"

"Figurines. Yes. Before I forget, Charie told me to invite you to a small dinner party. You've quite won her over, lad. My daughters, as well."

Sean had a great deal of respect and admiration for Charity Barnum. Despite her stern appearance, she possessed a lively sense of humour and always had a witty backchat, no matter how transparent, or insensible, the tease. Furthermore, she'd taught him how to speak like a gentleman, even though his blasted tongue frequently betrayed him by revealing his provinciality. If he could only find a woman like Charity Barnum, Sean often thought, he'd gladly relinquish his bachelor status.

He heard the echo of little Charlotte's voice: *Please, Sean, you must promise to find Petit Ange and kiss her awake.*

Upon reaching the shores of America, Sean had settled in Brooklyn, across the East River from New York, then initiated a search for the beautiful, albeit elusive, ropewalker. Months later, after listening to Sean's effusive praise, Barnum had renewed the search, vowing he'd hire a "live angel who walked on air" for one of his many exhibits. However, it soon became apparent that the lovely, golden-haired *danseur de corde* had no desire to walk an American rope, much less be kissed awake by a spectre from her past.

Angelique Aumont issued forth a deep sigh, then a second sigh.

She might as well get her wiffles over with now. Soon her corset strings would be knotted so tightly any huffs and puffs would be impossible, or—at best—painful.

Seated directly in front of her bedroom dressing table, she darted a glance toward the gown her Tante Bernadine had selected for tonight's dinner party. Several unladylike ruminations filtered through Angelique's brain, most having to do with a cow's defecation, but the word she chose to murmur was: "Drab."

"Wot did you say?"

"I said my gown is drab!"

Angelique stared up at her friend—and maidservant. Tante Bernadine had sent Angelique the funds for her journey to America while Madame Kelley's generosity had paid Gartrude Starling's way. Wanting to get the "lay-a-the-land" before she sought out a "Yankee circus," Gartrude had joined Tante Bernadine's large staff of minions.

"Dull, dreary, colourless," Angelique added, almost spitting.

"But the black'll make your hair shine more yella'."

Instantly contrite, Angelique jumped to her feet. "*Merci*, Gartrude. Tante Bernadine says no one should have hair the colour of mine. Of course, my mouth, my eyes, and my chin also displease her. Too bold, I suppose."

"You cannot alter what God has provided," Gartrude replied pragmatically.

"True. But I can alter that hideous gown."

Thirty minutes later, a froth of lace—pinched from one of Angelique's many petticoats—decorated a bodice that was now décolleté. Long fitted sleeves had given way to puff sleeves, and artificial flowers enhanced the twenty-inch waistline.

Angelique's busy fingers flew across the black material, stitching row upon row of pleated ruffles. Once flounced, the gown was no longer ground-length, so a pink taffeta crinoline peeked from below the modified hemline.

"God-a-mercy!" Gartrude exclaimed. "Your auntie will put on a tantrum when she sees wot you've done."

"Unfortunately, Tante Bernadine suffers from a gastric disorder and cannot attend Charity Barnum's dinner party."

Gartrude nodded. "We heard she'd overeaten herself and suffers from the belches."

Angelique giggled, aware that her aunt's recurrent bouts of indigestion were a constant source of amusement for the servants and frequently led to forbidden festivities. She was also aware that Gartrude usually played ringleader when those … ventures … were sampled, swallowed, and rued the next morning.

Truth be told, Angelique suddenly felt festive—the very same feeling she experienced when she saw a loose balloon skim the rooftops and float toward the sun. She only hoped that tomorrow morning she wouldn't rue tonight.

Escorted by her uncle—an astute businessman who was nevertheless overwhelmed by his acerbic wife and her seven cats—Angelique entered P.T. Barnum's ornate mansion.

Like almost everything Barnum did, his mansion had been designed to attract attention. Called Iranistan, or "Oriental

Village," it looked like a sultan's palace, executed in rust-coloured sandstone, capped with domes and spires, adorned with intricately carved arches that framed the broad piazzas on each of its three floors.

Two of Barnum's daughters, Helen and Caroline, greeted Angelique with air-kisses that narrowly missed her cheeks.

Following the girls, Angelique ascended a carved walnut staircase, leading to a huge central dome at the very top of the mansion. The sitting room boasted a circular divan that could accommodate forty-five people. Diamond-shaped windows were set with panes of coloured glass, casting an unusual glow, turning the room into an implicit fairyland.

Charity Barnum approached. Her warm welcome could have been uttered in Greek or Hindi, yet somehow Angelique managed to stammer an acknowledgment as she stared at the man who stood beneath a window. The pane cast a reddish hue, but the sun had already begun its descent, so the flickering colour merely tinted his thick ebony hair.

Deciphering her guest's avid gaze, Charity laughed and said, "Would you like an introduction, my dear?"

"*Mais oui,*" Angelique replied, her head bobbing like a child's teeter-totter. At the same time, a portion of her brain sternly told her heart to stop swinging like a pendulum.

She maneuvered the room carefully, as if she trod a lofty rope, but her mind raced. Would Monsieur Kelley call her Petit Ange and reveal the circus background Tante Bernadine had tried so hard to hide? Would Monsieur Kelley even recognize the Nouveau Cirque girl he'd wooed so briefly? Angelique's lips tingled with the memory of his kiss.

Charity accomplished the introduction, but again Angelique didn't hear one word through the cloud of imaginary bees that seemed to buzz 'round her gilt curls.

Instead, she focused on Monsieur Kelley's ice-green eyes. Until his eyes were hidden by his bow, which, in her opinion, was nothing more than a mock nod. And yet perhaps his arrogance was merely indifference. Perhaps he did not recognize Petit Ange after all, for he raised her glove-clad hand to his lips, kissed her cotton knuckles, then murmured, "'Tis a pleasure to make your acquaintance, Mrs. Aumont."

"*Miss* Aumont." Charity smiled wickedly and gave Monsieur Kelley a wink, just before she excused herself to welcome six new guests.

Angelique stifled a gasp. Charity had obviously cast herself in the role of ... what was the English word? Matchmaker. Did Charity not know that this blasted snake in the grass— this man who looked so *bon* in black trousers, starched shirt and gray vest—was already married? Perhaps "snake in the bosom" would be a more appropriate designation, considering how his gaze devoured the mounds of her breasts, rising above the froth of lace at her bodice.

"Our host has spared no expense on his home," Monsieur Kelley stated, his voice low. "Marble fireplaces, gilded ceilings, elaborately carved doors, and all sorts of superfluous paraphernalia."

Angelique blinked, surprised by his choice of subject. "Do you envy Monsieur Barnum his possessions, Monsieur Kelley?"

"Not at all. But I do envy him his business acumen. While he was in France...."

Monsieur Kelley paused, as if waiting for her reaction to the word "France." Angelique kept her face expressionless.

"While he was in Paris, the estate of a Russian prince was auctioned off. There were many valuable pieces, including silver flatware, a gold tea set, and some rare china. The items could have commanded enormous bids, but their value had been diminished by the fact that they bore the prince's monogram and coat of arms."

Angelique stifled a second gasp. Bloody oath, she and Monsieur Kelly could have been situated in Eden, rather than Fairfield, Connecticut. Lulled by the snake's deceptively hushed tone, she suddenly realized that his hand cradled her elbow. *Snakes have no hands,* she thought incoherently.

And yet this reptilian rascal was expertly guiding her toward the walnut staircase.

His fingers were as gentle as she remembered, and the gesture felt familiar, even after all this time. She wanted to pull away, express indignation at his assumption that she'd yield to his grasp, but curiosity overwhelmed her. He hadn't finished his anecdote, and she suspected that he was leading up to something profound ... something personal. She would not, could not, admit that she enjoyed his warm palm against her elbow, his fingers lightly, almost negligibly, stroking her arm. Truth be told, she could no more sever Monsieur Kelley's silky, webbed filaments than a bee could sever the complex filaments of a spider's web. Hopefully, once she found her voice again, she'd be able to *sting* her way free.

"Barnum bought the prince's entire lot," Monsieur Kelley continued, leading her out onto the third floor piazza. "The prince's initials were P.T., so Barnum had an engraver add a final B."

"What about the coat of arms?"

"It could have been created with P.T. Barnum in mind, for the motto on the escutcheon read: 'Love God and Be Merry.'"

"Is that your motto as well, Monsieur Kelley?"

"Yes. But I have not been very merry."

"Why?"

"Because a ropewalker, whom I loved with all my heart, did a moonlight flit."

"Equilibrist."

"I beg your pardon?"

"Equilibrist, not ropewalker."

"What, may I ask, is the bloody difference?"

"A ropewalker walks. An equilibrist performs." Raising her chin, Angelique asked the question that had burned her tongue ever since Charity Barnum's introduction. "Could you not love God and make merry with your wife?"

"Ah," Monsieur Kelley replied.

"Do you mean 'ah, the equilibrist discovered my secret' or 'ah, 'tis the reason she did a moonlight flit'?"

Her venture into idiomatic English caused Monsieur Kelley to issue forth a burst of laughter that could surely be heard by the couples below, circling Monsieur Barnum's opulent fountain. "Hush!" Angelique stamped her foot. "Why do you chortle like a peagoose?"

"I have niver heard of your peagoose, darlin', but I would imagine it honks. A peafowl is an ornamental pheasant, the peahen is the female peafowl, and the peacock has a greatly elongated tail that can be erected and spread at will. I am fairly certain they niver chortle. 'Tis the hyena that chortles."

Angelique tried to maintain her composure. She had, of course, learned the word peagoose from Gartrude, and now she felt like one. "Why does my misery incite a chorus of chortles, Monsieur Hyena?" she asked indignantly.

"'Tis happy I am that you're miserable, Mademoiselle Peahen."

"Oh … oh!" Enraged, she turned to leave the piazza, but he gently grasped her shoulders and pulled her against the length of his body. She could not see his face, yet she felt his tense thigh muscles and wondered how that was possible. Wouldn't her multiple petticoats ensure an impenetrable obstacle?

"I have been disconsolate, too, Angelique," he murmured over her shoulder, into her ear, "niver knowin' how me stepmother accomplished her flummery."

"I did not say I was discon…. Stepmother?"

"Aye, lass."

"The lady in mourning was your stepmother? She said her papa had died and left her a small fortune. She gave me a portion of her inheritance. I did not want to take it, but she became so agitated, I truly thought she'd swoon if I refused."

"Hortense faints at her convenience, and the only thing she mourned was my neglect, once I'd seen you. Her papa is alive, or at least he was, though I suspect he became a wee bit paddywhacked when his daughter discovered the loss of her favourite reticule. I pray daily that my stepsister Charlotte was able to maintain an innocent demeanor, for it was little Charlotte who pinched Hortense's beaded reticule, filled with her da's boodle. Thus, I was able to leave France and—"

"But the lady swore … she said God would strike her dead if she wasn't a Kelley. *Mon Dieu,* that wicked woman wed your papa!"

"Aye, lass. That pawky bitch wed me da, Timothy Kelley. Hortense and Tim were made from the same tatter'd cloth. 'Tis lucky we were cut from a stronger fabric, Angelique, for I swear by all that's holy that I'll not be losin' ye again."

Sean's beguiling brogue whiffed inside her ear. Her back was still against his broad chest, and she felt his fingers trace her bodice, as though he contemplated the fit of her gown. Apparently satisfied, he circled her heart breast with his first finger. Her nipple grew taut and quivered, not unlike the magic jumping beans sold to Cirque gillys. Angelique shivered with delight, even as she realized that she must immediately annul this *affaire d'amore.*

Bloody oath, but she missed the Nouveau Cirque, missed her freedom, missed her independence. Just like her damnfool corset, she was now restricted to drab ladylike activities and drab gowns. Tante Bernadine had even picked out a drab, albeit wealthy, fiancé.

However, all thoughts of her suitable suitor fled when Sean turned her around and traced the soft, moist, inner edges of her lips with his tongue. Eagerly, she opened her mouth, shut her eyes, and pressed herself so close to his body she could smell whiskey, tobacco, and boot leather. A moan forced its way up her throat. Her heart felt the gravitational pull of a forward somersault. She had never performed the forward, and that very thought caused her to pull away.

"I am a virgin," she confessed in French, her cheeks hot, her eyes downcast.

"I niver doubted that for a moment," he replied, tucking

an errant curl behind her ear. "We shall be wed before we—
"

"*Non.*"

"What do ye mean, no? Are ye sayin' you'll not marry me?"

"I am saying that our marriage will be a ... what is the English word? Hindrance? Obstacle?"

He snorted. "I cannot be dissuaded, if that's what's frettin' ye."

"Sean, you know nothing about my family ... my life ... my corset," she cried.

"Corset?"

"My aunt, who is also my guardian, tolerates my uncle's friendship with Monsieur Barnum. She admires and respects wealth, but she abhors Monsieur Barnum's menial background. And his fame."

"This is America, lass. Your aunt can refuse to bestow a blessing on our marriage, that is her God-given right, but she cannot forbid it."

"You would wed me without permission? Without a marriage portion?"

"Who has been filling your head with such twaddle, Angelique? In Brooklyn, where I reside, one does not speak of dowries. Still, you bring me a great gift...." He paused and gave her the most beautiful smile she'd ever seen. "Someday I shall own a circus, the finest in all the world, and you shall perform. But only if it pleasures you to do so. If it does not, you can run our household and raise our daughters ... like Charity Barnum."

"Suppose we have sons?"

"We will have daughters, but they'll not play the equilibrist."

"What will they play, *mon* Sean?"

"Equestrians. Should our wee lasses fall from their horses, 'tis not such a lengthy journey to the ground."

"I would rather count the stars."

"And so you shall, as soon as we are wed."

Angelique looked up at his face, at his earnest expression

revealed by the capricious moonlight. *I would follow this man to the ends of the earth,* she thought. She heard music. Monsieur Barnum's black pianist, Old Blind Joe, who could hear a song once and play it perfectly. She knew that Monsieur Barnum's entertainment, prior to Charity's sit-down dinner, included excerpts from a melodrama called *The Drunkard,* which portrayed the evils of alcohol.

Meanwhile....

"This time I have the carriage, Monsieur Kelley," she said. "My uncle drove us here in a brougham. I propose that we leave Madam Charity's 'small' dinner party, congested by so many people that we shall not be missed, then find a secluded place to plight our troth ... and return one half hour later."

"*Non,* mademoiselle," he teased. "What I have in mind for ye would take far more than half an hour." A solemn expression briefly transformed his face. "In truth, lass, we must say our vows first."

"After we prove how much we love God, may we be merry? *S'il vous plaît,* Sean?"

He let loose with another delighted burst of laughter, just before he lowered his head and gave Angelique a kiss that seared her lips and sealed their bargain.

THREE

Tante Bernadine's "picture room" boasted ornately framed portraits and a billiards table. Angelique had the distinct feeling that the people depicted in her aunt's paintings were not truly related, yet the men and women who graced the walls had always provided a strange sort of comfort.

This evening, however, they looked tragic and seemed to avoid her eyes.

Seated on the floor, surrounded by Tante Bernadine's seven cats, Angelique watched tears drip from her chin and stain her saffron-coloured evening gown. She had complained of a sniffy nose, a croupy cough, an aching head, a rotting tooth, even—somewhat desperately—a broken-winded gastric disorder, yet her aunt still insisted that she, first meet, then dine with her "intended."

A hungry Tuesday meowed and rubbed against Angelique's drawn-up legs. Thursday was asleep atop Angelique's belly. Friday played with a ball of yarn while Monday chased a billiard ball. None of the cats, including Sunday, Saturday and Wednesday, seemed perturbed by Angelique's shuddering sighs and sobs.

She had been weeping steadily for two hours, and the cats, clever creatures, had probably decided she had no tears left. They were "on the dot," as Gartrude liked to say. After all, how much salty moisture could a person—even a woman—produce?

Enough was enough! Angelique shook her head, spraying the last of her tears over Thursday and Sunday. A sleepy

Thursday hissed, but Sunday only gave Angelique a haughty glare, then washed his whiskers with one dainty paw.

Flexing her fingers, Angelique allowed her mouth to quirk at the corners. After years of hauling herself up and down a rope ladder, her hands were neither dainty nor delicate. In fact, she possessed a man's hands. Perhaps Monsieur Macy would consider her paw too rough to flaunt his ring of engagement; a ring that bore his family crest and motto: *abusus non tollit usum.* Abuse does not take away use.

Love God and Be Merry. It had been a full fortnight since the Barnum dinner party, yet Angelique had only seen Sean Kelley once—during a tea given by Charity Barnum. Tante Bernadine had attended the event, but Charity, still playing matchmaker, had managed to squire Angelique into her husband's private study, an orange-coloured, satin-walled library.

There, Sean had given her a kiss that left her breathless. And yet he seemed preoccupied.

"Mr. Barnum will hand over the funds for my traveling circus," he finally stated, "should Jenny Lind prove to be a success."

"Jenny Lind?"

"The concert singer."

"*Oui,* I know who you mean. My aunt says her character is 'simplicity and goodness personified.' Why would Mademoiselle Lind make a difference?"

"In order to pay her wages, Barnum has mortgaged the contents of his American Museum and borrowed all he could."

"But why would she not be a success, *mon* Sean?"

"Barnum himself doesn't know, but Jenny has a host of … attributes … which might lead to the wreckage of his enterprise."

"Can she not sing? Monsieur Barnum has said she would be adored, even if she had the voice of a crow."

"He can make that claim, aware that the glowing reviews from her Liverpool concert have been pushed into print. Do you know Jenny's life story, lass?"

"Of course. Who does not know her story? A poor and lonely little girl, Jenny oft sang in the street. One day she was overheard by a famous *danseur,* who arranged for her to audition at Stockholm's Royal Theater."

Sean remained silent for a moment. "Jenny is a bastard, Angelique, the illegitimate child of a woman named Anna Marie Fallborg. Jenny was born in secrecy and taken, under cover, to the home of distant cousins. She was then given away to a childless couple. The *maid* of a professional dancer overheard Jenny singing to her cat, and the rest is common knowledge. Except…."

"Except what?"

"She has described herself as having piggy eyes and a big broad nose."

"Is it her appearance or her illegitimacy that bothers you?"

"Both," he replied truthfully. "Did ye know that the Danish children's book author, Hans Christian Andersen, wrote stories about her and for her? 'The Ugly Duckling' and 'The Emperor's Nightingale.' I must keep the newspapers busy with those very details, so they will not dig up a scandal. I've also suggested that Barnum initiate a Jenny Lind Song Contest. Two hundred dollars shall go to the winning ode, which will then be set to music. I'd like you to win that prize, lass."

"Me? *Mon Dieu,* I can barely think in English, much less write it."

He grinned. "I'll write the ode for you, and your beauty shall do the rest. I cannot imagine Barnum passing up the opportunity to display a beautiful woman."

"Is that an honest ploy?" she asked, blushing at his compliment.

"*Honest* ploy?" Sean roared with laughter, then held out his arms and pressed her face against his vest. "Following Jenny Lind's opening night, we shall be wed," he murmured. "Does that make you happy?"

"*Non!*"

"You keep saying no to me, Mademoiselle Peahen," he teased, holding her at arm's length. "What bothers ye now?"

"My ... aunt...."

Angelique could not find the words to tell him that Tante Bernadine was already busy planning her niece's wedding to Monsieur Arthur Macy, who lived in a village called South Carolina. Jenny Lind's New York performance was several weeks away. Sean needed Monsieur Barnum in order to establish The Sean Kelley Circus. Angelique did not want to divert his attention from the task at hand—selling Jenny Lind to the public and keeping the details of her birth a secret.

Even though they'd only been in each other's presence three times, Angelique understood Sean well enough to know he'd give up his *cirque,* his dream, if he believed their future together was threatened.

"I've told ye before, lass," he said softly. "Your aunt cannot dissuade me."

Angelique managed a nod and a smile.

Somehow I must keep Monsieur Macy waiting for my answer, she thought. *Somehow, I must poke my feet.*

"Mr. Macy is waiting, my dear!"

Tante Bernadine's strident voice interrupted Angelique's reverie, even though she had not yet gotten to the best part; the part where Sean had soothed her fears with his experienced hands and warm lips.

She shivered at the memory.

"Are you cold, my dear?" Tante Bernadine picked up Thursday and cuddled the cat against her flat bosom.

Not sure whether the question had been directed at her or the cat, knowing that, despite her shivers, her face was flushed, Angelique simply followed her aunt into the hallway.

Tossing Thursday back into the picture room, Tante Bernadine set a brisk pace toward the staircase.

"Don't drag your feet, Angelique," she called over her shoulder. "Mr. Macy admires punctuality and would not appreciate a slowpoke."

"I do not care what Monsieur Macy admires or appreciates, Tante." Trying to keep new tears at bay, Angelique took a deep breath. "I will never marry him, for I am in love with another man."

Tante Bernadine halted so abruptly, Angelique very nearly plowed into her.

"Have you been playing the whore behind my back?" Tante Bernadine asked.

Angelique squared her shoulders and fibbed with a reply she'd soon regret.

"*Oui,*" she said.

Monsieur Macy was old … thirty-five, maybe even forty. Angelique felt a flush of anger colour her cheeks, eclipsing the splotch from her aunt's slap.

Did Tante Bernadine honestly believe Angelique would marry this *grenouille* … this frog?

He was no more than five feet, six inches tall, with a head that seemed too large for his narrow shoulders and thin body. His eyes bulged. His nose was flat. His brown hair seemed too luxurious for his age, and he possessed wide, fat, frog lips. Even if Angelique had not loved Sean, Monsieur Macy would have repulsed her.

Perhaps, she told herself, his disposition did not match his froggy exterior. Perhaps she judged him unfairly.

Tante Bernadine's hisses still echoed in her ear. "You must make certain Mr. Macy is charmed by your bodily assets. We need him to wed you within a few weeks, for you might be with child. Men put such store in breasts, my dear. Thus, I give you permission to strut and preen … in a ladylike fashion, of course. Furthermore, you will not leave this house until the day of your wedding."

For the first time in her life, Angelique wished her gown was more demure. She watched Monsieur Macy's gaze linger on her décolletage as he bent to kiss the back of her hand,

and she felt an urge to slap him senseless.

Speaking directly to Tante Bernadine, Monsieur Macy said, "She'll do."

"I'll do what?" Angelique asked recklessly.

"Her hips are too small," Monsieur Macy continued. "However, she looks strong. I am a widower. My last wife died giving birth to twins."

His voice contained a controlled anger, but Angelique didn't know if his ire was directed at his wife's demise, or at the fact that she had presented him with twins before she'd conveniently—and probably exhaustedly—expired.

"How old are your twins?" Angelique asked politely, swallowing an impolite rejoinder. "Are they boys or girls?"

"Girls. They are six months old. I need heirs, sons…." He paused as his mud-coloured eyes touched upon her hips again. "My first wife was barren," he said, strolling over to the piano. "Do you play, Miss Aumont?"

Bloody oath! Had his first wife died from exhaustion, as well? Angelique bit her lip to keep from asking. "No, Monsieur, I do not," she replied.

But I can dance across a rope, she thought, tempted to giggle at the absurdity of the situation. Her one saving grace, and apparently her only escape from this marriage of convenience, was small hips.

"You shall learn how to play," Monsieur Macy said. "I like music."

"I cannot learn," Angelique retorted, "for my *hands* are too small. However, I compose verse and have written an ode for Jenny Lind, P.T. Barnum's 'Swedish Nightingale.' I hope to win Monsieur Barnum's contest, a two hundred dollar prize, since I am, at present, bereft of funds."

Despite Tante Bernadine's loud gasp, Angelique continued. "Would you care to hear my verse, sir?" Sean had not yet delivered the ode he'd mentioned, but this morning Gartrude had recited a poem that was circulating among the servants. "In my verse, I pretend I am Monsieur Barnum talking to Mademoiselle Lind, and this is what he says.

'They will welcome you with speeches and rockets ... and you will touch their hearts and I will touch their pockets ... and if between us both the public isn't skimmed ... then my name isn't Barnum and yours isn't Lind.'"

Monsieur Macy's eyes were cold. "I admire wit, my dear," he said, "as long as it's not directed at me."

"My niece meant no disrespect, Arthur," Tante Bernadine cried. "She doesn't even know how you earn your living."

"How *do* you earn your living, Monsieur?"

"I own a large plantation, Miss Aumont, and many slaves."

"I do not believe in slavery."

"My slaves have been discombobulated recently, for I have purchased an elephant to plow one of my fields."

"An elephant?"

"It was P.T. Barnum who arranged the sale."

"You are acquainted with Monsieur Barnum?"

"He is my *friend* and business partner. In return for his advice and help with my elephant, I loaned him ten thousand dollars so that he could fulfill his contract with Jenny Lind. Do you understand, Miss Aumont?"

"*Oui,* Monsieur Macy, I am no ninny. And although we have just met, I realize that *you* are no altruist. What did Monsieur Barnum pledge in order to secure your loan? His museum? More elephants?"

"No, my dear. He pledged his soul."

True to her word, Tante Bernadine kept Angelique a prisoner, although her jail cell was spacious, her fellow inmates one uncle, seven cats, and a bevy of servants.

Somehow, Tante Bernadine had discovered that Sean was Angelique's "lover." Perhaps she had intercepted a letter before Angelique and Sean had begun using Gartrude as their courier; before they'd begun using false names.

Drawing a tiny peahen in a cage, Angelique now signed her letters "Mademoiselle Paonne." Sean was "Monsieur Hyene"—even if he didn't chortle much anymore.

Although Barnum was pleased with Sean's tireless efforts, Jenny Lind was a conundrum. Solving the riddle of the Sphinx, Sean wrote, would be easier than solving the riddle of the Swedish Nightingale.

Not knowing that she cringed from attention, Barnum, with Sean's help, had mounted an inspired campaign. As Jenny's steamship approached the docking area at the foot of Canal Street, every wharf, window, and rooftop along the waterfront crawled with "a sea of humanity." Unfortunately, once Jenny had descended the gangplank, she was almost trampled. Then, safe inside Barnum's carriage, over two hundred bouquets were thrust through the windows, drowning everyone with perfume and petals.

"Ye would not think me a lad if ye could smell me," Sean had written, "and poor Jenny was frightened out of her wits."

She was now living at Irving House, the most elegant quarters in the city, and Sean hoped she would honour her contract, since apparently she had gotten cold feet halfway through her voyage and begged to be taken home.

But, he wrote, all of this was not Angelique's concern.

Of course it was her concern! The colder Jenny's feet got, the longer it would take for Mademoiselle Peonne to escape from her prison and join Monsieur Hyene.

Angelique heard the unmistakable footsteps of her aunt. Quickly, she thrust Sean's latest missive beneath her pillow. He had included the Jenny Lind ode on a separate piece of paper, but she had not read it yet, and she had a sinking feeling she'd have to decipher the poem tonight, by candlelight. Damn and blast!

"I want you to stay by my side," Tante Bernadine said without preamble. "You must learn how to manage a household, my dear. Mr. Macy has a large staff and will expect you to oversee their various duties."

"Monsieur Macy has slaves!"

"Slaves are unpaid servants, Angelique, and Mr. Macy expects—"

"An heir! He wants sons, Tante, and my hips are too small."

"Fiddle-faddle! The next time he visits, we shall pad your hips."

"I suppose that's an *honest* ploy!"

"Of course. Just as your 'padded belly' will be an honest ploy."

"What makes you so certain I am with child?"

"The wages of sin—"

"I have never earned those wages. I fibbed about my *affaire.* I cannot offer you proof of my chastity, Tante, but this morning my bleeding began."

"Flowers," Bernadine said, her cheeks crimson. "In America we call it flowers. And if you are not with child, Arthur Macy will soon pad your belly."

"Monsieur Macy will never get the opportunity, for I would rather sleep with a toad! No, a newt!"

Angelique was prepared to endure her aunt's face-slap. However, she was not prepared for her aunt's smile.

FOUR

Charity Barnum handed Angelique a cup of tea and a handkerchief.

"Warm your stomach and dry your tears," she said.

"But why did Sean leave? Please tell me."

"It's really quite simple. Jenny Lind's opening night was a success. My husband kept his promise and gave Sean the funds for his traveling circus."

"But why would he leave without *me*?"

Charity walked over to the window and looked out, her head bent, as if she contemplated the verdant lawn below. Then she made an about-face. "Don't you know that your wedding is the talk of New York, child? Your aunt picked Grace Episcopal Church as the site, a reception will be held at the Metropolitan Hotel, and my husband will provide the entertainment."

Angelique felt the colour drain from her face. "I know nothing of this. I never said I would wed Monsieur Macy. In fact, last night I incurred his wrath."

"And how did you do that?"

Angelique's hands were shaking so badly, she placed her teacup and saucer on a small table. "Monsieur Macy began to … to…."

"Seduce you?"

"*Oui.* Frightened, I reached out blindly. The first thing my hand encountered was his hair. Only it was a—"

"Wig," Charity guessed.

"*Mais oui.* His pate is bald, and he was very angry, so this morning I made my escape."

"How did you escape?"

"I dressed like my maid, Gartrude. We are the same height and I hid my hair beneath her hooded cloak. Tonight Gartrude will pack some of my clothes and my letters from Sean, leave the house as Gartrude, and meet me here. I am truly sorry, Madame Barnum, but I could not think of any place else to go. I have no money and your house was near-by."

"Please call me Charity, Angelique, and my husband has money for you."

"He does?"

"Yes. Two hundred dollars. You won the Jenny Lind Song Contest."

Charity walked over to the piano and picked up some sheets of music. Then, in a small but clear voice, she sang Sean's *Ode To Jenny Lind.*

Oh Jenny Lind … oh Jenny Lind,
Your magic, angel's voice,
Hath claimed the hearts of all our men,
All smitten long past choice.

We beg of you to stay with us,
With always one more song,
For you have won our very hearts,
Your lilting voice so strong.

Fair tribute to your beauty, and
The angel's voice your own,
Your gift to us, beyond all doubt,
When nightingale hath flown.

All hail the Swedish Nightingale,
Of beauteous form and song,
Our favored choice, this angel's voice,
May she remain here long.

Charity smiled sweetly. "Ordinarily I sing hymns, and God does not care what I sound like, so I might have been off-key." She placed the music sheets on the piano. "My husband plans to make your last verse the chorus."

"Sean's last verse." Angelique looked down at the floor. "Sean wrote the ode," she confessed. "The money is his, not mine."

"I suspected as much. Nevertheless, Phineas will hand over the two hundred dollars if you give him permission to use your likeness on posters and music."

Lifting her teacup from its saucer, Charity took a delicate sip. "I'm glad you came here, child, but why did you not make your escape earlier? Did your aunt threaten you? Was that a nod, Angelique? What did Bernadine say?"

"She said Monsieur Macy would ask for his loan back, the ten thousand dollars he loaned Monsieur Barnum. Monsieur Macy said Monsieur Barnum pledged his soul, but I am not certain what he meant by that."

"He meant Iranistan."

If possible, Angelique's face grew even whiter. "By running away, I've ruined everything. Monsieur Barnum will lose his soul and you will lose your home. Oh Madame Barnum … Charity … I am so sorry. Perhaps they have not yet discovered my absence. Perhaps I can return and—"

"Nonsense! Mr. Macy's loan was repaid, with interest, after Jenny Lind's second concert. Still, I appreciate your sacrifice … and so will my husband."

"I don't understand." Staggering toward an armchair, Angelique sank onto it. "Will Monsieur Barnum find Sean for me? Does he know where Sean is?"

"No. But Sean left a map, detailing his route. You see, Phineas promised to purchase elephants for Sean's circus, from the dealers who supply his wild animals. Unfortunately, they cannot go to a store and say 'Six elephants, please,' so it might take some time."

"A map! Then I will follow Sean, meet up with him, and explain away the misunderstanding."

"You will do no such thing! You cannot travel across the country unescorted. I have a better plan in mind, but I want to discuss it with my husband first. For now, you must rest in one of our guest bedrooms. I would imagine you are exhausted."

Despite the fact that she had spent a sleepless night, Angelique wasn't tired. Maman had made a journey of the heart, following Papa to Paris. She would make a similar journey … even though the ends of the earth might be a wee bit farther.

Sean Kelley celebrated Saint Valentine's Day by hiring an equestrian.

Maureen O'Connor was beautiful, despite the anguish that tinted her blue eyes almost purple. In truth, Sean had a feeling his own eyes reflected her deep sorrow.

Except when they touched upon Maureen's son. Sean was impressed by the fact that the dark-haired, blue-eyed little boy didn't try to hide behind his mother's skirts. Instead, Brian O'Connor stood directly in front of Maureen, as if he'd fiercely attack anything, or anyone, who threatened her.

Sean hunkered down. "And how old might ye be, lad?"

The boy held up six fingers.

"And what will ye be doing while your mum rides the horses?"

"Whatever ye wish me to do, sir."

"Can you ride?"

"Of course," he replied, as if Sean's question was ludicrous. "But…" the boy paused and looked up at his mother. "But I want someone to learn me how to tame the cats."

"*Teach* you," Maureen corrected, "and we've gabbed about this before, Brian, over and over again. 'Tis the reason why I left my last position," she said to Sean. "The owner of the circus believed it would be good for business, puttin' a wee lad inside a cage filled with Bengals. I told him what-for, and he sent me packing."

Sean felt his face flush, for he had been thinking the very same thing. While no Tom Thumb, Brian O'Connor—even at six—had a devil-may-care demeanor. He was, Sean concluded, a man inside a boy's body.

"Folks think I'm daft," Brian said earnestly, "but I can talk to lions and tigers, and they understand every word I say."

Maureen pointed to an ugly scratch on her son's arm, beneath his rolled-up sleeve. "One tiger did not understand your words!"

"Yes he did, Mum. Mr. Browne's whip made him forget."

"Ye must snap a whip to tame the cats, Brian," Sean said softly.

"True, sir, but Mr. Browne struck the tiger's nose."

"You were in the ring? Performing?"

The boy shook his head. "We was practicin'. I know how to snap the whip, sir, but I'd never hurt a cat. Just like Mum would never hurt a horse."

"Which is why I hired your mum," Sean said with a grin. "And I believe I have more than enough chores to keep you occupied."

"I'm good at chores," Brian bragged. "But someday I'll tame your cats."

Watching Maureen O'Connor and her son walk toward the Cook Top, Sean hoped that "someday" would come soon. He desperately needed a star attraction.

And he needed the elephants Barnum had promised to deliver.

Traveling from town to town by horse and wagon, Sean found that many roads were impassable, especially during rainstorms. If swollen streams blocked the road, elephants could double as wagon-pushers. With elephants, Sean could erect a huge canvas tent. Right now, more often than not, he presented his show outside, usually in a farmer's field. And although his loyal troupe was willing, Sean wouldn't allow them to perform during turbulent weather.

He had heard of an elephant named Matthew Gray. Matthew Gray plowed a plantation owner's fields. The owner, who lived in South Carolina, wanted to sell Matthew Gray to the highest bidder. Apparently, his field hands feared a whipping less than they feared the huge, four-footed, flap-eared mammal.

Sean had been all set to visit the plantation and make a bid, until he learned the name of the owner. Arthur Macy. Angelique's husband. Sean would die a thousand deaths, or push a thousand wagons across a thousand swollen streams, before he'd set eyes on the woman who had married for wealth rather than love.

While he suspected her aunt had something to do with Angelique's decision, that didn't negate the fact that she had betrayed him. He had *not* believed the newspaper story—had, in fact, been writing a letter to "Mademoiselle Peonne"—when Barnum entered the room and announced that he would provide the entertainment at Angelique and Arthur Macy's wedding reception.

"Do you think the happy couple would enjoy excerpts from *Romeo and Juliet*?" Barnum had asked.

"I think Mrs. Macy would prefer *Beauty and the Beast*," Sean had replied bitterly. "Or *Blue Beard*."

Perhaps his new equestrian could mend his broken heart, Sean thought, picturing the masses of red hair that framed Maureen O'Connor's porcelain complexion and dark blue eyes, aware that below her neck and shoulders her breasts and hips were well-rounded, her waist as small as a whiplash popper.

During her audition, she said she was a widow. But a vivid blush had stained her cheeks, and something in her voice didn't ring true.

The last thing Sean needed right now was an irate husband.

Of course, there was always Panama Drayton. The statuesque trapeze artist had made it very clear that she'd be willing to perform with Sean beneath the wagons. But even if he had been tempted, the strong man, Bobby Duncan, had already staked his claim. Well structured with cast-iron muscles, each brain cell Duncan lacked was stored inside his powerful arms and shoulders. Sean didn't want to tangle with "the strongest man in the world," nor did he want to lose him, for it was the sideshow exhibits that kept his circus afloat.

After opening in Brooklyn, he had toured New England, and at one stop in Waterville, Maine, so many people lined up to buy tickets that his troupe had given continuous performances, starting in the wee hours of the morning, ending late at night.

But those early shows had been confined to buildings and tents. People preferred to sit under a roof, even a canvas roof. In order to make a profit, Sean needed huge audiences, which meant an oversized tent, and it was difficult to raise up and tear down an oversized tent without the help of elephants.

The one snag to staging a circus in an oversized tent was that the people in the back rows had a hard time seeing the show. Sean had discussed this with Barnum, who offered the perfect solution. Enlarge the ring where the acts were performed. That, Sean insisted, was out of the question.

"The diameter for circus rings is thirteen meters," he told Barnum. "Circus horses all over the world are trained to perform in rings of that size. If every circus had a different size, horses would have to be re-trained every time they appeared with a new company."

"Then add a second ring," Barnum replied.

Sean planned to add a second, then a third ring. The most popular acts would perform inside the center ring.

But three rings would make it difficult to hear the clowns' silly gibber-jabber, so he would initiate yet another daring innovation. His clowns would perform their routines with no dialogue at all—in pantomime.

First, however, he needed a star performer. And more exhibits. Barnum had promised Sean two camelopards. Camelopards possessed long spotted necks, but they also had long black tongues, allowing them to encircle tree branches and eat the leaves that would otherwise be out of reach.

I'll wager Americans have niver seen a camelopard, Sean thought. *In truth, I've niver seen one meself.*

He shut his eyes as a headache galloped inside his skull.

Once, not too long ago, he had pictured Angelique as his star performer, her rope stretched tight across the tent's top, drawing every gaze toward heaven.

If you're very good, he had told Charlotte, *ye can capture a dream.*

Had Sean been able to "capture" Angelique, he would have filled his circus posters with her likeness.

And he would have introduced her to the world as Dream Angel.

FIVE

"Will you please, please be quiet!"

"I am sorry, Mademoiselle Lind."

"Not you, Angelique, the bird!" Jenny Lind pointed to a small birdcage. Inside, a canary was singing its heart out. "Get rid of that bird. It's giving me a headache. I want it gone from my dressing room before I return."

Sweeping up her long skirts with one hand, Jenny turned toward the door.

Angelique leaned over to pick up a discarded shawl, and heard the door slam. She could usually determine Jenny's moods from the strength of her slams. This evening Jenny was very angry.

"And what am I supposed to do with you?" Angelique asked the bird.

Thanks to Charity, Angelique had become part of Jenny Lind's entourage. Monsieur Barnum had been reluctant at first, but when Charity reminded him of *their* difficult courtship, he boomed his big laugh and agreed to make Angelique one of Jenny's two personal tour servants.

Angelique often wondered if she wouldn't have been better off setting out on her own. Jenny was spiritual and devout, but she hated thanking people, disliked staying at a table after she'd finished eating, was wracked with headaches and rheumatism, and plugged up her ears with wool stoppers at night to "shut out the noises of the world." She could be sweet, and generous—at Christmas she'd showered everyone with gifts—but Angelique knew that, as the tour progressed,

Jenny was growing increasingly distrustful of Monsieur Barnum. Angelique also knew that Jenny's advisors had pleaded with her to break her contract. After several months of touring, Angelique could speak English with only the smallest trace of an accent. But since she was a servant—and French—everyone assumed she couldn't understand what they said, and she heard things she wasn't supposed to hear.

Tonight Jenny was angry because someone had told her that the venue for her Tennessee concert would be a tobacco warehouse. Before confronting Barnum, she'd peppered her servant—and the poor canary—with indignant epithets.

Still, Angelique gladly endured the singer's insults. Because she was close to Sean. She could *feel* it. Even better, she had overheard Monsieur Barnum teasing Jenny, asking if she'd like six elephants to share her stage ... before he delivered them to a friend in Missouri. Jenny had *not* been amused, and Angelique had a feeling Barnum would soon lose his famous singer.

So, just in case, she had asked to borrow Sean's map. Then, using one of Sean's old letters for paper, she'd drawn a copy. The next stop on Jenny's tour was St. Louis. On the map, near St. Louis, Sean had inked a big black X.

A knock sounded at the door, and without thinking Angelique said, "Enter."

The furniture was suddenly dwarfed by a tall stranger whose over-large hands clutched a bouquet of flowers ... and a cowboy hat.

Stifling a yawn, Angelique repeated the words she'd said at least a hundred times before. "Miss Lind prefers that flowers be delivered to a children's hospital. If there is no children's hospital, any hospital will do."

"Yes, ma'am. Problem is, these ain't my flowers."

And that canary ain't my bird, Angelique thought, her mouth quirking at the corners. "If you did not purchase the flowers," she said, "who did?"

"I dunno, ma'am. A gent outside the theater give me four bits to make sure these here blooms got brung to Jenny

Lind's room. Are you her?"

"Yes," Angelique fibbed. "But please return those … uh, blooms … to the gent, and tell him what I said about hospitals."

"Cain't do that, ma'am."

"Why not?"

"I need the money."

"Suppose *I* give you six bits…why are you shaking your head?"

"Ain't never took no money from a girl, ma'am, and don't plan to start now."

Intrigued, Angelique gestured toward a chair. "Won't you sit down, sir?"

"I'll sit if you take these here flowers, and I ain't no sir. Roy Osborne's the name."

"I'll take your flowers if you take my bird," she retorted. "And please call me … Jenny."

"Yes, ma'am."

"Jenny!"

"Yes, ma'am."

Angelique swallowed a laugh, then placed the cowboy's bouquet on top of the dressing table. Roy Osborne, now seated, stared at the canary. Angelique stared at Roy Osborne.

Harsh weather-lines spun out from his blue eyes. Deep furrows connected his nose to his mouth. His long, sun-streaked brown hair was tied at the nape of his neck with a piece of string, and he was perfect for what she had in mind.

But first, a few questions.

"How old are you, Mr. Osborne?"

"Dunno, ma'am. More than my fingers an' toes put together, I reckon. How old are you?"

"As old as my fingers and toes put together," she replied. "Why do you need money so badly, Mr. Osborne? Are you not employed?"

"I was, ma'am, but my horse died."

"Oh, I'm sorry."

"Me too, ma'am."

"How much does a horse cost, Mr. Osborne?"

"Reckon I could git one for fifty, ma'am, a good horse for seventy-five."

"Dollars?"

"Yes, ma'am."

"I think I'd want a good horse," Angelique murmured, watching Monsieur Osborne squirm in his chair.

"Ma'am … Miss Jenny … I'm sorry, but I gotta' git. You see, I'm in a … well, a hurry … a big hurry."

"And why are you in such a big hurry?" She watched his face redden. "Oh. The water closet is down the hall."

If possible, his weathered cheeks turned even more ruddy. "No, ma'am, it's not that. My wife … she's expecting our first young'un, an' I want to be there when it's birthed. We live near St. Louie. I finished up a cattle drive an' was headin' home when some bastard … 'scuse me, ma'am … when some bastard…" He smiled sheepishly and shrugged. "Guess I cain't think of no other word, ma'am, just like I can't seem to call you nothin' but ma'am."

"What did the bastard do to you, Mr. Osborne?"

"He shot my horse, ma'am, and stole my pay."

"I'm sorry."

"Ain't your fault."

"There! You didn't call me ma'am. That's a good start."

"A good start for what?"

"Suppose I gave you two hundred dollars? Could you buy two horses, saddles, blankets, maybe some food?"

He shook his head. "I don't take no money—"

"From a girl. Yes, I know. But would you consider taking money from a woman who offered you honest employment?"

"No, ma'am."

Angelique felt tears blur her eyes. "Mr. Osborne … Roy … I need you to help me find my husband. He's somewhere in Missouri, but I have a map, and if you help me, I'll let you keep both horses." She followed his gaze, and saw that he was looking at several large trunks, stacked in the corner of the dressing room. "I'll only take one gown, one pair of shoes, one pair of gloves, and one bonnet."

The grin he gave Angelique made him almost handsome. "Seems like you're in a big hurry too, ma'am. Already got me a saddle and bedroll, but if you grab up them flowers and that yella' bird, we'll find us some horses."

He tilted her chin with his callused finger. "Do you ride, Miss Jenny?"

Non, she thought.

"Not yet," she replied.

Watching circus equestrians perform, Angelique had always believed that riding a horse would be easy as pie.

She should have known better, especially since she'd never baked a pie. In fact, she had never cooked anything at all. Circuses had Cook Tops. Tante Bernadine employed a cook.

Roy Osborne couldn't cook, either. If she'd had any money left from the horses and gear, Angelique would have given it over for a nice hot cup of tea. Roy's coffee tasted like gooey mud, and his hardtack tasted like … well, to be perfectly honest, she had never tasted anything that tasted like hard-tack. It was saltless. It was bread. It was hard. And if she ever described it to Sean, that's all she could say.

She and Roy were getting closer to the X on Sean's map, even if she *had* delayed their journey by bouncing up and down on her saddle, not to mention falling off her damnfool horse so many times she'd lost count.

And *she* rode the seventy-five dollar horse!

Angelique heard the echo of Sean's voice: *Should our wee lasses fall from their horses, 'tis not such a lengthy journey to the ground.*

She heard her reply: *I would rather count the stars.*

Tonight there were a multitude of stars overhead, and a full moon provided enough light for a rope to be strung between two trees. Coiled across Roy's saddle was a rope, only he called it a lasso.

"Want more coffee, Miss Jenny?"

"No. No, thank you." Angelique wrinkled her nose at the thought. "But I would like to borrow your lasso, *s'il vous plait.*"

"Is that Swede talk, see-vu-play?" Roy nodded toward the canary, which for some reason Angelique couldn't fathom, he had insisted they take along on their journey. "The gent with the blooms said you was a Swedish bird, Miss Jenny. Knew a Swede once. Big yella-haired fella, same color hair as that there bird. Nice fella. Why do you want my lasso, Miss Jenny?"

"I thought I might string it up between those two trees and walk on it. If the rope is tight enough, I can do back flips. If it's really guyed out ... stretched ... I can try a forward somersault, which has never before been done by a woman."

Roy removed his hat, scratched his scalp, tossed the remains of his coffee into the fire, listened to the hiss, and put his hat back on. "Okay," he said.

Once they had strung Roy's lasso as tightly as humanly possible, he hoisted her up onto the rope. Immediately, Angelique clung to a tree. Damn and blast! Too many months had passed since she'd played the equilibrist.

Then she felt the magic.

Her bare feet practically skimmed the rough rope as she danced to the middle. Her calico gown was a hindrance, but she had removed every petticoat, leaving her chemise and drawers. Dare she remove her gown? No. She trusted Roy, but knew him well enough to know his cheeks would turn bright crimson, and he wouldn't watch. She wanted him to watch. She wanted the night critters that inhabited the woods to watch—owls and possums. She wanted the fish in the stream to watch. She wanted God to watch.

This is what she had been born to do!

SIX

Maureen O'Connor didn't have a husband.

Sean had found this out when he and Maureen shared a bottle of whiskey. They had been inside the silver wagon, where, after a show, Sean counted his greenbacks, coins and receipts.

"I believed the lies of Aaron Fox," she said. "Aaron looks a wee bit like you, except his eyes are as blue as the bunting on an American flag." She peered into Sean's face. "Your eyes are as green as ... well, the flag of Ireland, I suppose."

"Maureen ... sweetheart ... let me help you back to your wagon. No more spirits, lass, for you have a show tomorrow and must be balanced."

She tried to snap her fingers, and failed. "I have jumped through hoops of fire, atop a horse, with Brian in my belly, resting against my heart."

"Yes, Brian told me. And 'twas your horses who jumped, Maureen, not you, though had I been there, you would *not* have performed. 'Tis lucky you didn't miscarry, lass."

"At the time I did not care if I fell off. I love ... loved him so much."

Sean patted Maureen's shoulder, knowing he could have her if he wanted her, knowing he wanted her but would not have her.

"I thought myself wed," she continued. "but the man-wife words were falsely spoken by Aaron's friend, who wore a borrowed frock coat and clerical collar."

With that, she gave a whimper, shut her eyes, and pitched

forward. Sean caught her before she fell, carried her to her wagon, then placed her on her bed.

Poor Maureen, still in love with the man who had betrayed her. Just like Sean was still in love with the woman who had betrayed him.

The Irish can only love once.

Raising his arm, Sean shaded his eyes. In the distance were two figures on horseback. As they drew nearer, he could see that the smaller figure—a lass—held the reins with one hand and carried something in her other hand. A birdcage?

He couldn't quite make out the girl's features, yet his heart began to pound, and he staggered backwards until he felt the silver wagon's slats against his spine.

Was he brainsick? Of course he was. The girl who rode the dappled horse wore a floppy bonnet, a tatter'd gown, slippers tied her feet with string, and dirty gloves. She looked a wee bit like his small angel … except Angelique had never learned how to ride.

He remembered one of her letters, in response to his second vow that their daughters would be equestrians. "Someone else will have to teach the children," she had written, "for I have never, nor will I ever, ride a horse. Should I fall from my rope, the net is flexible. A horse's back is not, nor is the ground. In truth, Monsieur Hyene, I would rather walk."

A capricious breeze lifted the girl's bonnet from her head. As it spun toward the ground, she made a futile attempt to catch it.

Sean shut his eyes, then opened them again, but the lass—closer now—still looked like Angelique. The same robust breasts and shoulders. The same golden hair, now cascading down her back to her waist. And he would wager the elephants Barnum had not yet delivered that her eyes were gray-green.

Maybe he *could* wager his elephants. Shifting his gaze, Sean saw several large, dark shapes advancing, almost blocking out the sun. Even though they were farther away than the girl and her companion, the ground shook.

Once again, Sean focused on the two horseback riders. The elephants were expected, but what would Angelique be doing in the middle of a Missouri farmer's field? Perhaps her companion was her husband, Arthur Macy. Perhaps, unable to sell their plow-elephant, Matthew Gray, they had decided to visit the Sean Kelley Circus and ask for a bid.

The idea was so ludicrous, Sean laughed. Even if true, Arthur Macy—wealthy beyond measure—would have used a carriage to transport his young wife. He wouldn't want her beautiful rump bruised. Furthermore, the girl's companion didn't look like a rich plantation owner. Clothed in buckskin, his long legs straddled an animal that could only be described as a nag. Or crow bait.

Maybe the two figures on horseback were merely figments of his imagination, Sean thought, the result of yet another long, lonely night with his whiskey bottle.

But then why was his circus troupe joining him? Why were they staring across the farmer's field? A few watched the lass and her companion, but most watched the humped blobs that shaded the sun, and the troupe's joyous expressions confirmed what Sean had already deduced.

P.T. Barnum was, at long last, delivering the elephants.

Duncan the Strong Man, Jack the Giant, Morgan the Skeleton Man, Grace the Giantess, and Charlene the Bearded Lady, all grinned from ear to ear. Other performers duplicated their grins.

The clowns smiled through their painted frowns.

Maureen, Panama, and Cuckoo the Bird Girl had made a circle by joining hands, and were now dancing a wild jig.

Quite a few roustabouts had tears running down their weathered cheeks.

Only the goat, Natasha, expressed dismay—by bleating indignantly. Fearless Natasha could jump through hoops while riding around the ring on the back of a horse, but apparently the smell of elephant was not her cup of tea.

Sean laughed at the image of his goat, sitting on her haunches, delicately sipping from a china teacup.

"Why do you chortle like a hyena?" asked a familiar voice.

"What do you have in that cage?" Sean countered. Which wasn't at all what he wanted to say. But it was the first thing that came to mind since he couldn't tell if she sported a wedding band beneath her dirt-encrusted gloves.

"Cage? Oh, birdcage. A canary. It sings as sweetly as Jenny Lind, but has a much better disposition."

"You sound very … American, lass."

"And you sound flummoxed, Monsieur Kelley."

"Odd way to greet your husband, Miss Jenny," Roy muttered, climbing down from his horse, retrieving the birdcage from Angelique's outstretched fingers, then heading—reins and birdcage in hand—toward the roustabouts. "Even for a Swede," he called over his shoulder.

"Husband?" Sean quirked one dark eyebrow.

"An honest ploy, Monsieur."

"And did ye change your name and nationality?"

"*Non.* I am still French, and proud of it. I could be Mademoiselle Peonne or Mademoiselle Petit Ange, if that is your desire. But if you do not help me off this blasted horse, I shall be Mademoiselle Sore Derriere."

"As long as you are *Mademoiselle,* I care not," he replied.

"Ah," she said.

"Do you mean 'ah, the circus owner has lost his wits' or 'ah, Sean Kelley is a bumptious noodlehead'?"

"You thought me married to Monsieur Macy, Sean, and I cannot fault you for that. It's the very reason why I embarked on my 'journey of the heart.' Because you *are* my heart, and without a heart, one cannot live." She smiled wistfully. "I can dismount on my own, but I crave your touch, so won't you please help me?"

As he reached up, she brought her right leg over the saddle horn. A lion roared, and the horse shied, and Angelique pitched forward. She landed on top of him, and they both went down together, all in a heap.

Sean held onto her shoulders and rolled them over, away from the horse's hooves, until she was on the bottom and he was on top.

"Ooof," she said. "I think you weigh more than an elephant."

"Perhaps a baby elephant," he teased, pressing his palms against the ground and lifting his weight from her body. Then, he simply couldn't help himself. Her face was so close to his. Slowly, deliberately, he traced her mouth with the tip of his tongue until he felt the soft, moist, inner edges of her lips yield.

As he reluctantly ended the kiss, he could see that an adorable blush stained her cheekbones. He could also see that her gray-green eyes were focused on something to the left of his shoulder. Turning his head, Sean followed her gaze.

A woman had hunkered down near them. She had brittle, rust-coloured hair, and wore enough paint to challenge the clowns. Her breasts were bulldozed forward, aided by a tight corset. Above her stood an ebony giant.

"The roustabouts're wantin' you, Sean," the woman said. "And your friend might have to pee," she added with mock politeness.

"Thank you, Panama." Sean rose to his feet and helped Angelique rise. "Do ye have need of the donniker, lass?"

"*Non,*" she replied with another blush.

"Please help the roustabouts secure the elephants," Sean told Jack the Giant, "and offer the men who have herded them something to eat and drink. There should also be a gilly with the face of a bulldog. His name is Barnum. Tell him to make himself at home." Then, gently grasping Angelique by the elbow, Sean led her toward the silver wagon.

Once inside, she said, "Two women just stared at me with daggers in their eyes. One is quite beautiful, with an abundance of curly red hair. The other was the woman who asked if I had to pee."

"You have nothing to fear from those women, Angelique."

"I did not say I feared them."

"I swear by all that's holy that I have not slept with another lass since the first time I saw you ... dancing across a wee rope."

"A rope! Sean! I have performed the forward somersault!"

"And where would ye be doin' that?"

"In the woods. My ... escort ... and I guyed out his lasso, between two trees. Why do you look at me like that?"

"When I hired my ropewalker, I asked why he couldn't somersault forward as well as backwards. I was told that backflips allow your shoulders to flex naturally, and swinging arms give additional momentum. Somersaulting forward reverses natural reflexes, and the arms are no help because they get in the way."

"I wrap my arms about my chest so they won't catch between my legs."

"Nevertheless, it's too dangerous."

"Nevertheless, I *will* perform it."

"May we discuss this later, Angelique?"

Just like their first meeting, his eyes undressed her, discarding her tattered gingham gown, her four petticoats, her chemise, and her flannel drawers.

"'Tis not somersaults I have on my mind," he said.

"Have you *changed* your mind, Sean? The night of Charity Barnum's dinner party you insisted we must be wed first."

"Your cowboy believes I'm your husband."

"I told you. That was an honest ploy."

Sean laughed, then cradled her chin with his hand. "You have been my wife since the day we met, lass, for after that I could not imagine myself married to anyone but you. We don't need a man in a frock coat and clerical collar to say the words that will bind us." He kissed the long lashes that shaded her cheekbones. "Although hundreds of miles apart, we were still bound to one another." He traced the graceful arc of her neck with his thumb until he reached her gown's bodice buttons. "I promise we shall have a ceremony, but for now ... may we love God and be merry?"

Angelique replied by helping him remove her clothing, then his.

Oh, what a glorious sight, she thought, gazing immodestly at Sean's nakedness. Jenny Lind's voice might be God-given, but Sean's body was, too, and Angelique knew that if she ever composed another ode, her own ode, she wouldn't dwell on nightingales. Roy Osborne liked to share his knowledge of critters and birds. He had told her that the nightingale's song was trilled by the male. So she would play the peahen, instead ... because she wanted to sing.

Together, she and Sean sank to the wagon's floor. As he straddled her hips, his mouth found her heart breast and his tongue teased her nipple. With fierce abandon, she moaned her first song and began to writhe.

"You must stay motionless as long as ye can," he whispered, "but prepare yourself for a backflip rather than a forward somersault, me darlin', for I do not want your arms wrapped 'round your chest. In truth, I'll have need of your hands."

Sean knew that Angelique was already aroused, but he wanted to make her wet, and the method he had always employed with a more experienced woman might frighten her. 'Twas a dilemma he'd solve eventually. For now, he traced her lips with his thumb. Opening her mouth, she sucked his thumb like an infant. He responded in kind, sucking her fingers one by one. Then he lightly caressed the area between her thighs. Wet, but not wet enough.

Angelique sang her second moan. What on earth was Sean waiting for? Heat coursed through her, and she knew that as soon as he penetrated the fire would totally consume her. She wanted the fire to consume her.

As if he'd read her thoughts, he maneuvered his body until his knees were between her thighs, spreading them apart. Then he placed his thumb, the thumb she had just sucked, directly above the core of her womanhood. He slid his thumb lower, then higher, then lower, until he had established a rhythm.

She gasped and began to quiver. Covering his thumb with her fingers, she adapted to his up-down motion, but made him press harder, until she was on the verge of losing all coherent thought.

Apparently, he didn't want her to lose all coherent thought. Removing his thumb, he bent forward, kissed her chin, then parted her lips and thrust his tongue inside. She felt his tongue caress the inside of her mouth while he rubbed his hand across her breasts, stopping every now and then to lightly scissor her nipples with his fingers. Once again, she began to tremble.

He abandoned her mouth in order to say, "Now I have need of your hand."

Kissing, then licking her palm, he guided her hand downward, until he was fully in her grasp. Why had she not thought of this herself? Eagerly, she began to insert his spit-wet, engorged tip. Tilting her head all the way back, she arched her hips. He unclasped her fingers while she urged his entry, crying his name, crying for all the lost months of their separation.

Suspended between pain and pleasure, her senses focused on the searing intrusion of his body into hers. Then pleasure began to dominate, and her pain diminished. She sang her third moan, a duet, for Sean had joined in her song, and his wetness soothed the last remnants of her pain.

After their passion had been spent, she covered her face with her hands and began to sob.

"What's wrong?" Sean asked anxiously. "Did I hurt you? Are you all right? Angelique, answer me!"

"Jenny Lind once said that she could never forget the seriousness of life, thus she preferred sorrow to joy."

"*That's* why you're weeping, you daft colleen?"

"My tears are tears of joy, Sean, and I've shed a few for Jenny."

* * *

Angelique stood on Roy's guyed-out lasso, only this time the rope had been strung tightly between the tops of two circus wagons. All the performers watched. So did Barnum. Jack the Giant stood nearby. Sean had told him to try and catch her, should she fall. She didn't plan to fall.

Once he'd accepted what he called her "daft notion," Sean had offered to play ringmaster.

"La-deez and gen-tul-men," he began, then paused to wink at Brian O'Connor. "And children of all ages. The Sean Kelley Circus proudly presents Dream Angel, the first female equilibrist to perform a forward somersault. Picture tossing an egg into the air. Imagine stretching a piece of sewing thread out in front of you, then trying to catch the rotating egg. What happens if you miss?"

Barnum, who had been sitting on the ground, jumped to his feet.

"I know what you're thinking," Sean continued. "You're thinkin' Dream Angel has eyes to see where she'll land while an egg doesn't. But Dream Angel's legs will come between her eyes and the rope, permitting no optical help with her landing. The forward somersault requires the utmost in bodily coordination, muscular precision, and faultless technique, and has never been successfully completed by a woman. Pre-senting ... Dream Angel."

Angelique leaped toward the sky. At the same time, she lowered her head. Wrapping her arms about her chest, she felt her body rotate. All she could see were her knees. Her golden hair whipped around her throat as she landed slantwise and teetered on the rope's edge. Then, with the greatest effort of her young life, she restored her balance.

The *cirque* performers applauded wildly. Barnum looked dazed. Sean helped her down from the rope and gave her a kiss—the best applause of all.

Sean had "traded" a sturdy stock horse for Roy Osborne's nag, and insisted Roy keep Angelique's seventy-five-dollar-horse to tote his gifts.

The gifts were for his wife, Maggie. Female performers had contributed several opening spec evening gowns—in so many garish colours, Angelique wondered if Maggie would don them anywhere but in the privacy of her own bedroom. The gowns were enveloped by a quilt that boasted a circus motif.

Sean had given Roy enough food to feed a small army, after Angelique had attempted to describe hardtack, and Barnum had given Roy money—to make up for his stolen wages.

At first Roy protested, but nobody could gainsay Barnum, especially when he insisted that Roy deserved every cent for "delivering a valuable cargo."

"More valuable then all them there elly-phants?" the cowboy had asked.

"Ummm … I'll have to think about that," Sean had replied, then chortled like a hyena when Angelique's elbow poked his ribs.

Roy made only two requests—the yellow canary, which he said would be for his new son or daughter "so he or she will never be alone, without no singing." And some elephant dung, so he could prove to everyone that he'd truly seen the critters.

When the last of Roy's trail dust had disappeared, Sean excused himself to help feed the cats, and Barnum turned to Angelique.

"I want you to finish Jenny's tour," he said bluntly, "and by the time we return to New York, the press will be singing your praises."

"Are you joking, Monsieur Barnum?"

"Not at all. You are the only woman in the world who can do a forward somersault, and you look like poetry in motion when you perform. So I'll offer you the same terms I offered Jenny … one hundred and fifty thousand dollars, payable in advance."

"What about Sean?" she asked, stunned.

"You shall be my protégé," Barnum replied, "but Sean can

be your manager."

"His circus—"

"Can be run by someone else until the tour is finished. I have a man in mind, and I'll be happy to pay his salary. If Sean wants to direct the Sean Kelley Circus himself, which you and I know he might prefer, I'll give him my most popular American Museum exhibits. In fact, I'll promise him anything he wants ... except Tom Thumb."

Later, in the privacy of their wagon, Angelique told Sean about Barnum's offer.

"Do ye want to accept, lass?"

"Aside from the money, you could choose the museum attractions that would increase business, and I'd return to our *cirque* a star."

"Did Barnum happen to mention when you would return?"

"He said two, maybe three years. He wants me to perform in London, Sean, for the *Queen*."

"Then say yes, Angelique."

"Would you travel with me?"

"Of course. You are my heart," he replied, repeating the words she had uttered earlier. "And without a heart, one cannot live."

"But one cannot live without a dream, either, and your circus is your dream. *Your* circus, Sean, not Barnum's."

He shook his head vehemently. "You are my dream, lass."

"*Non.*"

"There you go again, saying no to me. *You* are my dream, Angelique, and I will follow you to New York or London or—"

"I meant I shall tell Monsieur Barnum no, my Sean. Not because of hearts and dreams, but because of our afternoon in the silver wagon."

"We can make love in London, lass. We can even make love in Buckingham Palace..." he grinned "...after you perform for the Queen."

"But I cannot perform the forward somersault when my belly is filled with your son."

"My daughter! What makes you think you're with child, Angelique?"

"Silly peagoose! If we did not make a baby this afternoon, we might tonight. Or tomorrow. Or the day after tomorrow."

"You would give up the money? The fame?"

"I give up nothing, Sean. All I want is you. And now, would you please hush, so that we can love God and be merry?"

EPILOGUE

Brooklyn, 1855

"It's a girl," said the bearded lady, "but her's not breathing." Carefully, the bearded lady extended the lifeless infant toward Angelique.

"Ye did your best," said Sean, stepping forward and patting the bearded lady's shoulder. "There was no midwife handy, and our wee one came early."

Brian O'Connor had been crouched outside the wagon. Now he burst through the doorway and raced across the narrow interior. Grasping the baby, he held her by her ankles and slapped her slippery bottom.

"Brian!" Sean shouted. "Are ye brainsick?"

"Brian, *s'il vous plait*," begged Angelique.

"Hush," he warned. "Listen!"

The baby girl mewed piteously. Then she sneezed, screwed up her tiny mouth, and wailed. Brian placed her upon her mum's bosom, and the babe's yowls subsided.

"*Merci*," whispered Angelique.

"There was something in a book 'bout spanking a dead baby alive. You always say reading's a waste of time, but I'm glad I read that book."

Gazing up at Sean, Angelique said, "You promised me a wee lass, Monsieur Hyene. Did you mean it, or are you disappointed she's not a boy?"

"Of course I meant it, Madame Peonne. Why on earth would I want a boy like me, another noddlehead?"

"And when should we begin her riding lessons, *mon* Sean?"

"Soon," he replied with a grin.

The bearded lady had not yet recovered from the shock of seeing a dead baby spanked alive. "It's a miracle," she said.

As if she understood, the baby gurgled.

Sudden tears streamed down Sean's face. "Me daughter," he bragged, "sounds like a calliope."

"What's a calliope?" Embarrassed by Sean's tears, Brian counted his toes.

"A musical instrument. I shall buy one for our circus; that'll increase business tenfold. Wait till ye hear the calliope's whistle, lad. 'Tis a siren one cannot fail to notice. Seductive, tempting, irresistible."

"Seductive, tempting, irresistible," Brian repeated. Then he took a deep breath. "I'm nine now, sir. When are you going to let me tame the cats? Taming the cats has always been my dream."

Sean's gaze shifted to Angelique. "If you're very good, he said, "ye can capture a dream."

The exciting story of the Kelley and O'Connor
families continues in Denise Dietz's
Dream Dancer
coming from Avid Press in January 2001!

Calliope Kelley, the daughter of Sean and Angelique Kelley, is known as the Dream Dancer...her beauty and skill on horseback have become legendary.

Her two passions are her father's circus, and Brian O'Connor...and when a deadly enemy begins sabotaging Sean's circus, Calliope must risk everything—even her love for Brian—to save it.

Miss, Trixie's Fancy-Man

by Linda Colwell

CHAPTER ONE

Trixie Muldoon stood on the upper landing, poised in her scarlet silk dress. Smoothing down the black lace that edged her low cut bodice, she looked about the large, open area. Jaunty piano music and raucous laughter floated upward, as did the appreciative smiles of several patrons.

Trixie scanned the room, noting that her girls were flitting about, engaging the gentlemen in coquettish conversation and teasing them into relinquishing a tidy sum for more intimate services. Business was good, and she took satisfaction in the fact that hers was a clean, honest house—if a house of ill repute could ever be called clean.

Just then she noticed Giles, the manservant, answering the door. The chilly March wind swooped in, bringing with it the smell of frosted pine and smoke, and a tall stranger who immediately looked up at Trixie. He paused in the doorway, and his hair, the color of the sun, was framed against the blackness of night. His eyes, even at a distance, spoke of the sea her mother had so lovingly described. He wore a black suit and matching string tie, and sported a vest of gold satin brocade. *A fancy-man—no doubt about it!*

He stepped inside and closed the door behind him. "Ma'am." His lips moved, forming the word, though she could not actually hear it above the noise of the room and the pounding of her heart. He tipped his hat and smiled.

Trixie acknowledged him with a nod, but the sudden weakness in her knees kept her bolted to the spot. She'd been upstairs checking the supply of fresh linen. Now she regretted being caught on the landing with all eyes on her.

Shaking off the self-consciousness, she descended the steps, taking each one carefully. She knew how to be poised and demure, even if she was quaking inside.

"Good evening, sir, I'm Miss Trixie. Welcome to my House. I don't believe we've had the pleasure of entertaining you before. I'm sure you will find that we have many lovely ladies here. They're all very anxious to please you."

Up close, she confirmed that his eyes were indeed a deep blue. She noticed the little crinkle lines around them when he smiled, and that his lips were full … and well practiced at the art of kissing, she suspected. Trixie had to admit that his was a most appealing face. *But what of it? Why should she even give him a second thought? She wasn't in the market—and even if she were, she would run from a fancy-man like him!*

The man stared for another moment and then finally spoke. "I'm Chase. Chase Summers." He looked her up and down. "As far as your girls are concerned, there can't be none as pretty as you!"

She felt the warmth creep up her cheeks. Was she actually blushing?

"I don't entertain gentleman, but I'm sure you'll find someone here to your liking. We also have games of chance, music, and of course the best liquor in Independence."

He continued to smile as he removed his hat and handed it to Giles. "I've taken a fancy to you, ma'am. What's your price?"

Anger shot through Trixie like a bolt of lightening, but she quickly reined it in. What did she expect? She was a Madam.

"I'm sorry, I must have not made myself clear. I do not entertain gentleman."

Mr. Summers cocked his head and winking at her, he flashed what he no doubt thought was a winning smile.

"Why not allow a gentleman to entertain *you* for a change?"

There was no question that her face had turned as crimson as her dress. How dare this man! "Sir, if I could find a true gentleman, I might consider it." She boldly locked gazes with him. "Please avail yourself of our offerings if you choose. If not, then I bid you good evening."

Chase Summers threw his head back and laughed, drawing attention to himself and Trixie. "Yes, ma'am," he finally said. "I'll do just that." He turned his back on her and walked away.

Trixie watched him as he made his way to the gaming tables. She shook her head. *A fancy, gambling man—nothing but trouble.*

What difference did it make anyway? He was a stranger to her, and his money was just as good as the next one's. She headed towards her office and living quarters on the opposite side of the house.

Once inside the office, she sat down at the ornate, mahogany desk, and looked at the lump of fool's gold. She thought about "Uncle" Roscoe Jenkins. He'd chuckled when he gave it to her. He told her she should always distinguish between the fake and the genuine article. She picked it up and held the cold, rough-surfaced lump in her hand.

The old prospector had said she reminded him of his niece back East, and insisted she call him Uncle. Roscoe was an old man who actually treated her with the respect he'd have shown a niece. That was refreshing and endearing, in spite of his cantankerous nature—and all that talk about a gold mine! She'd warned him more than once to be quiet about it, though in truth, she doubted there actually was a mine. Still, men had been killed for less. She hadn't seen old Roscoe for a week or so. She hoped he was all right.

Dropping the shiny rock on the desk, she stood, smoothed her skirts and, throwing her shoulders back, Trixie headed for the parlor.

Scanning the smoke-filled room, her gaze came to rest on the fancy-man. He was seated at the poker table studying his cards. Lola, one of the more voluptuous girls, sat on his knee with her ample bosom pressed against his cheek. She whispered something in his ear and he chuckled.

An unreasonable anger shot through Trixie, and she suddenly found Lola's behavior repulsive. Besides, Lola was wasting her time on a fancy-man like that! Trixie marched over to the table, ignoring the lazy layer of smoke that irritated her eyes and nose. "Lola, may I speak to you for a minute, please?"

The painted girl with the soulful brown eyes looked up at Trixie. "Now?"

"Yes, please come to my office."

Reluctantly, Lola disentangled herself from Chase Summers after whispering a final message in his ear.

He looked up at Trixie with a surprised, questioning gaze. Then he gave Lola a playful slap on the backside.

Trixie ignored him. Turning crisply, she made her way to the office, with Lola following closely behind.

Once inside, Lola flounced her skirts, giving off a faint whiff of cheap perfume, and sat down in a huff. "I don't understand, Miss Trixie. I had that cowboy lined up. He would have paid good money, too!"

Trixie looked Lola squarely in the eye. "I'm sure *that one* hasn't got two nickels to rub together. Do as you please, but there are other gentlemen looking for entertainment."

Lola cocked her head. "Are you telling me to stay away from him, Miss Trixie?"

What are you telling her? Trixie asked herself. *And why did you call her away?* Suddenly she realized the foolishness of her own behavior. Trixie heaved a sigh. "I know his type—dirt poor and all show. I just didn't want to see you wasting your time, that's all." Trixie waved her hand in a dismissing motion.

A knowing look crept over Lola's face. "Oh, well why didn't you say so, Miss Trixie! If you want that cowboy for yourself, why I won't mind a bit." She grinned. "In fact, me and the girls was wonderin' why you don't already have a man of your own!"

"Lola, that's not it at all!" Trixie realized she had put herself in a very foolish position. "Besides, whether or not I have a man is my business. I choose not to entertain customers—that's all any of you need to know." She hesitated for a moment, not wanting to sound unduly harsh. "Run along now. I have a headache."

"All right, Miss Trixie, whatever you say." Lola grinned, showing her deep dimples. "I figure you could make an exception if you wanted to, though." She giggled. "I'll go get me another man warmed up."

Trixie felt her own cheeks flame as Lola left the room. She had just made a complete fool of herself! Why was she allowing that fancy-man to rattle her?

She frowned when a knock sounded at the door. It was probably Lola again. The girl just didn't know when to leave well enough alone.

"Come in!" Irritation tinged Trixie's voice.

The door opened slowly and a slip of a girl, with long, golden hair stepped cautiously inside. She couldn't have been much more than twelve. Her dress was faded with age and it was ill-fitting, giving the impression that she'd recently gone through a growing spurt. It was a little girl's dress and her body was budding into that of a young woman.

Her sad, young face was partially camouflaged by a garish rouge-colored paste on her cheeks and lips. Blotches of rice powder clung thickly to her forehead and chin, topped off by a strong scent of vanilla flavoring, which the girl, no doubt, had dabbed very generously behind her ears.

"Who are you?" Trixie's voice was gentler.

"My name's Amy, and I want to work for you."

Trixie's stomach turned. Another one—so young. "Have a seat, Amy." She motioned to the sturdy chair in front of her desk.

Hesitantly, the girl made her way to the chair and sat down. "Yes'm."

"Do you have any idea what you are asking of me?"

"Yes'm. I do. I want to be one of your girls—work in your house."

The sadness in the child's large blue eyes tore at Trixie's heart. "Why, Amy? Tell me why a beautiful young girl such as you would want to ruin her life?"

The girl sat up straighter and tilted her chin. "It seems to me you haven't ruined your life, Miss Trixie. You have pretty clothes, money, a nice house. I want those things too."

"Is that the real reason you want to sell your body to men?"

Amy looked down at her lap where she was twiddling her thumbs. "What does it matter? Ain't I pretty enough?" She looked up, once more tilting her chin defiantly.

"You are too young; much too young!"

"I might look young, but I'm sixteen."

"Oh, I doubt that, and I certainly wouldn't hire anyone who wasn't honest with me!"

Just then another knock sounded at the door.

Trixie sighed, figuring that it was definitely Lola this time. "Come in!" She didn't bother keeping the impatience from her voice.

Chase Summers stepped inside the office. He glanced at Trixie, then at the young girl and a look of disgust crept over his face. "Lady, you are a piece of work!"

"What do you want, Mr. Summers?"

"Procuring young'uns for your line of work? You ought to be ashamed!"

Trixie glared at him as anger sent sharp little sparks through her veins. "Mr. Summers, you don't know what you're talking about!"

"I've got eyes! I see what's going on here. Being a lady of the evening is one thing. I always say live and let live. But when it comes to young'uns, that's where I draw the line."

"I draw it there too, Mr. Summers—not that it's any of your concern. Now, will you please just leave?"

Indecision washed over his handsome features. "You mean this isn't one of your—?"

"Of course not! Now get out of here before I call Giles!"

Pink crept up his cheeks. "All right, ma'am, I'll go." He

tipped his hat to Trixie and to Amy, and then ducked out of the door.

Trixie told herself she shouldn't allow this stranger to upset her so. She turned her attention back to the wide-eyed girl seated in front of her. "Now, Amy, do you want to tell me the real reason you have come to me?"

The girl fell silent as she first looked down at her hands and then at a painting on the sidewall. "My family needs the money," she finally said. "My Pa got sick and died. Ma was takin' in sewin' and she was washin' people's clothes, but she's sick now. Someone has to make some money. I have three brothers and sisters to feed."

Trixie gazed at the girl and saw that she was now getting the truth. "Who was your daddy?"

"Leroy Dixon." The girl's voice sounded sad, defeated. "I reckon you might know who he was. We heard he'd come here a few times."

Trixie remembered Leroy. He had been a fairly regular visitor to one of the girls. Trixie's conscience flared. She did not like to think about women and children sitting at home while their fathers or husbands were spending their money at the Pleasure Palace.

"What can you do, Amy? Can you sew like your mother?"

Trixie saw hope rise in the girl's clear blue eyes. "Yes, ma'am. Ma says I can do just about as good as her."

"Do you go to school? Can you read and write?"

"No, ma'am. I did start to school once, but I couldn't stay. Ma needed me."

"I would like to hire you to do my mending. I'm afraid I am a terrible hand at sewing. Never did take to it. I'd also like you to go to school, learn to read and write. If you do all of this I will pay you four dollars a week."

"Four dollars! But, Miss—"

"Do you mean to haggle with me, Amy?"

The look of relief on the girl's face made Trixie's heart skip a beat. At this moment, she felt better than she'd felt in a long time.

"Miss Trixie, I just don't know what to say. I can't believe this."

"Will this be all right with your mother? Did she know you were coming here?"

"No, ma'am." Amy glanced down at her hands again. "I wasn't going to tell her that I was working here. I was going to tell her that I was helping out at different people's houses."

"I don't want you to deceive your mother. You must tell her the truth and get her approval. Do you think that will be a problem?"

"I'll talk to her, ma'am."

"Tell her that your only duties are to sew for me, and you will do so in my office and will not be exposed to any of the other parts of the house."

Amy nodded. "Yes, ma'am."

Trixie pulled a key from her deep pocket and unlocked the top desk drawer. She extracted a twenty-dollar gold piece. "Here is your first five weeks in advance. That should help you get some things your family might need. Oh, and one more thing, Amy. Our bargain will be forfeit if you should ever try to engage yourself as a prostitute. Is that understood?"

"Oh, yes, ma'am." A tear slipped down the girl's cheek. "I really didn't want to be one anyway."

"I know." Trixie rose from her chair and walked Amy to the door. "I'm glad we've come to this agreement."

Staring at the closed door after Amy left, Trixie wondered if the girl would come back. If she didn't, it was all right. She felt good to have used her money to help Leroy Dixon's family. She just hoped Mrs. Dixon would accept it.

Trixie fixed herself a cup of tea and sat by the fire to warm herself from the sudden chill that had swept over her. This really was a dirty business. How could she ever have thought otherwise? There was a time when she had wanted to defy society, she had something to prove; but that fire had died and the reality of her situation had become all too clear.

Maybe that's why the fancy-man had impacted her so. She was feeling unusually vulnerable, melancholy this evening. *That has to be it*, she told herself, as the memory of his quick smile flashed before her. She couldn't afford to let any man have that effect on her—especially one who was so obviously unsuitable.

She smiled ruefully. "Unsuitable" was not a word a Madam could afford to bandy about, since her lifestyle and her profession were considered the ultimate of unsuitable!

It would be a scar that she would always carry on her heart, her soul, but it was also one she wanted to banish from the public eye if possible. If only she could take back the last few years, set back the time and do things differently… But then, what could she have changed? It would all have unfolded the same way again.

No use crying over the past. The only solution was to set a different course for the future. It would take time and money, but she would do it. Someday she would walk away from all this; leave it and everything connected with it behind.

Again the fancy-man flashed before her, and she just as quickly banished him from her thoughts again. There was no room for the likes of him in the future she planned.

CHAPTER TWO

Chase Summers slammed the massive oak door behind him. Who did that highfalutin Madam think she was? He'd turned on all of his charm, and she'd turned him down flat! Miss Trixie was one maddening redhead! She was also a very attractive one, with those bewitching green eyes and haughty attitude.

He didn't know what had come over him, but for a moment there, he wanted to reach out and touch those coppery tresses to see if the fire there was hot to the touch. He wanted to taste those lush lips that looked almost swollen—from too much kissing perhaps? Though she said she didn't entertain customers, he wondered if the remark was aimed only at him. What was wrong with him? He'd never had a problem getting women before—and they weren't always "ladies of the evening" either!

He had to push this Miss Trixie right out of his mind. She was only a means to an end anyway. He'd heard Roscoe Jenkins hung around Miss Trixie's Pleasure Palace. Old Roscoe had loose lips. One of Chase's acquaintances had heard him speak of his gold mine in California—and the friend had said the old man seemed to have plenty of money to spend when it came to playing poker. Chase figured the elderly man wasn't going to have that mine for very long. He might as well be the one to relieve him of it.

A pang of conscience hit him. He'd never set such a scheme in motion if he thought the old man had any intentions of going back and working his claim. He wasn't a thief!

Word was, Roscoe Jenkins had taken all he wanted from the rich vein and had left California, never to return. So the gold was just there, waiting for someone who truly wanted it, needed it.

Though good, decent folk, Chase's parents had been dirt-poor farmers. He'd labored long and hard alongside his father and brothers. But he'd known that farming wasn't for him, at least not when he was young and there was a whole world out there. He had a fire burning inside of him that could not be quenched. He felt driven to explore, experience the world.

He'd left when he was seventeen—had struck out to make his fortune. Now he was thirty-one and that fire wasn't so all-consuming. He'd made a living as a gambler, but he was tired of it. Tired of going from town to town, tired of the seamy side of life.

More and more he yearned for the chance to secure a future, to put down roots and build a home, a life. He chuckled. He supposed his upbringing had finally caught up with him. If he'd ever voiced such sentiments, his fellow gamblers would, no doubt, have a good laugh at his expense.

Chase just needed that one big score and he could make a fresh start. He'd move to California, stake that gold claim. He might even settle down and have his own family!

Chase was itching to meet Roscoe and challenge him to a few hands, sort of lead him up to playing for the mine. Chase again thought of Miss Trixie. There was something about her. Maybe it was the fact that it had been awhile since he'd been with a woman. Yes, that must be it. Even Two-Ton Gertie would probably look good to him about now. He chuckled to himself. He was in no position to allow any female to get next to him. He had a job to do. Any woman, especially a Madam, would only get in the way!

He realized that he, a gambler by profession, had over-played his hand when he went to Miss Trixie's office and accused her of procuring children. He had hoped to lay the groundwork for an introduction to Roscoe Jenkins, but

instead, he'd jumped to conclusions and had further alienat-
ed the woman who would be his best link to Roscoe Jenkins.
One thing for sure—he wasn't going to let that gorgeous
redhead keep him from meeting Roscoe.

At least he had been lucky this evening at poker. He
stepped inside his boarding house and this time he didn't
have to dodge the proprietor.

"Here you are, Mrs. Oglevy. This should pay me up till the
end of the month." He tipped his hat at the rotund, older
woman and proceeded up to his room.

The next afternoon there was another tap at Trixie's door.
It was Amy, devoid of all the rouge and rice powder of her
former visit. Clearly, she had been crying. She stepped forward and placed the gold piece on the desk. "My ma says I
have to return this."

Trixie's heart sank. "Did she say why?"

The girl looked down at her feet. "Well, not exactly."

"Nevermind, Amy, I can guess." Trixie stood up, scooped
up the coin and put it in her pocket. Unlocking the desk
drawer, she took two more coins and dropped them in her
pocket. "Come on, Amy, I want you to take me to your
mother."

"Oh no, Miss! I couldn't do that. She wouldn't allow you
in the—" The girl clapped her hand over her mouth as the
crimson crept up her cheeks.

Trixie flashed a smile. She was beyond allowing the label to
hurt anymore. "I know how the good wives feel about me
and the business I run. Just take me to her, Amy. I think I
can help." She laid a comforting hand on the girl's arm.

Amy sighed and nodded her assent.

Trixie chose her more demure, black cape. She didn't have
the time or inclination to change into something subtler
than the blue satin dress with the low cut bodice that she was
wearing.

Amy led Trixie out the back door and eventually down a

garbage-strewn alley, the stench causing Trixie to pull a handkerchief from her pocket and cover her nose. A well-fed rat darted just in front of her and she stifled a cry. She hated the filthy things, but she didn't want to show her fear to Amy.

"It's just over here," the young girl said, pointing to a door that looked as though it should lead to a storage room instead of a home.

No wonder the girl was so desperate, Trixie thought. She remembered living in a similar type hovel and experiencing the same hopelessness.

Amy opened the narrow door and motioned Trixie inside the dimly lit room. The ripe odor of unwashed bodies and dank mildew was about as bad as that which she'd encountered outside in the alleyway. Since she did not want to offend the family, Trixie put her handkerchief in her pocket.

When her eyes became adjusted to the light, Trixie saw a woman propped up in bed in the corner of the room. Wispy strands of her lank, dark, hair streamed away from her pale, pinched face. "Has she seen a doctor?" Trixie asked Amy.

The girl shook her head.

Of course she wouldn't have. They had no money. Trixie looked around the room and saw a raggedy, unwashed boy of perhaps ten. "Go fetch the doctor immediately," she instructed him.

Startled, the young man stared at her.

"You heard me, go get him now!"

"Go on, Willy! Do as the lady says." Amy spoke with authority, confirming what Trixie already knew. Amy was carrying all the responsibilities on her young shoulders.

"Who's there?" the woman in the bed rasped. "Who's barking out orders to my son?"

Willy looked at Amy then he turned and headed out the door.

Trixie approached the bedside. "It's me, Mrs. Dixon. I'm Patricia Muldoon, but you would probably know me as Miss Trixie of the Pleasure Palace."

"You! Get out of my house. I've got no use for your kind!" The strained, hoarse words resulted in a coughing spasm.

"Ma, please, don't say those things! She's a nice lady!"

"Lady?" the woman croaked. "That ain't what we call 'em where I'm from."

Trixie reminded herself that the woman was ill and she was only spouting the same line as all the other respectable women. It was expected of them.

"Look, Mrs. Dixon. I know what you think of me. But truth is, I have some money that belongs to you." Out of the corner of her eye, she saw the startled look on Amy's face. She continued. "I may be a lot of things, but I'm not a thief. Your husband got lucky at poker once and he gave me some money to hold onto for him. He didn't want to gamble it away. I gave your daughter some of the money to give you. I figured you might not want me in your house."

"That's not the story the girl was telling! But you are right. I don't want you in my house." The woman's large, blue eyes glared at Trixie.

"Well, I guess you'll have to get up out of that bed and throw me out then." Trixie turned away from Mrs. Dixon and Amy's shocked expressions.

"Amy, get a scrub bucket and some soap. That is if you have some?"

"Yes, ma'am, I think we still have some."

"Have you any food in the house?"

Amy's face flushed. "We ate the last yesterday."

Trixie looked at the sunken-faced Mrs. Dixon. "You are a stubborn, foolish woman. What does it matter where the money comes from when your children are hungry?"

She pulled one of the gold pieces from her pocket. "Amy, go to the mercantile and buy the supplies you need."

"Yes, ma'am," the girl said, breathless with excitement.

Mrs. Dixon started to say something, but Trixie turned a wilting glance on her and she shut her mouth.

"It's your husband's money, woman, and your kids need to be fed!" Mrs. Dixon looked away, fixing her gaze on the wall.

Just then two younger children, a boy and a girl, came through the door. Their little arms were filled with sticks of wood and kindling and their faces bore patches of crusted dirt and fresh scratches from the spiky branches.

"Well, now, you are just in time!"

They stared at Trixie.

"Can you two make a fire while I tidy up the place? The doctor will be coming to see your Mama."

Nodding their heads, they proceeded to the fireplace.

Trixie took off her dark cape, exposing her shoulders and cleavage. There was no time to worry about it now.

She picked up a broom and started sweeping. After filling the bucket from the pump that was gratefully inside the ramshackle hut, she set it by the fire to heat.

When it was warm, she filled a small basin, took a cloth and a piece of soap. "Here," she said, placing it next to the bed. "I imagine you'd like to freshen up before the doctor gets here. Do you need me to help you?"

Mrs. Dixon shot her a resentful stare. "No, I can manage by myself!"

"I figured as much," Trixie muttered as she set about looking for some more cloths for dusting the house. A small wood-burning stove stood in the corner, so she had the younger boy start a fire in it. She glanced about her. It would have to do, though Lord knew the woman's bed could use some clean sheets and blankets.

Trixie smiled to herself. She dare not send to the Pleasure Palace for those articles, though she would have gladly spared them. Poor Mrs. Dixon would die of apoplexy for sure!

Dr. Beasley arrived about the same time Amy returned with two sacks of groceries. The frail girl was straining to carry them.

"Doctor, please tend to Mrs. Dixon and send your bill to me."

The doctor nodded. He had treated Trixie and her girls before for various illnesses and he'd shown himself to be a kindly, fair-minded man.

"Now, Amy, I think we need to fix something to eat."

"You know how to cook, ma'am?" Amy stared wide-eyed.

"Well, of course I do! You don't think I was born a Madam, do you? There was a time—"

Trixie heard the wistful quality in her own voice and regretted it. What was the matter with her? For now, at least, she had a good life! She did as she pleased, had a lot more independence than the women who looked down their noses at her.

Soon Trixie had bacon sizzling and potatoes frying and had just put a pan of biscuits in the small oven. The smell of hot coffee mingled with tantalizing smells of the food and filled the room with a pleasant aroma.

Dr. Beasley walked over to Trixie. "I've given Mrs. Dixon some draughts. I think she can recover, but she needs cleaner surroundings, good food and rest." He shook his head. "She just doesn't have the resources."

Trixie thought for a moment. "Would the vacant Turner place at the edge of town do?"

Doctor smiled. "I reckon it might at that."

"I'll see to it, Doctor. Now how about some supper?"

Mrs. Dixon eyed Trixie when she took her a tray of food, but she didn't shove it away. Trixie suspected that the respect the doctor had shown her made Mrs. Dixon ashamed to say too much.

Besides, the woman was probably so hungry, her hardened stance left her once she caught sight of the hot biscuits and bacon, fried potatoes and scrambled eggs. She took a quick slurp of coffee and then tucked into her meal.

After everyone had eaten and the dishes were cleared away, Trixie pulled a chair up to the bed.

"Now it's like this, Mrs. Dixon—your husband only came to my place to gamble. He wasn't there for the women." Trixie knew she needed to keep the man's memory intact for his family. Why not stretch the truth a bit? "He left money with me for safekeeping. I'm going to use the rest of it to get you and your family into the old Turner place. You'll have fresh air and sunshine there."

The woman just stared at her, but the hatred in her eyes had softened. Trixie saw that beneath the illness and hardships etched on her face, there was a woman who had lovely eyes and fine, delicate features.

"I am in need of someone to sew for me. I would like Amy to do that and, also, I'd like to see her in school. For sewing and for going to school, I will pay four dollars a week. I hope that will be satisfactory. I will increase that to five dollars a week if your other children go to school too." Trixie saw the woman taking it all in; a flicker of hope seemed to shine in her faded blue eyes.

"If you don't want me to be seen coming to your house to drop off my mending, then Amy can come to me and I will let her in my office by the back door. She will not be permitted in any other area of the house. The choice is yours."

The woman stared at Trixie and a tiny smile quirked the corners of her lips. "If my Leroy trusted you to keep his money, and you were honest enough to bring it to me, well then I reckon I'd be all right to have you call at my house."

Roscoe Jenkins gazed at himself in the watery mirror. He saw the lines and the unhealthy color. He'd been feeling poorly of late. Figuring it was the liquor, he'd gone easy on it—but he still didn't have the stamina he'd once had. Of course, he wasn't getting any younger, so what did he expect? He smoothed down the collar of his freshly laundered shirt and slicked down the gray cowlick that stubbornly grew near the balding area on top of his head.

He'd been staying away from Miss Trixie's, but now he looked forward to a night at the gaming tables. The pain in his chest was gone this evening. He knew he'd been overdoing it, not only with the drinking, but with the women too. He grinned, remembering how the ladies at the Pleasure Palace always made him feel special.

Even Miss Trixie herself gave him special treatment, though in a different way. He thought about his niece, Jade, back in Boston. He hadn't seen her for years, but he figured she must be about the same age as Miss Trixie.

Where Miss Trixie had flaming red hair, little Jade was dark like his sister, with large green eyes. Yet there was something about Miss Trixie that reminded him of his niece. Maybe it was the green eyes and the fact that both were spirited young women. At least that's what his brother-in-law said about Jade, and certainly Roscoe had seen Trixie when she set her mind on something. She could be one stubborn woman!

Miss Trixie had treated him very kindly, though, and at the same time had been the soul of propriety. He reckoned she wasn't in the business of flesh peddling anymore. At least not where she herself was concerned. Of course she ran the House, and a damned good one it was too! He thought about brown-eyed Lola and the way she made him feel. Then he thought about the gaming tables and realized that he was looking forward to a good game of poker even more than the obvious charms of Miss Lola. "I must be gettin' old!" he said to his image in the mirror. After sniffing the pleasant aroma, he slapped on some bay rum after-shave and was ready to tackle the evening.

CHAPTER THREE

Trixie felt a deep satisfaction as she left the Dixon home. Things had worked out well. It may be too late for her, but it wasn't too late for Amy. Not even the ripe odor of garbage in the alley could discourage her. She did, however, decide to go around to the front street, which would afford her a better-lighted walk home.

Night had fallen and the bustling town was alive with activity, as people had begun to converge on Independence to prepare for the wagon trains' April departures.

Trixie was grateful for the boardwalk that at least covered part of her distance home. Pulling her cloak closely about her, she attempted to keep out the creeping dampness that came with the night. The scent of pine, mud, and horse dung clung to her nostrils as she hurried on her way.

"Well now, who have we here?" A rangy-looking cowboy stepped in front of her, blocking her path.

Startled, Trixie came to an abrupt halt. She knew how to handle amorous cowpokes, but this one had caught her off guard.

"Step aside!" She glared at him.

The man guffawed, sending off waves of rank breath that sickened Trixie. He set his feet farther apart as if to ensure that she could not pass. "Well, that's right unfriendly of you, seein's that it's your business to entertain lonesome cowpokes like me." He reached out and grabbed her arm.

Trixie tried to jerk away but his grip was too tight. Her cloak fell open, exposing her scant bodice.

"Well now, I see you are dressed for work." His free hand reached toward her cleavage.

The rotten smell of his unwashed body hit her in the face. "Let go of me, you miserable jackass!" She pulled back, this time managing to break free. At the same time she delivered a kick, that, had it hit its mark, would have rendered the man temporarily helpless.

Unfortunately, he did a mincing sidestep, and then lunged at her again.

"Get your filthy hands off of me!" she shrieked as he grabbed her with both arms and yanked her against him. Her heart pounded and a raw, numbing fear shot through her veins. She was aware of a crowd forming. They seemed to be fascinated with what was transpiring and not particularly interested in helping her. *Oh God! Were they actually going to stand by and do nothing while this vile man assaulted her?*

Suddenly out of the corner of her eye, she saw a flash of gold brocade and she heard a crunching thud as a well-delivered fist made contact with her attacker's jaw. The disagreeable man went sprawling on his behind, hitting his head against a post in the process. The blow knocked him out cold.

Then Chase Summers was offering Trixie his hand. "Are you all right, ma'am?"

She quickly pulled her cloak about her, noting that his was a most pleasant scent: sandalwood and lye soap with a touch of pine. Strange that she would be aware of it under these emotional conditions.

"Yes, thank you, Mr. Summers." She could hear the quavering in her voice, but she refused to give in to the tears that threatened to spill.

"In that case, ma'am, I'd be happy to escort you home."

A refusal was on her lips, but she realized she was shaken and could truly use the company. "Th-thank you, Mr. Summers."

"Ma'am, you shouldn't be out on the streets after dark like this."

"Why not, Mr. Summers? Do you think it will damage my reputation?" She tossed a challenging glance at him. But then, he wasn't the enemy. He'd just rendered her a kindness. "I'm sorry." She glanced away because at that moment she wanted him to put his arms around her, to comfort, soothe her as one would a frightened child. But there was no room in her world for such vulnerability. "That was uncalled for. I don't usually venture out at night. I had some business to attend and it took longer than I had expected."

She placed her hand over his arm for the remaining walk and instantly felt his body heat against her gloved fingers. The warmth coiled through her like white heat, and it took all of her will to maintain a cool, calm demeanor.

They made small talk along the way and garnered several stares and a few snickers, but she held her head high. If Chase was aware of the attention being paid to them, he didn't show it.

Soon they were at the door of the Pleasure Palace. "Won't you come in, Mr. Summers? The least I can do is buy you a drink."

"The last time I was here you threw me out," he chuckled. "Are you sure it's safe for me?"

"I'm sorry. I had a headache that day and I'm afraid I over-reacted. Of course, you did jump to conclusions." Trixie smiled and directed him through the back entryway. "Feel free to avail yourself of all that the house offers." Feeling her cheeks flush, she quickly glanced away.

Chase followed Trixie down the hallway to the open area where they were greeted by the eternal layer of smoke from the numerous cigar and pipe smokers.

"Enjoy yourself, Mr. Summers." Before he could respond, she turned away and walked over to Lola who was draped across Roscoe Jenkins.

"Miss Trixie!" Roscoe stood, almost spilling Lola onto the floor.

"How are you, Uncle Roscoe?" Trixie greeted him with a kiss on his weathered cheek. "I haven't seen you around. I was concerned."

"Well now, that's right sweet. I was feeling poorly, but am fit as a fiddle now. I'm ready to whup these ol' boys at poker, by God I am!"

"Look no further, mister, I'd love to engage you in a game!"

Trixie heard Chase's voice behind her. She whirled around. "Roscoe's a friend of mine, Mr. Summers," she said, hoping to impart the idea that he was off-limits to a professional gambler like Chase Summers.

"You wouldn't mind introducing me, would you? Did I hear you call him uncle?"

"That's just an endearing term. We aren't related."

"Who's this young feller?" Roscoe didn't attempt to conceal his curiosity.

"This is Chase Summers. Mr. Summers, this is Roscoe Jenkins." Trixie felt the anger rising. She didn't like being used and it certainly seemed that was exactly what was happening here. Though she was indebted to Chase for rescuing her, she didn't like him using that indebtedness to finagle an introduction to Uncle Roscoe.

"I heard you liked to play poker, Mr. Jenkins. I've been known to turn a card or two myself. How about a few hands of stud?"

Old Roscoe broke into a laugh. "I say quit your palavering and let's cut them cards!" Roscoe slapped Chase on the back, and then sat down. Chase smiled and took a chair across from the older man.

Trixie didn't trust Chase when it came to card games. He was clearly a fancy, gambling man. Roscoe wouldn't stand a chance. She shot Chase a warning look, which only caused him to raise an eyebrow and wink at her. The man was most infuriating!

She called Lola aside.

The dark-eyed girl looked wary. "Did I do something wrong, Miss Trixie?"

"Of course not, Lola. I just want you girls to keep an eye on Mr. Summers. I don't want him cheating old Roscoe."

Lola flashed a toothy, dimpled grin. "Why sure, Miss Trixie. I'll stay close to Roscoe. He's taken quite a fancy to me and he does pay generously."

"See that Mr. Summers and Uncle Roscoe have a drink on the house. Oh, and ask Vanessa to entertain Mr. Summers." As the words came out Trixie disliked herself for saying them. *God, she needed to get out of this business!*

She went back to her office and put on water for a cup of tea. She could imagine Vanessa, with her long blonde tresses, hanging onto Chase. He would enjoy every minute of it. Vanessa, with her fragile, china doll face and willowy features, was one of her most sought-after girls.

When the tea was ready, Trixie sat down on the chair by the tiny window and propped up her feet. She took a sip of the hot, aromatic brew. Suddenly she was very tired. Tired from all that had transpired that day and tired of running a bawdyhouse. She kept coming back to the same conclusion. She'd had to turn-off her conscience, but it came back to haunt her from time to time.

She had paid the price for her lucrative profession and so-called independence. She couldn't walk down the street alongside the proper ladies of the town. She wasn't welcome in church, though she sometimes stole in at night and lit a candle for her darling mother.

Mama, forgive me, but I would do it all over again. It paid for the medicine, the good food that kept you alive a bit longer. Besides, once Mrs. Arlington spread the lies about Trixie, there was no decent job to be had in St. Louis or anywhere in Missouri. The high society woman made sure Patricia Muldoon would never work in a decent household again, as a governess or even a scullery maid—and all because Mr. Arlington couldn't keep his hands to himself and Patricia had gone to his wife and told on him!

Curtis Walters had come into Trixie's life on a day when the cupboard was literally bare and the landlord was on the verge of evicting them. Curtis was elderly and liked being seen with a beautiful young woman on his arm. A childhood injury had left him impotent, and disinterested, so he had no real physical need for a woman. However, in the eyes of the world, she was his mistress, and he thoroughly enjoyed that illusion. She had been well compensated financially even though it left her reputation in shreds.

It wasn't that Trixie wanted marriage. She hadn't found a man yet that would make her want to pull off his boots, wash his underwear and bear his children. Of course that option was pretty much closed off to her now anyway, though occasionally a presumed "soiled dove" did land a husband.

Neither did she crave the acceptance of an unforgiving society. Mostly, she just wanted to feel clean again, to walk with her head held high and not be sneered at. Deep down inside she knew the truth, but she also knew no one would ever believe it. Besides, even though she didn't sell her own body, she ran a business where other women did.

There was no getting around that. The only way to feel normal again would be to leave this place, to make a fresh start somewhere far away. Even then she would always run the risk of meeting up with someone who'd known her as Miss Trixie. But it was a chance she'd have to take.

She'd been saving her money. She was getting closer to the day when she would once again be Miss Patricia Muldoon instead of Trixie of Miss Trixie's Pleasure Palace.

She took a long sip of the sweetened tea. Yes, it was what she wanted, what she was working toward. Chase Summers' teasing smile flashed before her. She couldn't allow that fancy-man to turn her head and keep her from her goal.

Chase studied old Roscoe's face. He knew he had the old man beaten, but he also knew that Roscoe needed to be cultivated a bit. It wouldn't be too smart to beat him right away.

Chase slung his cards face down on the table. "I'm out! You got me, Roscoe!"

The old man laughed and Lola planted a big, red kiss on

his lips. "You ain't been too lucky with the cards tonight, Chase. Maybe you'll be luckier with the ladies?" Roscoe winked at Vanessa who was lounging on Chase's knee.

"You may be right at that." He flashed a grin at Vanessa, then at Roscoe. "I hope you will give me another chance tomorrow?"

"Why, sure thing, young feller! I'll meet you here same time!"

Roscoe stood up then, with Lola in tow, and hand in hand they headed upstairs.

Vanessa stared deeply into Chase's eyes, a sly grin on her face.

"Would you like to go upstairs, lover?" She stood up.

Chase gazed at her for a moment, then winked. "Can't do that, darlin'." Using an exaggerated sweep, he placed his hands on his chest and flashed a forlorn smile. "Alas, my heart belongs to another. You are prettier than dew on a daffodil, honey, but my little lady just wouldn't understand."

The painted smile on Vanessa's dainty lips drooped. "Are you sure?" She looked taken aback, then a lazy, knowing grin flashed across her face. "Who's gonna tell her?"

"No one would have to tell her. She's got eyes in the back of her head, *that one*! Now you run along, darlin'."

As Vanessa sashayed away, he asked himself why he'd done such a fool thing. He hadn't been with a woman for some time and this one was really quite attractive, even if she was prostitute. Still, it didn't sit well with him to have to pay for companionship! He didn't usually have any trouble attracting a female.

So was that why he kept remembering that copper-headed wildcat called Miss Trixie? She'd turned him down—something he wasn't used to. Was that why she dominated his thoughts? He'd have been laughed out of the Pleasure Palace if he'd told Vanessa that the 'lady' he was referring to was none other than her Madam, Miss Trixie. He recalled her pointed words again, *I don't entertain customers!* So what was she doing in this business then? He could understand if she were old and frumpy, but it seemed to him this prime specimen of womanhood had retired much too early. That also made him foolishly happy, because he didn't like the idea of another man touching her.

He felt the redness creeping from his neck up to his ears and beyond, and was glad no one seemed to notice. For all his joking and bravado, he had a mother and sisters whom he greatly respected, and he knew that many women ended up in the prostitution business because they had no other choice.

He should be the last person to judge anyone. Look at him—a gambling fancy-man. He'd heard the label more than once and he supposed he lived up to that reputation— but he also knew he probably wasn't the rake, the charlatan many thought him to be. He was just a man trying to make a big score so that he could retire and, in effect, end up with a life similar to the one he'd left behind. No one could have convinced him of that when he was seventeen, but there it was.

He was tired of traveling, living day by day. He wanted to put down roots. Once he had a good living, he wanted a woman by his side to love him, as his mother had loved his father. He wanted a helpmate to bear his children, someone to cuddle next to him on a cold winter's night.

"Chase, you must be gettin' old," he whispered to himself.

CHAPTER FOUR

Trixie walked out into the front parlor for one last inspection before going to bed. She didn't see Chase Summers—not that she cared. At least that's what she kept telling herself every time his face and ready smile flashed before her. Again, she willed herself not to think of him and to get back to the business at hand. She just wanted to make sure he wasn't taking advantage of Uncle Roscoe. As she surveyed the room, she saw that the poker game was over.

Then she saw Vanessa and was mildly surprised. She figured she would be upstairs with Chase. Vanessa was hanging on the bar, striking a pose, no doubt to enchant male admirers. Trixie approached her.

"I thought you'd be entertaining Mr. Summers."

"Oh, him!" Vanessa snorted in disdain, spoiling her ladylike image. "That fancy-man's already got himself a woman."

"Oh, I didn't realize—" Of course she should have known that a handsome charmer like Chase Summers would not be wanting for female companionship—even if he was a gambling man! He probably had some poor schoolmarm's heart in his unscrupulous hands! Grudgingly, she had to admire the fact that he was faithful, but then she remembered how he'd propositioned her the first evening he came to the house. So it appeared he was faithful when it suited his purposes. *What is that fancy-man up to?*

Why should she care anyway? She was an independent woman, and the only way to stay that way was to avoid men—particularly the likes of Mr. Summers.

"Well, Vanessa, I'm sure there are other gentlemen here who would be more appreciative of your charms."

As Trixie walked away, she heard a voice behind her and felt a hand on her shoulder. She reeled around. "Mr. Summers!" She took a backward step. "I thought you'd gone."

"I left for awhile, but now I'm back. I thought you might join me for a late dinner at the café across the street."

"I'm afraid that isn't possible, Mr. Summers."

"And why not? Have you already dined?"

"Come, let's speak out there." She motioned to the hallway. "There's less smoke and it's a little more private." Once outside the room, she stopped and leveled her green-eyed gaze at him. He stood so close, she was very aware of his masculine scent mingled with that of sandalwood.

"I can tell you're new in town." She found herself smiling, in spite of the tinge of sadness that swept over her heart. "I wouldn't be welcome at Mrs. Green's Café. I'm surprised a man such as yourself wouldn't know that."

"And why not?"

"Really, Mr. Summers, isn't it obvious? Women in my profession are not welcome in so-called 'decent' places of business—at least not during regular business hours—and certainly not where families might go."

Chase threw his head back and chuckled. "You mean you'd let that stop you?"

"Mrs. Green is a nice lady. I don't want to hurt her business and that's what I'd be doing if I stepped foot inside there this evening."

"If she was a nice lady, she'd be more welcoming to you."

"Not if she wanted to keep running that café! Besides, I have my own cook. I have no need to go across the street."

"Are you inviting me to have dinner with you here then?"

Trixie was caught off-guard. "Well, no, that wasn't what I was doing." Then she remembered Uncle Roscoe and she realized she would like to learn more about Chase's poker game with him. "However, if you'd care to join me, I will have Cook prepare a bite for us in my private dining room."

She hesitated for a moment, telling herself that this was a huge mistake. "Will the lady in your life mind? I wouldn't want to cause a problem."

"Well now, I'd be much obliged." Chase made a sweeping bow. "My lady won't mind a bit." He flashed his devilish grin. "In fact, I think she'll be pleased." Then he raised his left eyebrow. "Private dining room? I'm impressed."

"I have a suite next to my office." Trixie frowned. "That's an odd thing to say, Mr. Summers. Most ladies don't like their men fraternizing with anyone in a house of ill fame— even if it is a 'dinner-only' invitation."

"You seem to think you know an awful lot about me, ma'am. Me having a lady in my life and all...."

"I try to make a point of knowing something about the people who frequent my House. It's just good business. As I said, though, this is just a dinner invitation, so your lady will have no reason to be upset."

"You are showing a total immunity to my charms. I must be losing my touch!"

"How can you lose something you never had?" Trixie regretted the cutting words, but then, he did need a bit of comeuppance. "Now if you'll excuse me for a moment, I'll speak with the cook."

Chase Summers threw his head back and emitted a deep laugh. "You wound me deeply, ma'am!" He held his hand over his heart in a dramatic fashion.

Trixie turned and headed down the hallway to the back of the house, glad to escape the uncomfortably personal nature in which the conversation had drifted. Perhaps he'd just mentioned a lady friend to Vanessa to put her off. Strange, though—few red-blooded men would have turned Vanessa down

Trixie asked herself why she had agreed to dine with Chase Summers since he was nothing but trouble? Oh yes, Uncle Roscoe. That was it. She'd tell him to go easy on the old man. Roscoe wasn't exactly right in the head at times. She'd not have him taken advantage of!

Later, Trixie watched Chase as he cut into his thick, juicy steak. The dim lamp's glow caught the gold in his hair, giving him the look of an angelic being. But Chase Summers was far from that! She'd have to be careful. She'd never allowed any man to get truly close to her. That was dangerous ground; territory she had no intention of treading. Yet this man had been dominating her thoughts like no other.

She thought about her dear, sweet mother and the man she'd chosen to marry. Trixie's father had been an Irish charmer, a heavy-drinking, gambling, fancy-man to the core. He'd left when Trixie was seven years old, so she had memories of him—his quick smile, boyish charm. But in the end, all that love she thought he had for her and her mother had apparently been a sham. He left, never to be heard from again.

Life had been very hard after that. Kathryn Muldoon worked long backbreaking hours and had scrimped and saved to give her Patricia an education. Yet there was always a sadness about her, something that no one, not even Patricia could dispel.

Trixie knew her mother never lost hope of again seeing her 'Andy'. She died still believing that someday he would return. Trixie had always believed he had gone for good, but she never told Mama that. She let her have her dreams, and in fact, as angry as she was at him for leaving, she'd always love her Da.. Still, Trixie vowed that she'd never let the same thing happen to her.

Trixie studied Chase in the flickering lamplight. "So, Mr. Summers, I hope you were not too hard on Uncle Roscoe. He is a special friend of mine. I wouldn't want to see him taken advantage of." Trixie cut off a small piece of the succulent steak.

"Uncle Roscoe? Special friend?" Chase raised a well-formed eyebrow.

Trixie sighed. "Not *that* way!" She glared at him. "Not that I have to defend myself to you, Mr. Summers. I think I made it clear that I only run the business end of this enterprise. I do not entertain customers."

"I must say, I find that rather strange."

"It's my business and I couldn't care less how you find it."

Trixie took a sip of hot tea. Chase Summers had a maddening habit of probing into things that weren't any of his business.

He nodded and smiled. "I am chastened, ma'am, truly I am!"

Ignoring his mock humility, she continued. "I believe I was asking you about Uncle Roscoe. I hope you haven't taken all his money?"

Chase chuckled. "Me take all his money? Ma'am he took mine! That old coot can take care of himself. You needn't be worryin' your pretty little head about ol' Roscoe."

Trixie looked him in the eye. "I like Uncle Roscoe and I don't want to see him hurt. Do you understand?"

"Yes, ma'am, and I can assure you that you have nothing to worry about where I'm concerned."

Trixie studied his sincere countenance. "Very well, Mr. Summers, I'll take you at your word."

When the meal was finished, Trixie was surprised and relieved that Mr. Summers thanked her politely and then took his leave. She'd expected him to at least try to kiss her. Having grown accustomed to such behavior in her line of work, she was grateful and though she didn't care to admit it, perhaps a little disappointed.

After saying goodbye with a handshake at the door, she made her way past the salon, back to her own suite. She felt suddenly very alone. Had she actually wanted him to ask to stay with her? *Of course not!* Yet, something deep, primitive within her had come alive in his presence. Something she'd never felt before.

In bed that night, she kept seeing Chase Summers' golden hair and ready smile. He had all the charm of her father.

That must be why she was attracted to him! He was the same type of man too, someone who could never be counted on. She would have to keep reminding herself in the future when she was in Chase's presence.

Trixie kept herself busy the next two weeks. Chase came in almost every day and played cards with Roscoe. He seemed to be true to his word. Maybe he wasn't quite the devil she'd made him out to be, but she still kept up her guard. In spite of that, she would get a funny, giddy feeling inside when she'd catch sight of him.

This was especially true when their gazes met, which was often. Those blue eyes embraced and held her each time. She fought the feelings, the urges, that the sight of him evoked. She could not afford to get involved with a *ne'r do well*. She would not suffer the same fate as her mother!

On the following Tuesday, Trixie went to the Dixon home and found Mrs. Dixon looking much healthier. She was sitting in a chair and greeted Trixie with a ready smile when Amy admitted her to the house where they now lived. With Giles' help they had moved into the old Turner place the Friday before. This was the first time Trixie had visited the family in their new surroundings and she found the house to be clean and pleasant. Mrs. Dixon, or Mae, as she insisted on being called, now treated Trixie with respect.

"I have brought some sewing for Amy." Trixie offered the bundle to the girl. "I want to hear all about school. How you and your brothers and sisters are doing."

Amy and her siblings launched into eager details. Afterwards, Trixie pulled candy sticks from her pocket and gave one to each of them.

"Miss Trixie," Mae spoke up when there was a lull in the conversation. "I have a proposition for you. I'm feelin' much better now. If you have extra sewing, like maybe some of your ladies need things mended or made, well I'd be happy to take care of that for you."

"Oh Mae! That would be wonderful! Have you thought this out? It might require entering my establishment; people might talk about you."

"Shucks. Let 'em. I didn't see none of them respectable ladies coming around in my time of need. You were our angel of mercy. I reckon I'd be right proud to work for you. Besides, that Mr. Giles is a fine man, a true gentleman. I don't reckon I'd mind running into him on occasion."

What was this? A budding romance? Trixie gazed at Mae Dixon, who now had color in her cheeks. She was an attractive woman. Trixie smiled to herself. Giles had been a bit distracted lately. Was this the reason why?

Trixie knew the value of allowing people to earn their way. That's why she'd made stipulations to the money she'd given Amy. Truth was she could use someone like Mae to do the sewing in her house. Her girls tried to do their own, but most of them were lacking in that talent.

"Mae, when the doctor says you are ready, I will hire you. You come and see me at that time and we'll discuss pay, your hours and so forth."

"Thank you, Miss Trixie."

Trixie left the house feeling good about Leroy Dixon's family. She was especially happy about the possible romance between Mae and Giles. Perhaps they, at least, could fall in love and have a happy life together. Perhaps Trixie would have to settle for seeing such good things happening to the Mae Dixon's of the world and enjoying them vicariously.

Roscoe looked at the map, staring at the 'X'. People thought he was a fool, but by God, he'd gotten gold out of there. He got out a fresh sheet of paper and made a copy of the original. "Can't have too many maps," he chuckled.

He'd have one copy on him. Should he leave the other one in his room? It didn't seem like a good idea. Then a thought suddenly struck him and he got out another piece of paper and an envelope.

Dear Lawrence and loving niece, Jade,

Here is a copy of my map for safekeeping. I have found gold and I know there's a lot more. Hold onto this and should anything happen to me, I hereby give you the rights to the mine and all that is in it.

Roscoe Jenkins

Then he wrote on the map itself, *I, Roscoe Jenkins, grant the bearer of this map the ownership of my gold mine claim.* Suddenly, Roscoe clutched his chest as the pain hit him, threatening to cut off his breath. Beads of sweat popped out on his forehead and a wave of nausea swept over him. Putting the letter aside for a moment, he reached for the bottle of whiskey and put it to his lips and took a long drink.

The warm liquid seared a hot path as it slid down his throat. In a moment the pain eased and he could breathe better. That was a close one! He knew his ticker was acting up. He would never survive a trip back to his gold mine in California.

Besides, he liked it here in Independence with Lola and the other girls at Miss Trixie's. They treated him with respect. He chuckled. As far as he was concerned it was respect. Others might call it something else. Then his thoughts grew more serious.

Miss Trixie was special. He wanted to do something nice for her too. He thought for a moment, then he took out another envelope and wrote her name on it. He took the other copy of the map and, and in his spidery scroll wrote, *I, Roscoe Jenkins, grant the bearer of this map the ownership of my gold mine claim.*

He put the map in the second envelope, and placed it in his pocket. He'd give it to her for safekeeping and tell her if anything happened to him, it would belong to her. Yes! It was a capital idea! Shucks, there was enough gold there for his relatives back East and for Miss Trixie if any of them ever decided to strike out for California! When the time came, they'd all figure it out. "Haw, haw!" He slapped his knee. You had to get up pretty early to outsmart him, Roscoe

Jenkins!

Having resolved that, he felt better. Now he just had to get the other one mailed to his brother-in-law and niece. He also needed to take a little better care of himself, give his heart time to rest. He'd been hitting those gambling tables heavily. That young Chase Summers was a pretty good gambler, but he was no match for someone like Roscoe. The old man chuckled to himself as he fingered the envelope with Trixie's name on it.

Ol' Chase's eyes would pop out if he could play for such stakes. He'd been dropping hints left and right. Maybe Roscoe would give him a chance at it before he turned the envelope over to Miss Trixie.

Suddenly a truly brilliant idea struck him. He took out one more envelope and scrawled on the front, *Roscoe's Map*. Then he wrote '*Surprise*' in the middle of a blank piece of paper and stuffing it into the envelope, he licked the flap and sealed it.

"Haw, haw!" He wheezed and stomped his foot as a coughing spasm hit him. He reached for the whiskey bottle again and nearly strangled as he took a swig.

Finally the coughing subsided, but it left him temporarily out of breath. He willed himself to calm down, take it easy. Save his laughs for later when ol' Chase figured out he'd been suckered.

Shucks though, with the way Chase played, Roscoe could have put a copy of the actual mine in there and would never have had to worry about losing it! He knew how to hide an extra ace or two if it came to it! Then another idea came to him. It would be the king of all practical jokes. Roscoe loved a good joke and from what he could tell, ol' Chase did too.

Yes, he would sweeten the pot when he played with Chase Summers again. Before he did, though, he would make sure he gave Miss Trixie the real copy.

First, he had to get himself rested up. That Lola had about worn him out—or was it the other way around?

Roscoe sauntered over to the lumpy bed in his rented

room and stretched out. He'd spend the next day or so planning for the grand finale. He might play a couple more times with Summers; really whet his thirst, line the young upstart for the kill. Roscoe chuckled to himself. It would be fun.

CHAPTER FIVE

Trixie gazed at her ledgers, but she just couldn't concentrate. She kept seeing the smiling, devilishly handsome face of Chase Summers. Taking a deep breath, she could almost smell his tantalizing, masculine scent. She stopped, stretched, and rotated her neck from side to side to get out the kinks. Then she stood and walked over to the window and looked out onto the side street.

Large, wet snowflakes swirled on the blustery day. Sometimes winter seemed to go on forever. Varying shades of grays, dull whites and mud that always ended up on the entryway floors—ah, but that was the least of her worries!

Worries? Now why had she thought that? She had a good income, her girls seemed happy enough with their lives—in fact they considered her something of a heroine. She thought back to the day when she'd become a Madam.

Strange how it had all come about. She had a small nest egg Curtis had left her and she saw how the girls were maltreated. The rambling house in Independence was up for sale and Trixie's reputation as Curtis' mistress had preceded her there and had closed most doors to her. So there seemed to be a mutual need.

She bought the house, fed the girls, cleaned them up and named the place Miss Trixie's Pleasure Palace. Curtis had always called her 'Trixie' and the name seemed to fit the chosen profession. She had never looked back—until now. It was ironic that she was branded as a 'soiled dove' when no man had ever actually touched her. But who would believe that?

Though, strictly speaking she wasn't one of them, Trixie identified with the downtrodden ladies of the evening. She was branded just as surely as they were.

Again she thought about getting away—starting over where no one knew her name. It was a dream, but when she heard people talk of their upcoming journeys to California or Oregon, a part of her wanted to stow away with them! She had the wanderlust, the desire to be free of this work, this reputation.

She wanted to scrub Missouri from her until her skin was pink and raw. Someday she would make the break! When that day came, her name would no longer be Trixie, the Madam. She'd simply be Patricia Muldoon.

She thought of Chase Summers. He was totally unsuitable, undependable, just like her father had been! Yet, she couldn't stop thinking about him, wondering how it would feel to have his lips pressing against her own—to feel his firm, lean body possessing hers.

In spite of the business she ran, such thoughts were foreign, intrusive to her. She did not like being caught up in such raw emotions. In order to survive, she'd had to be in control, plan her steps carefully. These feelings were like a tidal wave, threatening to sweep her along, away from all that was familiar.

Just then a knock sounded at the door, awakening her from her musings. "Come in," she called out.

Roscoe stepped inside, a sly grin on his face. He held an envelope in his hand. "Miss Trixie, I have something for you—for safe keeping."

She walked over to him. "What is it, Uncle Roscoe?"

He pushed the envelope toward her. "It's the map of my gold mine. I want you to keep this and if anything should happen to me, it's yours to do with as you see fit."

Trixie was stunned. "Oh, Uncle Roscoe, I don't know what to say."

"Just say you'll put it in a safe place and keep it for me, that's all you have to do. You've been good to me, Miss Trixie—always kind and thoughtful. I trust you and I want you to have it when I'm gone. I'll never go back to California. The trip's too hard!

Besides," he scratched his head, "I'm havin' way too much fun here with the girls. Don't reckon I'd like bein' back in California nearly as much." He started laughing and wheezing until it grew into a full-blown coughing spasm.

"Here, come and sit down." Trixie helped him to a chair and got him a glass of water. "Uncle Roscoe, you need to slow down. I'm afraid you're going to kill yourself with all the gambling—not to mention the girls!"

"Haw, haw! I reckon if I die, I'll go with a smile on my face! What more could a man ask for?" He took another slurp from the glass.

Trixie patted Roscoe's shoulder and gave him an affectionate hug. "All right, if this is what you want, I'll put the map in my safe. But just one more thing, be careful of that Chase Summers. I think he's pretty slick, a real professional gambler. Don't let him trick you."

"Shucks, Miss Trixie, that young whippersnapper ain't got nothin' on me. I've been hidin' aces up my sleeve since before he was born! Haw, haw! He makes a right good opponent. I'm just havin' fun with him and the fun ain't over by a longshot. No sirree!" Then he peered at her strangely and another grin split his weathered face. "You ain't sweet on him are you?"

Trixie could feel her cheeks redden. "Of course not! I just don't want to see you taken advantage of."

"Well, Miss Trixie, I don't want to see you taken advantage of neither. But it seems to me, he ain't a bad feller. Maybe you should give him a chance."

"A chance for what? Really, Uncle Roscoe! That fancy-man would be real trouble if I let him. No, thank you! There's no room in my life for the likes of him."

"Well, I don't mean to pry, but it seems to me there ain't

much room in your life for any man. How come?"

Trixie didn't like such personal questions, even from old Roscoe. "I'm happy with things just as they are."

Roscoe shook his head. "Well, you don't look it to me. Just don't seem natural. No, it don't seem natural at all. And I don't care what you say, I think you're sweet on ol' Chase and I think he's right taken with you too! I've seen the way the two of you have been makin' cow eyes at one another!"

"Uncle Roscoe! I have no idea what you're talking about." She felt herself blush.

"Never you mind denyin' it. I know what my eyes seen. Haw, haw! Ain't no law agin' it, Miss Trixie. You need to loosen up and let your feelings go. Ain't good to keep 'em all pinned up inside. Now you think about what your old Uncle Roscoe has told you!"

Trixie studied the sealed envelope after Roscoe left. Did everyone read her as well as he? Were her growing feelings for that fancy-man so apparent? She tried to push the conversation from her mind and concentrate on the envelope in her hand. Was there really a map to a bonafide gold mine in there? It didn't matter—it was Roscoe's property. She went over to the wall safe that was concealed behind a painting. She pushed the painting to the side and turned to the appropriate numbers on the lock. It clicked open. Quickly, she placed the map inside and closed it. As she did so she heard a knock and Chase Summers' voice.

Trixie whirled around realizing that Roscoe had left the door open. Chase stepped into the room, the perpetual smile on his face. She quickly moved the painting back into place.

"What do you want, Mr. Summers?" She noticed the snowflakes on the shoulders of his great coat and the brim of his hat, which he promptly removed in her presence. She could smell the cold, pungent, pine-scented air and she felt an urge to run to him—to brush the icy patches from his shoulders and kiss the snowy flakes that dotted the planes of his face. She restrained herself, hoping he couldn't read thoughts.

Apparently he could not. He seemed more intent on what it was he had hidden behind his back. A teasing smile curled his lips as he pulled his right hand around in front of him to reveal a small bouquet of white lilies.

"What on earth…?"

"For you, lovely lady."

Momentarily tongue-tied, Trixie just stood and stared at him. She felt her face flush as an anticipatory shiver creep up her back. The irony of white lilies was not lost on her. He was giving her this purest of all flowers. "Where did you manage to get lilies when the snow is flying outside?"

"Oh, I have my connections." He grinned and winked at her.

"I'll just bet you do. Come over here and warm yourself by the fire." She reached for the lilies, and clutched them to her breast. She felt her heart, beating, leaping beneath her bodice. The sweet scent filtered up to her nose and caused her heart to do a joyful little flip.

Chase hesitated for a moment, his gaze locking with hers. Feeling the warmth of him so close, and knowing if he tried to kiss her she would readily go into his arms, she glanced away. A delicious shudder rippled through her. She didn't dare look him in the eye now.

"Have a seat. I'll get you something to drink." She motioned to one of the chairs next to the fire. "You look like you're freezing!" She tried to make her voice sound light, witty, but inside a battle was raging. Fight though she may, she wanted to surrender to this golden god, this thoroughly maddening man. She wanted to know the feel of him touching, kissing her until she could scarcely breathe.

"Yes, ma'am, a shot of whiskey would taste mighty good if you have any on hand."

Trixie forced herself to walk to the other side of the room to her liquor cabinet. She kept a bottle there, though she rarely drank it herself. Before retrieving it, she took a small, empty vase, filled it with water from a nearby pitcher and put the lilies in it. She sniffed them again; their pure, sweet scent touching that indefinable longing that had gripped her of late.

"They really are lovely flowers, Mr. Summers," she said through stiff lips. "Thank you."

"It's still Mr. Summers, is it? Why don't you call me Chase?"

"Of course—Chase."

She took the whiskey bottle from the cabinet and poured two shots into a glass and carried it to him. It took all of her concentration to still her shaking hands.

"Aren't you going to join me?"

"No, I don't think so." Her voice had a particularly breathless quality.

"Ah, come on, Miss Trixie! I've never seen such a straight-laced Madam in all my born days!" He cocked his head to the side and gave her a devilish grin.

"And I imagine you've seen plenty of them too, haven't you?" She didn't try to conceal the sarcasm in her voice. Now she was on safer ground. His remark had helped her slip back into her Miss Trixie role.

Chase threw his head back and laughed. "A few, darlin', but none like you!" He set his drink on the tea table.

Trixie put her hands on her hips. "And what is that supposed to mean?"

He looked up at her with his dreamy, blue eyes, and she felt the swirling sea that her mother had spoken for. He reached for her hand and suddenly she did not have the will to pull away.

"It means, sweetheart, that you are the prettiest thing I ever saw." His voice was soft, smooth, like yards and yards of velvet.

She couldn't think straight when he was this near. It took all her resolve to try to pull away, but he wouldn't release her hand.

"You really don't want to do that." He gave her a gentle tug and she found herself suddenly sitting in his lap. She turned slightly so that her breast was resting against his chest and she could feel the beating of his heart, synchronized with her own.

She couldn't help but look into those hypnotic eyes of sapphire blue and when she did, she drew closer until their lips were only inches apart. She closed her eyes and for the first time in her life, she gave herself over to being kissed.

His lips were soft, pliant, gentle against her own. He pulled her even closer. She felt giddy, lightheaded as her breath came out in a deep sigh. She put her arms around his neck, and her hands found the silken strands of his hair. Ah, the absolute freedom and wonder of running her fingers through it, she thought, as she sank further against him, totally surrendering to his kiss.

She felt the warmth of his tongue smoothing against her lips, seeking permission to probe more deeply. She opened to him, reveling in the absolute wonder of these new feelings.

Her skin felt like liquid silk as his hands smoothed over the surfaces, beckoning, pulling her to a deeper union. She felt one hand slip up to her low cut bodice and cup her breast. A shiver rippled through her and she heard herself whimper.

She breathed deeply of his manly scent mingled with the ice and pine and she could only think of this very moment as it both taunted and soothed her hungry soul. All that had happened before or might happen in the future didn't matter. Here, now—nothing else mattered.

Suddenly, he pulled back. Confusion, vulnerability and surprise flashed across his face. He seemed momentarily speechless. Then the unsettled look was replaced by the cocky, confident demeanor Trixie had grown to associate with this fancy-man.

"Sweetness, you are some kind of tiger!" He winked at her and chuckled.

It was as though he'd thrown cold water in her face. Quickly she pushed herself away from his lap. "As I told you before, I don't entertain customers." She tried to sound firm, but she heard the quaver in her voice and realized how foolish she must sound.

A frown creased his brow. "You must have been somethin' when you did.".

"I think you've warmed up enough, Mr. Summers, now please leave. I have work to do."

He drained his glass then stood, eyeing her up and down with his devastatingly blue gaze. His grin returning, he pointed at her as though she had been a naughty child. "I told you to call me Chase."

"I may call you something a lot worse if you don't get out of here and leave me alone!"

"Yes, ma'am. I love you too!" He ducked out of the door before she could throw a nearby book at him.

CHAPTER SIX

A few days later, Chase headed for the Pleasure Palace. He was ready to take Roscoe on for high stakes. The old man had tossed out the offer. It was what Chase had been waiting for. Soon the wagon trains would be pulling out, heading for the California gold fields and he intended to be on one, with his gold map in his pocket—compliments of Roscoe Jenkins.

The old man was going to lose that mine sooner or later, so it might as well be to Chase. So far Chase was the only one who had been losing. Of course it was by design. He had lost his small bankroll to Roscoe just so the old man would let his guard down. It would be worth it when Chase gained that gold mine. He'd find a way to get to California once he had that map in his possession! Getting it was the thing that required timing, finesse. He was up for the occasion.

Of course he would have to be careful around Miss Trixie. She protected old Roscoe like a tiger protects her cubs. Tiger. That red hair of hers reminded him of a jungle cat and she had a temper and passion to match. What a woman! He hadn't been able to banish the memory of the feel of her soft body next to his, the willingness, even innocence of her kisses. He'd never allowed any woman to get under his skin. He traveled light and that was what he intended to keep on doing until he got his gold mine. Then he'd find himself a good woman and settle down.

So why did he keep thinking of Miss Trixie? He wondered

what had made her choose the life she had. She seemed different, not like the others. There was a certain shyness, innocence about her. But she was still a Madam. Even if she didn't "entertain" gentleman now, she obviously had in the past. So what had made her stop? Once thing was certain, her resolve had weakened the other day.

He shook his head. Was he getting soft on a prostitute?

He mustn't let that happen, though he would not be adverse to spending an evening in her very desirable company. There was no girl in her house who could compare. It had been a very long time since he'd been with anyone as pretty, and for that matter, as interesting, as Trixie.

Again, he remembered the feel of her warm body next to his, the sweetness of her lips. "Well why not?" he said aloud. "She's had plenty of practice!" Something inside of him felt a momentary shame for having said it. Why should that be? Her past experiences would only made her better at the art of lovemaking. After all, it wasn't as though he wanted to marry her!

He suddenly realized that he wanted very much to make love to her, and he would, by God, before he left for California to claim his gold mine—the one he was going to win from Roscoe Jenkins!

Roscoe looked up from his cards, a sly grin on his face. He was really whupping up on ol' Chase. "Four of a kind!" He slapped his cards down on the table and began raking in the money.

"This just ain't my evening," Chase shook his head. "You've about cleaned me out, Roscoe."

Roscoe knew this was the time. He reached in his pocket and pulled out the envelope. "I'll tell you what I'm going to do, young feller. I'm going to put up the contents of this envelope. I don't think I have to tell you what's in it, do I?"

Chase stared at him.

Roscoe could tell the man was trying not to act too surprised, but he could see the young pup was practically salivating. Of course he knew what was in it! Or at least what was supposed to be. This was going to be fun!

"I see you have about twenty dollars left, Chase. I got all your money and I'm feelin' generous this evening. I'm going to put up this envelope against the money you have left. We'll cut the cards once. The one with the highest card wins."

A light came on in Chase's eyes and Roscoe could hardly conceal his glee. He loved the joke he was playing on the young scamp. He wanted Chase to think he'd finally gotten the upper hand and had him, Roscoe, right where he wanted him. There'd be no harm in it. There wasn't any law against Roscoe purposely losing. Chase wouldn't be losing his investment, so no harm done.

After ordering another round of whiskey, Roscoe was the first to draw. With sleight of hand he switched it for the card up his sleeve. The Two of Hearts. He was leaving nothing to chance. "Ah shucks!" Pretending to be disgusted, Roscoe slammed down the deuce.

Chase remained calm in spite of the excitement raging inside of him. For a moment he considered actually drawing from the deck, instead of using the Ace he kept up his sleeve. The only way he could possibly lose would be if he also drew a two. Then they'd have to do it all over again. He decided not to risk it. He pulled the Ace from his sleeve and revealed it as the card he had supposedly drawn.

Lola's surprised squeal pierced the room, then all fell silent."Well I reckon you done won this fair and square, Chase." Roscoe leaned forward as he handed him the map. "I would suggest you wait till later before you open it. Don't want to go givin' people ideas. Don't want to be flashin' it around." Roscoe rubbed his chin thoughtfully.

"In fact, let me suggest that you go see Miss Trixie when we're done here. That little lady is plum sweet on you. Man, you're a fool if you let her slip through your fingers! But mind you, you'd better have honorable intentions or you'll answer to me!"

Chase stared at Roscoe, unable to believe what he was hearing. "I think you've been hitting that whiskey a little too hard, Roscoe. The last time I saw her she was ready to throw a book at me. Fortunately I dodged and got out of the room in time."

"You don't say?" Roscoe wheezed, still trying to talk in low tones. "By God, that proves it! Ever heard of love taps, boy? If you have any brains, you'll go to her tonight."

Chase looked at Roscoe a slow grin washing over his face. "You really think so?" Chase knew that spending the evening with Trixie would make this a perfect day!

"Hell's fire, son. I know so. I know women. I know all about 'em. That little lady has a mighty hankerin' for you. Do you know how many men would love to be in your shoes and she won't give none of them the time of day? Mind you, though, you treat her right or you'll feel my boot if you don't."

Chase grinned at Roscoe. "If you will excuse me, I have to call on a certain red-headed lady." He tucked the envelope in his inside pocket and headed for Miss Trixie's office. He resisted the temptation to rip open the packet there and then, choosing instead to savor the moment and open it later.

When he knocked on Trixie's door, he heard her sweet voice bid him to enter, and his heart did a funny skip. He touched the area where the map was concealed in his jacket. He had no intention of telling Miss Trixie about it. In fact he'd have been smart to have left the place right after winning it. But Miss Trixie had awakened a fire in him. He'd stayed away, but now that he'd gotten what he wanted from Roscoe, he just couldn't leave without tasting Trixie's lips one more time.

If he played his cards right in this particular game, he'd come away a winner here too. Even without Roscoe's encouragement, he knew he would have ended up here at her door anyway.

The room was bathed in a soft lantern's glow. Trixie was

sitting by the fire sipping something from a fancy teacup. Her long cascading hair looked like burnished copper as it spilled over her shoulders and down her back.

He heard her breath catch when she caught sight of him. She was clad in a dressing gown with what appeared to be a flannel nightgown beneath it. Strange way for a lady of the evening to dress, but then he reminded himself that she did not entertain gentlemen. Maybe she had actually been telling the truth about that. One thing was certain; she had not been expecting him.

Uncertainty pricked at his confidence. He had come here with the idea of making love to a tiger, and instead, he was looking at an innocent looking, demure pussycat!

"Miss Trixie, I—I just wanted to stop by maybe for a drink, if that's all right?" *Damn! He was acting like a schoolboy. What was the matter with him?*

"I was just having a cup of tea. As you can see, I'm not dressed for receiving visitors." She seemed torn by indecision and fell silent. Then she spoke. "I suppose a drink would be all right. There's tea in the pot, or if you want something stronger, help yourself to some whiskey from the liquor cabinet."

For a moment he actually considered the tea. Then he came to his senses. "Whiskey sounds just fine." He turned his back on her and went over to the cabinet. Why had he come here? He shouldn't have listened to Roscoe! He'd won the map, so why hang around and risk Miss Trixie finding out? The growing hardness between his legs answered that question for him.

He retrieved the whiskey bottle and poured himself at least a double shot. "I'm sorry if I've dropped in at an inconvenient time." *Ah, hell, he was sounding worse by the minute!* He walked stiffly over to the chair directly across from her, hoping she didn't notice his awkwardness. Why didn't she have a settee here by the fire? A man couldn't do much, sitting across from her. It dawned on him that that was exactly why there was no settee there.

He settled back against the brocade chair and took a long sip of the fiery liquid. It burned as it slipped down his throat, but it also helped ease his tension.

Then he looked at Trixie. She was gazing directly at him with those wondrous green eyes. Again he gazed at the fiery red-gold of her hair spilling over her shoulders, with some of it draping against the swells of her breasts.

The lantern's glow accentuated her alabaster skin, making him question anew. *How could this lovely wholesome looking creature be anything other than a proper lady?* He'd heard of men falling for soiled doves, and he'd always gotten a good laugh out of it, labeling such fellows as desperate and dumb. Suddenly it wasn't so funny any more.

He took another drink of his whiskey, but his eyes never left her. What was she thinking? Maybe she was waiting for someone else! That's why she told him to come in, in that demure voice!

But then if she were expecting someone else, she'd have told him to leave. Besides, she had kept reminding him that she didn't entertain customers.

He set his glass down and rose to his feet. "I guess I'd better be leaving," he said, though he knew it would be the most difficult thing he'd ever done.

The look of disappointment that washed over her face hit him like a scalded dog. In two quick strides he was in front of her, pulling her up out of the chair and into his arms. He only saw the glow in her eyes and the smile on her face as she melted against him.

Her lips sought his hungrily, pressing against him. He felt her fingers lacing through his hair, touching his face. *Oh, she was good, really good!* Then he felt ashamed for even thinking it as his lips trailed kisses down her neck. She felt so soft, innocent, smelled of the pure lilies he'd given her. Even the high-necked collar of her gown seemed to proclaim a virginal innocence.

Suddenly she stepped back from him. "Wait. Please tell me the truth. Is there a woman your life?"

He could hardly believe his ears. Since when did a prostitute even care? "I have been with many women, but I travel light, so until I met you there was no one. Now I can't seem to think of anything but you!" He reached out and took a strand of her fiery-colored hair between his fingers. "I do believe you have bewitched me!" He smiled and reaching out, he chafed his thumb against her soft cheek.

At first she looked surprised, then a sweet smile swept across her face and she stepped back and began undoing the buttons of her bodice. Her fingers fumbled, betraying her nervousness.

My, it must have been a long time for her. Good man, Chase! He complimented himself for his prowess and at the same time he asked himself how he could have gotten so lucky—a gold mine and this gorgeous woman all in one night!

He couldn't help but gape at her as she nervously undid the last button. Then she pulled the gown slowly away from her shoulders, revealing creamy skin, as the gown slid down her form, and pooled at her feet.

Chase's breath caught in his throat. *Venus rising from the Sea,* he mentally called on something he remembered from his school days. Trixie was indeed a good comparison to a goddess. He gazed at her perfect breasts and graceful form. *Was this a dream?*

She stepped back into his arms then and rested her head against his chest, clinging to him. He felt her shudder and he wasn't sure if it was from passion, the cold, or just plain fear. Once thing for sure, she was trembling.

He picked her up in his arms then and headed for a doorway that he assumed led to the bedroom. A soft lamp's glow highlighted the plump bed, covered with a white lace comforter. The coverlet had already been turned back.

It *was* as though she had been waiting for him! He quickly reminded himself that a turned back bed was hardly proof. Besides, what did it matter? He wanted this gorgeous creature and she was obviously willing.

He gave the comforter a tug, pulling the covering halfway

down the bed. Then he deposited her gently on the cool, smooth sheets. She watched him with eyes brimming with desire as he peeled off his shirt, then his trousers. Her breath caught in her throat, when he was at last devoid of all clothing. He saw her eyeing him, all of him and it heightened his desire. He felt the resulting hardness pulsate as he slipped in bed beside her.

Quickly, he reached for her, his need washing over him like rushing waves of warm water. He had to have her. He wanted her like no other woman he'd ever known.

Her lips we so soft, giving, seeking. She moaned when he again trailed kisses down her neck until he found her waiting breast. He suckled it, taunting, teasing as he felt her shiver beneath him. Her breath rushed out as she wound her fingers through his hair. Pulling his face to hers, she sought his lips, probing deeply with her tongue until he felt dizzy with desire.

He again kissed her neck, traveling further this time to the other breast, then beyond, reveling in her sweet scent. Passion and raw need gripped him and he could wait no longer. Slipping above her, he again sought her mouth with his own as the rest of his body took possession of hers. He was startled by her cry of pain.

To Chase's amazement, she cried out again, then she began to moan softly in husky pleasurable tones. His heart pounded a primitive beat and his breath rushed out in gasps. He couldn't stop now. Their bodies were exultant as they moved in unison, reaching for the heights of pleasure.

Finally in one great wave, he released, satiated, filled to capacity, totally consumed by emotions he'd never before experienced.

He rolled away, settling himself on the pillow as she snuggled against him.

Why had she cried out like that? Why would there have been any pain at first? He had been gentle. Then the truth dawned on him. He'd just made love to a virgin! A virgin Madam? He'd never heard of such a thing!

CHAPTER SEVEN

Trixie stretched and sighed when she opened her eyes the next morning. She felt languid, sensual, different that she'd ever felt in her life. She reached out to the other side of the bed as the events of the night before rushed over her like a soft breeze. The spot was empty, only Chase's lingering, masculine scent remained.

Chase? Where was he? An uneasy feeling crept over her. She had taken leave of her senses last night. It was simple, really. She was in love with a fancy-man!

Suddenly a yelp from the sitting room caused her to jump from the bed. Grabbing her dressing gown and slipping into it, she ran to see what had happened.

"Damnation!" Chase held a piece of paper in his hand and he was staring at in disbelief. An envelope lay on the floor next to his foot. Trixie glanced at the picture that hid the wall safe. For a brief moment she thought he had broken into it and had taken the envelope Uncle Roscoe had given her. Pushing aside her foolish suspicions, she went to Chase. "What is it?"

"Look at this! Just look at this!" He thrust the piece of paper in her direction. There was one word scrawled in the center of the page. *Surprise!*

"That damned ol'liar! I can't believe I fell for such a stunt!" Chase grabbed the paper from her hand, threw it on the floor and stomped on it. "Well, he's not going to get away with this. You can't cheat people like that!"

"Who are you talking about, Chase? What's happened?"

He turned to her, his eyes a stormy blue, "Roscoe Jenkins! That's what! He cheated me in a poker game. He told me we were playing for a map to his gold mine. No wonder he did-n't seem too upset about losing it." Chase began pacing. "Damn! I won it fair and square….Well, in a manner of speaking anyway." A niggling suspicion crept over him. Ol Roscoe probably palmed that deuce so he could lose. He'd lost on purpose just to play a horrible joke on Chase.

After fastening her outerwrap more securely, Trixie put her hands on her hips and glared at Chase. "You mean you tried to cheat that old man out of his mine! Well, it seems to me you got what you deserved."

"Well he won't get away with this!"

"And just what do you plan to do about it?" She stepped up and glared at him eyeball to eyeball.

She saw the realization dawn in his eyes. He'd been hood-winked and there was precious little he could do about it.

"Look, Chase, just let it go. I don't need trouble in my place. I run a clean house. The old man played a practical joke on you—that's all. You won, so you really don't have any complaints. It's not like you lost any money."

Trixie was concerned about Roscoe. She didn't think Chase was the type who would do physical harm to the old man, but she couldn't be certain. What did she really know about this man that she had just made love to? What could she have been thinking last night? The answer came swift and sure—she had been thinking with her heart, not her head.

She saw the disappointment in Chase's eyes and that wounded her deeply. How had she developed such a soft-ness, a need for this man?

Mama, she silently whispered, *it must have been this way with you and Da.* She reached out and touched Chase's cheek. "Don't worry, I promise you it doesn't matter. It'll be all right."

He looked at her and suddenly his gaze softened; the mus-cle in his jaw relaxed. "How can you possibly say that? You have no idea—"

"I may have a much better idea than you think." She went into his arms and kissed him willingly, wantonly. It felt as natural as the sunshine on her face on a warm spring day.

She saw the disappointment in his eyes and her heart squeezed.

"I love you, " she whispered.

Chase's stance relaxed, softened. "I don't know exactly how it happened but it seems I am falling in love with you." His lips planted feathery kisses on her cheek and her nose as he leaned over her, his blue-eyed gaze holding her captive. "Furthermore, I do believe I made love to a virgin last night. How can that be?"

"It's a long story, Chase. I'll tell you all about it some other time. Right now, I'm thinking Cook should be sending some breakfast. She always sends way too much, so there'll be enough for both of us."

A few minutes later, Trixie opened the door to the cook who carried in a lavish breakfast tray. Trixie was about to help herself to some coffee when Lola's voice sounded from the hallway. She pushed past the serving woman, almost knocking the tray from the elderly woman's hands.

"Miss Trixie! Have you heard the news? Old Roscoe was found dead in his room this morning! They say it looked like it was his heart that took him!"

"Oh, no, not Uncle Roscoe!" Trixie felt as though someone had knocked the breath from her.

Immediately, Chase was at her side. "Here, darlin' have a seat. He guided her to the settee near the window. "Just leave the tray there," he motioned for the cook to put the tray on the small dining table.

"Poor old Roscoe. I'm gonna miss him!" Lola wailed as tears spilled down her cheeks. "He was awful good to me."

"We're sorry for your loss, Lola, but right now I think Miss Trixie needs some time to take this all in. I'll see to her."

"All right, Mr. Summers." Lola looked at Trixie. "I'll talk to you later, Miss Trixie."

"Yes, Lola, later. We'll talk."

After Lola and the cook had gone, Trixie turned to Chase. "I don't know what to think, or say."

Trixie saw that Chase, too, seemed saddened by the news and she felt relieved.

"I'm sorry this happened. I'll miss that old cuss! I guess I gave him a good laugh before he died. Maybe the excitement was too much for him." Chase shook his head. "I guess that is the end of the gold mine map. Unless—"

"What are you thinking, Chase?"

"Well, I did win that map. Maybe the real one is in his room somewhere—or maybe it was. Damnation! With all the talking that old codger did, I'm sure his room has been searched, stripped by now."

Trixie saw the deep disappointment in his eyes and she turned to butter. "Why is that map so important to you?"

Chase chuckled. "It's the map to a gold mine for God's sakes!—to a new life in California."

"I thought you were the type who liked to gamble, travel light. A gold mine would be lots of responsibility."

"It's the kind of responsibility I'd welcome. My pa was a farmer, worked hard all his life. I was restless, left home, but I'd like nothing better than to have a new chance. I'd settle down, make that money work for me. It would help me get a fresh start, a new life! A man gets tired of traveling and wants something better; wants to put down roots, share his life with someone!"

Trixie thought her heart would burst. "We have the same dream, Chase. We want the same things and we're in love, aren't we?" She reached over and wrapped her arms around him.

"It sure looks that way." He stroked the long strands of her hair.

"You don't have to go looking for the real map. I have it. I can turn the business over to one of the girls, and we can walk away. We can both get a fresh start in California and we can do it together."

He gazed into her eyes. "*You* have the map? Are you sure

it's the real thing and not another one of Roscoe's jokes?"

"Well I never actually opened the envelope, but I'm sure Uncle Roscoe wouldn't play such a trick on me."

"Don't you think it would be wise to check just in case?"

Trixie didn't want to think Roscoe would ever try to trick her, but she knew Chase was right. She should check. She got up and went into the sitting room. Pushing the painting aside, she set the appropriate numbers on the tumbler and opened the safe. She took a deep breath before reaching in and pulling out the envelope.

When she turned, Chase was right behind her, so close she bumped into him. "Open it, let's see what kind of man ol' Roscoe was."

Trixie's fingers trembled as she opened the envelope. She pulled out the piece of paper and when she unfolded it, there was indeed a map, with a large X marking the mine's location and scrawled on it the words that would transfer ownership to the bearer of the document..

Tears welled up in Trixie's eyes as Chase took the map from her hands. Dear old Roscoe. He'd just given her the means to have a new life. And now, she also had the man she loved standing next to her. They would share it.

Suddenly Chase picked her up and swung her around. "Whoopee! Hot damn! We're gonna be rich, darlin'. We're gonna have a good life, a new start in California."

"Yes, and I'll no longer be Trixie the Madam, I'll be Mrs. Chase Summers!" The words slipped out before she could even weigh them.

"That is if you want to marry me. You do want to marry me, don't you Chase?"

He set her down but held her so closely she could feel his heart beating against her own. An easy smile settled on his handsome features. "Yes, if that is what you fancy, sweetness, you will be my bride."

His lips found her own eager ones and she wondered how it was she had lived all these years without this wonderful fancy-man! "Chase, promise me you will never leave me,

that we will be together forever. I don't give my heart lightly. I play for keeps."

"Yes, we will always be together, my sweet, Trixie."

"In that case my love, the name's Patricia...Patricia
Muldoon."

*Can love continue to blossom for
Chase and Trixie?*

Watch for **Toward the Sunset**
by Linda Colwell,
coming in March 2001 from Avid Press.

*Gold Fever seizes the hearts of four people and propels
them to the gold fields of California.*

After being jilted by her fiance, Jade Whitman strikes out
on her own to claim the gold mine left her by her Uncle
Roscoe. But an uncooperative wagonmaster refuses to
allow a single woman on his wagon train.

Just how far is Jade willing to go to gain her passage and
what awaits her at the end of the trail?

Passion's Legacy

by Sally Painter

The saga of the Bates family, begun in
Shadows of Love,
continues with the story of Maria Bates.

Prologue
– Allensville, North Carolina, June 5, 1858 –

"At least he was tidy about it." Sheriff Hanson slipped the makeshift noose from the dead man's neck.

"My uncle was an orderly man." Andrew Bates jerked the blanket from the small cot and covered Jonah Bates's prone body. "Thelma does not need to know how he died."

"He hanged himself in his cell. How do you expect me to keep that quiet when we have newspaper journalists from all over the South in town? Hell, we have them from as far north as New York. The trial was scheduled to start in a few days, the defendant is dead, and you want me to keep it a secret?"

"At least allow me to tell my cousin first, before everyone in town knows. Hasn't Thelma suffered enough with her mother dying and now her father taking his own life?" Andrew replied.

"What a mess. Ole Jonah just couldn't face the humiliation of his trial." Sheriff Hanson shook his head.

Andrew clenched his fists by his sides but his outrage broke through.

"Damn, you, George! I tried to tell you that he wouldn't stand trial. Granted, I expected him to break out of jail— not *kill* himself." Andrew swallowed back the other words he wanted to hurl at the Sheriff.

"Had one of my best deputies watching him."

"So what did your deputy do? Sit and watch my uncle rip

the sheets into strips and tie them into a noose?" Sarcasm dripped from Andrew's words.

"I don't know, but I sure as hell intend to find out. My men are searching for Deputy Williams right now."

"Searching? My uncle's suicide makes it *all* very tidy. Doesn't it George? Saves the town of Allensville a sensational trial of one of their most prominent citizens." The bitterness in Andrew's voice was impossible to hide. He cleared his throat and turned from the body.

"My deputies cannot be bribed. I don't care what your uncle promised Williams, he wouldn't have left his post. Not Williams."

Andrew glanced back at the sheriff. "What makes you think it was my uncle doing the bribing?"

"Now wait a minute, Andrew. You insinuating this was more than a suicide?" The sheriff pushed his hat from his forehead, revealing a thick crop of dark hair, and stared from the covered body to Andrew. "You think he was *murdered*?"

"What do you think, George? You're the law officer here. It's your deputy who's missing. It's your prisoner who's dead." Andrew swiped his hat from his head and raked his trembling hand through his hair. "My uncle was a coward, but I don't think he'd take his own life. I think he had an escape planned and whoever was supposed to help him didn't." He plopped his hat back on his head, hiding his unruly hair.

"Now see here. Just because there was all this white slavery commotion going on up at your place, doesn't mean there is some kind of conspiracy here surrounding his death. I think Jonah just couldn't face the humiliation of a trial."

"It's your district, George. If that's what you want to say happened, fine with me." Andrew pushed the metal door open and left the cell.

As he stepped outside the jail, his heart pounded harder. The sun was just rising above the tree line. Allensville gave the illusion of being a peaceful Southern community, not at all the hub of the impassioned crowd that had been held at bay for nearly three weeks. Once they heard the news, the crowd would grow wild with speculation and stories about Jonah Bates's suicide.

Andrew was grateful his sister, Celeste, was not there. He would send a courier with the news to the MacGraft home as soon after he told Thelma. He swung up onto the horse's back. Dread hammered out his heartbeat. How was he going to tell his cousin that her father was dead?

"Are you just gonna leave?" The sheriff rushed out of the jail after him.

"There's nothing here for me to do. I'm going home." Andrew reined the horse.

"Well, damn. I would have expected more from you, Andrew Bates. After all, it was *your* sister your bastard uncle tried to sell into slavery."

"My sister is safe with her new husband in Virginia. Now that Uncle Jonah won't be on trial, she doesn't have to come back to Allensville and face all this. My aunt is dead and now my uncle. My cousin is the *only* person I'm concerned about at this moment. I have to bring this news to her. Or would you rather have that chore, Sheriff?" Andrew glared down at the flustered man. Sucking in a deep breath, he released the bitterness in his final words to the lawman. "You tend to your business and see that my uncle's remains are turned over to the undertaker and I'll tend to what's left of my family."

Chapter One
– Allensville, North Carolina, September 12, 1858 –

"You cannot be sincere, Andrew." Thelma Bates paced the length of the study. Andrew could sense her feelings. Her life had crumbled around her. First, her mother had died and then her father, arrested and awaiting trial had taken his own life. Marriage might be good for her. She'd lost so much. If she married the right man, then she could start a new life.

"My father did the same thing to your own sister. How can you do this?"

"It's not the same thing. I'm *asking* you. My sister, Celeste, was not consulted about her arranged marriage."

"I cannot cope with all this." Thelma's green eyes darkened with a painful glint. Andrew reached over and closed his hand over hers. His cousin bowed her head, struggling for control.

"It's only been five months, Thelma." Andrew drew her into his embrace. "Grief takes a long time to heal. You've lost too many people in such a short time. You cannot continue to blame yourself for what he did."

She pulled away from his attempt to comfort her and paced over to the large window overlooking the west pasture.

"How did all this happen, Andrew? How can life fall apart so quickly? A few months ago—" Her voice broke off. "It's obvious you want to be rid of me, Andrew. Marrying me off is the easiest way to do that. Now that my parents are dead, well, I guess you have what you always wanted."

"What would that be?" He turned to stare at her, challenging her with his glare while trying to veil his hurt.

"Bates Manor. You'd been seeking a way to wrestle it from my father." She smiled slightly. "Yes, I know all about the lawyer you hired in Wilmington. Word gets around. Especially among the slaves."

"Is that what you really think, Thelma?"

"Don't call me that," she seethed.

"What?" Andrew stared at her. "Don't call you Thelma?"

"I've always hated that name. That was the name Papa gave me and insisted I go by. Mama called me by my middle name, Maria, whenever Papa wasn't around. That's my real name. Now that he's gone," she choked back the tears, "I insist you call me Maria."

"Your mother called you Maria? I never heard her call you that."

"Of course not. It was just between Mama and me. Papa would not have allowed it. There's no telling what he would have done had he known. He could be cruel." She looked away from him.

"Very well." Andrew paused and smiled slightly. "Maria. That will take some getting used to."

"Not for me." She shrugged. "As for Thomas Murphy…" She moved to stand in front of him again. Her green and white pinstriped gown rustled with her movements. "I have no intentions of marrying that boy." She tugged on the puffed sleeves and adjusted the cuffs.

"Oh?" Andrew chuckled under his breath and sat down in his uncle's chair behind the oak desk "Why do you dislike Thomas so much?"

"He's young and has a lot to learn about being a man. When I marry, I want to marry a man."

"Then why don't we make this easier, *Maria*? Who is it you wish to marry?" Andrew watched the emotions stir over her refined features. When had his cousin grown up? It seemed like only yesterday he'd watched her long curly red locks bouncing behind her as she rode bareback across the pasture, with her father cussing the stable boys for letting her go off like that—as if anyone could have stopped her.

She frowned at him. Sadness tinted her green eyes. Andrew looked away and pretended to look at the stack of papers in front of him. He felt responsible for her and the pain she'd suffered over the last year. He should have suspected his uncle was involved in something illegal. He should have stayed at Bates Manor and fought his uncle for the estate. Instead, Andrew had taken a job with Brent MacGraft.

He glanced up at his cousin.

"So?"

"What?" She blinked while a bewildered look vexed her face.

She was a full-grown woman with a mind of her own. With her controlling father out of the way, Andrew could see why so many young men had petitioned for her hand in marriage.

"Who's the lucky man you wish to marry, cousin?"

"I—I—" Her voice dropped off. Pain pierced the depths of her liquid eyes.

He stood from the desk and retraced his steps to her.

"I'm sorry." Andrew rushed on, trying to soothe her hurt.

Tears glistened in her eyes and she looked away from him.

"I don't blame you for anything, Andrew." Her attention snapped back to him. "If I blame anyone, I blame my papa for everything he did. He shamed our family. Mama couldn't take the humiliation. She literally died from it. And now, how do you think I can possibly hold my head up in this community? Why do you think I stay inside this house and don't go out? Because of the mourning period?" She bowed her head. Her reddish curls fell over her face.

"Papa sold white women to other men. He was part of that vile business—God." She covered her face with her hands and sobbed. "How do you think I can live in this community when everyone knows the horrible truth?"

"No one is holding you accountable. Why, I've had three petitions for your hand this week alone. No one blames you for your father's—"

"I'm his seed," Maria sobbed.

Andrew put his arm around his cousin's narrow shoulders and once more pulled her into his embrace.

"My heart aches, Andrew." Her voice was muffled against his chest. " I cannot stand living here another day." She pulled from him and swiped the tears from her face with the backs of her hands. "I want to leave. I want to go far away. I want to go where no one knows me or my father."

"What?" Andrew's hands closed over her upper arms and he practically shook her. "You cannot mean that, Thel-*Maria*. How can you leave? I need you to help me with the plantation. There's talk of war and—"

"I do mean it, Andrew." She pulled from his hold and stared at him with the resolve shining brightly in her eyes. "I've thought about this a long time and it's the only way I can continue to draw breath. I have to go some place where no one knows my father and what he did."

"Where would that be? Your father was a powerful man. He had political connections not just in North Carolina, but in South Carolina as well. He shipped his crops to England from Wilmington and Charleston. He was a very well known man."

"I know, but no one has ever heard of *Maria* Bates," she smiled triumphantly, "and if anyone asks if I'm related to Jonah Bates, I'll lie. Maria is my real name. It's the name Mama wanted for me. She hated the name Thelma almost as much as she hated my father."

This revelation halted Andrew. He'd never contemplated the relationship between his aunt and uncle. He'd had little use for either one of them, especially when they'd sent his sister to live in England when she was only a child.

"Well, you do have the income from your father's businesses."

"But they are now yours, Andrew. They always were yours and Celeste's. My Papa stole so much from ya'll. I don't want any of it."

"Don't be absurd, Thel- Maria. Even if my sister made it quite clear she doesn't want any of it. Bates Manor belongs to the three of us."

"Celeste is being generous. I don't want any of it, Andrew. It feels as though it's covered with the blood of all those women, my father…" her voice trembled, "…sold. Don't you see? I can never do enough good in this world to repay for his sins."

"They are not *your* sins. You do not owe anyone anything."

"But I do. I ate his food. I wore the clothes his money purchased. Everything I've had—"

"Stop this!" Andrew shook his head. "You'll drive yourself insane with this. The money from the crops and the mill has nothing to do with the white-slavery ring."

"Sure it does, Andrew. Who do you think planted and harvested those crops? Who do you think fell those trees and hauled them to the mill? Slaves. Oh, their gender and color are different from the women my father sold, but it's all the same. I see that now, so clearly." She sobbed and collapsed in his arms. "I can't live here anymore, Andrew. You must let me go."

"I can't. You're all the family I have left here in Allensville and I could use your help here with the plantation. You've always had a good head for figures. You could help with the record keeping." He held her at arms length. "I've given up all my other interests to concentrate on Bates Manor. This is all that's left of both of our fathers. We can rebuild what my father lost and your father destroyed. You can marry whomever you wish. You don't have to live here. Just don't run away. Running only makes matters worse."

Chapter Two

"Watch your step there, boy. You almost tripped me up," came the gruff voice from the darkness. Maria flattened her back against the barn door, lest the men walking a few feet ahead discover her.

"It's so dark I can't see my hand in front of my face."

"That's why we chose tonight to do this, you fool—no moon."

"I know that," came the sullen reply. "Why you think I got them dogs penned up earlier today? So we got nothing between us and them unsuspecting—"

"Shh! Keep still. We soon be down there at the slave row, don't want them hearing you. Besides, we ain't going to be greedy. Only one goes tonight."

"What? I was counting on at least five."

"You want Miss Tessa to get suspicious?"

"Shucks, she's a Yankee. What does she know about slaves or how many she inherited with this plantation, anyway?"

"Well, I damn well suspect she found out how many David Renault owned when she attended his funeral, or when she came back down here a few months ago. I don't think that one lets much get past her."

"Don't imagine nothing wants to get past that pretty thang. Still, she ain't getting here until next week. So, what's the harm in stealing 'em all tonight? Makes more sense. Do it all at one time and be done with it. Hell, we could even sell 'em back to her and she'd never know the difference."

"Are you just plain stupid? The harm is in raising suspicion and making folks nervous. We do it my way, one or two every month or so. You get greedy, boy, and we get caught. It's that simple. Don't want no slave catchers coming around looking to bring them home."

"Slave catchers?" The youth's fear trembled in his voice. "Lordy, don't want them leeches in our neck of the woods. Why you go and say a thang like that?"

" 'Cause, you go taking more than one every month or so and folks will get jumpy. Miss Tessa might go and hire herself a slave catcher and that'll be the end of our little enterprise."

"I heard tell of one of them catchers, Garrett Lawson."

"Oh now, he is one catcher I never want to meet face to face."

"I heard tell how he beat this slave so badly that when he returned the slave to his owner in South Carolina, the owner refused to pay. Said his slave wouldn't ever be worth a penny all crippled up like he was."

"Yeah? What did Lawson do?"

"He beat the slave owner and took up his money and left."

The low whistle breezed past Maria as the two shadows walked around her hideout. She held her breath, squinting her eyes tightly together. Their footsteps stopped and Maria opened her eyes, certain she'd been discovered.

The men seemed to be looking at the manor.

"Well now, appears like ole Whitned has done made himself at home, the bastard."

Maria squinted at the lamp glow coming from the window in the study. Her stomach knotted at the thought of the arrogant overseer guzzling down David's fine port. David had prided himself in his private stock of liquors. Her heart pounded harder as she visualized him sitting in David's chair with his feet propped up on the furniture, smoking David's cigars and wearing his clothes.

Maria clasped her hands tighter together and gritted her teeth. She couldn't do anything about the pilfering of David Renault's estate. That responsibility now belonged to Tessa

Renault and she was still in Baltimore.

"Yeah, well, that's gonna change real soon, ain't it? Once Miss Tessa gits herself settled in there," came the voice, followed by the grinding boot heel.

"Hey, I heard there's this free Negro in South Carolina who owns more blacks than most whites do. Now, I didn't know no Negro could own slaves."

"Yeah, I know of him. Runs a big cotton gin down there. Done joined some white church. They let him and his family sit down on the first floor with the rest of 'em."

"You're a liar."

"I swear on my papa's grave, it's the truth. I also heard his slaves run away regular-like. Once, he hired ole Garrett Lawson. Now you'd think him being like them, having been a slave himself, that he'd done treat them better 'cause of it."

"Well, slap my face and shoot my dog, I ain't never heard tell of such a thang."

"Enough talking. Let's git this done. There are men waiting for us just over the border in South Carolina."

"Stupid slaves, thinkin' we gonna lead them to freedom. It's a good plan, Jeb, best you ever had, to pretend we's the Underground Railroad."

"Hush, you idiot, don't want 'em hearing you."

The voices moved away from the barn as the men made their way towards the slave quarters. Maria chided herself for taking a short cut through the Renault estate on her escape from Bates Manor and a lifetime of humiliation.

The entire world was upside down. Nothing was as it should be. She longed for things to be the way they'd been— even if it had been an illusion of reality. At least she'd had a mother and father. At least David had been here. A tear slipped down her cheek. It was so hard to believe that they were all dead.

Maria swiped at the path of her tears and strained to hear the night prowlers as they made their way to the slave quarters. They were not the typical night raiders that plantation owners vigilantly guarded against. These men worked on the

Renault estate and had once been guards against such a raid.

It wasn't her concern, Maria vowed, yet she stood frozen in the shadows of the barn. So what if these men took slaves and sold them in South Carolina to another planter? Chances were the slaves would be just as well off as remaining here.

Tessa Renault was a Yankee. She knew nothing about running a plantation or dealing with slaves and overseers. Maria sighed. Tessa was either very brave or very naive.

The flickering light from the house caught her attention as the silhouette moved in front of the window. Let Whitned take care of his men. Let him explain how slaves disappeared right under his nose. Besides, how could she stop men determined to steal slaves? Maria shuddered at the thought of what they would do to anyone who tried to interfere, especially Jonah Bates's orphan daughter. When her father had been alive no man would have dared to harm her. She straightened her shoulders. It didn't matter. None of it mattered now. Nothing was going to stop her!

Chapter Three
–Charleston, South Carolina, September 17, 1858 –

Garrett Lawson stepped off the gangplank onto the dock and took a deep breath. Charleston never changed. The ocean breeze rustled through the palmettos and up the street. He swept the dock with a trained gaze and looked beyond the crowd. The majestic homes—with piazzas, widow's walks, and luscious private gardens walled from curious eyes—overlooked the harbor. Garrett took a deep breath, glad to be back.

The dockside along East Bay Street was filled with disembarking passengers eager to climb into the awaiting carriages. The unsuspecting would never guess war was in the air.

To the untrained eye, it appeared to be a typical dock in a typical Southern port. To the unwary, the commotion going on about two hundred feet from where he stood went unnoticed. But to Garrett Lawson, one glance at the young Negro woman and her two companions told him all he needed to know. She was a runaway and they were raiders.

After nearly three years of chasing them down, Garrett had developed a checklist. Shoes were either missing or in poor condition, clothing unusually dirtied, and overall appearance was unkempt, often haggard. It was not difficult to spot them, just that the average person was blind when it came to a Negro. The typical white man or woman never saw beyond the dark silhouette. He sneered. Probably the only way they could continue to stomach their "peculiar institution."

"Hey girl. Just stand here while I git some tobaky for my pipe." The raider turned to his cohort. "I'm going over to Broad, won't be long. Watch the girl." The man tossed the chain to his companion, a young white man, who dodged it. The chain clattered to the dock and he scrambled to pick it up.

Garrett watched the youth, placing his age somewhere near twenty years. He looked almost as travel worn as the slave. Slave raiders. They were as easy to spot as the runaways. Disgust churned in Garrett.

"Garrett." The man leading the woman down the gangplank hailed. Garrett glanced at the couple as they disembarked the ship. Dressed in a gray pinstriped suit, the man touched the brim of his top hat.

"Jamison." Garrett returned. The woman with Jamison lifted her parasol and gave Garrett a fetching smile.

"Do call on us while you are in Charleston, Garrett. Perhaps dinner one evening?" Louisa Jamison touched her tongue to her upper lip before disappearing behind her parasol again.

"I'll try. Depends on how long my business keeps me here." Garrett frowned at her, wanting no part of whatever it was she was offering. He'd heard the rumors about the flirtatious Louisa and her indiscreet liaisons.

"When we return home, I'll be sure to let your family know you're well," Jamison added.

Garrett groaned, imagining how that conversation might run. His family would complain how all of Newport News frowned upon their only son's chosen profession. Then they would remark how they hoped all other planters, including the Jamisons, never had a child who chased runaway slaves for his living. His mother would probably faint and his sister would no doubt defend him for the thousandth time, claiming her brother had always been an adventurer. Then she'd comment on how dangerous his chosen occupation was. Her final defense would be how he was aiding the

Southern cause.

Garrett nodded goodbye to the Jamisons as they hailed a carriage. He could travel all over the South, but his past always seemed to follow him.

His attention quickly shifted back to the raider left to watch over the slave. As much as he loathed his past, Garrett hated raiders more. Just what were these two doing in Charleston with a runaway? Were they here to meet their buyer? If so, they were braver than any raiders he'd ever seen. Their transactions were usually done under the cloak of night on some deserted back road, not in broad daylight in a large city like Charleston.

"Just sit over there on that crate a spell. He won't be long." The man absently tossed the chain onto the nearby barrel.

"Hey! You wanna play?" A dockhand flashed a gap-toothed grin and shuffled a deck of cards in front of the raider. "We're playing right over there. You can watch yer slave from over there. She ain't going nowhere. Where could she go? You'd catch her 'fore she got far."

The man's face twisted with his dilemma and finally he turned to the black girl, pointing his finger at her. "Don't you try nothing. I'm going right over there." He nodded in the direction of the row of barrels a few feet away.

The girl's face was drawn with fatigue. Her eyes held a dullness that reflected her resignation to her fate. Slowly, she nodded then bowed her head.

"Don't make me mad, hear? I'll beat you if you so much as let one foot touch the dock. Understand?"

She jerked her head in a nod and twisted the long braid of her pigtail between her fingers. He sauntered off, glancing back at her a couple of times, giving what Garrett assumed was meant to be a warning glare.

Garrett leaned against a nearby stack of crates and lit a cheroot. Slowly, he moved into the shadows to wait for the other raider to return. The girl sat as though she were a statue. Garrett knew she'd probably not had anything to eat since being stolen from her plantation. He took a long draw on the cheroot and expelled the smoke.

The card game grew and soon there were boisterous shouts followed by bouts of laughter. Garrett smoked the cheroot and planned his next move. He could take the slave now, but he wanted to turn the raiders over to the local authorities. Raiders were not tolerated in the South, and were dealt with swiftly.

The movement around the stacked bales of cotton a few feet from the slave alerted Garrett. This time, he saw the woman who peeped around the bales. She glanced about the dock then moved from her hiding place. He straightened. Now, what was this debutante about?

Her wavy red hair was neatly pinned and tucked underneath a wide-brimmed, straw hat. Unlike most of the women, she was not carrying a parasol. Garrett's gaze swept her pale blue dress. He noticed the fine chintz fabric with stylized flowers that graduated into darker hues to the hem of her dress. The way her sleeves tiered to her wrists, revealing the fine white lace cuffs of an under blouse confirmed his conclusion. It was a very expensive gown.

Even her gloves were detailed with a fine satin edging. A woman of such obvious wealth not carrying a parasol or at least a gauzy shawl threaded from one arm to the other arm was an oddity. Perhaps she'd been in a hurry.

She moved from her hiding place and took brisk steps towards the slave. Now just what was she about? Her attention was trained on the card game with a quick glance in the direction of the slave every now and then.

Her face, partially hidden by the matching hat, was defined with elegant features offset by wide eyes that could be green. It was difficult to tell at this distance. Her stride quickened as she neared the slave.

Taking one last draw on the thin cigar, Garrett tossed it over the seawall. He was not about to let anyone interfere in his plans. He was too far to hear her low entreaty, but he saw the slave snap alert at the woman's voice. A look of relief brightened her face.

Keeping her stare trained on the gambler, the slave quietly lifted the chains from the barrel onto her lap. She wrapped them in her paisley skirt, and then slipped in a fluid motion from the barrel onto the dock.

Garrett moved from his perch and wasted no time moving through the crowd. Trying to keep the women in sight, all he could see was the wide-brimmed hat. As he wove his way through the bustling dockside, he glimpsed her profile, and then her bell-shaped dress.

His stare jumped from one side of the stacked crates to the other. Where was the slave? It was as though she had disappeared. The young debutante moved slowly up the wide walkway heading towards the Battery.

Garrett glanced over at the young gambler just as he looked up from his game. The youth's face turned whiter than the bales of cotton stacked around him. Garrett caught his hurried look in the direction of Broad Street and, as though it were all being orchestrated, the other raider rounded the corner.

Grabbing up his winnings amid the angry protests of his fellow gamblers, the youth scrambled from the game. He ran around the barrels and nearly collided with his cohort.

"Where is she?" came the gruff voice.

Garrett's attention flashed over to the woman. She didn't glance back. Instead, she opened her fan and leisurely moved it in front of her. She didn't appear to be in any hurry and meandered up East Battery. The raiders' voices grew louder. Garrett's attention shifted to the raiders.

"I don't know. I turned just for a moment and she was gone."

"A moment?" came the snarled question and the raider moved around the massive stacks of crates and barrels, searching for the slave. He cursed under his breath.

Garrett stood a few feet from them and glanced around for all the places the girl could hide. What had happened? Where could she have gone? He recounted the whole scene from the time the woman had approached the slave.

His gaze skipped over the constant flow of people. Where was the woman now? He searched the sidewalk and spotted the blue hat in the distance. She'd continued towards the Battery ignoring the commotion going on behind her. Garrett found that odd, since the two men were creating quite a stir with their frantic search for the girl.

"Damn you, I'm gonna kill you," the older cursed.

"Wasn't my fault," the youth began, but he must have seen the murderous glint in his cohort's eyes because he pivoted and darted into the crowd.

"Git back here!" The man ran after him, pushing through the crowd.

Garrett decided to follow the woman instead of the raiders. She was the key to this. He walked towards East Battery and soon caught up with her. He stopped a few feet from where she stood by the seawall across from White Point Gardens and turned his attention to the raiders.

The older one had caught up with his cohort and they'd resumed their frenzied search along the Battery. Running through the crowd, they knocked a finely dressed gentleman onto the promenade and several women screamed. The debutante glanced over her shoulder, but quickly turned her attention back to the wide harbor dotted with ships.

Instantly, the crowded Battery turned into a free-for-all. The raiders broke from the fight, but several men chased them into the park. The younger raider jumped over a bench and sprinted across the walkway while his companion raced towards Meeting Street. Those in pursuit divided, with several running after the youth along South Battery and the rest cutting across to Meeting.

The ocean breeze ruffled past Garrett, drawing his attention back to the woman. Now just what was she about? He took a few steps closer, bowing his head to get a better glimpse of what she was trying to do. She leaned to one side and lifted her skirts. It was such an odd thing to do, especially in public.

She shifted her weight again and the hoop skirt swung out.

Intrigued, Garrett moved closer. Suddenly, he saw underneath the hoop skirt. His eyes were playing tricks on him. He squinted and nearly laughed out loud. There, underneath the woman's hoop skirt, crouched the slave. She appeared to have her hands locked around the woman's shins and wouldn't come out despite the debutante's attempts. She tried to swing her hoop skirt again so the slave could crawl from underneath the dress, but the slave didn't budge.

The woman leaned over and whispered something in the direction of the slave. Garrett could barely see the young Negress when the skirt swung out to the side again. She must have locked her arms tighter around the woman's legs because the woman grasped for the post along the seawall and steadied herself.

A slow grin stretched over Garrett's lips. He'd never witnessed anything like it. He folded his arms over his chest, anxious to see how this woman was going to disentangle herself from the frightened slave.

"Raci." Maria regained her balance and tried to move her feet, but the slave weighted her. "You have to let go or we can never leave here. I can't help you if we're discovered."

Had she been crazy? What had she thought she'd do once she rescued the terrified slave? It had been such a spontaneous reaction when she'd recognized poor Raci with those despicable men. Self-conscious, Maria glanced around to see if anyone had witnessed what she'd done.

The commotion of the raiders had begun to settle and no one was paying any attention to her—except, Maria's heart stopped, the most handsome man she'd ever seen.

Had he witnessed the slave's escape? Had he been watching her try to coax Raci out from underneath her skirt? Heat raced up her neck and fanned her cheeks. Composing herself, Maria stiffened against the trembling slave wrapped around her legs. Slowly she opened her fan and fluttered it in front of her, cooling her scorching cheeks.

Who was he? She could not resist glancing at him. He touched his hat in a gesture of greeting and bowed slightly.

Maria gasped and quickened the rhythm of her fanning. He was as tall as her cousin, maybe taller. His hair was light brown and held a slight wave to its thickness. He was dressed finer than any gentleman she'd ever seen. There was something about him….

She looked out across the Charleston harbor, letting the wind whip over her. She wasn't sure what it was, but there was something in the way he looked at her that told Maria he was not what he appeared to be—a gentleman. No gentleman would let his stare travel so freely over her.

Had he seen her steal Raci? Was that why he was staring at her? If he were a true gentleman, then he'd turn and leave her to her business. Maria glanced at him again. He unfolded his arms and started towards her. Her heartbeat pounded to her head.

"We have to go." She tried to lift her legs, but Raci tightened her grip. Maria glanced up to see where he was and gasped. He was weaving his way through the crowd. His stare was centered on her. "You're like a Georgia tick, Raci. Let go before we're both caught and thrown in jail." Maria jerked her leg and instantly regretted it. The slave's weight nearly sent her headfirst right into the arms of the handsome stranger.

"There now, Miss." His laughter was so deep and Southern, Maria's heart surely melted. He steadied her with strong hands around her waist. Raci tugged on her leg and Maria gasped, catching herself before she let out a startled scream. "You don't want to end up in the harbor." He flashed a wide smile.

"Oh, thank you, sir. It's just so … *hot* … today. I nearly fainted." Maria fluttered the lace fan faster while lifting her hand to her throat. Her pulse throbbed hard under her fingers

"Allow me to escort you to a bench over there in the shade." He cupped her elbow in his hand, but Maria quickly pulled free of him.

"I'm fine here."

"Where's your parasol, dear lady?"

"Dreadful me, I left it behind."

"A woman as delicate as you should always carry a parasol." His eyes were a warm brown. Maria felt she would easily lose herself if she stared much longer into them. She pulled her stare from his and glanced down at her trembling hands. She moved the fan faster stirring the air against her cheeks.

"Why is such a fine lady as yourself out and about unescorted? Did you escape your chaperon?" he asked, his voice barely above a whisper. He leaned closer. "I daresay you have a father or brother worrying himself sick looking all over Charleston for you."

"No." Maria looked away, struggling against the tears welling in her eyes. Damn him. He didn't even know her but had managed to reach in and grab the one bitter place in her heart.

His handsome face darkened.

"Did I say something to upset you?"

"I don't even know you, sir. How could you upset me?"

"Forgive my ill manners." He removed his hat, sweeping it in front of him in a gallant bow. "Garrett, my dear lady, Garrett Lawson."

Maria's knees weakened and had it not been for Raci clinging to her, she would have fallen to the walkway right there. Raci tapped her on the leg.

Maria shifted her weight, trying to get the slave to calm down and know that she, too, recognized the man's name. He was the one she'd overheard the raiders talking about. Garrett Lawson was a ruthless slave catcher who would return any slave for the right price.

"Mister Lawson." She trembled as she extended her gloved hand. He bowed over it, properly feigning a kiss just above it.

"Are you from Charleston, Mister Lawson?"

"No, ma'am." He straightened, but continued to hold her hand longer than respectable. Finally, he released it. "I'm a traveler. The South mostly, sometimes the North."

"Is that so?

"Allow me to escort you to your destination." He offered his arm. Maria steeled herself against his charm, trying to ignore how handsome he was. His nose was neither large nor small, but the perfect size for his face. Dark eyebrows framed his brown eyes and whenever he turned like he just did, his side profile was enough to inspire any artist. Her pulse sharpened.

"Who said I had a destination, Mister Lawson?" Maria smiled stiffly and feigned interest in the harbor, focusing on the ships anchored in the rolling high tide waters.

"We all have destinations, Miss...." His smile widened.

"Bates," she supplied, then moved the fan, trying to focus on something, anything other than Garrett Lawson. He was everything she abhorred, yet, something inside her quickened. His brownish hair framed his tanned face, and whenever he smiled like that, her heart skipped a beat.

"Bates? Are you from Charleston?"

"Yes. Charleston," she lied, telling herself it wasn't really a lie since she'd been there a few days. She'd gone to the only place she knew, The Charleston Hotel. Her father had always stayed there. No one had asked about her family when she'd registered. Maria felt comfortable in the huge, block-wide hotel—at least until she decided what she was going to do.

"Then allow me to walk you home, Miss Bates," he interrupted her thoughts.

"Well, thank you for your kind offer, sir, but I am not going home just yet. Good day." She turned her back to him, hoping he would honor her dismissal so she could get Raci out from hiding and—Where was she going to take Raci? Maria had heard of secret routes with houses along them. There was a regular route, which led to the North, but she had no idea how to contact them. She bit her lower lip when she realized he'd not taken his leave.

"Was there something else, sir?" She glanced at him.

"Well, just one thing, Miss Bates."

"Sir?" She turned, holding the fan poised in front of her.

"I was just curious." He paused.

"Mister Lawson?"

"How long do you intend to keep that slave under your dress?"

Chapter Four

"Although I cannot imagine a nicer place to find oneself."

The glint in his eye warmed a path all the way down to her groin. Maria's pulse drummed hard in her throat as her stare locked with his. Desire mingled with danger fluttered through her. She quickly reminded herself of his horrid reputation. He was a vile man of numerous evil deeds.

"I imagine it is getting rather stifling underneath all those crinolines—or are you wearing one of the newer hoop petticoats?"

Maria gasped. He certainly was a lewd man.

"Aren't you afraid she'll just keel over?" His deep voice soaked into her like the hot afternoon sun. He was more than a rogue with a horrid reputation. He was a scoundrel!

When he leaned closer and cupped her elbow with his hand as though to guide her, Maria's legs trembled and Raci's arms tightened around her. His touch sent her heart racing. Her breathing was short and fast. Maria quickly pulled from him.

"You take too many liberties, sir. Please take your leave." She fluttered her fan and tried to cool the heat rushing through her.

"I've never seen anything like what you did. What are you planning to do with her? Take her home and make her *your* slave?"

"I don't know what you're talking about, *Mister* Lawson. You are making yourself a nuisance."

"Am I?" He chuckled and bowed his head so he was look-ing right into her eyes. "My dear debutante, you have no idea just how much of a nuisance I'm going to be to you until you turn that slave over to me."

Raci pounded her fists against Maria's legs.

"Oh!" Maria's voice was a shrill pitch in response to the sudden movement.

"Miss Bates?"

"Sir. You've made a mistake. I think your imagination exceeds any I've ever known."

"And if you think I'm going to just turn and walk away while you steal a runaway from those raiders, then you are more naive than you appear, Miss Bates."

What had she been thinking? She'd had no plan. When she'd seen Raci, Maria had not thought beyond the terror and plea she'd seen in the young girl's eyes. She'd *had* to save her from those raiders. Now she might lose her to the worst person possible.

"You're a slave catcher aren't you?" She spat, hoping her disgust was mirrored in her eyes.

"I see you recognized my name."

"Everyone knows your name, Mister Lawson. You prey on the helplessness of slaves like Raci and the desperateness of their owners."

"Raci? Is that her name?"

"What would you do?"

"Return her to her owner, of course."

"For a fee?"

"Yes, ma'am. That's how I earn my living." His amused expression contradicted the fierceness in his voice.

"I see, so it really is about the money, then, is it not?"

"Everything is about money, Miss Bates."

Managing to shift her weight slightly from Raci's hold, Maria locked her knees. "Then how much would you say it is worth to forego the usual challenge of finding the rightful owner and returning Raci to him?"

His eyes glinted with a mischievous spark, not at all the

greed she'd expected to see in their depths. "You think I am that easy, Miss Bates? Is this how you face your challenges in life?"

"Sir?" She raised her chin.

"Buy your way?"

"It is clear you're a man who can be purchased, sir. Your occupation suggests that. So I ask again, what is your price? Name it."

"What if I said one thousand dollars?"

"I'd say you're also a thief." Maria felt the blood drain from her and pool at her feet.

"Too much? But how do you put a price on what you want?" He leaned in so his breath fell on her cheeks. "I could easily receive that much for Raci. I could sell her as a breeder, judging by what little I saw of her. There's a free Black not far from here who runs a cotton gin. I understand he also has breeders. Many of them are his own offspring. He turns a nice profit. I'm sure he could always use another breeder."

"That's disgusting!" Maria covered her gasp with her hand and tried to move from him. Raci must have realized the need to move, too, because she released her hold so Maria could walk.

Taking smaller steps than normal, Maria walked away from the slave hunter. He was quickly by her side.

"I'm not letting you just walk away with that slave, Miss Bates. She's coming with me."

Maria couldn't look at him. She wanted to run down the long expanse of the Battery and across the park and back to her hotel, but he reached up and his hand closed over her arm.

She glared up at him and met his wicked smile. He was not at all what she had imagined such a notorious slave catcher would look like. He didn't wear the disheveled dirty clothes like the raiders. Instead, he wore a fine linen shirt and one of the cleanest cut suits she'd ever seen. Her fingers itched to touch the fine wool of his black jacket. Instead, she jerked her arm from his hold.

"You, sir, are a scoundrel. Please take your leave before I—" She flipped her fan open and tried to block herself from him.

"What? Call for help? Whom would you call out to?" he whispered in her ear. His breath sent delighted shivers over her. "That slave is not yours. What you are doing is illegal."

Maria moved away from him, managing to take tiny short steps with Raci somehow keeping up with her. Her heart tugged at the thought of the frightened girl. There was no way she'd allow this vile man to take Raci. Panic seized her. Her mind was jumbled with fearful thoughts. He just might sell Raci to the breeder, which was a worse fate than being returned to the Renault plantation.

"There she is!" came the familiar voice.

"Git her!"

Maria looked up and so did Garrett. The two raiders had managed to free themselves of their pursuers. They ran towards them, pushing people out of their way.

"Please." Maria looked up into his face. "Please save us."

Garrett Lawson looked from her to the approaching men. Their yelling and pushing through the crowded Battery created another protest, but the men were unyielding and came towards them.

"I'll handle this. You and that slave stay put, hear?" Garrett turned from her and started for the men.

Maria didn't waste any time.

"Get up, Raci. The slave raiders are back." This time the slave obeyed and skittled out from underneath Maria's skirt. Maria grabbed the younger woman's wrist and dragged her into the swelling crowd.

"Now see here, gents." Garrett Lawson's voice pitched above the noisy crowd, but Maria didn't stop to look back; she pushed her way through the Battery with a terrified Raci in tow until she found a carriage. The driver assisted the women into the carriage.

"200 Meeting Street." Maria handed the driver her money and he jumped back into his seat and flicked the whip over the horse's head.

The slave lifted her large brown-eyed stare up to Maria's, panting and trying to catch her breath. She quickly looked away, as though suddenly realizing the offense she'd made.

"It's all right, Raci." Maria laid her hand on the girl's shoulder. "We are going to get out of here."

Raci nodded her head and glanced back. People were rushing past them towards the Battery to see what the ruckus was about.

Maria had no idea what she was going to do with the slave, but knew she had to get Raci out of sight as quickly as possible. She cursed herself for having given her real name to that despicable Garrett Lawson. She would have to leave Charleston before he discovered she was not a resident and tracked her down. For a man such as he, finding her would be a simple task.

Biting her lower lip, Maria paused outside the hotel entrance, along the expanse of porticos. She felt so tiny beside the massive columns. She turned to Raci.

"I want you to go to the back of the hotel through there, see?" She pointed to the side street that ran alongside the hotel. Raci nodded her head, but her eyes were large with renewed fear.

"It's going to be fine, Raci." Maria grabbed the girl by her shoulders. "I can't take you through the lobby, dressed like you are. You look like a runaway. It would arouse suspicions. I'll let you in through the side entrance and you can get cleaned up in my room. I will get you some fresh clothes, then we'll leave tonight."

Raci nodded, but hesitated. "Miss Thelma?"

She glanced up. "I have a new name, Raci. It's Maria."

The black girl nodded. "Yes'm. Miss Maria, then, just why are ya doing this?"

"Because it isn't right, Raci. It's like I woke up from a long nap and realized just how wrong our world is."

"Yes'm, but where are you going to take me?"

"To freedom, Raci." Maria smiled hoping to calm the girl's

fears. "Up North."

"Can I not just go home, Missy Maria, to my mama and papa? I's missin' them sumpthin' terrible. They thought those men were Underground and that's why they sent me with 'em. They thought I was going to freedom, but I never been away from my mama and papa. I didn't want to go in the first place. Be so happy to go home. Please, Miss Maria?" Raci brushed the tears from her eyes.

"If that's what you want, Raci, I'll take you home. Don't be frightened. We can do this. You just go around the back and wait for me to open the door. Can you do that?"

Raci nodded and Maria steered her towards the corner. She stood watching as Raci made her way to the side door and stood waiting on her. Satisfied Raci was all right, Maria entered the hotel lobby, frowning at the full-length mirrors reflecting her blue gown as she walked towards the wide staircase.

It was an unusually quiet afternoon; she could hear muffled sounds from the dining room. The clerk glanced up from his newspaper, peering over the top of his spectacles. Maria started up the staircase to the second floor.

"Miss Bates?" His voice halted her. Maria paused on the first riser and turned slightly towards the clerk.

"Yes, Mister Stevens?"

"There was a man here earlier asking for you. Said he was your cousin, Andrew."

Her heart pounded in her chest. Andrew had followed her here? How had he found her? What would he do? Insist she return to Bates Manor?

"My cousin? Did he say what he wanted?" Maria tried to calm her voice, but it sounded nervous to her own ears.

"No, ma'am. He took a room upstairs next to yours. He just left to see if he could find you in the park. I assume he'll be returning soon."

"Thank you, Mister Stevens. Please tell my cousin I will be out most of the afternoon, but would like to have dinner with him around seven o'clock this evening."

"Yes, ma'am." He nodded his bald head. "I will be glad to tell him, Miss Bates."

"Thank you." Maria tried to compose herself. She managed to climb the staircase to the second floor, and then rushed down the hall to the servant's staircase.

She peered down the stairs and listened to make sure no servants were about, then lifted her skirt and descended to the landing below. The door to the street was at the end of the short hallway. Maria rushed over to the door. They could not risk staying in the hotel. Andrew was here to take her back to a life she could no longer live. Anger filled her veins. Why couldn't Andrew understand she wanted to be left in peace?

Maria's hands trembled as she fumbled for the doorknob. What would she do with Raci? Return her to a life of slavery? Wouldn't that mean she was no better than those she abhorred?

Maria opened the door, determined to find a way to free Raci *and* the girl's parents. When she pulled the door open, Maria screamed as the raider rushed inside, clamping his hand over her mouth. Writhing under his strong hold, Maria saw past him to where the other raider held Raci with her arms pinned behind her back.

"We're here to reclaim our merchandise." The man's foul breath fell over her. "You gonna regret the day you interfered in our business, Miss Bates."

Garrett Lawson blinked against the harsh light streaming in through the window. He jerked into an upright position, but quickly regretted it when the hard pounding in his head pushed him back against the pillow.

"Easy, Garrett," came the familiar voice. "You had a bad blow to the head."

"Jamison?" Garrett frowned up at the man.

"Yep." Jamison smiled widely and pushed a brandy into Garrett's hand. "This time try sitting up slower." He helped Garrett rise into a sitting position on the settee. "Good thing

I sent Louisa ahead and went back to find you."

Garrett took a gulp of the brandy. The oily liqueur rolled warmly down his throat.

"What did you say?" He put the glass down on the nearby table.

"I went back to the dock to speak with you. I didn't expect to find you in the middle of a brawl, much less hit on the head and lying face down.

"I don't know what you're talking about." Garrett moved to stand and once more was brought back against the couch by the fierce pounding in his temple.

"Those two men knocked you unconscious. What were they about?"

"I was knocked unconscious?"

"I had you brought here to my home." Jamison sat down in the chair beside him and sipped his drink.

"You came back to speak to me?" Garrett tried to clear his mind, but the pain distracted him from what Jamison was saying. Jamison's confused expression only dumbfounded Garrett more.

Jamison had always been a rather straightforward man with little to say. Garrett didn't even know the man's first name. What was it? Edgar? He'd always known him as Jamison. He'd been the kind of neighbor who blended into the scenery and daily life without much interaction except for social functions, and then he'd never expressed his opinions.

"I know why you're in Charleston." Jamison's blue eyes were dull as though trying to mask his thoughts from Garrett.

"Is that so?" Feeling stronger, Garrett stood from the settee. What had happened to Maria Bates and the slave she had stolen from the raiders? Had the raiders caught up with the women? He blocked the imaginative scene from his mind. Maria Bates would be in grave danger if that had happened. He needed to find her.

"Where's the map? What was the address you were given

for the Charleston location?"

"Map?" Garrett narrowed his glare on Jamison. "What are you talking about?"

"Come on, Garrett. What was the address?"

"Thank you for all you've done. I can never repay you. Perhaps I can treat you and Missus Jamison to dinner one evening while you're in Charleston. How long did you say you were staying?"

"Indefinitely."

"Well, I'll call on you later this week. I cannot thank you enough for coming to my aid. I apparently needed your help." He extended his hand and Jamison was quickly on his feet. He clasped Garrett's hand with a strong grip.

Garrett released the man's hand, noting he didn't have a single callous. He frowned at Jamison, surmising he'd rarely done any physical labor. To have the kind of success Jamison had with his plantation required hard physical labor. Obviously, Jamison was one of those planters who didn't do any physical labor on his own land, completely relying on his slaves and overseer. Jamison had always struck Garrett as the kind of man who'd spent his life keeping records and attending socials. His handshake bore out that summation.

"You're good." Jamison's pale face broke into a wide grin.

"What does that mean, Jamison?" His dislike for the man grew.

"You don't take risks and you certainly don't trust anyone." He stared at Garrett as though expecting Garrett to confess something.

"I have some business I need to attend to." Garrett chose to ignore the comments, not wishing to get into the discussion Jamison was determined to have. "Thank you again."

Garrett looked around the room searching for the exit. Whatever Jamison thought he knew, Garrett had no intention of confirming or denying. He glanced into the foyer and saw the ornate lead glass door panels where the brilliant afternoon light played along the stained glass panes.

"I'll see myself out." He espied his hat on the marble table beside the door and walked over to it.

"You really are going to make this difficult for me, aren't you?" Jamison was on his heels. "You can't leave just yet, Garrett."

"Why is that?" Garrett stepped around him and into the foyer.

"Because I'm your new contact."

Chapter Five

"I's scared." Raci's voice trembled in the darkened warehouse. "What's they gonna do with us?"

"It's all right, Raci. We're going to escape before they return. I think I might be able to slip from these knots. Can you wiggle free of the ropes?" Maria tugged against those binding her hands behind her back.

"No, ma'am. They's so tight my hands is numb. I don't like dark places. This ole warehouse is so dark, Miss Thelma. I mean Miss Maria. Keep forgetting you done changed your name." Her laugh at her own mistake was shrill and giddy.

"Try not to think about the darkness, Raci."

"Can't help it. I's trying. I think, 'well, I'll close my eyes,' but that don't help none. Just as dark."

"Just a little longer, Raci, I'm almost free." The lapping water of the harbor rocked the stilted building.

"I can't swim neither, you know. Feels like the tide is rolling in, and Lordy, I hope this old building ain't going to fall into the ocean. Oh, Lordy!" Her voice pitched a piercing octave.

"Hush up now, Raci. You know that isn't going to happen. This building would never have been built if that were the case."

"Yes'm. If you say so Miss Th – Maria. I just knows if I could jump outta my skin and run home right now, I would."

"Well, me too, Raci." Maria shook her head. "But we can't,

so try and loosen the ropes by wiggling your arms."

The loop was secured with tight knots, but she managed to wiggle her hand through it. The coarse rope scraped her skin and Maria felt the ropes give under her struggling. Her hand slipped free and Maria gasped. She quickly freed her other hand.

"Oh, Lordy, you did it, Miss Maria! You did it!" Raci's voice was loud.

"Shh!" Maria hurried over to the girl and started tugging against the ropes.

The slave's hands were like ice. Maria glanced around the dark space for a knife, all the while trying to push the hard knots apart. The hemp relaxed under her insistent tugging.

"Oh!" Raci exclaimed and jerked free of the ropes. She rubbed her hands together. "I never been so happy to see my hands!"

"Come on," Maria insisted and they raced towards the end of the warehouse. Sunlight streamed around the uneven door. Maria's heart pounded faster. She could almost feel the sunlight she knew would glare into her eyes when she threw open the door.

She reached for the metal bar that kept freedom just beyond their reach, anticipating the sea breeze and the rush of afternoon heat from the cobblestone streets. Freedom! Excitement coursed through her.

Her fingers trembled against the rusted metal and she lifted the handle, letting it fall against the weathered wood. The door creaked open. Golden sun blasted into the warehouse. The two women half-gasped and half-laughed. Maria moved to step over the threshold but froze in her movement when the brilliant light darkened.

Shielding her eyes, Maria looked up into the silhouette towering in front of them, blocking their path.

"What are you doing?" The deep voice boomed from the shadow. Her heart pounded icy pains and shattered her momentary elation.

Raci gripped Maria's forearms with both hands. Her long,

thin fingers were like bands of steel, but Maria was so focused on the man in front of them she didn't try to free herself from Raci's desperate grasp.

"Mister Lawson." Maria straightened her shoulders and swallowed the dryness in her throat. "Please excuse us." She tried to step around him, but his muscular frame blocked their avenue of escape.

"Are you well?"

Maria squinted up at him. The harsh sun glared around him like shards of gold.

"We will be just fine if you will get out of our way so we can go home." She hoped she sounded indignant and not as terrified as Raci had. She reached over and gently pried the girl's hands from her arm. Raci finally relented and loosened her grip, but didn't turn loose of Maria's arm.

"You certainly may go about your business, Miss Bates, but I will be taking the girl."

"Ouch!" Maria yelped when Raci's fingers bit into her arms again. "*Raci.*" She pulled free of the girl and jerked her arm when the girl tried to latch on to her again.

"Now see here, Mister Lawson, you are becoming a nuisance. Step aside." Maria tried to peer around him into the street, but he shifted his weight, blocking her view. Maria crossed her arms over her chest.

"The girl is a runaway. I will see that she is taken care of."

"No you won't, sir!" Maria stood in front of Raci like a shield.

"Miss Bates, your kidnappers will be returning soon. I cannot assure you I can hold them off this time for another escape."

"You will not take Raci back."

He leaned forward so that his face was in the shadows of the warehouse and she couldn't see his grin.

"I never said I'd take her back, now did I?"

"We were discussing purse earlier." Maria would try to bargain. He had a price; she just needed to discover what it was.

"And I told you before, you don't have enough money."

"Then perhaps something other than money?" Maria shocked herself as well as Garrett Lawson, whose smile broadened to reveal his white teeth. Raci gasped beside Maria, but she ignored the slave's shock and continued her barter with the slave catcher.

"Just what are you offering me?" He moved closer. Maria swallowed the pulsing knot in her throat.

"I think we could come to agreeable terms, sir. But we should hurry from here before those despicable men return. A place more suited to our private discussion?"

"I know a place. Come." Not allowing her time to protest, Garrett Lawson grabbed her arm and, with Raci still latched on to her other arm, Maria stumbled between them. He hurried them from the warehouse towards the street.

"Where is this private place?" She huffed beside him as they ran down the nearly deserted street.

"Right here." He stopped beside the awaiting carriage. Before she could speak, his strong hands came around her waist. For a brief moment, Maria's heart fluttered with the contact. He lifted her into the carriage. Before Maria could turn to comment on the rough way he'd handled her, he slammed the door in her face.

"Take her to the Charleston Hotel, no stops and hurry." He tipped his hat and turned to Raci.

"What are you doing?" Maria protested and tried to scramble from the seat and out the door, but the carriage jerked away from the dock and bolted down the street.

"Miss Maria! Missy Maria! Help me!" Raci screamed at the top of her lungs, but Garrett held the girl by the wrists.

Maria groped for the door handle, but the carriage bounced over a pothole, sending her painfully onto the floor.

"Slow down!" She pounded against the seat. If she ever saw Garrett Lawson again, she was going to make him rue the day he ever met her.

"Please, boss, I knows you one of those slave catchers. I's a good girl. Please don't sell me to no breeder. Please!" Tears streamed down the girl's cheeks. "I wants to go home to be with my parents."

"Here." Garrett reached in his waistcoat and retrieved a handkerchief. He handed it to her. She stared at the monogrammed linen. "Go on. Take it." He held it closer. Timidly, she took it from him and wiped her eyes. "I can't take you home, Raci. I can't. But I can take you somewhere else. And I may be able to help your parents. Now I can't promise, but I will try."

"What?" Her shocked expression made him laugh.

"If you can be calm, I'm going to take you to a friend of mine tonight. He'll see that you are taken to Canada."

"Canada? Where is dat?"

"North, Raci, far North. It is a separate country. You will be free there."

"What? But my mamma and papa....I wants to go home." The girl looked up at him, but quickly averted her stare.

"I will try, Raci. I will try. I can't promise you that. I can only promise you freedom. But you can't tell anyone. You'll have to stay at a house, though, until tonight. But you cannot tell the owner, Jamison, anything—or any of his slaves. Understand?"

"Yes. But I don't understan', Mister Lawson. You's a slave catcher."

"Not everything is how it appears, Raci. And not all people are as bad as their reputations." He shook his head when she offered his handkerchief back.

"Keep it, Raci. In years to come, you can show it to your children and tell them a slave catcher gave it to you." He laughed out loud at her startled expression.

"No, Massah. I be telling them it holds the last tears I ever shed as a slave."

When the carriage finally slowed down, Maria managed to climb into the seat and look around. They were on Meeting

Street and almost at the hotel.

When they stopped, the doorman was quick to open the carriage door and hand her from the carriage. Maria stomped around to the front of the carriage.

The driver glanced down at her, but before she could tell him what she thought of him and that he'd best take her right back to the warehouse, he flicked the whip over the horse's head and the carriage bolted from the hotel.

"Get me a carriage." She turned her anger on the unsuspecting doorman.

"Yes, ma'am." He rushed down the street to the waiting taxis and motioned for one. A carriage stopped in front of the hotel and he handed Maria into it.

"Take me to East Bay Street." She knew she'd be able to find the warehouse area again. She had to find Raci.

"Thelma?" Andrew ran across the street. "Hold up there, driver." He opened the street side door and peered in side. "It *is* you, Thel—Maria. I've been looking all over for you."

"Either stand aside, Andrew, or get in." Maria leaned over and called up to the driver. "Let's go."

Andrew jumped inside the carriage as it pulled from the curb.

"Where are we going?" He removed his top hat and sat down across from her.

"To stop a bastard slave catcher from selling Raci to a breeder." She enjoyed watching the surprised look wash over Andrew's face.

"What did you say?" He blinked at her with his stare narrowing on her.

Chapter Six

"I need a place for this slave, Jamison. Do you think you could let her stay out back in one of your cabins until later tonight when I can come back for her?" Garrett stood in the foyer with Raci cowering behind him.

"Well now, Garrett. You know I told you that's why I'm here—to help you with the railroad—only I didn't think you believed me. You sure as hell don't waste any time, now do you?"

"I don't know what you are talking about, Jamison. I just need a place to stow this slave until I can arrange a deal with a breeder upstate. If it is too much ask, I'll find someone else."

Jamison laughed. "Garrett if you want to play your hand this way, I'll go along with you. But sooner or later you are going to realize I'm telling you the truth."

"Whatever you say, Jamison. Her name is Raci. I want her to be here when I come back. If she isn't, I will kill you. Don't mind adding it to my other sins. I figure I'm already going to be burning, so one more flame isn't going to matter."

"Well, she'll be here, of course. Why wouldn't she be? Damn, you really do have your role down pat. I give you credit. No wonder you are one of the best conductors around and have yet to be discovered. I think you have the highest count for getting slaves out of the South than any other."

"I don't know what the hell you keep talking about, Jamison. I'll be back for her after dark. Her name's Raci. Remember, I don't let any slave get away from me. Ever."

He turned just in time to see the horrified look on Raci's face. Garrett winked at her and instantly saw the girl understood what he was doing. She released a deep breath.

"She needs something to eat. If you have some extra hot water, that would be good too. Clean slaves bring a higher price. Anything I get over a thousand, I'll split with you for your assistance. Fair enough?" Garrett didn't wait for an answer and started for the door.

He paused and turned to Raci.

"Now, see here, girl. You are just staying here until I return. If I come back and find you have somehow run away, I will track you down. You know my reputation. If I have to come after you, I won't be merciful when I find you. Understand?"

She nodded her head and looked away.

"Good." Garrett glanced over at Jamison who stood with his hands in his trouser pockets and an amused look on his face.

"Glad you find this so entertaining, Jamison. I will kill you if anything happens to my merchandise."

"She'll be here when you get back." Jamison shrugged his wide shoulders and chuckled. "You are quite the actor, Garrett."

Garrett sneered at him and left the manor. He hurried down the steps to the street and sucked in the late afternoon air. The tide had gone out and life had slowed along the Battery.

He would start with the hotels. Over the years, he'd discovered that hotel clerks know everyone and everything about their cities. He'd soon learn if Maria Bates was her real name. If it wasn't, he'd find out what it was.

Garrett turned down Market Street heading for Meeting. He'd start at the Charleston Hotel since it had the most affluent clientele. If Maria Bates were a local of any standing, she would be known at this hotel. If not, then Garrett would try the Mills House Hotel. He paused. Would she be the type to delight in rubbing elbows with the artists down at the King Henry Inn? Just who was this Maria Bates and what had she planned on doing with Raci?

"They are not here. Please, Maria, let's go." Andrew held his hat in his hands as Maria walked the length of the alley one more time. "They're gone, Maria."

She turned to face him and released a heavy sigh.

"You're right. He's taken her away." Tears welled in her eyes. Andrew put his arm around her and pulled her into his embrace. He was the closest thing she'd ever had to a brother, although until the last year, Andrew had held great resentment towards her.

Perhaps he felt guilty and that was the reason for the change in the way he treated her. She felt guilty for being the brat she'd been most of her life. Since her father's death, the two of them had leaned on each other and mended the old hurts and angers.

"I'm sorry, Maria. I truly am." He walked her towards the carriage. "Let's go back to the hotel. You need to rest some. You've had a busy day." He handed her into the carriage and climbed in beside her.

"I feel like such a failure, Andrew. I set out to change my life and amend what my father did, and the first opportunity I had, I let that scoundrel get away with Raci."

She swiped the tears from her eyes and Andrew retrieved his handkerchief and offered it to her. She shook her head and he returned the handkerchief to his coat pocket.

"What's this slave catcher's name? Do you know?"

"Garrett Lawson."

"Lawson?" Andrew's pallor whitened. "Are you sure?"

"Yes. Why?" She stared at her cousin as he tried to mask his reaction, but it was clear to Maria that Andrew knew Lawson not just by reputation but personally.

"Oh, no reason. Just surprised he's in Charleston. I understood he mainly worked in Virginia and North Carolina.

Never heard of him coming this far south."

"Well, I didn't know slave catchers had territories. He acted like he travels all over the South. I suspect he works wherever he wants." She paused. "Do you know him, Andrew?"

Andrew sat up straighter as though her question had alarmed him.

"Now why would you think that?" His blue eyes veiled what his voice couldn't hide. He knew Lawson.

"Just the way you said his name, like you knew him."

"I met him once." Andrew shrugged.

"Oh? When was that?"

"A few years ago in Virginia, when I worked for MacGraft Shipping."

"Did he use MacGraft Shipping for his slave catching business? Were he and his slaves passengers?"

"Once, on Brent's ship. Lawson and one of the slave's he'd caught were on board."

"Oh." Maria frowned. "I want to catch up with Mister Lawson and give him a piece of my mind. He doesn't appear to be the kind of man who would be a slave catcher. I mean, he acts like one, but he seems to be a man of breeding. I find him a contradiction."

"Well, he is." Andrew nodded. "He comes from a very prominent family in Newport News."

"I wonder how his family feels about his occupation?"

"I guess they aren't pleased he didn't go into the family business. I heard they feel being a slave catcher is a lowly job not suited for his social standing. They disowned him."

Maria watched the emotions play over Andrew's face. She could only imagine what deep pains he'd suffered over the years of being at the mercy of her father.

"I think disowning your own child is more despicable than being a slave catcher," Maria voiced.

"I believe his sister still has contact with him. She would never disown her brother, from what I hear."

"Well, cheers for her. I'm glad he has someone in his family who still believes in him." Andrew raised his eyebrows at her last comment and Maria trained her attention to the street scene outside the carriage. It was late afternoon. The streets were nearly empty as everyone retired to their homes and prepared for their evening meals. Her stomach rumbled and Maria remembered she'd not had anything to eat since early that morning.

She fell silent the rest of the ride to their hotel lost in thoughts about Garrett Lawson. Why was she relieved his sister had not abandoned him? Why did she care? Maria could not deny the strong attraction she'd felt to the scoundrel. If only he were not on the wrong side of life, she might have found him to be—

She shook herself mentally. Such musings were pointless.

Maria wondered about his sister. What type of person was she? Did she support slavery? Just what would make a sister stand by her brother when their parents had turned against him? Did she think her brother performed a service to the South by being a slave catcher? Did his sister not see what a wretched thing it was that he did?

Would Maria have felt that way a year ago? She was a different person now. She had been forced to change because the safe world she'd been raised in had been shattered. It had been a world built upon lies. She had just begun to find out what the real world was like, and so far, Maria did not like it much.

When Andrew handed her down from the carriage, she suddenly felt very tired.

"I'm hungry and exhausted, Andrew. I think I'll have something sent to my room then take a nap. Shall we meet for dinner around seven?"

"I will take care of having something sent up, you go rest." He smiled and put her hand in the crook of his arm.

Garrett Lawson stood across the street and watched Maria Bates step from the carriage. Now just who was that with her? He looked familiar. She turned and bestowed a brilliant smile on the man as he put her hand in the crook of his arm. Garrett's breath caught in his throat.

She shook her head and the late September afternoon sun caught in her red hair. His heart pounded harder. Garrett closed his eyes and tried to shake her from his thoughts. He had no time to get school-boyish over any female, much less this slave-stealing woman who had interfered with his life. He didn't have time to deal with a runaway. Not now. This had put him off schedule and he had much to accomplish in the next few days.

He had to meet his contact tonight. Well, Raci would just have to go with him. If Jamison were in fact his new contact, then he would apologize to him later.

Garrett tossed the dying cheroot onto the cobblestone and ground it out with his boot. At least he didn't need to worry about Maria Bates, as it appeared she had someone looking out for her and she'd not be interfering with Raci anymore.

Taking a deep breath, Garrett wished circumstances could have been different. If only life's choices were so simple. He was about to turn back towards Church Street and Jamison's home when he noticed the two men entering the side door to the hotel.

At first, he didn't think anything about it. Then he saw the taller man slap the shorter on the head. His pulse spiked. It was the raiders. They had come back for Maria, of course— she could identify them, and these idiots had not fled the state like any smart man would.

Instead of following them, Garrett decided to counter them by entering through the front and surprising them.

When he entered the hotel lobby, Garrett quickly met the look of the clerk. His footsteps echoed in the large lobby and a few of the guests looked up from their conversations, and then turned back. He didn't stop in front of the counter.

"Yes, sir." The clerk smoothed his hands over his baldhead. "Can I assist?"

Garrett halted with one hand on the banister. "I was to

call on Miss Maria Bates. Can you tell me what room she is in?"

"Well, sir, you must know we don't give out such information to strangers."

Garrett frowned and took the short steps over to him. Without a word, he retrieved his wallet from his breast pocket and pulled out a few bills.

"Let me introduce you to some old friends." He handed the money to the clerk. "Mutual friends, aren't they? Which means I'm not a stranger."

"Does the number 224 sound familiar to you? Up the stairs and to the left."

"Thank you." Garrett returned his wallet to his pocket and started up the stairs. He controlled the urge to take the steps two at a time and rush to her rescue. Surprise was on his side. He would reach Maria Bates in time, he reassured himself.

When Garrett reached the landing, he broke into a run, glancing at the number on the doors until he found 224. He stopped and put his ear to the door, listening. There was no sound coming from within. Was he too late? Panic threatened to override his good judgment and he willed his heartbeat to slow.

He lifted his hand and rapped on the door. There was no response. He knocked again. This time a muffled voice responded, followed by faint footfalls.

"Yes?" Her voice sounded sleepily from the other side.

"The desk clerk, Miss Bates. A word with you, please?"

He heard the key in the lock turn yet the door didn't open.

"Mister Lawson?" Came her muffled voice.

Garrett heard her fumbling with the key, but before she could turn the lock, he shoved his way into the room.

She stood with her dressing gown slightly askew, revealing a shapely thigh and long tapered leg. Garrett closed the door and turned the key in the lock, pulling the key from the door and holding it up to her.

"No sound. I'm not going to hurt you." He stood staring

at the way her unpinned hair cascaded about her shoulders, tumbling to her waist. The emerald silk dressing gown clung to her shapely form, and Garrett cleared his throat, struggling to control the involuntary response rising in his body.

"What the hell do you want?" She backed away from him.

"Shh." He put his finger to his mouth and took a step towards her.

"Stay away or I will scream."

"You don't want to do that unless you want the raiders to know exactly which room is yours."

"Raiders?"

"Yes. I saw them just a few moments ago. They entered through the servants' door."

"Oh my God!" Her pallor whitened. "Why would they come back? Do they think I'd bring Raci back here?"

"Perhaps. But I suspect they're here to make sure you never tell anyone about them."

Her green eyes reflected the deep green of her dressing gown and widened with the thought.

"You mean," she gulped, "they are here to kill me?"

He nodded and moved closer to her, but she backed away from him.

"How did you find me?"

"I track people for a living, Miss Bates. Finding you was easy compared to finding a runaway slave."

"Why did you track me down, Mister Lawson? You have Raci. What is it that you want from me?"

"Nothing, dear lady. I'm here because I was worried about you and my fears for you are climbing the back staircase as we speak. Please dress so I can help you out of here before they discover which room is yours, Miss Bates."

"Oh, so you were worried about me? Is that why you threw me into a carriage and sent it flying down the street like a demon-chased coach? I suffered several bruises from that rough treatment."

"I'm sorry, but you have interfered in something you don't understand. These raiders are incensed over losing Raci twice to you. You can identify them. Do you understand what I'm saying?"

"Yes." She seemed unconcerned by his warning. She crossed her arms over her generous breasts, pulling the silk material tautly over the two hardened tips.

The effect was not lost on Garrett. He clenched his teeth together and tried to douse the rapid fire this unconscious movement had stoked in him.

"You don't understand, Miss Bates. These men are desperate."

"Mister Lawson, you are a slave catcher. Why should I believe you for one second?"

"Because I'm here. Why else would I be here? As you pointed out, I have Raci. What purpose would it serve for me to come to you this evening other than to warn you? I could have gone on with my business. Regardless of what you think you know about me, understand this: those two raiders are here this very moment searching for you. When they find you, they are going to kill you. They seem to be the type who will have sport with you first, but rest assured, they *will* leave you dead. Now get dressed and hurry."

"You must think I'm a fool, Mister Lawson. Leave before I call out for help."

Garrett took the short steps to her and grabbed her by her forearms. He pulled her to him, pressing her into his hard body. Every sense in his body startled alert at the warmth of her softness. He struggled to keep his mind on the emergency at hand.

"Listen to what I'm saying. I will say it only one more time. You're in danger. You cannot expect these raiders to act with honor. Do you find that so difficult to understand? They recognized you. You are a witness to their crime. Do you understand what I'm saying?

"You must leave with me now, or you will be killed. Do you think they fled in fear? They won't let you spoil what they've established. Do you think they do this alone? They are here and I'm sure their cohorts are not far behind. Think.

You're a runaway of sorts, from what Raci has told me. You ran away from your home in North Carolina to live in Charleston. I don't know why and I don't care. These raiders are desperate. They won't stop until they have silenced you."

Maria's heartbeat pounded in her head. Her throat dried. Was it fear that ravaged her body or was it his muscled body pressed so firmly and intimately against hers? His hardness rose against her stomach. She gulped and her stare locked with his. She was unable to mask the fire quaking in her.

"Get dressed, now!" He pushed her towards the wardrobe and turned his back to her. "Something you can travel in. Hurry."

Chapter Seven

Maria didn't move. Why should she believe this man? He was a *slave catcher*, of all things. He was not a man of honor, yet coming here, if he were telling the truth, was an act of honor. What if it was a trick? What if he planned to harm her? Confused, Maria stood staring at the wardrobe. Maybe she should call out for Andrew.

A noise from the hall alerted them. Garrett put his finger over his lips and drew a pistol from his waistcoat. Trembling, Maria followed him to the door on tiptoes. He pushed her behind him, using his body as a shield when the sounds stopped in front of her door.

Maria pressed against his back, letting the strength of his hard body fill her with courage. Slowly, she peered around him, listening. If only his profession was not so despicable, Maria groaned mentally. How could he appear to be so caring and honorable? It was a contradiction.

"What are you doing?" came the hushed voice. "I was going to knock on the door."

"Are you really so stupid? Do you think she is going to just open the door and let us in? And what if it's the wrong room? We're going back outside to wait. She has to leave some time. When she does, we'll be waiting for her. One way or the other, she's ours."

The voice drifted back down the hall. He lowered the pistol and laid it on the nearby console. Maria collapsed against his back. He had been telling the truth. How could a man with his reputation be the same man standing here? Surely there was some mistake. There had to be. She was so confused. The sob jerked from her involuntarily.

He turned and pulled her into his arms. He held her tightly while stroking her hair. Maria fought the flood of tears, but the sobs racked her body. She clung to him, realizing how close she had come to being murdered. Fear, mingled with the brunt of realization, shook her to the core.

Had Garrett Lawson not warned her, when she and Andrew had emerged from the hotel for their evening meal she would have been assassinated. Andrew would have defended her and possibly been killed too.

"Oh God." She stood on tiptoe and wrapped her arms around his neck. Maria molded her body to his, taking comfort in his closeness. He was a strong man, she thought as her fingers threaded into his wavy brown hair.

"Shh. It's over. They won't come back inside this evening and you won't leave. I'll stay here and keep you safe. I promise." He smoothed her hair and tightened his arms around her. "I won't leave you by yourself."

His scent greeted Maria's nostrils as she buried her head into the curve of his neck and shoulder. Everything about him excited her. She knew she should be afraid of him, but he had saved her. He was not the man she'd heard about. This Garrett Lawson was someone very different.

His hand traced the curve of her face and she lifted her head from his shoulder. Her hands glided from his neck as she relaxed from tiptoes and rested her head against his chest.

His heart pounded wildly against her ear and brushed his thumb underneath her eye, tenderly pushing the tears from her face. Maria looked up through blurry eyes and saw the passion reflected in his handsome face. His dark eyes sparked with hunger so deep, Maria trembled. She'd never felt such intensity.

His lips were just inches from hers. It was so easy to lift onto her tiptoes again and meet his kiss. He bent over to her.

It was a natural need born of base desire. Her mind swirled, sensations bombarded her as his lips touched hers. His kiss was surprisingly tender, almost reluctant.

Maria returned his kiss with a feeling of urgency pounding in her chest. She tasted his lips and wanted more. He pressed his lips harder against hers. Her eagerness excited her beyond thought. She must have him.

Unaware the sash of her dressing gown had come untied, Maria startled when he crushed her to him and the roughness of his clothes brushed her naked body. Delighted shivers tingled over her. Incredible luscious sensations ignited everywhere her body touched his.

His tongue separated her lips and she welcomed him, allowing him full possession of her mouth. He demanded more as his hand moved down the curve of her neck and slipped between the space of silk and flesh to cup one of her breasts. Her gasp was a small catch in her throat beneath his kiss. His hand was large and warm. Maria's mind reeled. She was drunk with sensations. His tongue claimed hers and danced frantically around her attempts to possess it. His other hand slipped from her waist to close over her other breast and Maria felt she would burst into flame.

She curved herself into his hardness, grinding her hips into his, trying to ease the ache pulsing between her legs. Her movement incited him, and his hands slipped from her breasts and down her back, cupping her buttocks.

Shocks of heat and ache throbbed harder when he met her hips, grinding himself into her. Suddenly, he lifted her from the floor and pressed her into him. Maria was oblivious to being carried to the bed until he lowered her onto it. The springs groaned under his weight.

He pulled from her kiss, letting his lips track moist kisses down her neck to her hardened nipple. Her gasp filled the room. His tongue flickered over her breast, finally resting once more on her nipple as his lips closed tightly over it. The sensation pulsed to her groin and Maria kneaded his back with her hands.

Unable to stop himself, Garrett groaned against the sweet taste of her flesh. He wanted her. He needed to feel her hot passionate touch. She had incensed him beyond all logic and reason. He was a man possessed as he tugged against his coat, lifting slightly from her, long enough to toss it to the floor, followed by his brocade vest.

His gaze traveled the sultry length of her torso to the reddish tuft of hair that tickled his smooth stomach.

"You are so beautiful!" The words rushed from him in a throaty whisper.

"Garrett," she moaned.

He jerked the ascot from his neck.

"You've put me under a spell." She writhed under him, sending Garrett beyond all possible control. He clawed at the buttons on his shirt, yanking one from its place, sending it bouncing across the room. Frustrated, he pulled the shirt over his head and threw it from him. Her undulating hips hurled him into a heated response and he moved over her, still wearing his trousers.

"I want you, Garrett Lawson. I've never wanted any man this way in my life." She stared up at him from beneath hooded eyes. "Please," she murmured, and her eyes fluttered closed again.

It was all Garrett could do to unfasten his trousers. He could not wait, but his trousers caught on his boots and he cursed. Standing from her, he removed his boots and socks and at last, his trousers and long underwear fell to his feet. He stepped from his clothes and stood naked in front of her.

Maria lay looking up at him. She let her gaze wander over his muscled body. He was beautiful. She gulped when her gaze moved below his waist to his stiffness. She had no idea a man could be so huge.

Her heartbeat pounded loudly in her ears. How was her body going to accommodate him? She didn't care. She had to have him. She had to know what it was like to be his. Nothing mattered at that moment but being with him. She didn't care who he was.

Garrett lowered himself over her again and trembled when she let her hands glided over his back. His muscles flinched under her touch. His weight pressed down into the mattress as his knee found its place between her legs.

He scattered short hot kisses over her face in a consuming trail to her lips. Once more, his kiss possessed her. She was moist and hot waiting for him to do what a man should do. She knew what it was. She'd been raised on a farm, but Maria didn't know how it was supposed to feel. If this was what it felt like for all people, Maria marveled that any progress was made in the world and that men and women were able to have a life beyond such intense passion.

He shifted his weight and guided himself between her legs. She tingled expectantly, knowing that he would ease the heated, edgy need growing between her legs.

"You have excited me so much, my lovely lady, I cannot contain my passion any longer. Please forgive me," he whispered hotly in her ear.

"You better not contain anything, Garrett Lawson, or I will feel cheated." Her own voice sounded husky to her.

He groaned and pressed his throbbing hardness into her. The searing pain shot through her like a hot coal and she struggled from him, but his hands were on her shoulders as he pressed her into him.

Maria cried out and then the pain blasted beyond discomfort into something else. It eased, settling into a moist hotness that ground out its own need. Her hips rolled and beckoned him deeper and deeper. His breath blistered her neck. He grabbed her buttocks and ground himself deeper into her.

She could not press against him hard enough. Maria dug her hands into his lower back, urging him deeper until she felt she would scream her need to reach fulfillment. Unexpectedly, jagged waves bolted through her groin and up her spine, rippling and pulsating higher and higher with each thrust, until the sensations reached her head and exploded in a shudder of delightful waves.

His passion erupted in her and he shuddered with her. The two of them lay panting and rocking as their passion uncoiled in delightful, smaller quakes.

"Oh, sweet heaven," he panted in her ear. "I've never felt such intense pleasure." He kissed her ear and held her to him, gently rocking her.

Maria could feel him pulsing inside her and relaxed her legs, unlocking them from around his waist, momentarily embarrassed that she had allowed herself to be in such a position. Shame washed over her, followed by guilt then confusion. She tried to pull from him and turn her face, but he wouldn't let her.

"No. Don't turn away from me, Maria. Please," he whispered, "it was all my fault. I had no right. Had I known you were a virgin, I would not have seduced you so thoroughly. I pushed you beyond any woman's resistance."

Maria stiffened. How was it this man could continually surprise her? Was he really Garrett Lawson? Could it be he was an imposter?

The knock on the door alerted them. Maria jumped, but he kept her close to him.

"Maria? Are you dressed?"

"My cousin." She looked through blurry eyes. "We were to dine together this evening." She whispered.

"Send him away. Don't endanger him further." Garrett breathed.

"Maria?"

She pulled from him taking the sheet with her. Groaning, Garrett reached for her. Lying on his stomach, he let his arm relax against the mattress. The sheet caught under his leg, halting her in her path. Lazily, he lifted his foot releasing the edge of the sheet. Maria gathered it about her underneath her arms and glanced back at him. Her heartbeat jumped to her throat.

He lay with his arms and legs spread out, his head turned sideways to watch her. Her gaze traveled down the length of his long, naked body, burning a trail down his tanned back to his buttocks. Her mouth dried and the heat washed over her anew. She quickly found his stare and the lazy smile spreading over his lips.

The anxious knock jolted her from her moment of appreciation followed by Andrew's tensed voice.

"Maria? Are you all right?"

"Yes." Her voice was still weak from her passion. "Yes. I'm fine. Just tired." She rested her head against the door, missing Garrett's warm arms around her.

"Are you not dressed for dinner?"

Maria covered the threatening laughter with her hand. Garrett's low chuckle fell over her like a sultry summer breeze. She heard him shift in the bed, but didn't dare look over at him, lest she give herself away.

"N-no, I'm not. Please go without me. I'm going to bed early."

"Are you ill?"

"No. I'm not ill."

"Did I wake you?"

"Well, yes. I will see you in the morning."

"I will go on without you then, as long as you are feeling well."

Maria flattened her hand against the door. "I feel very well."

Another low chuckle behind her sent excited shivers cascading down her.

"Good night, then." Andrew's voice held concern and disappointment in its baritone depths.

"Good night, Andrew."

When she turned toward the bed, Maria was startled to find Garrett had risen and donned his pants. Was he leaving? He pulled his white linen shirt over his head and buttoned the remaining top button.

Maria padded over to bed and watched him, unsure what had happened. Anger had replaced the sensual warmth in his face with harsh lines. He glanced over at her while tucking in his shirttail.

"Andrew?" His voice was harsh and absent of warmth.

"Yes, my cousin. I told you about him." Was he jealous? Maria startled and felt a twinge of pleasure. Garrett was jealous over her?

"*Andrew Bates* is your *cousin?*"

Maria nodded.

"Why didn't you tell me?" His stare hardened. Her heart slammed against the walls of her chest. She didn't like the sound of his voice at all.

"What's wrong? Do you know my cousin?" Her knees weakened. She closed her eyes, certain she would hear the words she feared the most.

"Yes." Garrett bent over to pick up his waistcoat. "I also know about your father, *Thelma.*"

Chapter Ten

If Maria had ever believed in a God, she didn't at that moment. Had there been a God, he would have protected her from the pain Garrett's look sent shooting through her heart. Had God truly been forgiving, she would have been spared the legacy of her father's illicit deeds. And had God been with her that moment, Garrett Lawson would not be looking at her like that.

Taking a deep breath, Maria tried to still the frantic whirling of her thoughts and emotions.

"What do you mean?" Her voice trembled. She watched him sit down on the edge of the bed to put on his socks.

"You should have told me who you really are." He bent over to pull on his boots. He finished and stood from the bed.

"I haven't lied to you, Garrett. My real name *is* Maria."

He frowned at her. Could this be the same man who'd made such passionate love to her only moments earlier? Could this truly be happening? Maria collapsed on the edge of the nearby chair, trembling with the shame of her heritage.

"You have lied to me. You pretended it was Raci's welfare you were concerned about when all along you had other plans for that girl. "

"What?" Maria's attention snapped up to his stare. "How can *you* of all people, a renowned slave catcher, possibly be indignant? You are going to sell her to a breeder for God's sake."

He glared so hard at her, Maria was sure he'd burn her flesh with his stare.

"My sister, Nan, was one of your father's victims. Fortunately, Brent MacGraft and his agents found her before the white slavers managed to get her on board a ship bound for London. That was two years ago and my sister has never recovered. Never." He spat and stomped across the floor.

Maria felt as though the very air had been knocked out of her.

"Oh, Garrett," she wailed, watching helplessly as he reached for the door.

"I will take care of the two men outside, but after that—" his voice broke, "our association ends. To be with you, Maria, is a betrayal to my sister and all she's suffered at the hands of your family."

Maria's lower lip trembled. She stared at him in disbelief. This was not happening.

"Garrett," she sobbed, "how can you leave me after what we shared? Don't you know me at all? Don't you realize that I'm not like my papa?"

"Can you possibly imagine my sister's reaction if I were to tell her about you and that I've fallen in love with you?" he asked with pain and desire clashing in his brown eyes.

He opened the door and without looking back, left, slamming it behind him. Maria sat numbly listening to his footfalls on the back staircase.

"In love?" she whispered. Had he said he was in love with her? "Oh, Garrett." She bowed her head. The tears streamed down her cheeks. What was she to do now? Everything she had tried to run from had not only followed her here, but also had created the one thing she'd vainly tried to prevent, destroyed her opportunity for happiness. The one man she'd felt she could love had just walked out of her life.

It wasn't fair. She raised her hands to her face and smothered the heart-wrenched sobs. None of it was fair. She loved an infamous slave catcher. Her thoughts turned over the irony of his profession and the near fate of his sister. How did Garrett Lawson reconcile the two? How could he be such a hypocrite?

Maria had no idea how long she sat there with the sheet wrapped around her, crying, thinking, and crying some more. When she came to herself, she started to rise and change into her nightgown when she glimpsed the curled edges of the folded paper, jutting out from underneath the bed.

Instantly, she realized it must have fallen from Garrett's clothes during their lovemaking. The excited flutter rose to her cheeks, then crashed in grief as she realized it would be the one and only time she possessed Garrett Lawson like that.

She swallowed the burning knot in her throat and reached over to pick up the folded paper. She lit the nearby lamp and unfolded the paper. Maria brushed the new tears from her cheeks and struggled to focus on the paper.

"A map?" She squinted down at the crude drawing. "What an odd thing to have, Garrett." Maria tried to make out what it meant. There was no writing on it to distinguish anything. There was a long road leading from the city that branched off in two directions. A tree was drawn on one of the roads and an arrow pointing along the road. Next there was a series of wavy lines that must represent a creek, with an arrow drawn perpendicular to it. Another division of the road was marked with several arrows, more landmarks, and a crude drawing of a house with a large X in the center of it.

Maria shook her head. What did it mean? What was at the house? Why did Garrett have such a map? Sudden fear burst in her.

"Oh my God, Garrett, no." She wailed. Could he have taken this from Raci or some other runaway? Of course. Maria looked at the map again. She'd heard of such maps that mark the next safe house along the Underground Railroad. Could Garrett find it without the map?

Indecision and fear were not going to stop her. She had come to Charleston on a mission. She had to do something to cleanse her soul of her father's legacy. Hadn't she just been made a victim of that legacy this very night? She must get to the safe house before Garrett did and warn them.

Garrett Lawson stood in front of the deputy sheriff as the two raiders were led to the jail cells.

"But where's the slave they stole, Lawson?" the deputy sheriff insisted. "We can't hold them without evidence."

"I'll be back with the evidence in fifteen minutes, Deputy. Then I'm taking my cargo and returning her to her owner. Do you have any problems with that?"

"No. As long as you give me a sworn affidavit and this woman, Miss Maria Bates, does the same.

"She will. You can call on her at the Charleston Hotel in the morning. Her cousin is with her. He knows the slave as well.

"Since I know your reputation, Lawson, I'm trusting you are telling me the truth. I'll keep them locked up until you return with the Negro."

"Thank you, Deputy." Garrett shook the man's hand and left the building. He could go on with his business knowing Maria was safe from the raiders. His chest tightened at the vision that unwillingly flashed across his mind. He hailed a carriage and climbed in. "Church Street." Garrett settled back in the seat. How was it possible that a woman so tender and passionate could be such an accomplished liar? Maria Bates had learned from one of the best, her father.

Garrett took a deep breath of the air, trying to clear her from his mind, but he knew it was hopeless. She had left her imprint on every part of him, his sense of smell, his touch, his mind, even his hopes and especially his heart. God, she had sliced right through his heart and into his very soul. The only thing that could save him was his work.

When he arrived at Jamison's house, Garrett found the couple had just sat down to their evening meal. He politely refused Louisa's insistence that he join them and told

Jamison he'd come for his parcel.

Jamison excused himself from dinner and led Garrett to the back.

"She's in the cabin where our cook and family live." Jamison held the lantern up to light their way through the backyard. The three small cabins were hidden from view along the back of the walled property, obscured by shrubbery and Palmetto trees.

"Kinda strange traveling with her at night, isn't it Garrett?"

"Not at all." Garrett stared at the brick cabins, which appeared in better condition than most, probably because they were in the city and within visual distance of the main house. They were tiny, not more that a hundred square feet in each one, and when Jamison barged into the cabin unannounced, Garrett followed him inside and quickly realized just how small they were.

Inside the cook's cabin, Garrett counted six adults and eight children. Raci sat in the corner of the room as though in a trance. Garrett cringed at the crowded condition of the cabin and his disgust for Jamison elevated. It never ceased to amaze him how slave owners who prized their slaves as one of their most valuable possession could abuse them to the extent they did. The stench nearly gagged Garrett.

"Seems your slaves are sick in here, Jamison.

"Just that one over there, I sent for the doctor earlier."

"Yellow fever?" Garrett frowned and the cabin filled with gasps.

"Shut your mouth, Garrett. You want to start a panic through the city?"

"Come on, Raci. I'm taking you home."

She jumped to attention with the biggest smile Garrett had ever received.

His thoughts jumped to Maria and her seductive smile. His throat burned and he swallowed the twisting knot against his rising emotions. How was it possible to miss someone so much? He led Raci through the backyard and to the door in the wall, which led to the street.

"Why the hurry, Garrett? Come have a bite to eat before you leave."

"I need to be on my way. We have a long night's ride."

"Hell, yeah you do and then some." Jamison slapped him on the back and Garrett stiffened under the man's familiar gesture.

"Look, Jamison," he turned to the man, "I don't like the way you have fourteen human beings crammed in a one room shack. It's no wonder they're sick. I don't like the way your hands have no calluses. And I sure as hell don't like the way your wife propositions me every time you are out of hearing range. In brief, Jamison, I don't like anything about you. So keep your damn hands off me." Garrett glared at the other man, fighting his rage by balling his fists by his sides.

In the gold reflection of the lantern, Garrett could see the indignation rise in Jamison's eyes.

"Hell, boy, you leave your runaway slave at my place all day and this is the kinda thanks you give me?"

"The only reason she's still here is because you were hoping to use her for whatever game it is you're trying to play."

"Now, boy, I don't know what you are blabbering about. I was trying to be accommodating to you."

Garrett couldn't take any more. He pushed Jamison against the wall, pressing his arm into the other man's throat, choking off his air. "I told you before, I'm not playing. I offer this warning only once. Stay the hell away from me. If you see me anywhere, turn and walk in the other direction. Understand?"

Gasping for breath, Jamison managed to nod.

Enraged, Garrett slammed him harder against the brick wall, glaring into the startled expression that froze Jamison's face. His eyes were wide with a flicker of fear quickly masked in their depths. Garrett shoved from him and grabbed Raci by the wrist, pulling her behind him and out the gate.

"You's mad, boss?" she stuttered as they stepped onto the street.

"Yes, Raci, but not at you." He managed a slight smile.

"Come on, we're taking a carriage ride. It's waiting for us around the corner."

"Why's it way down there?"

"Because I don't want Jamison to know where we're going."

"And where is that, Massah?"

"A brief stop by the sheriff's office so he knows I'm telling the truth about the raiders locked up in his jail."

"They is? Did you do that, Mister Lawson?"

"Yes, I did, Raci."

Her grin was as wide as her face.

"Then once we are finished there, Raci, we're taking the road to freedom." Garrett reached inside his coat pocket to retrieve the map, but his fingers didn't meet the expected thickly folded paper; instead, his pocket was empty.

He stopped a few feet from the carriage. Raci walked ahead of him, then turned to stare at him. The street lamps hissed brightly in the early evening darkness.

"Lawsy, Massah, you look whiter than any white folk I ever seen."

Garrett searched his other pockets. Empty. He paced the short distance to the carriage then turned, nearly colliding into Raci who was hard on his heels. He paced back to the corner of the street and searched the ground.

When had he seen the map last? He mentally retraced his steps during the day. It had been a long day—not at all what he'd planned. His stomach rumbled at the thought he'd not had anything to eat since leaving the ship that morning.

When he'd left Raci with Jamison earlier that afternoon, Garrett had gone to the Sailor's Home and picked up the envelope left for him. The map had been inside as promised. He read it in the privacy of his carriage before refolding it and shoving it into his pocket. Then he'd gone to The Charleston Hotel. His heart pounded harder at the memory of what had happened there. God, she was an exciting, fetching woman. He swallowed and forced his thoughts back to the map.

Garrett had a gift for being able to completely recall any-thing he read or glanced over. It had served him well over the years. Being able to find the safe house tonight was not the problem. The problem was if the map fell into the wrong hands, their operation and all involved could be in danger.

"Massah?" Tense lines etched Raci's youthful face.

Garrett walked over to her and nodded to the driver.

"Let's go." He handed Raci inside the carriage.

"But what's wrong?" she insisted as she settled into the seat across from him.

"It's nothing, Raci." The carriage lurched forward.

Their business at the jail didn't take long.

They were soon back in the carriage. They left the police station, turned off Broad onto Meeting Street, and headed away from the city.

Garrett rode in silence, staring out at the dark night. The smell of fall hung in the cool air, mingling with the rem-nants of the humid day. He took a deep breath through his nostrils and released it. Leaning his head against the leather seat, he closed his eyes.

It would soon be over and he could go back to Virginia. It had proven more difficult than he'd expected. Garrett lamented he had not spared himself the most painful expe-rience of his life, falling in love with Maria Bates, daughter of the most despised criminal of their time. The tumultuous feelings overwhelmed him. Garrett opened his eyes. He had to get out of here before his emotions broke over the dam he'd put in place. He nearly jumped from the carriage before it came to a complete stop.

He turned to offer Raci a hand.

"Why's we stopping here, Massah?" The fear in her small voice pierced his heart.

"It's all right, Raci, no one is going to harm you." They stood in silence while the driver guided the team of horses and turned the carriage around in the road and headed back to the city.

Garrett stood listening until he was certain the carriage was not returning to follow them.

"This ain't the way to North Carolina. I knows that much. No moon tonight, but see that star? It should be over there when I look at it from my porch. So I knows we not going right."

"You're a smart girl, Raci." Garrett left the road and moved toward the scrubby dwarf trees forever bent into jagged shapes making one feel the wind even when there was none.

The horse was where he'd instructed the boy to leave it. Garrett led it to the road and mounted then extended his hand to the slave.

"I's never ride no horse, Massah. Can I just run beside ya?"

The image her request created was amusing, but Garrett covered his smile with his hand. He extended his other hand again.

"You don't have to do anything but hold on, Raci." He didn't wait for her to decide, and reached down, plopping her behind him on the mare's rump. Her tiny arms grabbed him around the neck. Garrett quickly disentangled himself, guiding her arms to his waist.

"Now, hold on. We have about a ten-mile ride."

"Just where are we going, Massah?"

Chapter Eleven

His eyes had grown accustomed to the dim light and Andrew Bates paced the length of the darkened room. The sound of an approaching horse alerted him. He drew his pistol from his waistcoat and peered out the window.

Two figures had dismounted the horse and were walking up the overgrown pathway. He recognized the shorter one as a Negro girl, but he couldn't make out the man.

The partially open front door creaked on its rusty hinges and the pair entered the abandoned house.

"Stand right there and don't move," Andrew ordered and took a step closer. He fumbled for a matchstick in his breast pocket.

"We were just out for a stroll," the voice recited the coded message.

"Then let me light a lantern to help you find your way," Andrew responded with his portion of the code.

"Why don't we do it together?" came the designated answer.

Andrew released his breath and lowered the barrel of his pistol. He struck the match against the mantle chasing the darkness from the corner and looked over to his new contact.

The man stood with Raci peering around his arm. He lowered his pistol and took a deep breath. The flame sizzled against the fuel soaked wick, illuminating Garrett Lawson's frowning face and the shocked face of the Negro girl.

"Lawson?" Andrew nearly burned his finger and shook the match flame until it extinguished.

"Bates?" Lawson mumbled and shook his head. "I don't understand." At first, Garrett feared it was an ambush. Andrew was Maria's cousin. What was he doing here?

"Well, hell, neither do I."

"You?" Garrett jeered and walked into the room, peering around as though he expected someone to jump from the darkness. Satisfied, he returned his pistol to his inside coat pocket.

"Just me." Andrew held his arms out from his sides and returned his pistol to the side holster strapped to his chest. "No one else is here."

"That's not exactly true," came the woman's voice from the darkness. Both men turned.

"Maria?" Garrett breathed, searching her determined expression. His body responded to her nearness and he groaned. Would he ever be free of her?

"What are you doing with that?" Andrew's voice broke through Garrett's musings, and he, too, saw the pistol she held with both hands.

"What are you? Andrew's accomplice?" Garrett asked and started for her, certain she would not harm him.

"Stop right there. I'll use this. I swear I will, Garrett."

"Maria, put the gun down." Andrew spoke from behind Garrett.

"What are you two doing here? Are you selling Raci to my cousin, Garrett? And you condemned me because of something my father did? What a hypocrite you are, Garrett." Her voice trembled and he knew she was crying.

"Maria, I'm sorry. I shouldn't have left you the way I did."

"Maria, no." Andrew moved towards her.

"Stay back, Andrew. I don't want to hurt you, either. But this is bigger than family or *friends*. This is Raci's life and doing what's right."

Andrew stopped a few feet from Garrett.

"Raci, get over here behind me," Maria ordered the slave, who was quick to obey.

"I expected this from Garrett, but you, Andrew? I can't

understand how you could be a part of this."

"What do you think is going on, Maria?" Andrew took a cautious step towards her.

"Stay back."

"They's taking me up North," Raci spoke up, "to Canada."

"What?" Maria glanced back at the slave then raised the pistol higher. "Stay back."

"What are you going to do with Raci, Maria? Sell her yourself?" Garrett's voice was cold. Her heart pounded heavily.

"I told you before I was taking her home."

"No, you never told me what you were doing with her."

"Maria, we aren't the villains here," Andrew tried, but she pulled the hammer back on the pistol.

"No!" Garrett cried out. "You can't. He's your blood."

"I will kill anyone who tries to stop us. Raci is going with me. I'm taking her back to her parents. That's where she wants to go. Isn't it, Raci?"

"Yes, ma'am. I's never wants to go to Canada, but Massah Lawson, he says I have my freedom and he will try to get my parents there too."

"He's lying!" Maria glared at Garrett. His life crumbled in the wake of her glare. He'd been wrong. Maria had done an honorable thing and he had colored her by what her father had done to Nan and all the others. And Raci. She had been trying to help Raci.

"Maria," he spoke softy, "I was wrong. I was so wrong. I've regretted every minute since leaving you."

Andrew frowned at him then his cousin.

"Very good, Miss Bates." Jamison spoke from the open doorway. The faint light fell over his face. A satisfied smirk spread over his face as his stare met Garrett's.

"That's right Garrett. I *am* playing a game. A game of cat and mouse. Guess who's the cat." Jamison pointed a pistol at Garrett. "We're working together. Maria Bates, daughter of the renowned Jonah Bates, what better way to exonerate herself than to help uncover the Underground Railroad in Charleston and see that the criminals are brought to justice."

"Maria!" Andrew sounded as though the breath had been knocked out of him.

"It's not true." She shook her head with a pleading look at Garrett. "He's lying. All I've tried to do is save Raci. I don't even know this man."

"Oh, my sweet Maria, you wound me." Jamison raised the pistol higher.

"Don't listen to him, Garrett. He's lying."

"It was so easy, Garrett. Hire a couple of raiders, find a willing partner to make an impromptu rescue, then have you find them just as they are escaping the warehouse. It was all so perfect and you took the bait. You took it better than I had planned."

Garrett searched her face for a sign of betrayal. He replayed the events the way Jamison described them. He hadn't seen Raci until Jamison appeared on the gangplank and he'd not seen Maria until that time. When he'd tracked them to the warehouse, they were just walking out after having untied themselves.

"Don't listen to him, Garrett," Maria begged. "Please don't. He may have planned it, but it wasn't like that. I was played just like you. I was." The pistol shook in her hands.

"I know my cousin, Garrett." Andrew joined her. "She would not do such a thing. Maria came to Charleston to start over. She felt guilty about her father's crimes and came here seeking absolution."

"And she has attained it." Jamison stepped around the men.

Garrett couldn't pull his stare from hers. She was so beautiful. Was she lying?

"Now, gentlemen, if you will turn and face the wall." He ordered and stepped beside Maria. Before she knew what had happened Jamison jerked the gun from her grip. She met the look of betrayal in Garrett's eyes and knew she had to do something to clear the confusion. Just who was this Jamison person and how had he known she would rescue Raci?

She glanced over her shoulder at Raci, then down at Jamison's feet as he backed from the men. Maria glanced up at Raci who followed her stare and nodded. Just as he took another step back, Raci stuck her foot out from beneath her skirt. Maria dove on top of him, wrestling for the gun. The hammer released and the sound was deafening.

Raci tackled him and pounded her tiny fists at his face. Jamison yelled and struggled with the two women.

"Let go of the gun, Jamison, or I'll shoot you right here. I'd just as well do it now and get it over with." Garrett's voice boomed over them and the entangled bodies froze.

Maria stared up at Garrett. The look in his eyes chilled her blood. Panting, Maria jerked the gun from Jamison. Andrew helped her to her feet, then turned to assist Raci. He slipped the gun from Maria and put his arm around her.

Maria drew Raci to her.

"Thanks, Raci. You're a brave girl." Maria squeezed her shoulders.

"What are you going to do now, Garrett?" Jamison challenged. "No sheriff in the South is going to lock up a white man who was only trying to stop the Underground Railroad."

"Is that what you think is going on here, Jamison?" Garrett's laughter shocked Jamison and Maria.

"It isn't?" Maria blinked.

"Do you want to tell them, Andrew or shall I?"

"No, I think you have earned the pleasure of the moment, Garrett." Andrew smiled.

Garrett flashed a wide grin and pulled a gold object from his coat pocket. He held it in the lantern's light. "Treasury Department, Federal Agent. And we're arresting you, Jamison, for operating an illegal underground railroad."

Andrew flashed his badge, too.

"That's ridiculous, everyone knows your reputation, Garrett. It's a perfect cover for an underground conductor."

"It *was* a perfect cover for a Federal Agent, but then most covers don't last as long as this one has." Garrett shrugged.

"I'll have to find a new one." He looked at Andrew. "Perhaps as a conductor for the underground railroad?" He laughed at the irony of it all.

Maria watched how the laugh lines creased around his eyes.

"Keep an eye on him while I get the irons." Andrew left the house and Garrett stood with the gun pointed on Jamison, toying with him the way a cat would a cornered mouse.

"Go ahead, Jamison, try it."

"You're framing me. The two of you are framing me." His voice rang with the incredulous realization of what had just happened.

"Now Jamison, which would a court of law believe? Tell me. Two agents of the federal government or a man who knowingly hid a runaway slave in his home all day while the sheriff was holding the two men *you* hired to steal that slave? Do you think the raiders will turn state's evidence against you to save their own skins?" Garrett's laughter only grew louder the more Jamison fumed.

Andrew returned carrying the shackles and stooped down to put the irons around Jamison's ankles.

"You can't get away with this." The prisoner huffed and tried to jerk from the shackles Andrew locked around his wrists.

"Appears we just did."

"I work for some powerful plantation owners," Jamison warned.

"Then maybe you'll have some plea bargaining power if you give the district attorney their names."

"Why would I do that? We're helping the government."

"Underground Railroad helping the government?" Andrew laughed.

"I don't work for the underground, damn you! You do."

"No, I work for the Treasury Department, Jamison. I think that fall addled your brain a bit." Garrett wasn't going to let up on the man.

"You set me up from the beginning, on the ship."
Dawning understanding hit Jamison. "Why you son-of-a-
bitch! You played me like a poker game, didn't you? It was
all a grand scheme to make me show myself and the men I
work for so you could protect your sorry ass underground."

"If you go around claiming that, Jamison, they might
forego a trial and commit you to an asylum instead. I'd be
careful if I were you," Garrett warned with a wry grin.

"Come on." Andrew jerked Jamison to his feet. "And Raci?
You come with us. I think Garrett and my cousin need some
time alone." Andrew shoved the baffled Jamison through the
door.

"You can't frame me like this!" Jamison yelled once they
were outside.

Maria heard the horse's snort followed by the sound of
hooves as they rode away from the house and down the road
towards the city. She stared at Garrett, searching his face for
the truth.

"How did you find this place? How did you know about
us if you weren't working with Jamison?" He moved closer.

"I found the map after you left." She shrugged and nervously clasped her hands together. A long silence ensued. It
was so awkward to be alone with him again, after the way
he'd left her.

"Garrett?" Her voice quaked. "Are you really an agent?
And my cousin, Andrew?"

"It's true." Garrett moved closer to her. "Maria, can you
ever forgive me?"

She looked so beautiful. Beaded sweat rolled down his
spine. Garrett needed to taste those lips or he was going to
go insane with the fire roaring in him. He took another step
closer.

"What you did was a brave thing." He wanted to tell her
how proud he was, but she interrupted him.

"But the Underground Railroad? You were going to take
Raci to Canada? You and Andrew?"

"Yes, my love." Garrett stepped over to her. "We have a lot

to talk about." He pulled her into his arms and let his hand thread through her long silken tresses. He caressed her cheek with the back of his other hand, tilting her face up to his.

"But how can you be both an agent *and* work for the underground? How can you do that?" Her lips trembled as he leaned over and let his lips brush against hers.

"The question, my sweet," he said against her lips, "is how could we *not*?" His lips covered hers.

Maria drew her arms around his neck and welcomed him back. She had grieved his leaving her and feared she'd never have the opportunity to explain. In their kiss, their passion rekindled, and Maria knew what was between them would create a new legacy, all their own—a legacy of love.

The Bates Family Saga continues in Sally Painter's
Shadows of Passion,
coming in April 2001 from Avid Press....

The story of one family's passion for freedom continues when Andrew Bates turns his back on his heritage
to follow what he believes is the only path to real freedom.

Running Bates Manor by day and a stop on the
Underground Railroad by night, Andrew soon finds
himself at odds with his beautiful new neighbor, Tessa
Renault.

After inheriting her cousin's plantation in North
Carolina, the Baltimore socialite's sense of adventure
quickly fades when she discovers several of her
cousin's slaves have run away.

Turning to the one man she can trust, Tessa is per-
plexed with Andrew's reluctance to help her track the
raiders. She's soon convinced he's the one stealing her
slaves and selling them to unsuspecting plantation
owners across the state line.

Enraged, Tessa sets out to entrap Andrew but soon
finds herself ensnared within the
SHADOWS OF PASSION.

The
Mystic's
Promise

by Kelley Pounds

Prologue

Nueva España
Province of New Mexico, June 1674

Through shimmering heat waves Sebastián de Navarra watched the half-naked boy stumble, fall, and push himself up again. The water gourd tied at his waist bounced too freely to be anything but empty. Desperation dogged his every step until finally he collapsed face down in the drought-scorched grass.

If Sebastián allowed more than memories and imagination to bridge the distance between this mesa and the valley below, he knew he would feel the soft wheeze of final breaths as if they were his own. He would hear the gentle slowing of a heartbeat until it stopped, releasing an exhalation of spirit deep into the earth.

Forgive me, Isabel. Forgive me for seeing you too late.

"A messenger?"

Yanked from the past, Sebastián turned his head slightly to acknowledge Tito's question, but he could not drag his gaze from the boy. "*Sí.* Perhaps a Tiwa Indian slave from one of the eastern pueblos."

His black Andalusian mare arched her neck into her chest and fought the bit as he spurred her into motion. Tito Pasquale followed, cursing the crow-hopping antics of his newly broken *mesteño.*

When they reached the valley floor, Sebastián dismounted
at the boy's side. Crouching, he turned the *niño* over, and
despite his determination to remain untouched, a relieved
sigh escaped when he found the child still breathing. Dark
hollows shadowed the boy's eyes. Bones tented the slack
parchment of his flesh. Sebastián perched an elbow on one
knee and touched his mouth to the back of his wrist.

Tito slapped him in the shoulder with a water skin.
Sebastián took it, pulled out the cork, and poured a tiny
amount of water into his palm. He soothed the warm liquid
over the child's cheeks and forehead. His eyes fluttered open.
Fear jumped into the obsidian depths, and Sebastián saw his
own unshaven Basque face reflected there. The boy gasped
and tried to pull himself back.

"Shh." Sebastián laid a hand on his shoulder and held up
the water skin, arching his eyebrows in question.

Eyes narrowed, the *niño* looked at the skin, then back at
him. Thirst won the battle with distrust, and he pushed
himself up on his elbows. Tito steadied him and helped him
sit, while Sebastián held the skin to his mouth. As thirsty as
he was, he drank carefully. Only a drop or two leaked onto
Sebastián's fingers.

When the boy finished, Sebastián corked the water skin
and set it aside. "Where are you from?" he asked in Spanish,
hoping the boy could understand.

El Niño merely stared at him, suspicion creeping back into
his eyes. *Sí*, he understood. He just chose not to answer.

Sebastián fished a strip of dried venison from the pouch he
kept hidden in the folds of the *faja* sashed about his waist.
He took a bite, and as he chewed he watched the boy's
changing expressions. He also noticed the leather thong
looped around his neck. Attached to the thong was a small,
flat, intricately tooled leather pouch, which he clamped
tightly to his side with one emaciated arm. The Spanish-
made purse contained no food, or the *niño* would not guard
it so jealously, so fearfully, while looking at him with such
miserable expectation.

He didn't need second sight to know the *niño's* pouch most likely contained an important message—one for which the boy had been threatened with death, or worse, if it did not reach its destination.

"Hungry?"

At the boy's eager nod, Sebastián gave him the uneaten portion of venison. *El Niño* promptly bit off a huge chunk.

"What kind of fool would send a child his age on such a mission alone?" Sebastián asked Tito in their native Euskara.

"A cruel one," Tito replied.

Sebastián nodded. "One with enough impudence to believe his authority above the laws of God, nature, and the Apaches."

Tito smiled. "One with money."

Compassion crumpled beneath the weight of Sebastián's more mercenary emotions. Long ago, in the land of torment and regret known as Spain, he had buried his wife and turned his back on his gift. He made his way in the New World by feeding on the superstitions of wealthy patrons all too eager to believe legends of the visionary El Místico. The mystic. A man who dowsed wells and fortunes. A man who spoke to spirits. A man who beheld death before its appointed time.

In truth, he could do none of those things anymore. Only keen observation, quick wit, and a talent for the theatrical served him now. Even so, his reputation flourished among a population whose parched souls craved hope like the desert he now called home craved rain. If Sebastián had learned anything in his thirty years, he had learned that no soul craved false hope more than the hungry, thirsty soul of a cruel man with money.

As for his own soul? Since Isabel's death, he'd lost hope of finding anything to sate it.

Sebastián returned Tito's smile. "Perhaps the boy would like to come back to our camp and meet the others. Rest, good food, and good company are sure to earn his trust."

Chapter One

Foothills of the Manzano Mountains
A few weeks later ...

Esperanza Salazar crept along the flat adobe rooftop, her path illuminated by the full moon. Pilfered bags of dried maize and beans hung by their drawstrings over her shoulder, and the added weight made her more careful than usual to keep each moccasined footfall light and soundless over the span of her half-brother's bedroom. Only a few steps more and she would reach the apple tree that grew at the southeast corner of the *hacienda.*

When she was five, she had begged her mother to help her transplant the stunted *manzano* seedling her father had chosen not to save for his orchard. Little had she known that fifteen years later she would use the tree as her ladder to freedom from the Salazar family fortress—a fortress now ruled by her half-brother, Antonio. A fortress with no windows on the exterior walls through which she could escape, alone, into the world that existed outside the central courtyard.

Reaching the apple tree, she hid within its branches and peered down at her brother's soldiers, who had forsaken the relative safety of the stone watchtower for the cool night breeze. Laughter and wood smoke drifted up to her from where the three men drank and played some game of chance by firelight as they guarded the *hacienda*'s massive front gate.

Their drunken presence would provide nothing but a token threat to a band of marauding Apaches. Seeing the arrow that had pierced her mother's heart had taught her early how easily the Apache could shatter one's sense of security. But because Esperanza counted on her brother's growing complacence, which had also pervaded the attitudes of his soldiers since her recapture two years ago, she merely smiled at her good fortune and stepped out on the limb nearest the parapet.

Moments later she jumped to the ground, her bent knees absorbing the impact as well as the sound. Adjusting the sacks at her shoulder, and draping the cotton *manta* more closely about her face so no one would recognize her by the scar, she sprinted into the shadows of the juniper and piñon trees. Comfortable laughter told her the soldiers suspected nothing.

Her mission took her a league to the southeast, to the Pueblo Indian village of Cuarac, where the old Tiwa woman lived who had once been her *niñera*. Juana de la Concepción was like a second mother to Esperanza, and Juana's grandson had recently endured the amputation of his feet for refusing to carry ore out of Antonio's silver mine. With last year's crop failure, the continuing drought, and her brother's insistence that mining proceed despite the threat of famine, few of the other families had been able to help Juana and her grandson. So Esperanza did what she could by stealing small portions of stored tribute that the villagers had paid her brother in past years.

She kept to the shadows as she entered the village behind the mission church, Nuestra Señora de la Purísima Concepción, which loomed over the small valley like God's angry fist. Around the church, multi-storied dwellings stood like indistinct stair-steps, their windows dark, ladders drawn up for the night. But here and there lights peeked from tiny second-story openings.

She made it past the church, and had just reached the lower portion of the village near the creek bed when the moonlight caught the tonsured head of Father Montoya as he closed the door to Juana's dwelling.

Esperanza froze. She knew she should continue walking, head down, as if she belonged. After all, she had dressed as a Tiwa woman, prepared for just such an encounter. But now that such an encounter seemed imminent, panic flooded her chest. Father Montoya would tell Antonio, who might see fit to punish her disobedience by inflicting more pain on Juana and her grandson. At the very least he would lock her away at the *hacienda* to shame and punish her. She'd rather be beaten than imprisoned, and he knew it.

As Father Montoya turned from the doorway, his gray Franciscan robes swinging about his ankles, Esperanza ducked into the alley that led to the back door of the *casa de communidad.* She flattened herself against the wall and held her breath as she strained to hear the *padre*'s footfalls, but the muted noise of drunken revelry drifting down the narrow passage made it impossible to focus on any other sounds.

Finally, the priest walked past her hiding place, his thoughtful gaze never wavering from his path as his sandals crunched the gravel beneath his feet. Esperanza released her breath, and her heartbeat slowed to a more natural rhythm.

"What do you suppose the priest is about at this hour— last rites … or a midnight confession?"

Esperanza whirled. The *manta* fell from her head. Adrenaline-tinged fury replaced startled fear, and she pulled the knife from the belt at her waist.

"Who are you?" she demanded of the shadow standing in the back doorway of the community house. "You speak Spanish too well to be a villager."

"As do you," came the shadow's unruffled response. "And with such fine Castilian inflection."

"Reveal yourself."

At first he seemed to melt into the doorway itself, making his shape even more difficult to separate from the darkness. Then, with enigmatic grace, he stepped into the narrow slash of moonlight. Silver light kissed shoulder-length black hair, high cheekbones, a narrow nose, and long-lashed, almond-shaped eyes.

He held a gourd cup in one hand. The other he stretched out to his side, his cloak spreading like a raven's wing as he presented her his empty palm. Though he held no weapon, the way he studied her face, his gaze lingering on the scar along her left cheek, made her senses tingle.

Too late she pulled up the *manta*, tossing one end over her shoulder to better hide her face. "I've not seen you before. Are you a trader?"

He smiled, and the moonlight slid along a full lower lip and winked off white teeth. "Of sorts. And you?"

"I am the one asking the questions, not answering them."

He laughed and moved closer, slowly, gently, as if coaxing a wild animal into a snare as he held his free hand in full view. Long fingers, like those of a musician or a poet, tapered into the strong, square, capable hand of a warrior.

Instinct warned her to step back, to strike out, or even to run, but she stood her ground, entranced by the tall stranger despite herself. Never had she seen such a beautiful man exude so much masculine energy, so much personal power, without the added "persuasion" of physical force.

"Perhaps you are a trader of sorts as well," he said, moving ever closer, until he stood vulnerable before her, well within the reach of her knife, should she choose to use it. "Would you trade a kiss for my silence?"

The moment Sebastián spoke, he knew he had allowed his fascination with this woman and his drink-muddled brain to spoil his timing. Though he could not see her face clearly, for the moon was above and behind her, he watched pride raise her pointed chin, while anger lifted dark, wing-like brows and pinched her generous mouth. He only hoped he hadn't miscalculated her character so much that he ended up with six inches of steel in his gut for his mistake. From her stance and the speed with which she had moved to protect herself when he had first spoken, he had no doubt that she knew how to use the knife she held. Oddly, that—and the riddle of her scar—only added to her mysterious appeal.

"Who do you think I am?" she asked, raising her knife. "Who are you to take me for such a fool?"

"As to the first, I must admit I am at a loss. But I can see now that you are no common ..."

"*¿Puta?*"

Sebastián raised his eyebrows; he had not expected such plain speech. He had thought to let the implication go unanswered, to speak for itself. In truth, he had never believed her to be a woman of easy virtue, especially given the furtiveness of her actions and the heavy leather bags she carried over her shoulder. But he knew what she believed he thought of her, and so he must give her the response she expected. A denial would only add to her distrust.

"*Sí.*" He dredged up just the right blend of embarrassment and apology for his voice and expression. "And it is quite clear you are nobody's fool, señorita. Forgive me."

He watched the anger fall from her like a soldier's armor after a long battle. She lowered her hand, and though she still held the knife, she no longer threatened him with it.

"Close your eyes," she told him.

He tilted his head and studied her intently. The only clue to her thoughts was a slight upward tilt at one corner of that voluptuous mouth. She couldn't be about to do what he suspected, what he hoped for ... could she? Already he had learned how difficult it was to correctly assess this woman.

"Close your eyes," she repeated.

Finally, he did as she asked, and as she drew near, her warm breath caressing his face, the heat of arousal mixed with the prickling sensation of danger—a heady blend, for he knew he was still vulnerable to her blade.

Sebastián opened his eyes just enough to peek through his lashes. He watched her dip her first two fingers in his wine, then simulate a kiss by pressing a lingering touch near the corner of his mouth.

He could have easily overpowered her and stolen the treasure instead of accepting the token. But he refused to take by force what he would rather coax forth with skill and patience. Still, against his better judgment, he turned his head and touched his lips to her fingers. A quick flick of his tongue brought a startled gasp from her mouth. He savored the taste of bland mission wine flavored by the salt of her skin.

"Some day, perhaps you will offer an even finer vintage."

She stumbled back, eyes wide, the knife thankfully forgotten.

And then she fled.

Sebastián watched her run, the taste of her still in his mouth ... and in his mind. The fantasy of the two of them making love, their passion blooming to full body like the bold red *Rioja* he used to drink back home, bled into a new vision.

No!

But it was too late. The images decimated his self-control; he could not stem the flow.

The chimera ripped at his mind and stabbed into his temple. Soon, the only reality that existed was inside his head.

Death hovered like a black storm cloud in a tiny rock chamber, whispering, beckoning to the fighting soul of the delirious young man who lay on a cot before a corner fireplace.

An old woman soothed his fevered brow, but turned her attention to the young woman who set leather bags beside the pottery jars lining the wall. When she pulled the manta from her auburn curls, the light from the fire caught the puckered gash that spread from her left ear almost to the corner of her mouth.

"I don't know how much longer he will live," the old woman said, tears glistening on her cheeks. "And even if he does, he will never walk again."

The young woman touched the ancient one's face, and the grief she felt gave way to a twinge of relief for the impending end of the young man's suffering. But then a new emotion engulfed her—a raw, white-hot rage that radiated from the deepest recesses of her being.

"If it means the death of me, Juana, I will put an end to my brother's cruelty."

Just as the vision appeared, it vanished, and Sebastián collapsed, his ability to cope shattered after so many years of neglect.

For eight years he had kept the unwelcome gift locked away. He had starved it, he had beaten it into submission, only to have it once again break free and pillage the landscape of his psyche.

Why? Why now?

He sat up and gripped his head in his hands, remembering the woman whose name he didn't even know, but whose touch and taste had awakened the demon from his past.

What well-bred Castilian woman lurked in the shadows dressed like a peaceful Tiwa, yet fought with a knife like an Apache?

Surely this mysterious enchantress could not be the demure señorita Esperanza Salazar spoken of in such glowing terms in the message he'd intercepted.

No. Please let it not be so.

Chapter Two

Esperanza hovered in the open doorway to her brother's office. As yet he had not glanced up from quill and paper to acknowledge her presence, even though her form blocked much of the morning sun that lit the room's gloomy interior.

"You summoned me, Antonio?"

The nib of the turkey feather faltered, leaving a blotch of ink in its wake. Antonio jerked his head up and glared at her, thick black brows knitting together atop a long, narrow nose. He ran a hand through black hair liberally streaked with gray. "*¡Ay de mí!* Look what you made me do! Do you know how much I pay for a single sheet of paper?"

"I am sorry, Antonio."

"Why must you always lurk about like a savage?"

"A virtuous woman should be seldom heard and rarely seen," she recited, offering a sweet smile.

"You will not put me in a foul temper today, Esperanza." He sponged the excess ink from his pen and placed it carefully among others in one of the small drawers that opened onto the drop-front desk of his *vargueño*. "I have good news. Come in and sit down."

Esperanza did as he commanded, her nape tingling as she turned her back to the bow and quiver of arrows that hung above the corner fireplace. Though her brother's weapon was not Apache, it always called to mind the sickening sound of flint piercing flesh and the sight of a striped and notched hawk feather so close to her face.

Perching on a sturdy pine stool, she glanced at Antonio's document. She wished the symbols meant something to her, for she knew it must be another letter to the governor about the mine.

"My messenger returned late last night. Don Baltazar Cabrera sends word that he is quite taken with the idea of a marriage between our families."

Despite the cold prickles stinging her arms and hands, Esperanza forced herself to remain calm. She had known this day would come. Even an Apache's disfigured whore could be married off for the right price. But why now, when she had finally summoned the courage necessary to put an end to the suffering Antonio caused?

"So, how much did you offer him so that your precious honor might be soothed?"

Antonio merely smiled. "One thousand pieces of silver, plus household goods and two *fanegas* of piñon nuts, but the final sum is to be negotiated by his envoy."

"What? No request for a personal inspection?"

"No, thank the Blessed Virgin. You see, Don Baltazar is very old, and it is unlikely that he would be able to see you even if he had been strong enough to make the journey himself."

"So fortuitous for you."

"And for you."

She swallowed to moisten her throat. "When will this marriage take place?"

"It remains to be seen. But if negotiations go well, you and Don Baltazar's representative will accompany my soldiers when they escort the southbound supply caravan."

That left her little time to formulate a plan! Panic welled up in her chest, but she stuffed it back down. She must keep the promise she had made to Juana, and she could not afford to make Antonio suspicious of any changes in her behavior.

"So noble of you to escort me yourself, Antonio. Are you

certain he will marry me when I arrive?"

Antonio smiled, but his muddy brown eyes remained dead. "As long as I keep you under control while you are here, so that you do not further soil our family name in our own backyard, I do not care to contemplate what will happen when you reach Mexico City. You know as well as I do that if our father had been dead, I would never have rescued you from that band of savages."

He reclaimed his pen, pulled a fresh sheet of paper from one of the drawers, and returned his attention to his task. "I have invited our guest to stay with us, so make certain a room is made ready, and see that Inez prepares something appropriate for tonight's meal." He glanced up. "And have her set the table with the silver—not your mother's cheap *majolica*."

Though she seethed inside, Esperanza tilted her head just so and dropped a dramatic curtsy. When she rose, she found Antonio staring at her, his thin upper lip curled in distaste.

"A word of warning, dear sister. I expect you to be on your best behavior. Do not disappoint me, or you will regret it."

Soon. Soon, dear brother, we will see who has the most regrets.

"He rides a horse worthy of a king," gushed Antonio. "Look at those lines. And such spirit!"

Even Esperanza could not help but stare in awe at the prancing Andalusian Don Baltazar's representative rode as he neared the *hacienda*. But when he drew rein before the massive *zaguán* gate, and she glimpsed his face beneath the black, broad-brimmed hat, she felt the blood drain from her cheeks. Last night's pale moonlight had not lessened the impact of his features on her memory.

She should not have been surprised. She should have realized that such a man as this would not have come to Cuarac merely to engage in trade with the villagers.

As he dismounted, Esperanza noticed for the first time the

young boy who had accompanied him. The *niño* jumped down from his burro, loaded with what looked to be their guest's baggage, and rushed to take the Andalusian's reins. As the boy led the horse and burro to the corrals behind the *hacienda*, striding with purpose and pride as if he knew his way, she recognized him as Felipe, one of the Cuarac village children. She noted that his cheeks and arms appeared fuller, and he wore new clothes in the Spanish style.

Esperanza flinched when Antonio, who stood beside her in preparation to greet their guest, lifted his hand to her face. He tugged her black lace *mantilla* forward, closer to her mouth.

"No need to spoil your first impression," he whispered, his hot breath burning her ear.

Despite the hollow feeling in her stomach, Esperanza pushed the lace back over her shoulder. "I am not a *Morisca*, Antonio, to be enshrouded by veils. He will see the scar soon enough."

And he will know who I am.

Antonio clenched his jaw, but then stretched his lips in a smile and took a few steps forward to greet their guest. Esperanza watched the man stride confidently toward Antonio. He had forsaken his black cloak for a short, black velvet jacket that revealed a width of *point d'Espagne* lace chased with silver threads at neck and wrists. The white silk *faja* sashed about his waist accentuated lean hips and powerful legs encased in knee breeches and high boots. Esperanza could almost hear Antonio's teeth grind in envy of the man's display of wealth and style, because he merely wore black linen, while his *faja* had been woven from native cotton.

"Ah, señor de Navarra. It is so good of you to come." Antonio flourished a hand, directing their guest closer to the house, where Esperanza stood. "May I introduce my sister, señorita Esperanza Alejandra Salazar y Bustamante. Esperanza, this is señor Sebastián de Navarra of Mexico City."

As Esperanza met his gaze, she found recognition but no surprise. So he had known. Or at least he had discerned the truth more quickly than she had. Fearing he would denounce her to Antonio, Esperanza's knees trembled as she lowered her head and curtseyed, offering her hand for his kiss. After a long moment, when only warm evening air circulated about her hand, she peeked up to find him removing his hat and flourishing it before him as he bowed low over one extended foot.

"It is a pleasure, señorita Salazar."

Disconcerted by his snub of her hand, but relieved that he chose to keep their secret, she wobbled as she rose from her position. She glanced quickly at Antonio. Aside from the grim set of his mouth, he revealed nothing of the anger and disappointment she knew he must feel.

As their guest straightened, she met his gaze, searching for some reason for his refusal to so much as politely buss the air above her hand, when last night he had tried to blackmail a kiss. Though he watched her intently, as if devouring her every feature in this new light, she found no nameable emotion in his expression.

"Felipe looks well," she said to him, eager for some kind of response she could measure. "Perhaps my intended will not be the cruel, selfish ogre I had feared."

A startled, unguarded smile lifted one corner of señor de Navarra's sensuous mouth, and humor lit the depths of eyes the color of rich chocolate.

"Esperanza, apologize at once!"

"Truly, señor Salazar, there is no need," Sebastián said. "It is only natural for your sister to wonder about the character of her intended. And Don Baltazar admires a woman who is unafraid to speak her mind ... as do I."

Open appreciation lit his face, and Esperanza caught a glimpse of the seductive charmer she'd met last night. But just as quickly, he pulled the mask back in place over his emotions, as if he had suddenly caught himself responding too freely.

For some reason, the obvious rationale for his sudden restraint—that he should not be so bold with the woman he had been sent to claim as another man's wife—did not fully explain the change in his behavior from last night to today. True, last night he had been drinking, and she doubted he had known who she was, but Esperanza still could not help but wonder if there was something else to this man that she could not see.

"Shall we go inside, señor de Navarra?" said Antonio, leading the way into the cool, shaded *placita*. "Our cook has prepared a feast fit for the viceroy himself. It is a rare occasion when we receive such an honored guest."

"Don Baltazar could not say enough about your generous hospitality, señor Salazar."

Antonio stopped and turned, frowning. "Oh? In truth, I must admit I have never met Don Baltazar."

Esperanza watched señor de Navarra's smile fall, alarm registering in his eyes and in the sudden tightness of his mouth. But in almost the same moment he reclaimed himself, his expression changing to one of polite confusion.

"Forgive me, Don Antonio. The respectful way he spoke of you led me to believe he knew you."

The explanation, and the fact that señor de Navarra had addressed him as "don," seemed to mollify Antonio, who smiled as if he'd received a grand compliment. Esperanza was not so easily convinced, although she was impressed by his ability to so quickly assess her brother's weakness and use it to rescue his own blunder.

As Antonio turned and led the way once more, Esperanza forced eye contact with their guest, testing his reaction to see if her suspicions were correct. He glanced away and back again, more forcefully this time, as if commanding her silence.

Esperanza denied her promise with a smile and a lift of one brow. No doubt his secret was greater than hers, for she suspected that he had not come from Don Baltazar at all, but had intercepted her brother's note and had used the information to gain entry to their *hacienda*.

Yes, there definitely was more to señor de Navarra than she first realized, and she intended to discover the full extent of his secret. Perhaps it would even prove useful.

Chapter Three

"I cannot remember when I have been presented with a finer meal, señor Salazar."

Sebastián inhaled the aroma of cornmeal and spiced pork from the steaming *tamales*, but it was the elaborate, filigreed silver platter on which they had been served that begged for a finger stroke. When he glanced up, he found Esperanza watching him. He shifted his focus to the cook, who beamed at him as she presented Esperanza with her plate.

"My mother's recipe," Antonio informed him before taking a sip of his wine. "A traditional Christmas meal in our family. Inez is the only cook we have ever had to do it justice."

"I am honored."

"And the silver you are admiring is from my brother's mine."

This time Sebastián forced himself to hold Esperanza's gaze. She teased him with knowing eyes that were the unfathomable blue of the Bay of Biscay, her expression just as dangerous to navigate.

The scar, wider close to her ear and narrowing near her mouth, should have destroyed her beauty. But he found the flaw only added to her allure because it suited her personality: bold, incisive, provocative. Until now, no woman had ever unnerved him and aroused him at the same time.

Last night, after the vision's impact had paled, he had convinced himself that he was capable of reining the beast back in and locking it away again, as long as he kept his distance from Esperanza. But he had been a fool to think it would be so easy. Now that he knew his interest in her went deeper than a gourd cup of mission wine, now that he suspected she knew he was not who he claimed to be, he did not know quite how to proceed.

"Señor de Navarra?"

Jolted from his musings, he shifted his attention to Antonio.

"Is there something wrong with your food?"

"Perhaps his conscience troubles him," Esperanza offered.

"Conscience?" Sebastián replied, determined this time not to allow his inner turmoil to show on his face.

"*Sí*. Such fine fare on such magnificent dinnerware, while those in the village go hungry."

Antonio's fork clattered on his plate. "*¡Ay de mí*, Esperanza! Must you ruin yet another meal with your prattle about the starving villagers?" He turned a conciliatory smile on Sebastián. "Esperanza would only be happy if we were all reduced to surviving on our last *fanega* of seed corn. Please, señor, enjoy the *tamales*. My dear sister merely thrives on goading me about business practices she should not even attempt to understand."

"It seems simple enough to me, Antonio. By having your soldiers force so many of the villagers to work at your mine like slaves, you keep them from tending already failing crops."

"Esperanza …" came Antonio's warning voice.

"If there are no crops," she continued, "the people starve or run away, and there is no tribute for you, their *encomendero*. If this continues long enough, you will have no subjects left to meet your kingly demands. Besides which, your practices are illegal. But then, with a partner like the governor, an old family friend, perhaps the legalities of Indian labor are inconsequential."

"Esperanza!"

"Despite what you would like to believe, dear brother, I have yet to see a man survive on a diet of silver." She turned to Sebastián then. "As much as he might like to try."

Antonio stood, his face florid. "Enough! You would do well to show me the proper respect—at least in the presence of our guest." With a self-conscious glance at Sebastián, he returned to his seat. "Forgive the outburst, señor de Navarra. Please. Eat."

Esperanza said no more. With unflappable grace, she lifted a forkful of *tamale* to her mouth, no doubt because wasting her food by refusing to eat it would only be a slap in the face to those who had so little and for whom she cared so much. So much that she was willing to incur her brother's considerable wrath.

Sebastián could not help but admire her zeal for such a worthy cause. Years ago, before prison, before Isabel's death had taught him that the useless pursuit of noble ideals offered scant comfort for a broken heart, he might have felt the same way.

Silence held the room in a chokehold for the remainder of the meal, until finally, over dessert, Antonio broached the subject of Esperanza's marriage to Don Baltazar.

"As you are no doubt aware by now, señor de Navarra," he began in a tone that revealed his sorely tested patience, "my sister is not the meek and well-mannered young woman I led Don Baltazar to expect. She has reached twenty unwedded because of her sharp tongue, and because of certain other … distinctions … which few men will accept in a wife."

"Antonio, please."

Esperanza's vulnerable tone startled Sebastián.

Antonio rose and strode around the table until he stood behind his sister's chair and placed his hands on her shoulders. Esperanza visibly cringed, but tried to disguise it in the determined set of her chin.

"I had hoped that an older man, perhaps a widower, might be persuaded by a substantial dowry to overlook obvious flaws—" he gripped her jaw, and she gasped as he yanked her face toward Sebastián "—as well as some that will not be apparent until her wedding night. My sister is not a—"

"*Sí, sí.*" Sebastián held up his hand and forced a smile. "Out of respect for your sister's modesty, say no more, Don Antonio."

As much as he wanted to learn about Antonio's source of wealth and the opportunity for its exploitation, he had no desire to participate in the man's sick game of humiliation.

"I only thought it fair to be honest with you, señor de Navarra. It is my fervent hope that you and I will still be able to negotiate."

Sebastián looked at Esperanza, who stared at her lap. As if sensing his attention, she lifted her chin. The small display of bravado did not erase the shadow of mortification from her eyes.

Lifting his wine glass, he returned his attention to señor Salazar. "Please, Don Antonio, finish your *flan*. We will discuss such matters after señorita Salazar has retired for the evening."

Esperanza stood and moved away from Antonio, putting the table between them. "No, *señores*, I propose we discuss the matter now. As long as we are professing our honesty—" she directed her gaze at Sebastián "—I think it only fair that señor de Navarra know the whole truth before he makes his decision on whether or not to … accept my dowry on behalf of his benefactor.

"The truth is, señor de Navarra, I was stolen from my mother's arms after she had been felled by an Apache's arrow—the same arrow that gave me this scar. For thirteen years I lived with the Apache, first as a slave, and later as … how shall I say it?" She glanced across at Antonio, her glittering eyes expressing her scorn and defiance. "A warrior's whore. My brother has never forgiven me for bringing shame on our family name. Nor has he forgiven me for not escaping, or for not killing myself when I did not succeed, since—according to him—I was already damned."

Antonio watched her with an expression of paralyzed stupefaction.

"There, Antonio." She offered him a smile filled with mock innocence. "My humiliation and punishment are complete, and by my own hand. You should be pleased. Although I daresay you would rather I had not been quite so candid."

Once again she turned to Sebastián, baiting him with a devious smile. "And now, señor de Navarra, it seems only fair that since you know so much about me, I should know more about you. Is there any deep, dark secret you would like to confess?"

While Sebastián reeled under Esperanza's full frontal attack, scrambling for some kind of response that might save his life as well as salvage the situation, Esperanza turned again to her brother.

"Or perhaps, Antonio, since señor de Navarra shares your love for silver, you would like to tell him the location of your mine, since you will bestow that honor on no one else."

Chapter Four

As Esperanza stood firm under her brother's withering glare, she knew the danger of her bold wager. She waited, hoping against her life, which both men held in their hands, that she had not underestimated Sebastián de Navarra's greed ... or his dormant sense of honor.

A fraud and a thief he might be, with fancy clothes and a fine horse both intended to allay the suspicions of Antonio, who set great store in appearances. But she knew now that he was the one who had cared for Felipe, because just weeks ago the boy had been little more than a walking cadaver. He was the one who had diffused her brother's humiliation and allowed her to regain some sense of control, even if she had not been left with her dignity.

What would he do with the information she had provided? If he reacted the way she hoped, perhaps she might convince him to help her—for the price of her dowry, of course. If he would not, then perhaps he deserved to be denounced to Antonio for the trickster he was.

She had no more time to contemplate the question as Antonio advanced on her, his fists clenched at his sides, his face livid. Esperanza's stomach sank.

Sebastián stood and stepped in front of Antonio, forcing him to look up. "Don Antonio, please," he said in a laughing tone. "You said yourself that she enjoys goading you. No doubt her experience with the *Indios* has left her somewhat ignorant of proper behavior. But we are civilized men and must show her the way."

Esperanza noticed that he had gracefully stretched his arms out to his sides, palms open. But she knew now that his odd mannerism—the same one he had used last night—only pretended supplication.

"And if you are worried that her behavior will jeopardize our negotiations, do not concern yourself. Although I was sent here on Don Baltazar's behalf, I must tell you he finds the terms already offered satisfactory. He is extremely eager for a dowry and heirs." Sebastián laughed, the sound itself a ribald jest between men. "And if nothing else, I can attest to your sister's health and vigor. What man would not want such qualities in a young bride?"

Sebastián's tactic seemed to work, for Antonio turned his attention to her, his jaw still clenched but loosening slightly as he considered the words. Finally, he strode back to his chair. But before sitting, he pointed a shaking finger at her.

"One more outburst, Esperanza, and I will lock you in your room until the arrival of the supply caravan."

Pretending to show remorse, Esperanza ducked her head and dropped a small curtsey. She returned to her chair, and after a respectable amount of time had passed, she peeked up at Sebastián.

Thank the saints she had not misjudged him.

What game was she trying to play? Sebastián studied Esperanza, whose expression revealed a satisfaction he could not comprehend, especially since she had revealed something about herself that had obviously scarred her more deeply than the face wound she displayed to the world.

But if she knew he was not who he pretended to be, if she suspected he was only out to steal her dowry for himself, why bait him in front of her brother, then openly bait her brother as well? What could she possibly have gained by exposing her soft underbelly to two predators?

Unless she was trying to determine which predator posed the greater threat ... or which might be manipulated into serving as some sort of ally. A smile stole over his face as he realized that he had once again played right into her hand. He was too impressed by her bold maneuver to be angry for being used. No doubt it would only be a matter of time before she presented him with the true challenge for which he had just been tested.

He turned to Antonio, prepared to use the ammunition Esperanza had so deftly handed him behind her brother's back.

"Although your sister may lack a certain ... gentility, Don Antonio, she certainly does not lack intelligence. I had not planned to bring up this matter so soon, but I do indeed have a confession. I had my own reason for accepting Don Baltazar's request that I act on his behalf."

He finished the last bite of *flan*, savoring the smooth texture and smoky sweetness of the custard on his tongue, prolonging the suspense of his audience as he wiped his mouth on his napkin.

"Go on," Antonio prodded.

"Well, señorita Salazar was very observant when she noted my interest in silver." He smiled. "When Don Baltazar told me about the dowry you had offered, I confess I had a certain hope that I might gain something for myself."

Antonio lifted a brow and offered a guarded "Oh?"

"*Sí*. I am quite intrigued by this talk of your mine," he said, lifting his wineglass, "and I cannot help but wonder if you might have some need for a man of my special abilities."

Sebastián spared a glance at Esperanza, who was frowning at him as if she had misjudged him after all.

"And what might those abilities be, señor de Navarra?"

"Perhaps you know my reputation. You see, few know me as Sebastián de Navarra, but many know me as El Místico. The mystic."

The skin on Antonio's forehead drew back as recognition

dawned. "*Sí, sí,* I have heard of you." New interest lit his dull brown eyes. "Is it true that you used your magic to dowse the largest silver fortune ever found in any mine at Parral?"

In answer, Sebastián smiled and swirled his wine.

Antonio leaned forward. "You could do the same for me? The vein I have been mining has recently played out. My soldiers know nothing about mining, and with the recent problems I have had with my slaves, I have been at my wit's end as to how to find another. The governor is growing quite impatient."

"If the silver is there, Don Antonio, I can find it." He took a sip of wine. "Do you have a map?"

At the very least, a map could be copied and sold. Or, if he could get the map to his men, who camped not far south, waiting to waylay the passing supply caravan, perhaps they could use the map themselves after the ambush. Especially since Antonio's soldiers would have to be divided between caravan escort duty and guard duty at the mine.

Of course, the fact that Esperanza suspected his dishonest intentions would no doubt make everything much more difficult. He glanced over at her. Her expression of crestfallen bewilderment tugged at his heart, but he refused to give in to the emotions she stirred within him. He returned his attention to Antonio.

"As it is," Antonio said, "I worry that my threats and my punishments of the miners will not be enough. The location would surely not remain secret if I drew a map."

Sebastián laughed. "*Sí,* that is true." He set down the wineglass and allowed a thoughtful expression to fall over his face. "Hmm, I used a map to dowse the fortune in Parral...."

"Perhaps I could take you there," Antonio offered, his voice tentative.

Sebastián let several seconds elapse as he pretended to consider the solution. He did not want to appear too eager. "*Sí,*" he agreed at last. "I am certain to better envision the source of the silver at the mine itself."

"But you will have to be blindfolded."

Disappointment slammed the door on Sebastián's enthusiasm, but he forced a smile. "A reasonable precaution, Don Antonio."

Chapter Five

"Do not go, señorita Salazar," Inez whispered. "They say his own mother-in-law denounced him to the agents of the Inquisition. They say he used his powers to kill his wife."

Esperanza smiled as she dried the last silver platter and placed it atop the stack in the *trastero*, next to the flower-patterned *majolica* that had been part of her mother's dowry. The dishes would likely be part of her own as well, since Antonio hated the sight of anything that had belonged to Maria Bustamante. She could only guess that his hatred stemmed from the fact that her mother's background of wealth and breeding overshadowed that of his more humble maternal ancestors.

"You liked him well enough when he complimented your *tamales*."

"*Sí*, but I did not know who he was then."

"I have a feeling these legends about El Místico"— Esperanza waved her hand in the air—"are merely in his own mind." She pecked the frail woman on the cheek. "I will be fine, Inez. Go to bed."

With that, Esperanza left the kitchen and strode across the moonlit courtyard as if headed for her own bedroom. When she reached her door, she glanced back at the rooms surrounding the *placita*. No lights except the kitchen's winked from any of the shuttered windows beneath the shadowed portico. Veering right, she hunkered behind the tall hollyhocks that lined the perimeter of the *placita* until she neared the guest room door.

"I suspected you might visit me tonight."

Esperanza gasped, infuriated for being startled again by one as adept at lurking in doorways as she. "No doubt you 'envisioned' it," she retorted.

"Temper, temper, señorita Salazar. If you want something from me, insulting me is not the way to achieve it."

"My humble apologies, El Místico."

He folded his arms across his chest. "There is nothing humble about you, Esperanza. Least of all your apologies."

She tried to ignore the effect his muted voice speaking her name had on the pace of her heartbeat. "May we go inside before Antonio catches us out here together?"

"By all means," he said, unfolding his arms and stepping into the darkness as he flourished a hand before him.

Though her eyes had grown accustomed to the night, she was less prepared for the fantasy of being embraced in black velvet as she stepped past Sebastián and into his pitch black enchanter's lair. He shut the door, and her heart leaped in her chest.

She did not hear his footfalls on the packed earth floor, but she felt the air stir as he moved past her, leaving a scent in his wake that reminded her of a thunder storm's promise: charged and elemental.

She saw two sparks flare before flame danced on the wick of the candle at his bedside, illuminating his face and hands. He then reclined on his bed, and for the first time she realized that the drawstring closure at the top of his shirt gaped open, spilling lace over the boldly carved contours of his smooth brown chest.

"You may sit, but it will have to be on the bed. My hostess did not see fit to provide me with either chair or stool."

Esperanza contemplated his suggestion. Though she had sacrificed the role of shrinking virgin long ago, the way Sebastián made himself so comfortable in her presence left her feeling lightheaded and out of her depth. She continued to stand.

"I have come with a proposition, señor de Navarra."

She waited for his response, but he did not speak, which only increased her agitation—a reaction he probably relished, since she had come so close to betraying his secret over the evening meal.

"All right, I will be blunt, since that is what you expect of me. I know you came here to fleece my brother out of my dowry and anything else you might be wily enough to think of. What I propose is that you do something worthwhile to earn your spoils."

Sebastián laughed, a hearty sound that filled earthen walls.

"Shhh!"

"*Perdón*, señorita Salazar." He quieted. "How do you define 'worthwhile'? It has been my experience that anything that must be earned in such a dull manner is an even duller prize."

"You do not truly believe that."

"No?"

"Why do you pretend to be so bitter and jaded?"

Sebastián taunted her with a smile. "Bitter and jaded are two things I never pretend to be. Perhaps you just choose not to see me for who I really am."

"Perhaps I *do* see you for who you really are. Or at least what you could be if you did not spend so much time avoiding whatever it might be that has hurt you so deeply." She studied him for a moment, noting the tension in his jaw. "Is it true you murdered your wife?"

In one smooth movement he came off the bed. In two short strides he stood just inches away. He reached out to grab her by the elbow, but just before touching her, he curled his fingers back into his palm and put his hand down to his side.

"Perhaps you should leave."

The fury Esperanza saw as she looked up into in his eyes veiled the fear that touched her as he refused to do. "Ah, so that part of the legend is not your fabrication."

"I did not murder my wife."

"But she is dead, and you were blamed. That is why you are so bitter."

He released a disdainful puff of air and smiled with only one side of his mouth. "As you wish."

Esperanza could see the candle's flame burning deep within his enlarged pupils, those mirrors to his deepest self where his passion lurked in the doorway of his pain. Where he tried but failed to hide the belief that she might be the answer to his prayer … as if she might be his last hope for salvation.

He leaned closer, enveloping her in his elemental scent and the warmth that radiated from his body. She matched his progress, lifting her chin, holding his gaze, welcoming him into her own deepest self, but still he would not touch her.

"Esperanza …" he whispered, stirring the air above her lips as he closed his eyes.

Just as she closed her own, she felt him pull back. Opening her eyes, she found him turned away from her, furrowing one hand through his hair while he gripped the back of his neck with the other. She wanted to say something, but nothing seemed appropriate.

Finally, he faced her, the mask in place over the mirror once more. "You were about to tell me how I should earn my spoils?"

For a moment she could not speak. The change in him—the change in her because of what she had seen in his eyes for those few short seconds—squeezed her heart and left her bereft.

"I want you to help me destroy Antonio's mine."

He laughed again, but more quietly this time. "You claim to know me so well, señorita Salazar. You know why I am here. Explain to me why I would want to do such a thing?"

She shrugged. "Because it is the right thing to do."

"Ah, the right thing to do. I see. And I am such a noble man at heart, is that right?"

Sensing that he would be even more opposed to helping

her now, because of the vulnerability he had revealed to her, Esperanza did not answer. She merely allowed him to contemplate her words and his own in silence.

"No matter how enchanting the woman in need may be, señorita, noble causes are no longer my avocation."

"But they were at one time?"

He clenched his jaw.

"What about children like Felipe, in need of food from failed and neglected crops? What about old men who should be telling stories by firelight to those children, but instead are flogged for being too weak to shovel ore?" She paused for a moment to let the pictures she hoped she was creating gather strength in his mind. "What about young men with their whole lives ahead of them … who have their feet amputated, only to die of the dismemberment after suffering for days in fevered delirium?"

He turned away at that. "Destroying the mine will not put an end to your brother's cruelty, señorita Salazar. Besides, if it were not for this mine, you would not live in such comfort."

"I have survived far worse than being forced by necessity to repair a snagged lace *mantilla*, señor de Navarra. Suffering the death of a husband I had finally grown to love, knowing my brother hates me and would rather I had killed myself than surrender my maidenhead to a savage—these are the least of the 'comforts' I have lived with for the past two years. I am no longer afraid to do what needs to be done."

"Even if it means you will have to do it alone?"

"So, you are refusing to help me?"

He strode to his bed and reclined there, bending a leg and resting his arm atop his velvet-clad knee. "I already told you, señorita Salazar, your lost cause is not my own."

"Then perhaps Antonio would like to know why you are here."

"Perhaps he would like to know about this conversation. And should I give him my account of last night's encounter as well?"

Esperanza refused to believe he would let it end like this. "Go to the mine tomorrow, señor de Navarra. If you can refuse my request after you have seen with your own eyes the cruelties I have described, then I will know I have completely misjudged you."

She opened the door. A wedge of moonlight cut into the room.

"Esperanza."

Despite her disenchantment, his voice speaking her name did not fail to move her. She turned and looked at him, seeing a hint of the emotion he had shared with her when they had almost kissed.

"Why do you care so much what happens to these people?"

"Because no one should have to live without hope for a better future, señor de Navarra. Even a man like you."

Chapter Six

Blindfolded, Sebastián sat astride one of Antonio's horses. He beat back an upswelling of dread, refusing to succumb to the specters of the inquisitor's prison as Antonio tied the rope around his wrists behind his back.

"Forgive me, señor de Navarra," Antonio said. "That is not too tight, I hope?"

"No," Sebastián forced out.

"I know you must be disappointed about riding a strange horse, and perhaps I carry this too far by not trusting you to leave your blindfold in place, but one cannot be too careful."

"How right you are, Don Antonio," Sebastián said, his voice as tight as the ropes chafing his wrists. "I will merely consider it another grand adventure."

Moments later, the horse lurched into motion, and Sebastián tightened his knees so as not to topple off backwards. He felt the sun at his back for several minutes and knew the general direction they headed was west. But he would have known that by common sense alone. The only granite mountains nearby capable of supporting such rich veins of silver were the Sierra Morenas, which many now called the Manzanos for the Salazar *hacienda*'s apple orchard.

But just as a picture of their possible route formed in Sebastián's mind, the soldier leading his mount turned north, and the sun's heat touched his right shoulder and the portion of his jaw not shaded by his hat. At first he tried to keep track of their numerous directional changes, but as the hours passed and the sun rose higher, he could no longer tell where in the vast *cordillera* of the Manzanos they might be.

As they ascended ever farther into the mountains, he was at last able to distinguish sounds not made by their three-man party. The rasp of a boulder being dragged over ore, crushing it into rubble, sent chills down his arms. He listened to the screech and rumble of heavily loaded *carretas* as they trundled over rock. He leaned closer to the whisper of water in a wooden flume.

At last the horse he rode stopped, and leather creaked as Antonio and the soldier dismounted.

"We are here at last, señor de Navarra," Antonio said as he loosened the ropes at Sebastián's wrists.

"Quite some distance from the *hacienda*," Sebastián commented. It was all he could do to remain calm as the bindings fell away.

"Far enough," Antonio replied. "There. You are free."

Sebastián shoved up the blindfold. The first sight that met his eyes was a dead, emaciated Tiwa man hanging upside-down from a post and crossbeam. The man's spirit had not left long ago, for there was no stench.

Fury scoured through Sebastián's system. "Did you learn your sadistic tricks from agents of the Inquisition, Don Antonio?"

Antonio squinted, studying him with shrewd attention. "A rather effective punishment as well as a deterrent for those who see him, don't you think?"

"If you can refuse my request after you have seen with your own eyes the cruelties I have described, then I will know I have completely misjudged you."

Esperanza's words haunted Sebastián as he regarded the dead man, a hopeless symbol of a vanquished people. Still, he swallowed back his disgust as he dismounted, turning his intent gaze once more to Antonio.

Under Sebastián's scrutiny, the man offered an uncomfortable chuckle as he stroked the blaze on the nose of his mount. "Come. We leave the horses here; I don't want to chance them being crushed by a runaway ore wagon."

Rubbing his wrists, Sebastián followed Antonio and the soldier up a narrow red flagstone road, in which twin grooves had been worn from years of heavy *carreta* traffic. He marveled at the labor involved in such a road, for it had been built from rock that had to have been carted in from several leagues away.

As they drew closer to the opening of the mine, soldiers held whips in the crooks of their arms as they paraded amongst groups of miners loading ore into *carretas*. Piles of worthless tailings from the mine littered both sides of the road, and the surrounding canyon walls had been denuded of pines. At last the maw gaped before them, and Antonio stepped aside, allowing Sebastián to follow the soldier into a tunnel lined with shoring timbers and yucca-shaft torches.

"Do you sense anything, señor de Navarra?"

Sebastián clenched his jaw at Antonio's eager tone and forced himself to take in a slow, deep breath. Oh, yes, he would give señor Salazar the drama he craved, but he needed time to build suspense. He needed time to see the extent of the mine.

"It is too early to be certain, but …" He let the words linger, unfinished save for the distant rhythmic echo of steel against stone. "Perhaps if I lead the way?"

"Of course," Antonio replied.

Sebastián moved past the soldier, and when he knew he held the attention of both men, he lifted his hands out to his sides, palms forward, well aware that such a simple gesture seemed to add to the mystique surrounding him. With calculated grace, he strolled ahead, stopping every few steps to close his eyes and take in a deep breath as if to inhale some magical force from the earth itself.

Antonio dogged his heels, eagerly peering into his face at every pause. But when Sebastián, who peeked through his eyelashes, saw the man open his mouth as if to speak, he moved on.

He drew them ever deeper into the mine, past workers heaving pickaxes and climbing up and down the notched pine ladders that led into the labyrinth of stopes and tunnels. Soon, the expression on Antonio's face revealed his strained patience.

Sebastián paused one last time. He touched the wall, smoothing his hands over its jagged surface. A sudden blast of frigid air and a blow to the head knocked him to the ground.

Leave here! a voice thundered in his ear.

He rolled over, fighting dizziness as he strained to focus on Antonio and his soldier, but all he saw were the fuzzy multiple images of their surprised expressions illuminated by dozens of quivering torches. In the shuddering firelight, faces and forms of *Indios* began to materialize as if from a cloud, their bodies not made of bone and sinew, as were those working around him, but of haze and mist, hatred and fury.

The mine shaft filled with the rotten-egg stench of sulphur. The specters flashed like jagged bolts of lightning about Antonio and his soldier, but their impotent rage accomplished nothing, because the two men did not even imagine they existed.

"What is it, señor? Tell me what happened!"

As if the phantom blow had not been enough, the familiar stab to the temple folded Sebastián in half. He fought the onslaught, imagining himself closing every door, every gate, turning the key in every lock as he ran, but the pain battered down each defense and chased him through his own head. Images of a subterranean chamber invaded his mind, its vast walls, floor and ceiling lined with crystals of amethyst and nodules of silver.

Superimposed over the image of treasure, Sebastián saw bloody backs, legs, and faces along with dead, staring eyes. He heard the screams of men being whipped, tortured, and dismembered. Only the atrocities he'd assimilated in the inquisitor's prison could rival those he envisioned now.

Only the vision of Isabel's death had tormented him more.

Leave here! The apparition thundered again. As it struck Sebastián another blow, sending a crippling charge throughout his body, he recognized its enraged visage as the face of the hanged man outside the mine.

"What do you see, señor de Navarra?" Antonio gripped his arm. "It is here, *sí?*" His narrow face vented his greed in a zealous smile as he spread his hand on the same space of rock wall Sebastián had touched. "The treasure is here?"

Too consumed by pain to offer a coherent answer, Sebastian nodded as he lost consciousness.

Chapter Seven

"Esperanza!"

She jumped at Antonio's voice and looked up at Inez. Dropping the rolling pin amidst balls of tortilla dough, she dusted off her hands and rushed out into the *placita*. Inez followed on her heels.

When Esperanza saw Sebastián, weak and disoriented, being held up by Antonio and his soldier, her heart twisted in her chest.

"What happened? Was there an accident? Is he all right?"

"He found it. El Místico found the treasure!" Antonio turned his attention to the soldier and jerked his head to indicate the guest room door. "In there."

Esperanza stared at them as they half-dragged, half-carried Sebastián across the courtyard. When she came back to herself, anger and worry fueled her movements as she ran ahead to open the door. Once inside, they deposited their burden on the bed.

Esperanza touched Sebastián's forehead, dismayed to find it cold and clammy. She grabbed a blanket and spread it over him. When she rose from her task, Antonio and his soldier were already on their way out the door. She stormed across the room and caught Antonio's arm, whirling him around to face her. She pointed at Sebastián. "Did you do this to him?"

He yanked his arm from her grasp and slapped her hard across the face. "¡*Calmate*, Esperanza!"

She caught her balance, blinking back tears of pain and humiliation as she lifted her hand to her stinging cheek. "Did you do this?" she repeated, her tone deeper, but only slightly more contained.

Antonio narrowed his eyes. "I did nothing to him, dear sister, but why should El Místico's well-being at my hands suddenly be one of your pet concerns?"

Esperanza stepped back, realizing how wild her behavior must appear, realizing what conclusions her brother could draw about her feelings for Sebastián. She fought for a more passive expression. She must have succeeded, because Antonio lost interest in his study of her as he shrugged more comfortably into his jacket.

"If you must know, he collapsed."

"Collapsed?"

"Is that not what I just said? Do you think I would be so foolish as to do this to him myself?" He laughed. "To the man who will soon be taking you out of my sight?"

"But if he collapsed, how do you know he found the treasure?"

"I do not have time for your questions, Esperanza. I must go back to the mine. I have already ordered the *Indios* to begin the new tunnel, and I want to be there to see that my orders are carried out. Tend him while I am gone."

Her mind still brimming with questions, but knowing it was futile to ask them of Antonio, Esperanza merely nodded.

"Inez!" Antonio barked at the woman flattened against the wall just inside the doorway of Sebastián's room. "Prepare something that we may eat on our way."

"*Sí*, Don Antonio." Shoulders hunched, the slender woman dropped a tight curtsey and fled out the door. Antonio and his soldier followed.

Esperanza closed the door and turned to Sebastián. Sitting on the bed beside him, she removed the blindfold and stroked his black hair away from his face. His eyes fluttered open, and he squinted and blinked as if to focus, frowning with the effort. He lifted his head, but grimaced and let it fall back to the pillow.

"Antonio brought you back to the *hacienda*," she explained. "What happened? He said you found the treasure."

"*Sí*," he forced out.

"How? Did it fall on your head?"

One corner of his mouth lifted in a weak half-grin as his eyes drowsed shut and opened again. Frowning, he blinked, then turned his head on the pillow to stare at her more fully, his gaze narrowing as he studied her cheek.

"He struck you?" he asked, his voice soft and muddled.

When he lifted his hand to her face, Esperanza flinched, swallowing back a gasp. With his fingertips he touched what she knew must be an inflamed handprint, and though the contact was brief, a strange, tingling energy suffused her skin. In the same instant, the pain in her cheek and jaw flowed throughout her entire body and away, as if evaporating from her very pores. In place of the pain, something warm and magical filled her. She did gasp then. He must have felt it to, for he yanked back his hand as if his fingers had lingered a moment too long above a candle flame.

Too shaken to speak, she merely stared at him.

He returned her gaze, studying her through eyes filled with unbearable torment, as if the pain that had left her body had somehow found its way into his soul.

"I will see if Inez has some herbs for your headache," she said, and before he could stop her, before he could speak to her, she fled.

The headache and dizziness had long since passed, and Sebastián paced the floor in front of the shuttered window, waiting for full darkness to settle on the *hacienda*.

If he could still hope for any luck at all after the day's events, he would be reunited with his men long before

Antonio returned from his mine to find him gone and Esperanza's dowry missing—provided he could find it when he searched the man's office.

Any other riches he could have hoped to procure by carrying out the original plan would have to be taken from another victim far away from here, for he was a fool to have stayed this long. He was an even bigger fool for playing a game he could not hope to win against forces too strong to deny. And the strongest force of all was his inexplicable connection with Esperanza, who had stirred the sleeping beast. What he felt for her went far beyond the simple attraction he'd felt for other women since Isabel's death.

Sebastián stopped pacing and peered through the cracks in the shutters, just in time to see Esperanza herself, lantern in hand, headed across the *placita* toward his bedroom door.

For just a moment he watched her, the ache in his chest expanding as she tucked a strand of rich auburn hair behind her ear. The way she moved now, with a beguiling sway to her hips and a casual confidence he had never seen in her brother's presence, tormented his conscience.

Just before she stepped under the portico, Sebastián rushed to his bed, flung the blanket over himself, and closed his eyes. The door creaked open on rawhide hinges, and lantern light spilled across the floor.

"Sebastián?" she whispered. "Are you awake?"

He forced a sleepy groan and opened his eyes, squinting as if the lantern light offended. "What is it?" he asked in a raspy voice.

"I came to see if you were all right. If perhaps you needed anything before Inez and I retired."

"No," he said, letting his eyes drowse shut. "I will be fine."

She nodded and pulled the door halfway closed, but then she stopped. The door wedged open again, and Sebastián watched her through his eyelashes as she looked in at him, her head tilted. But then she shook her head and closed the door.

Sebastián released a pent breath and turned over on his

back. For an eternity he lay in the dark, staring at the pine beams in the ceiling, certain his heart had been ripped through his ribs.

Finally, he tossed aside the blanket, swung his legs over the edge of the corn-husk mattress, and donned his black cloak. After one last quick glance through the shutters to be certain there were no candles burning in other rooms of the *hacienda*, he opened the door, careful to lift it so the hinges wouldn't groan so loudly.

Keeping to the shadowed portico, Sebastián prowled around the perimeter of the *placita* to Antonio's office. Once inside, he spread his cloak over the shutters and lit a candle. He surveyed the room, taking in the *vargueño*, its open drop-front desk exposing drawers and shelves lined with papers; the corner fireplace, above which hung a bow and a quiver of arrows; and a bookshelf that had been built into the wall behind the door.

"If I were Don Antonio, where would I hide my sister's dowry?"

Taking a second look at the bookshelves, he noticed the lowest shelf had been stacked with only tall books, whereas the others contained a variety of sizes. On closer inspection, he discovered the shelf itself to be much shallower than the rest.

Crouching, he yanked out books, stacking them on the floor. When he'd emptied the shelf, he knocked on the back panel. The hollow sound told him it was false, and a grin spread across his face. "Not terribly original, Don Antonio. Somehow I expected more of you."

"You are perhaps looking for this?"

Sebastián almost toppled over as he spun on his heels and stared up at Esperanza. Her mouth set in a grim line, she dropped the wooden chest she strained to hold within a finger's width of his right foot. The weighty thud as the chest hit the dirt floor was punctuated by the clink of silver coins.

From the pocket hidden within the folds of her skirt, she fished a key and held it out to him, her hand shaking. "One thousand silver pesos, señor de Navarra. You may open the chest to see if I can be trusted to tell the truth."

Sebastián rose slowly, his gaze never leaving her face. The disappointment in her eyes tore at his heart. "Esperanza—"

"No. Do not say it. Do not tell me you are sorry. It is my fault for being foolish enough to put my hope in you. Just take the chest, take the key, and go."

"Esperanza," he tried again, but she held up her hand, tossed the key to the dirt, and turned to the door.

He grabbed her by the wrist and pulled her around. With wide, surprised blue eyes glistening with tears, she gazed up at him. And then she looked down at his hand clutching her wrist.

As if in a dream, Sebastián became slowly aware of the fragile bones in his grip, the warm skin, and the erratic pulse in the veins under the pad of his thumb.

He knew he should release her before a vision crippled him, but the longer he held her, the longer he looked at her, the more he wondered if the simple touch of her skin alone could be the force that would bring him to his knees.

Testing the beast within, he brushed his thumb back and forth across the veins in her soft skin, tentatively at first, then more boldly. His experimental strokes turned to circular caresses as each quick breath from her mouth came through moist and parted lips.

"Stop," she said, pulling her hand from his grasp and stepping several paces away. "If you must take my dowry, at least leave me with what little dignity I have left."

"Esperanza, you knew I did not go to your brother's mine as the man I used to be—the man you wish I could be again," he explained softly. "I went as El Místico the charlatan, seeking potential for exploitation. I came here as an actor, a fraud, I admit that, but something has happened to me. Because of you, eight years of relative peace are gone. *Eight years* I was without a vision to haunt my mind … until I met you."

She laughed and shook her head. "You are a man like my

brother after all. It is so easy for you to cast blame. Why? I have done nothing but try to convince you to help me—to convince you that there is more to you than this mask you wear. And you tell me that it is *my* fault you are leaving? That it is *my* fault you are having these visions? *What* visions, Sebastián? If you truly have these visions, what did you see at the mine that has made you want to run away? Or are you merely looking for a coward's excuse to steal my hopes along with the lives and futures of those I love?" She moved closer once more, forcing him to look into her eyes. "Do you honestly believe that a thousand pieces of silver are going to fill the emptiness within you?"

Her questions sliced him to the quick, laying open his shame. In the face of such an argument, what could he possibly say?

"Do you know what I saw when I went to your brother's mine, Esperanza? I saw great treasure. A vast subterranean chamber unlike anything I have ever beheld, the walls lined with amethyst and silver."

"And of course it was the silver you just could not wait to help my brother find."

He ignored her sarcasm. "And yet I am leaving, Esperanza. Why? Because I also saw what you told me I would see. Suffering and cruelty. But not in the way you think. I saw spirits," he admitted. "Spirits of the *Indios* who have sacrificed their very souls for your brother's greed."

"And that is supposed to make me understand, Sebastián? They sacrifice everything, and you sacrifice nothing? How convenient."

"How would you know what I have sacrificed? In truth, you know nothing about me—no more than El Místico has foolishly allowed you to see."

"Ah," she said, folding her arms beneath her breasts, "this is about your wife."

Rage ignited along his nerve endings. "Yes, this is about Isabel. Before her death, I had some control over the visions. I could call on them, use them without pain, but everything changed when I saw her die!"

He stopped and swallowed, studying her scar, realizing for the first time just how much they had in common. Only she had vanquished her demon, and he still ran from his.

"I was a simple man, given to simple crusades," he continued in a lower voice. "She knew this, and yet she left behind her wealthy family for me. She was carrying our first child when she died, and though I saw her death, I was too far away to save her."

"And that is when you turned your back on your gift." Her voice had softened as well.

He nodded. "But now," he said, studying her face, "since I have met you, the visions have returned, and they are controlling me."

"But why?" she asked. "Why me?"

"I have asked myself at least a hundred times—why you? Why now? All I know is that I thought if I kept my distance from you, if I did not touch you, I could lock the visions away again. But you are making it so hard for me, Esperanza. So hard to remain aloof. So hard to remain untouched myself."

Though his fear of physical contact remained, he had to reach out to her, to somehow let her know that he did not truly hold her responsible for his weakness.

He traced her scar from her ear to the corner of her mouth, feeling the puckers in her skin beneath the pad of his thumb. "You are unlike any woman I have ever known. What others would give anything to hide or disguise, you accept and embrace as though it were a symbol of your greatest strength. Perhaps it is. Do you know how much I admire your unconquerable spirit?"

She smiled and lifted her hand to cover his. "Then you must learn to gird your own spirit, Sebastián. You must unlock the door and give your gift free rein. By denying its liberation, you are only making yourself more vulnerable to its power."

"It is not that easy."

"No, it is not," she agreed. "Nothing ever is. Surely you must know that by now."

He sighed and moved across the room. Collapsing in the chair before the *vargueño*, he gripped his head in his hands.

"So what is it to be, Sebastián?" Esperanza asked softly, her voice impassive. "Do you stay and fight, or do you take the silver and run?"

Sebastián straightened in the chair, leaning his head back this time and closing his eyes. When he did, the image of a letter filled his mind, its face scrawled in Antonio's handwriting and marred halfway down by a blot of ink.

Frowning, he opened his eyes and looked at Antonio's desk. Atop a neat stack of paper, one leaf rested askew, its edges slightly curled. He picked it up, skimming it briefly. It was an unfinished letter to the governor in which Antonio complained about his growing frustration with the reduced production of the mine. The last sentence of the letter remained unfinished, the splotch of black ink smeared by a frustrated hand.

An idea formed. He turned to Esperanza. "Are you certain you do not know the location of the mine?"

She shook her head. "No. I have never been able to sneak away from the house during the day."

"Do you know anyone willing to risk helping us draw a map?"

Esperanza frowned at first, but then a tiny smile touched her lips and lightened her eyes. "*Sí*, I think so."

Sebastián rolled the ruined letter, then grabbed the bottle of ink and a quill from one of the drawers. He handed the implements to her. "Then let us go. But first, we put away the silver." He smiled. "Later we will decide if I have earned your dowry."

Chapter Eight

Esperanza gripped Sebastián's arm and felt his bicep tighten beneath her hand as he pulled her up behind him on the Andalusian. Ducking under his cloak, she tented the voluminous folds around her and over the horse's hindquarters in order to hide from the *hacienda* guards.

Eager to escape the corral, the spirited mare snorted and lunged forward, forcing Esperanza to grip Sebastián even tighter about the waist as she pressed her cheek against his back, listening to his heartbeat.

They hadn't gone far when she heard the metallic song of two swords being whipped from their scabbards.

"*¡Pare!*" one of the soldiers ordered. "Who goes there?"

Sebastián leaned into Esperanza's embrace as he pulled back on the reins. The Andalusian stopped and pranced in a semi-circle. "It is I, señor de Navarra."

"Where are you going at such a late hour?"

Sebastián's suggestive laugh rumbled in Esperanza's ear and tingled through her arms. "I met an enchanting young woman in the village when I first arrived, and I decided to see if I could convince her to go for a ride with me."

The guard laughed. "You will have to tell us if she was easily persuaded." With that, she heard the sound of their swords being resheathed. "*¡Buena suerte!*" the guard called out.

"It will be charm that wins her heart, not luck," Sebastián

quipped. *"Adiós,"* he said, spurring the Andalusian into a canter.

When they reached a safe distance from the *hacienda*, Esperanza pulled aside the suffocating folds of Sebastián's cloak and drew in a deep breath of cool, crisp mountain air scented by the juniper and piñon branches whipping past their faces. Despite the enormity of their purpose, she couldn't help the exhilaration that filled her heart and poured out as laughter.

"If I had known a simple horseback ride would please you so much,"—Sebastián turned slightly and smiled at her—"perhaps I would not have asked for a kiss that first night."

"And perhaps I would not have put my fingers in your wine."

Soon, peering over Sebastián's shoulder, Esperanza saw the moonlight showering over the parapets of Cuarac's mission church.

"Skirt the village and ride down by the creek bed," she told him. "We can hide the horse in the cottonwoods and come back up to Juana's dwelling from there."

He did as she directed, and after he had tied the horse and retrieved ink, quill, and paper, Esperanza led the way to Juana's house, one of the few homes in Cuarac with an outside door on the ground floor. Fully aware of Sebastián close behind her, his warmth spilling around her as they stood outside the rock house, Esperanza rapped her knuckles on the cottonwood panel.

"Juana?"

The door creaked open and Juana's aged face appeared in the opening. *"Sí, niña.* Come in."

Esperanza led the way into a room lit only by a small fire. Once inside, she folded the tiny woman in her arms and kissed her leathery cheek.

"I have brought someone, Juana." Esperanza turned to Sebastián. "This is señor de Navarra, and he has agreed to help me destroy Antonio's mine. We have come to seek Benedicto's aid," she said, her voice filled with a hope she soon lost when she did not see it reflected in the features of her *niñera.*

Juana shook her head. "He breathes, *niña*, but that is all. I am afraid he cannot help you."

Sebastián found the air in the close quarters too volatile to breathe. It vibrated with the jumbled emotions of grief and misery, relief and disappointment, most of which he found focused in the old woman's face as she turned her attention to him.

Pain began to build in his temple. But this time, instead of giving in to his instinct to run, bolting doors and gates behind him, Sebastián forced himself to take a deep breath as he imagined himself armoring his spirit and turning to face his fear.

What for eight years he had envisioned as a rabid beast, intent on eating him alive if he set it free, soon transformed into a tide of power, filling him with its essence, buoying him up until he rode its crest instead of drowning in its undertow.

"May I see your grandson?" he asked. "I would speak with him."

Both Esperanza and the old woman stared at him—Esperanza frowning as if questioning his wits; the old woman narrowing her eyes, considering, then donning an expression of understanding.

"He is on the pallet by the fireplace," she said, stepping aside for his progress.

The young man lay in death-like silence, but still his spirit fought the insidious whispers, which had grown louder since Sebastián's first vision. Sitting on the threadbare rug beside the pallet, he spread out paper, ink and pen. He felt Esperanza's presence at his side, no longer doubting, but offering quiet strength.

Filling his lungs with a deep breath, he reached out and

placed his hand on the young man's forehead. As he closed his eyes, he imagined himself on a pilgrimage across a landscape of light, searching for Benedicto's soul.

He found the young man, healthy and strong, standing in a small clearing of pine and spruce at the base of a mountain cleft. A spring flowed freely past Benedicto's uninjured feet as he gazed up the chasm and then into the sky. A concerned frown creased his brow, but then he turned, staring straight at Sebastián.

"They are angry," he said, seeming to accept Sebastián's presence as if they had known each other many years. He pointed to the sky. "Do you see? There are no clouds."

Sebastián followed his direction, noting that not a single cloud graced the turquoise sky.

"They want me to join them, but not in the sky so that we might bring rain back to the people."

"Who are they?"

"The ancestors," he answered. "The spirits who have forsaken the sky to haunt the mine."

It was then that Sebastián realized the voice he had heard in his first vision and again tonight was not the voice of death, but the collective expression of fury and oppression, an enormous storm that had taken years to brew.

And then he realized he stood on ground he had visited earlier in the day, when he had listened to spring water in a wooden flume. Except he saw no flume here. Nor did he see mountainsides devoid of trees. Benedicto had fabricated a perfect world for his escape, one that might have existed centuries ago, before his and his ancestors' enslavement. Perfect except for the spirits that would not give him peace.

"I need your help, Benedicto."

Cocking his head, the young man turned to face him more fully.

"Esperanza and I are going to destroy the mine, but we do not know where it is."

Like hail stones, a barrage of images hit Sebastián's mind: the spring, the flume, the chasm, the mine opening, the flagstone road—

"Wait!" he said. "Can you help me draw a map?"

"Come," Benedicto said, transporting them instantly to a subterranean ceremonial chamber, a *kiva* where the round walls had been painted with symbols of rain clouds and lightning. With a stick in the soft dirt floor, Benedicto sketched out a map.

Field and meadow, canyon and spring, Sebastián repeatedly dipped his pen and quickly copied each landmark and its location to the back of Antonio's discarded letter. He labeled the map in Euskara, for him the language of first and easiest thought.

"You must go now," Benedicto said, and his form began to shift into mist. "I will tell the others you are coming...."

Sebastián jerked out of his trance-like state, quill in hand, and shook his head. He glanced up to find Juana crying softly as she cradled her dead grandson's head in her lap.

Later, Sebastián stood outside the doorway, looking on as Esperanza gathered Juana in a tight embrace.

The old woman quickly disengaged herself. "Go, child. I will be fine. It is for the best." She patted Esperanza's cheek. "You and señor de Navarra should not be caught here, not with your map."

Wiping a tear from her eye, Esperanza nodded and strode away. Sebastián was about to follow when Juana gripped his arm in her crone's hand. He turned.

"My Esperanza has an independent and courageous heart," she said, "but she still needs someone to love her. Take care of her, señor de Navarra. See that she is safe."

The solemnity of the woman's charge shot a bolt of fear through Sebastián's heart. Even so, he could not refuse to honor the responsibility with which she had entrusted him.

"I will," he promised.

Chapter Nine

On the way back to the *hacienda*, Esperanza rode in front of Sebastián. Despite her grief-clouded mood, or perhaps because of it, she allowed herself to relax into the embrace of another human being for the first time since her mother's death. She permitted herself the foolish luxury of taking comfort from the feel of Sebastián's arms encircling hers, of his legs enfolding hers, of his warm breath in her hair and his broad chest sheltering her back. But permitting such trust also forced her to confront what she feared most—her yearning for love. And if she were honest with herself, she did not want just any love, she wanted *this* man's love. The kind of love he had once bestowed on his wife.

Too soon they reached the orchard, where they had agreed to part ways, and Esperanza's heart plummeted as the reality of the danger they faced shattered her fanciful thoughts.

Sebastián dismounted and reached up to help her alight. She landed with a soft crunch on a few dried apple leaves that littered the ground. Stepping a few paces away, she turned to look up at him.

"Sebastián …" she began, then licked her lips and folded her arms protectively across her stomach. "Perhaps I am asking too much of you after all. If you wish to change your mind, I—"

He pressed a finger to her lips. "I do not wish to change my mind. I will return by morning," he promised. "As soon as I have shown the map to my men and explained the change in plans.

She nodded, and with a wistful smile gave him permission to go. But he did not move. Neither did she stir from where she stood beneath the broad canopy of the oldest apple tree.

Though she knew better, she could not help but savor the beauty she found in his moonlit face. She longed to smooth back the lock of black hair that dangled between his eyes, to see if the lines of worry she saw on his forehead actually existed, or if she merely imagined them because she wanted so much for him to care.

"Ah, Esperanza, just looking at you is torture," he said, closing the distance between them. He unfolded her arms and took both wrists in his hands this time as he circled his thumbs across the veins. "Touching you is worse. I have to know if the vintage of your lips tastes as wondrous as I fear."

Esperanza knew he must feel the quickening of her pulse as desire flooded her bloodstream. With so much still unresolved between them, so much still unfinished, she knew she should not encourage further intimacy, but she couldn't muster a refusal.

After all, she was no innocent, nor did she feel obligated to remain chaste for the husband she doubted she would ever have. This man had seen to that, with his schemes and deceptions. Oddly, Esperanza could not bring herself to care that he had ruined her unwanted future—a future she now admitted she had not believed she would live to see—for she had always feared a second marriage would only mean trading one prison for another.

But now, as the soul he allowed her to glimpse in those chocolate brown eyes held her spellbound, Esperanza couldn't bring herself to care about the freedom she had always craved. Instead she craved only his touch. When he reached out to her face, tracing her scar with the backs of his fingers, something profound yet elusive filled her in the wake of his caress ... something far stronger and more soul-stirring than mere desire. Something that quenched her drought-parched heart.

Hope.

For the first time she realized that she, too, had been living without its illusory promise. Until tonight, the life-threatening cost of her crusade had not mattered, for her heart had been beating without any longing for fulfillment beyond her current tangible goal.

She moved closer to Sebastián, tilting her head to his, tentatively offering him what he wanted—what *she* wanted too. As if cupping a priceless chalice, he took her face in his hands. Though she was no inexperienced maid, even the Apache man who had claimed her as his own had never kissed her. So when his breath caressed her lips, promising pleasure if she would open to him, she felt for the first time like a beloved new bride.

What began again as a tentative sipping of lips, a tasting of tongues, a sampling of fragile emotions, soon became a complete surrender to intoxication.

Sebastián broke away. "My deepest fears are confirmed."

"What do we do now?" she whispered against his lips.

"We see if the rest of you tastes equally exquisite."

Taking a deep, shaking breath, Esperanza summoned her courage and undressed before him, forcing herself to watch his face as she slowly, painstakingly bared her body, along with her soul and her mind. *Take* me. *Accept* me, she thought, willing him to hear her, yet just as terrified he would.

As if he had indeed been listening to her thoughts, he embraced her, and the depth of emotion she found reflected in the mirror of his gaze spilled out of her heart and into her eyes. He kissed the tears from her cheeks, then kissed her mouth, stroking the taste of salt across her tongue.

Sebastián … ti amo. … I love you.

When Sebastián heard her admission, a whisper from her mind to his, he felt his heart turn over his in his chest. Consumed anew by his desire to taste her, to heighten the mystical experience of allowing his spirit to open to hers, he lowered her to the leaf-littered ground.

Like a man too long without sustenance, he devoured her neck, her breasts, and her belly with his lips and teeth and tongue. Pulling one of her knees to his mouth, he trailed kisses down the soft, tender face of her inner thigh. But as he placed the ultimate kiss, he felt more than mere lust, he felt her soul's dreams shudder through her body into his, overwhelming his senses with her very essence as a woman: fine and pure and noble.

I see your greed … is not … limited to silver.

When he heard her thought, he laughed deep in his throat and proceeded to show her that nothing limited his greed when it concerned his appetite for her.

Later, as Esperanza clutched Sebastián's cloak about her body against the chill of the mountain night, she watched him ride away until he and the Andalusian became one with the darkness. Finally, she forced her legs to carry her back to the *hacienda.*

Thankfully, the guards at the front gate were immersed in their liquor and a game of cards, and she had no trouble scaling the apple tree and stealing back into the *placita.*

Once inside her bedchamber, she fell back on her bed and stared up at the ceiling. "Oh, holy Mary, what have I done?"

Her bedroom door slammed open against the wall, breaking into her reverie. She gasped and knifed upright to see her brother's form framed in the doorway.

"Antonio … you have returned."

"Where is it, Esperanza?"

"Where is what?"

He stormed into the room and yanked her up by the arm. "My ink! And one of my pens is missing, along with the letter I ruined yesterday."

Esperanza's heart thudded in her chest and pounded in her ears. Not only did Sebastián have the map, he still had the ink and quill, forgotten in their intimate fervor.

"I—I do not know what you mean. I have not taken them."

"If it was not you, then who could it have been? Someone has been in my office and has stolen my things! You may be too stupid to use them, but you are not above taking them to try my patience."

Relieved he had not yet reached the only logical conclusion, she forced a shrug. Only then did she realize she still wore Sebastián's cloak.

"Are—are you sure you looked closely?" she forced out, stuffing down her panic, trying to think. "Perhaps you are too tired to see them. I am certain you will find them in the morning."

"I cannot wait until morning, Esperanza. I want the ink now."

"But why, Antonio? Surely it is too late—"

"I need it *now*." He shook her, then thrust her from him. "I must write the governor and tell him that I have not failed him—El Místico be praised."

Wide-eyed, Esperanza watched him stalk her bedroom like a caged beast. Taking advantage of his distraction, she unbuttoned the cloak and kicked it into the corner as she watched him grab the tin box of candles from the table beside her bed. Rummaging through the tapers, he found nothing. An enraged growl reverberated against the thick walls, and he threw the box on the floor. Tin clattered and candles rolled. He wrenched open drawers and doors and shoved aside furniture. She had just retrieved her knife from beneath her mattress when he upended that as well.

"You had no right to be in my office, Esperanza. You have no right to what is mine!"

"Truly, Antonio, I do not have your ink. And I do not see why you must find it tonight."

He whirled to face her. "It is not for you to 'see' anything, or to question my needs. As far as I am concerned, you cannot be gone soon enough. I have far surpassed my duty by you, for if it were not for you and your slut of a mother, I would not be forced to answer to that petty tyrant about a fortune that should be mine alone. Nor would I have to endure his threats to expose my crimes."

He advanced on her, his eyes narrowed and intent, his head tilted, and Esperanza fought the nausea that roiled in her stomach. She adjusted her grip on the hilt of her knife behind her back and set her weight into slightly bent knees.

"What is this?" he asked, yanking at a lock of her hair.

Esperanza yelped. Along with several auburn strands, he held a dried apple leaf.

His face hardened as he studied her more closely, running his gaze down her body. "Whose cloak were you wearing just moments ago, Esperanza?" The singsong quality of his voice knifed a chill down her spine. Realization erupted on his features, quickly followed by fury. "El Místico! I should have known you were the village whore my guards were joking about when I returned home."

When he pulled back his fist, she whipped her arm from behind her back. She arced it around her body, aiming for soft tissue between her brother's ribs. He shielded the slicing blow with his upthrust forearm, and blood spilled on the earthen floor.

Esperanza advanced on him again, but he caught her wrist and ground the bones together in his grip until she cried out, dropping the knife. Twisting her arm behind her and kicking her legs out from under her, he wrestled her face down to the floor. She bucked and writhed, but he straddled her legs. She flailed her free arm wildly, trying to pinch and scratch, then stretching to reach her fallen knife, but he caught that hand as well and clamped both wrists together in the small of her back.

"Where is El Místico?" he asked. "The guards did not report his return."

Esperanza refused to answer. Instead, she goaded him. "How does it feel to be cuckolded under your very nose, Antonio?"

He shoved her wrists farther up her back, and she cried out.

"I am not the first Salazar cuckold." He laughed. "Did you know you are not even my father's daughter? And yet he spoiled you as if you were his own. He spoiled *her* as well. Why settle for the son when you can seduce his wealthy, newly widowed father? But I do not blame him. I blame her."

He bound her wrists with his *faja*, yanking the knot tight. Then he leaned over and breathed into her ear. "Except for that disgusting scar, you look like her. It is a shame the arrow I used could not have pierced both your capricious hearts."

"You? You killed my mother?"

Memory flooded Esperanza's mind. Amid Apache war cries, firing muskets and dust, her mother swept her up and ran toward Antonio, calling his name. But then came the *whoosh*, the burning cheek, and the shaft protruding from her mother's chest. Esperanza stared at the striped hawk feather until an Apache yanked her up on his horse. As they rode out of the *placita*, she saw Antonio standing above the dead body of a warrior, holding the man's bow.

In that moment she realized the same notched hawk feather adorned one of the arrows in Antonio's quiver. *A souvenir.*

Rage blazed through her system. She butted her head up, but missed his face. He shoved her skull against the hard earth floor.

"*Sí.* And since you have soiled the Salazar name once again, I am going to kill *you*. But I will not end your life as quickly as I did your mother's, I promise you that. And this time there will be no witnesses."

Pain clubbed her head and her world faded to black.

Chapter Ten

South of the Manzanos, nestled in a cleft atop one of the peaks in the Los Pinos Mountains, Sebastián's five men slept surrounding the glow of a dying campfire. As he entered their camp, his mount nickered, and a hoof rang on stone.

Tito Pasquale jerked awake first. He pushed his burly frame up from the ground. "Why have you come back, Sebastián? Did the supply caravan already pass? Did we somehow miss spotting it?"

The others began to rouse as well, yawning and nodding their welcome to Sebastián, who returned their greetings in kind.

"No, my friend. There has been a change in plans. There will be no ambush, no kidnapping, and only the dowry itself in payment."

Blinking, Tito frowned. "Why? Is something amiss?"

Sebastián dismounted and turned a sheepish grin on his longtime companion. "You might say that, old friend. It seems I have rediscovered my conscience."

"What conscience?" one of the men quipped. "El Místico with a conscience? I do not believe it."

The others laughed, and Sebastián merely acknowledged their teasing with a wry grin as he held the attention of his friend.

Tito returned Sebastián's intent regard. "Is she pretty?" he asked at last, his voice laced with the self-amused defeat of a man afraid he might not only lose his best friend, but the fortune he had known better than to dream about in the first place.

"Beautiful," Sebastián admitted on a mock sigh.

"Damn," Tito replied, sitting on the trunk of a fallen pine.

"*Sí*, Tito, I know. It is a fine hell I have been living since I met her."

As Sebastián surveyed the faces of his men, laughter stilled and smiles straightened.

"Surely you are not serious," said Pedro, the one who had begun the teasing. He glanced at his companions, his expression incredulous. "We have been preparing to risk our lives against Antonio Salazar's soldiers so that you might suddenly decide to play the moonstruck fool?" He stood. "I did not cast my lot with El Místico to be duped out of my portion by a comely face."

"Then perhaps you should cast your lot elsewhere," Sebastián said, narrowing the distance between himself and the lanky Pedro. "For I am the leader here, and what I say is what we will do. There will be other gulls to pluck, Pedro, but this time we content ourselves with a thousand silver pesos."

As birds began to awaken to the promise of dawn, Sebastián stared the smaller man down.

"What would you have us do now, Sebastián?" asked one of the other five.

"We destroy Antonio Salazar's silver mine."

"He has a mine, and we are going to destroy it?" Pedro asked. "You truly have lost your senses."

"Since you say 'we,' I assume you have made your decision?"

Pedro sighed and looked away, effectively diffusing the tension between them. "*Sí*. As you say, there will be other gulls."

"How and when do you propose we destroy this mine?" Tito asked.

"As yet, Don Antonio suspects nothing," Sebastián said.

"So I will return to the Salazar *hacienda*, and señorita Salazar and I will leave with the escort for the supply caravan as planned. But instead of wasting time on an ambush, I want all of you to go to the mine. Meanwhile, Esperanza and I will steal the dowry and sneak away from camp in the middle of the night. The caravan guards will likely believe I have kidnapped her, and I will make certain they do not suspect that we have retraced our steps."

He turned to his horse. "I have a map that will lead you to the mine," he said, opening the leather bag that hung from his saddle. "I will entrust it to you, Tito."

When he reached inside, the stiff barbs of Antonio's quill rasped across his fingertips. A chill of foreboding scraped down his spine. He cursed under his breath, berating himself for forgetting to give the pen and ink back to Esperanza.

"What is it?" Tito asked.

"I must return to the *hacienda*," he said.

He yanked the map from the pouch. But just as he was about to hand the rolled paper to Tito, he saw Esperanza, heard her cry of pain as the flat side of a miner's pick hit her alongside the head.

"No!"

Not again. Please not again.

He slammed the door shut against the beast, and pain crashed into both temples at once. He closed his eyes and gripped his head, smashing the map against his skull.

"Sebastián?"

Fighting to drag a full breath into lungs suddenly too small, he forced his eyes open again. He peered up at Tito and the others, who gathered round, their foreheads creased with worry.

"You must unlock the door and give your gift free rein," he heard Esperanza say. *"By denying its liberation, you are only making yourself more vulnerable to its power."*

For her sake, he pulled in a calming breath and opened the door. At first, as he lurked in the darkened threshold, nothing appeared to him. But then, as he accepted the truth of what he was meant to see, the pain shafted from his head into his heart.

Pickax in hand, Antonio stood above her as she lay facedown on the granite floor. Sebastián could hear the beat of her heart, the sound amplified a hundredfold, but too slow for the true passage of time. Finally, the beating stopped, and she released her last breath deep into barren, unyielding rock.

"I will not let it happen again," Sebastián said, his voice quivering with the intensity of his emotion. "Tito, I need my weapons. We ride now. Antonio has taken Esperanza to the mine."

As the sun rose steadily in the eastern sky, Sebastián and his men raced north across the peaks and through the canyons of the Los Pinos range.

When they reached a wide valley between red sandstone bluffs and the southernmost evergreen-shrouded peaks of the Manzanos, Sebastián pulled up and unrolled the map. Five riders surrounded him, kicking up clouds of dust.

"According to this," he said, tracing a route with his forefinger, "we can reach the mine by traveling this valley until it narrows into a canyon. The *arrastres* should be at the mouth."

"What about soldiers?" Tito said. "They will be guarding these mills, will they not?"

"Perhaps we can avoid Salazar's men by hiding in the tree cover and skirting the mills before heading up this crevice." He pointed to the jagged line, north of the *arrastres* and the flume, which represented the chasm that led to the opening of the mine.

"And if we get past the *arrastres*?" Tito asked.

"Then it will be harder to avoid the soldiers as we get closer to our goal," Sebastián said. "With only six of us, perhaps we should distract them somehow. Although some will stay to guard the mine, enough might leave that our numbers will be equalized."

"As master of the merry chase," said Pedro, wielding musket and flintlock pistol, "I will do the honor of acting as both distraction and bait."

"*Gracias*," Sebastián said, clapping his hand on the man's shoulder. "The rest of us will wait until the soldiers are drawn away, and then we will sneak up the canyon to the mine."

They rode on, Sebastián leading the way through the junipers surrounding the mills, where burros trudged in circles, turning the columnar gears that dragged enormous ore-crushing stones.

A league or so north of the *arrastres*, they reached the spring. Hiding amongst the pines and spruce, Sebastián gave Pedro the familiar cue. Pedro nodded and spurred his mount, firing the first musket shot and following quickly with a ball from his pistol. He reloaded and primed as he rode, and when he disappeared into the forest, another two reports echoed off canyon walls.

Before long, ten mounted soldiers thundered down the flagstone road, then veered north in pursuit of the source of the gunshots.

After the last soldier vanished into the trees, Sebastián turned to his men. "Any kills will have to be quick, clean, and quiet, or Pedro has risked his life for nothing." Dismounting, he said, "We leave the horses here—they will be too hard to hide."

As he and his men ranged up both sides of the canyon, forest soon gave way to barren rock, forcing them to hide behind boulders and piles of tailings. Unlike yesterday, the soldiers did not stand over the workers with whips, but stood at the ready with firearms. Even so, one soldier after another fell to stealthy assassinations by Sebastián's men.

When Sebastián reached the mouth of the mine, one of the soldiers standing on a ledge across the canyon spotted him and lifted his musket. Suddenly he jerked and stiffened, then fell forward, revealing Tito behind him, bloody knife in hand.

Sebastián saluted his gratitude and ducked into the opening. For a moment he stood at the threshold, accustoming his eyes to the dim torchlight, preparing for both physical and spiritual attack. Breathing deeply, he opened himself to Esperanza's presence, focusing his thoughts on the treasure of her face. When he saw her, Antonio's *faja* like a noose about her neck, he began to run.

Images jumped into his mind's eye. Tunnels and pits, ladders and forgotten stopes. He flew through the maze, his mental map leading him to his beloved. Finally, he found an old, darkened tunnel that skirted the activity near the treasure of amethyst and silver he had dowsed just yesterday. He allowed the visions to lead him deep into the bowels of the mine, where the temperature rose and water dripped from granite crevices. Finally, dim torchlight and the sounds of her struggle led him to a forgotten room, a torture chamber where Antonio and his soldier wrestled her—weary, bruised, and choking—closer to the manacles chained to the wall.

Lifting his pistol, Sebastián pulled back the hammer above the priming pan and aimed at Antonio. "Release her! Now!"

Chapter Eleven

Esperanza stared at Sebastián, unable to believe her eyes. He had come! He had found her! Hope replenished her spirit. But even as newfound energy coursed through her veins, she pretended the weakness and despair that had been a reality only moments ago.

"Ah, El Místico, I am so pleased you were able to find the mine after all," Antonio said, his voice a mockery of their first greeting. "It will save me from having to hunt you down."

He yanked on the *faja* around Esperanza's neck, and she wheezed for air as he pulled her back against his chest and used her as a shield.

At the same time, the soldier lifted his own pistol and aimed at Sebastián. As the man tightened his finger on the trigger, Sebastián dove for the floor and shifted aim, shooting him in the chest. The soldier dropped his weapon and fell.

Esperanza used the moment to make her move. She stomped her heel down on the arch of Antonio's foot. Yelling in fury and pain, he released her. She whirled and jammed her knee into his groin, and he bent over, howling in agony.

Esperanza yanked the knotted *faja* from her throat and turned. "Sebastián!"

Sebastián's eyes widened. "Esperanza, run!"

But the warning came too late. From the edge of her

vision, she saw the flat side of a miner's pickax arcing up toward her. She swerved, but not enough to avoid the blow. Crying out, she crumpled to the floor.

Seconds later a strange sensation of unreality overwhelmed her. She no longer felt pain, only blood crawling over her scalp and warm granite beneath her cheek.

"No!" Sebastián yelled. "*!Dios mio, no!*"

Her feeling of ethereal detachment intensified as she pushed to her feet and turned to him, wanting to comfort him, wanting to tell him she was fine. But as he stared at her, shaking his head, his shoulders shaking as well, she knew something was indeed terribly wrong. When she looked down at where she had fallen, she understood, for she saw herself. Still unconscious.

Dead.

Antonio stood above her body, holding the pick that had killed her as he looked through her spirit to Sebastián. Voicing a growl of rage, Sebastían leaped at Antonio, slamming her brother's body against the wall. Antonio grunted from the force of the blow, but did not release his hold on the tool. Instead, he swept it close to the floor, scything Sebastián's legs out from under him.

Sebastián toppled, and his head whipped back, cracking against the granite floor. He tried to get up, but lost his balance and fell again. Antonio raised the pick above his head and brought it down. Sebastián rolled, but not fast enough. The iron point cut into his leg. An agonized growl ripped from Sebastián's throat as Antonio lifted the tool again, then lunged on top of him, using all his weight to push the wooden handle against his throat.

The eerie whine of a frigid wind filled the chamber, and Esperanza felt the spirits brush past her ... and breeze *through* her. She gasped and shuddered, still too accustomed to a physical state to accept such an invasion. Their formless bodies whirled about Antonio and Sebastián, and she could feel their frustration, their longing for release, their thirst for revenge.

"Call on them, Sebastián!" she shouted, not knowing where the idea had come from, only knowing her words held the answer. "Release them with a curse. You have the power."

For a long moment she feared his concentration on his struggle with Antonio had closed him to her presence. But then he dragged in a rasping breath and began to speak.

"I curse you, Antonio Salazar," he choked out.

The muscles in his arms shook as he pushed up on the pick, lifting Antonio, who tried all the harder to force his weight down. With a quick twist of his arms, Sebastián threw Antonio off. Rolling over on top of the smaller man, he forced the handle against his throat. Antonio's eyes widened, and he thrashed his legs, seeking leverage against the rock.

"I curse this mine," he continued, "that it shall never satisfy another man's greed. And I curse you to be tortured to death by those *you* have tortured and murdered."

With that, he shoved up from the ground, yanking the pick out of Antonio's grip.

Antonio scuttled back against the wall and used it to help him stand. His nervous laughter filled the chamber. "Your words are but empty threats, El Místico."

"We shall see, Antonio." Sebastián smiled. "We shall see."

The eerie whine escalated into a roar, and Esperanza watched in awe as the spirits began to take on recognizable features. Antonio screamed as they materialized around him. He tried to run, but they grabbed his arms and legs, carrying him, bucking and writhing, to the shackles. On a nearby table rested all the instruments of torture Antonio and his soldiers had used. When Benedicto turned to look at her, wielding a long, sharp knife, she had to turn away.

Antonio's screams soon ceased, and the spirits disappeared like fog under the heat of the sun. Silence expanded, reclaiming the forgotten room.

Esperanza watched Sebastián hobble to her body and fall to his knees. He gathered her limp form in his arms and wept. Lifting his face to where she stood, he stared right at her, tears rolling down his cheeks as he rocked back and forth. "I am so sorry, Esperanza. So sorry that I failed you, too."

Words would not come past the lump in her throat. She rushed to him and crouched behind him, enfolding him in her embrace. Closing her eyes, she rested her cheek against his shoulder blade, bereft to her very soul that she could no longer feel the heat of his body, or he hers.

She didn't know how long they remained thus, but she opened her eyes to a chamber suffused with gentle light. She and Sebastián lifted their heads. A feminine soul of exquisite beauty stood before them, emanating kindness and love.

"Isabel?" Sebastián whispered.

A soft smile was his answer. "She is what you need in this world, is she not, my love? A strong spirit to match your own? Hope for a better future?"

He nodded.

"Then do as I say, Sebastián, and she will live again." Isabel moved closer. "First, you must keep your promise to destroy this mine. Then, take Esperanza, and her dowry, to the church in Cuarac. Once there, you must bury the silver, the symbol of your greed and your loss of soul, under the altar floor."

"But Isabel, the Church—"

"I know, Sebastián. The Church has been the source of much pain for you. But if you want a life with this woman you love, you must relinquish the horrors of your past, even those you suffered because of my death. I am your past, Sebastián. The inquisition is your past. Greed is your past. Esperanza can be your future. Live for her, and I will see that she lives for you. Do you promise to do as I have asked?"

"*Sí*," he said, his voice a solemn whisper. "I promise."

With pick and shovel lashed to his saddle, and his injured leg bandaged with Antonio's *faja*, Sebastián sat astride his

Andalusian. He cradled Esperanza's body to his chest as he and his men, along with a hundred Tiwa miners, gathered near the spring at the base of the mine canyon. Only Tito and Pedro had not yet reached the rendezvous point, for after Pedro had lured the remaining soldiers into an ambush, he had stayed behind to help Tito place kegs of powder in the mouth of the tunnel.

Soon Sebastián heard the sound of a horse's hooves on the flagstone road, and Pedro appeared, Tito mounted behind him, clutching his hat to his head. Moments later an explosion reverberated against the mountainsides. The ground shook as an enormous cloud of dust and rock fragments blasted into a sky thick with the first storm clouds Sebastián had seen in months.

The miners' shouts of jubilation filled the air, but Sebastián didn't stay to rejoice with them. Assured of Tito and Pedro's safety, he turned the Andalusian and urged her into a gallop.

"Wait, Sebastián, I am coming with you."

Without slowing, he turned to glance back at Tito, who had reclaimed his own mount and was pounding after him.

"We have no time to waste, old friend," he shouted over the thundering hooves of their horses. "I need to you to go to the *hacienda*. There will be guards." He reined his horse through the obstacle course of pine and spruce. "Kill them if you have to, but get the silver."

"Where will I find it?"

"In Salazar's office. Behind the false back in the lowest bookshelf. Inez, the cook, will help you if you explain to her what has happened."

Tito nodded, and together they devoured the leagues. By midday, black bellies had formed on the clouds and thunder echoed through the foothills as they parted paths, Tito galloping the short distance north to the *hacienda*, and Sebastián continuing east to Cuarac.

Soon, Sebastián reached the mission church. Thunder boomed and lightning streaked through the sky as he slid off his horse and stumbled on his injured leg under Esperanza's weight. He kicked open the church doors, slamming them against the thick rock doorframe. The sound echoed throughout the vast space as he carried his precious burden up the aisle.

With his elbow, he swept embroidered cloth, candles, and silver monstrance from the altar. Eucharistic bread showered over the flagstone floor as he lifted Esperanza and laid her out on the smooth wood surface.

"What are you doing?" demanded the priest, who ran into the church from the attached convent. Trying not to step on scattered pieces of host, he rushed to Sebastián's side and attempted to lift Esperanza's body. "You cannot put her there!"

Sebastián grabbed the man by the front of his gray robes and thrust him away. "Touch her again, priest, and you will wish you had never been born."

As Father Montoya backed away, eyes wide, Sebastián ran back out the doors to retrieve pick and shovel. Yanking both from their lashings on his saddle, he raced back inside. He had not even come to a complete stop before he raised the tool above his head and slammed it down, breaking one of the flagstones in front of the altar. The sound boomed throughout the church, echoing the rolling thunder. Again and again he brought the pick down, shattering red sandstone.

By the time he had dug a hole deep enough for the chest of silver, Tito trotted into the church carrying Esperanza's dowry, his clothing soaked from the rain.

Breathing heavily, his leg throbbing, Sebastián leaned against the handle of the pick. "The map," he said. "Get the map from the pouch on my saddle. I will bury it as well."

Tito nodded and dropped the chest on the floor as he ran to do his bidding. Moments later he returned. As he handed Sebastián the map, a flash of lightning across the glassless clerestory window above the altar illuminated Esperanza's body.

Sebastián bent to place the map inside the chest, but found it locked. "The key. Did you find the key?"

Tito shook his head. "I am sorry. I did not see a key."

Growling his frustration, Sebastián wielded the pick above his head and smashed it down on the hasp and lock. Wood splintered and metal gave way. Opening the lid, he tossed the map inside, atop the silver coins. Closing the chest, he lifted it, dropped it into the hole, and shoved dirt in on top of it.

When Sebastián had finished, pain and exhaustion brought him to his knees. He knelt before the altar, holding one of Esperanza's hands in his own and draping his other arm protectively across her body. With every ounce of energy in his heart and mind, he willed his desire for her to heal through the conduit of his body and into hers. Time crawled by as the storm raged outside, and still he did not feel her body stir.

"Perhaps we did not get here soon enough," whispered Tito.

Sebastián ignored him, certain his heart would shatter if he acknowledged his own fear voiced by his closest friend.

Father Montoya stepped forward. "Shall I—?"

"No!" Sebastián shouted. "No," he repeated, his voice softer, but just as drenched in determination. "She *will* awaken."

A cold raindrop found its way through the clerestory window and fell against the back of Sebastián's neck. But he ignored that, too, as he peered into Esperanza's face, searching for some sign that Isabel had spoken the truth.

Another drop fell, this one splattering on Esperanza's cheek. And another, on her nose. Her brow twitched, and Sebastián leaned closer, elation unfolding so quickly within him he was certain there would be no room to contain it.

"Esperanza?" he ventured. "Esperanza, I need you. Not silver. Not gold. Not all the treasure in the world. Only you, and nothing else. I love you. *Please* come back to me."

He tightened his grip on her hand. Her answer was a twitch of her fingertips. And then she opened her eyes, staring first up at the clerestory window as another drop fell, this time on her lips. She slowly swiveled her head until she met his gaze.

He swallowed the lump in his throat as he reached up and held her face in his shaking hands.

"Do you feel that, Sebastián?" she asked, her tone weak and whisper-soft. "It's raining. The drought has ended."

"Saints be praised, it's a miracle!" the priest said, sketching the sign of the cross.

Tito's shout of triumph and jubilation filled the church to its pine-beamed ceiling. In the echo of the sound, Sebastián choked out a laugh and swiped away a tear.

"*Sí, querida mía*. The drought has ended. And my hope is alive."

Author's Note

Legends regarding lost Spanish mines and the ghosts that haunt them abound in the Southwest, and the Manzano Mountain area is no exception. So, breaking with "proven" historical fact, I decided instead to craft my story based loosely on the legends I grew up hearing from longtime residents of the Manzano Mountain area.

Esperanza and Sebastián are purely my invention, but the Pueblo village of Cuarac actually existed. Today it is a ruin, part of the Salinas National Monument, and is known as Quarai. Quarai was abandoned sometime in the 1670s, due in part to a drought so severe the people were forced to boil and eat rawhide.

Although there was mining activity in the Manzanos, historians claim it didn't take place until the 1840s. But once again, legend holds that there was indeed a curse on a lost Spanish mine in the Manzanos, and anyone who searched for it was doomed to die.

The legend and the curse will live on for two new lovers in *Amethyst Wish*, coming soon from Avid Press.

The Legend Lives On....

coming in May 2001 from Avid Press
Amethyst Wish
by Kelley Pounds

Two hundred years later the mythic love story of
Sebastian and Esperanza is told around campfires as the
Legend of the Lost Mine of Sorrows. Can this hidden
mine once again bring two wounded people together on
a journey toward forgiveness, self-discovery and love?

Brenna Kirkbride is determined to work her dead
father's mine and fulfill his dream of finding the legendary lost Spanish mine. She hires Aidan Shanahan, a
man with a questionable past—a man on a mission to
find the truth behind his best friend's murder.

But as secrets continue to be released like spites from
Pandora's Box, can Brenna forgive the most damaging
secret of all?

The Gillyflower Promise

by Colleen Gleason

I.

Father, are you mad? Beatrice of Callaway is barely ten years of age!" Bernard of Derkland frowned and finished off his tankard of ale, wishing his father would leave off grousing at him. If they'd only have one conversation where the man did not bring up suitable wives…!

"Aye, but if one judges by her mother, in five years she'll be a good breeder—and a generous dowry she brings." Lord Harold turned to look out over the rows of diners eating in the great hall of Wyckford Heath. They were guests at the week-long celebration of the wedding of the Lord of Wyckford's youngest daughter. "What of Theresa, daughter of Lord Enderman?"

Bernard gaped. Was not the man—his father—supposed to have some care for him? "Father, would you have that horse-faced shrew in your wedding bed? An' she hasn't a bride's portion big enough to make one forget that her temper is worse than a goat in heat." He drummed his fingers on the rough trestle table.

His father chuckled and traced an outline of his mouth with a thumb and forefinger. "Mayhaps you speak the truth. Even the dogs slink away when she walks thither." He chuckled again and bit off a chunk of roasted venison from its cross-shaped bone. Chewing thoughtfully for a moment, he drew his bushy grey brows together as if deep in thought. A moment later, his brows sprang apart as a new idea lit his face. "Mathilda, Lady Cretton, has a generous bride's price, an' she is not hard on the eyes. What say you that, Bernard? I'll speak to her father on the morrow."

"Only if you would like to find your firstborn son dead of mysterious causes," he shot back. "Did you not know that wagging tongues tell that she helped her first two husbands to an early grave? I'd as lief not be the third." Bernard stood, stepping backward over the long bench that lined the trestle table at which they ate. "Father, I know that 'tis important that I wed, but I should prefer to choose a bride of my own liking."

"An' choose her you shall, if you make a decision anon. 'Tis past time you wed, and if you do not make your choice, I will make one for you." Harold's countenance took on a firm cast that brooked no disagreement from his son.

And, in sooth, Bernard knew that the time for equivocating was gone. With his younger brother Dirick haring off with the new king in Aquitaine, and their middle brother wearing the robes of a simple monk, the necessity of wedding and breeding weighed heavily upon him. At one score and seven, Bernard had no excuses to offer. Duty beckoned.

"Aye, Father. I'll attend to it during our stay here."

With a curt nod, he strode off, out of the hall, pushing past the throngs of people and stepping around the begging hounds. He took long, hard steps that bespoke of his height and solid build, and as he left the noise of the hall behind him, his boots made echoing thumps in the empty passage-way.

If 'tweren't dark, and he weren't in unfamiliar territory, Bernard would mount his stallion and ride to clear his head. As 'twas, he could only visit the stables and talk to his favorite steed, Rock—saving the ride for the morrow.

Betimes, the weight of being heir to the vast lands of Derkland weighed so heavily upon him that he wished for the freedom of his brother Dirick, who could travel and live his life as he wished. But then that weight would lessen, as he recalled that his own brother had nothing to bring to a beautiful lady whom he might wish to wed, and that his prospects would not be near as numerous as Bernard's own.

An' he did love Derkland, Bernard reflected as he slipped into the stables, with all of her rolling green hills and thick forests, tiny thatched huts and fat woolly sheep. But most of all, he loved the soft brown noses of the fierce destriers that Derkland bred; the heavy, stamping hooves, and smart, shrewd eyes. There were none better than those from his father's stables, and none better than his own Rock—the grey-brown steed that was as solid as its namesake.

The stallion was glad to see him, and although he wasn't as gentle as a mare, he did toss his jet black mane and dance in greeting. Bernard shared some aged carrots and an apple core he'd sneaked from the kitchen earlier that day, patting Rock's velvety nose affectionately.

A soft cry from the depths of the stables reached his keen ears, even over the whuffling and stamping of the horses. Turning instinctively, Bernard thought to investigate, then halted. 'Twas likely only a man-at-arms finding his pleasure with one of the buxom serving wenches that adorned Wyckford Heath Hall.

He returned to Rock, allowing him to butt his head against his unshaven cheek, but kept his ears attuned toward where the sound had come. Bernard tried to return his thoughts to the path upon which they should be focused—finding a wife for himself, as his father's threat was not an idle one—but aught nagged in the back of his mind.

At last, with a frown at his foolishness, he gave Rock a quick pat and walked silently toward the back of the stable. In the case that it was just a randy man-at-arms rolling in the hay with his lady, Bernard could slip away silently and no one the wiser. But if, as the upright hair at the back of his neck warned, 'twas something more....

A dim light shone in the depths of the stable, and as he turned a corner, he found himself in a small room lit by a torch on the wall.

A girl sat in the hay, her skirts bunched around her as she bent her attention to something he could not identify. Her back was to him, with a long braid which fell from an intricate headdress that did not belong to a serving wench.

She turned, saying, "Leonard, if you would—" Her words ended in a small gasp as she caught sight of Bernard.

As she scrambled to her feet, her eyes wide in a face shadowed then unshadowed by the flickering torch, Bernard noted that she was more than a girl, and most definitely not a mere serving wench. Even in the low light, he could see the quality of her gown and the glitter of some jewels in her hair and at her well-rounded bosom.

"My lady, I did not mean to disturb you," he began, not quite certain how to proceed as she looked at him with such fearful eyes. He knew that his great stature and solidness was ofttimes disconcerting for women, and something about this female who—though fear shone in her eyes—stood as tall as her height allowed made him particularly conscious of his imposing appearance. He stepped backward to put space between them. "I meant only to assure myself that naught was amiss. I heard…your cry and thought to see if I could be of assistance."

She had a heart-shaped face, angelic and delicate, with ropes of honey-gold hair that glinted even in the dim light. As he stood there, caught suddenly by her beauty, he saw the fear lessen in her eyes. "You heard my cry?" she repeated, her head tilting slightly as she seemingly turned the words over in her mind. "You would have come to my aid?"

"Aye, of course, my lady." He didn't stumble on the form of address; 'twas obvious she was of noble title—but what was not so clear was why she was in the stables, alone, during a wedding celebration. And what was she doing in the hay?

Curious, he took a step forward without thinking about how this would affect her—but she did not move away; only gave the barest flinch as he came closer. "What do you here?"

She did not need to answer, for he saw for himself the large grey cat ensconced in the hay. Five tiny kittens, barely covered with fur and eyes still shut, nursed whilst the mother watched Bernard crouching next to her.

"They were born only today, and I came to see how they fared," the woman spoke, still standing behind him; now with the height advantage. "Cleome—'tis the cat's name—had a foot injured by one of the dogs, and 'twas only because Leonard—the stableboy—intervened that she lived to deliver this litter."

Bernard reached to pet the mother cat. The woman gasped and began to warn him—"Nay, she will scratch!"—but became silent when she saw Cleome's eyes barely flicker as Bernard traced a large finger over the top of her pointed head and down to rub her side.

"'Tis a miracle," she murmured, watching as his hand traced the thick fur down to Cleome's tail again and again. His hand was so wide and brown that it nearly covered the cat's entire abdomen, and she watched with fear and fascination combined as such a powerful appendage was used so gently.

I should be afraid, Joanna realized dimly, of this great man whose presence had filled the doorway. But she was not, and that was in itself a unique experience. Instead, she sat quietly and watched as he stroked the cat in silence, thanking the Virgin that she'd already covered the parcel in the corner with straw.

She glanced briefly toward the shadowed corner to reassure herself that 'twould not be noticed, then returned her attention to the countenance of the man, noting the tight, dark curls that covered his head in an unfashionably short style. His face was lean and sober, with deep-set eyes that had held no challenge when he'd greeted her earlier. The tan of his hand was echoed in the color of his face, and the wiriness of his dark hair in the short-clipped beard and moustache he wore.

"You have a gift," she said at last, breaking what had

become an easy silence.

He nodded once, turning a glance toward her that lingered over her face. "Aye. 'Tis my blessing that animals find no fear of me. My father—"

He was interrupted by the sound of someone approaching, and Joanna stood with a sudden fear clutching her middle, unable to keep a small gasp from her throat. If she were discovered alone with such a man.… It was Leonard this time, thank Mary, and she felt the discomfort in her stomach ease. But she must return to the keep now, as she'd been away too long and did not want to be missed.

Now ignoring the giant man—who watched her as she spoke to the stable boy—she told Leonard to keep watch of the litter and where to move them should aught disturb the mother and her kittens. Then, with a quick glance at the giant, she dropped the slightest of curtseys and began to take her leave.

"My lady, allow me to escort you to your destination, if you will," he offered, extending his arm.

Horror gripped her. "Nay! Nay, sir, but I must not be seen with—not be seen with anyone. I can find my way without assistance." She bent to gather her light cloak and, doing so, noticed that one of her braids had fallen from its mooring. Joanna bit her lip and reached behind to re-fasten the recalcitrant braid, knowing that if she returned to the hall and it was noticed, she would be the worse for it.

The giant stepped toward her, behind her, towering over her small frame as she attempted to twist her arms in the most awkward position. "Allow me, my lady." His voice smoothed over her as warm, deft fingers relieved her own of the rope of hair. In a trice, he had found its place and secured it with one of the jeweled pins her own maid had used earlier. Then, mercifully, he moved away.

"Th-thank you, sir." She hated that her voice quavered, but 'twas so foreign to have a man so close to her, so gentle, yet so imposing. "And now, I must return."

Bernard could only watch her go, hurrying down the hall of the stable. Though he felt uneasy with her request to depart alone, he abided by her wishes and stayed until she was safely out of sight.

Then he turned to Leonard, who now knelt beside the grey cat, and asked, "Who is the lady? What is her name?"

"'Twas Lady Joanna, my lord."

Bernard bit back a grin. At the least the young boy had recognized his station, although the Lady Joanna had not. "An' how does she know this stable so well?"

"She is my lord's daughter—the Lord of Wyckford's daughter."

"The sister of the bride, then?"

"Aye, my lord."

Then Bernard suddenly remembered that he had been invited to a wedding, and that his father would surely miss him by now...and that he had dallied long enough. And, betimes, he would now search out the lady to see if he could find her within the keep.

Unfortunately for Bernard, when he returned to the great hall, most of the men—bridegroom included—were in their cups, and the celebration had begun to wane. As the dancing slowed and the musicians had begun to disperse, and even the wine and ale began to dry up, the only entertainment that remained was to see the bride and groom off to the bridal chamber.

'Twas of little interest to Bernard to see the spindly-legged groom stripped naked and escorted to his bride's chamber, but he did not decline too strongly and soon found himself within the group of men doing just that.

They made the usual bawdy jests, drank jugs of ale and attempted to force more down the throat of the already dazed groom as others helped him out of his tunic, undertunic, and chausses.

"Give 'er all ye got," encouraged one man, slapping the groom on the bare skin of his back.

Another gestured to the groom's flaccid member, chortling, "Ye might need some help, there, eh, Will?"

"Eh, Will'll keep the bitch in line," grated a voice next to Bernard. "Not much more than a raised hand an' she'll be doin' your bidding as you please." The man, obviously well into his cups, swayed against Bernard, causing his perpetually-full cup of ale to slosh onto his tunic. "Have a care, sirrah," he warned, leaning threateningly into Bernard's face. "Ye've spilt on my new tunic!"

Bernard, used to dealing with confused drunks, merely turned away and chose to ignore him.

When he felt a hard shove from behind, however, he whirled, automatically clapping a hand to where his dagger hung. "Aye?" he asked, coming face to face with the man with the grating voice. "Did you wish to speak with me?"

He towered over the other man, who was not much taller than a woman and barely reached to Bernard's shoulders. "I said that ye spilled ale on my tunic, sirrah, and I would expect you to make recompense."

"'Twas your own clumsiness that caused it, man. Do you not make a mistake you will later come to regret." Bernard responded easily, but with a hard warning in his eyes.

From the belligerance in the other man's face, Bernard knew there might have been more of an altercation had not the father of the bride announced that the bridal chamber was ready to receive the groom. With a lethal look at Bernard, the slighter man with the grating voice—whom Bernard recalled was named Harmon—pushed none-too-gently away from him to stand beside Will, the groom.

The group of men tottered along the passageway, trading more bawdy comments and suggestions for Will, and Bernard followed their progression. He'd realized somewhere along the way that as sister to the bride, the young woman he'd met in the stables would likely be there at the bedding ceremony. And he wanted to see her again.

The door to the bridal chamber opened, and a flood of men pushed their way in. Joanna stood near the fire, chafing the icy hands of her sister, the bride, who was about to be disrobed.

The scent of men, and ale, and smoke, filled the room, along with stale, panting breath and loud exchanges. Joanna felt a familiar wave of anxiety at their closeness, the crowdedness of the chamber; and Ava, her sister, swayed slightly against her, clutching at her hand in the folds of her gown.

"Shh, 'twill soon be over," she murmured into Ava's ear, smoothing a hand over her shoulder even as she clenched the fingers on her other hand. "And when you and Will are alone—"

"Bring forth the bride and groom!" intoned the priest, pushing through the crowd of men.

A wave of bawdy laughter rose and roared, filling the room, as the men shoved Will forward as one body. The slim man stumbled, but caught himself on the tall spindle of the bed and grinned with the vacant eyes of one who had imbibed overmuch.

Joanna gently pushed Ava forward, and, blocking from her mind the memories of her own wedding night, began to assist her maid Maeve in removing the bride's clothing. She hoped to make the moment as brief as possible for Ava's sake, although what would happen in the chamber thereafter mayhap could be worse.

Ava's jewel-studded girdle jangled to the floor, and Joanna reached to pull her fine overtunic above her head. After handing it to Maeve to fold, she turned to unlace the sides of the bridal gown. As she worked her way to the far side of Ava, she glanced for the first time toward the sea of ogling male faces, and her attention fixed on one for the merest instant. 'Twas the man from the stable.

Joanna's heart slipped off its beat, then returned to a faster pulse. Her fingers became clumsy and it took her twice as long to unlace the second side as it had the first. What was he doing here? Dear God, if Harmon were to learn….

She felt the whiteness drain over her face as her head lightened with the surge of fear. Mary, Mother of God. But mayhap Harmon wasn't there…mayhaps he lay in his cups somewhere….

She raised her hands to lift the gown over Ava's head, and felt her own sleeves slip back to her shoulders, baring her slim arms. Maeve took it from her and Joanna turned to the last bit—the light, fine linen chemise that hid very little of the curves and dark areas of Ava's body. Knowing it was all that much easier if 'twere quick, she bent to take the hem, lifting it smoothly and easily up and over, leaving Ava beautifully nude in the midst of gaping, gawking, groping men for the merest instant. Maeve was mercifully quick with the fur-lined cloak, throwing it over Ava's shoulders and masking her nakedness.

Someone pushed Will, who stumbled again, this time into his bride; the noise of hoots and whistles deafened Joanna. She drew the blankets back from the bed and assisted her sister in slipping under the coverings as quickly as possible. Now she could do naught for Ava but pray that 'twould end soon, and that her husband would have a care when they were alone.

Backing away, nearer the fire again, Joanna watched as the priest raised the arms of the groom for all to see his nude body.

"There appears no reason that the groom should be unable to fulfill his marital duties," intoned the priest, and the room erupted with taunts and whistles as the evidence of Lord Will's virility swelled and rose to attention.

"Now, to bed with thee!"

Joanna turned to slip out of the room and came face to face with her husband.

"My lord," she choked. What she had feared was in his eyes—glassiness, but behind it, glinting sharply, lust.

"My tunic has been soiled," Harmon grated, his hand slipping around to grasp her arm. "You'll come to assist me in removing it."

"Aye, my lord," was all she could say.

Each of his fingers was a separate ridge, biting into the tenderness of her upper arm, and Joanna swallowed back a wince as he propelled her toward the doorway. *Mother of God....* she prayed silently—prayed that the man from the stable would not acknowledge her; prayed that Harmon would become distracted from his purpose; prayed that his overindulgence would get the best of him.

One, at least, of her prayers, was to be answered.

As they passed through the doorway, Joanna came face to face, briefly, with the giant from the stables. His expression was unreadable, but his eyes caught and held hers for the barest of instants before she dragged her own gaze away...as Harmon directed her toward her fate. Mercifully, the man said naught; just turned to look as they walked away. She could feel the weight of his stare behind her.

II.

Until she'd raised her arms to assist the bride in removing her chemise, the Lady Joanna had entranced Bernard with her shy beauty and graceful movements. He knew of her soft heart—just from their moments in the stable: the manner in which she'd treated him when she thought him less than a lord and the care for which she'd shown a mother cat told Bernard all that he needed to know.

In the bridal chamber, he'd stood to the side, sipping—not gulping—the bitter ale that must have come from the dregs of the barrel, watching her, suddenly wanting her…knowing that he must have and protect her. He saw the way candle-light glinted off her rich, burnished hair, wanted to touch the creaminess of her half-shadowed skin, and maddeningly felt the desire to feel her small hands cover his broad chest.

'Twas inconceivable that after so long, so many women, after so much nagging from his father, that he should find the woman he had to marry this suddenly. And he knew, clearly, that 'twould be she.

And then, Lady Joanna raised her arms to help Lady Ava off with her chemise. And Bernard found his attention fixed not on the newly bare body of the bride, but on the slender, upraised, bruised arms of her sister, Joanna.

Black and purple marks patterned the upper portion of her arms, both of them, leaving no doubt as to their origin. Bernard felt the loud, crowded chamber slide away, leaving him cold and stunned that someone—for it had to be another person—could have inflicted such pain upon a small, fragile woman.

He'd hoped to talk with her, to find a moment where he could ask her what or who…but 'twas not to be; for as soon as Joanna moved to leave the bedside of her frightened sister, she was accosted—nay, claimed.

Harmon. The whoreson.

Bernard could barely control his rage at the realization that this low-bellied snake not only had some claim to Lady Joanna, but that he doubtless had inflicted such bruises upon her person—or if he did not, then he knew who had. 'Twas all Bernard could do to allow the couple to pass by him at the chamber door, and remain passive. He looked closely at Joanna, catching her eyes—soft blue ones glazed with anxiety—as she passed, trying to send the message that he would stop them if she wished.

The way her gaze flickered away almost instantly bespoke of her fear, and Bernard forced himself to remain still, knowing that any action on his part would bear more ill toward Joanna.

They left, and Bernard had no choice but to follow the remaining men from the chamber. A heavy sickening settled in his belly as he stomped along the hallway with the other men. It took only one question to ascertain what he'd inherently known: Lady Joanna was wed to Harmon, Lord of Swerthmoor.

Anon, this morn, Bernard woke with a head fuzzy from little sleep and too much ale. The last person he wished to see, however, met him as he stumbled from his pallet—not the last of the men to rise, but near enough to it that his father must call attention to that fact.

"Good morrow, dear son," spoke Lord Harold Derkland, looking up at Bernard, but somehow managing to appear the taller. "And how fares your head this morn? 'Twould be aught

that I'd expect from your brother Dirick—such overindulgence—but not that I'd think of from you."

"Leave me be," growled Bernard, brushing past his father
on a mission to splash his face with water in hopes of washing the fog away.

His father chuckled, but followed along. They picked their
way among the pallets scattered over the rush-strewn floor in
an antechamber of the Great Hall, taking care not to tread
upon any outstretched hand or foot of the snoring men. "I've
found a wife for you, Bernard."

By the time his father spoke the unwelcome words,
Bernard's face was inside a barrel filled with water, so that he
did not have the breath to bellow his discord. But when he
pulled up, whipping his head back so that water sprayed—
even from his short curls, he turned to level a glare at Harold.

"Aye? Father, I'll find my own bride, I've told you!" He
swiped the arm of his tunic over his beard, then passed his
hand over the top of his head. More water rained down over
his face, and he wiped it again.

"So say you, and you haven't even looked at one yet,"
Harold griped. "But the one I've found is all that you'd ask:
well-landed, no history of ill-fated husbands, and quite easy
on the eyes."

"Father—"

"Maris of Langumont, she is. And her father a good man.
She'd make you a fine bride, son."

Bernard choked back his annoyance and looked at his
father. He meant only for his son's welfare…and he could not
know that Bernard had already found the woman he wanted
to marry. 'Twas not the fault of his father that she was already
wed. "Father, please. I beg you. Please leave off—at the least
for today." He had to find Lady Joanna … he had to speak
with her…if for no other reason than to see that she truly was
the woman he believed.

Lord Harold allowed his son to take his leave, but only after
wringing a vow that Bernard would sup with himself and

Lord Merle of Langumont that evening.

"Aye!" growled Bernard. "Anything to remove the leech that is my father from my neck!" He stalked off, ignoring the grating chuckle that echoed behind him.

Beyond the keep, the sun shone hot and bright—enough to make Bernard wince and his head throb all that bit more. His feet took him toward the stable—and that was as good a destination as any. If luck was with him, Bernard would find Lady Joanna tending to her cat. If not, then he would visit with Rock and hope that Leonard would have some direction for him.

Just as he was about to step into the welcome dimness of the stable, however, Bernard happened to glance toward the small herb garden that grew plentifully behind the structure. God must have caused him to do so, he thought, shifting his direction so that he was now walking toward the honey-gold head that bent over some small bush in the garden.

An' God was with him, for 'twas Lady Joanna that hovered over a growth of rosemary.

She started and sat back quickly on her heels when his shadow cast over her task. When she looked up and saw that it was he, she stumbled over her skirts, trying to get to her feet.

"My lady," he said gently, proffering a hand to steady her. "I mislike it that I have only to step near you and you are falling about yourself to get away from me. 'Tis not the reaction that I desire." He spoke without jest, seeing the apprehension in her face. "Why is that so?"

"My lo—sir, I—'tis only that—"

He stepped forward to grasp her small hand—which she had not extended toward his offered one, closing his fingers around her smooth skin. "'Tis 'my lord,' Lady Joanna. Lord Bernard Derkland…and I am most delighted to know you." And then, without giving a thought to her reaction, he slid his hand up her arm, pushing up the sleeve of her gown nearly to her shoulder. Rage surged through him at the sight of the bluish-green, black and purple mottles on her creamy skin.

"And I would kill he who would do this to a woman," he breathed through teeth clenched so hard that his head hurt. "Joanna, who?"

She jerked away, showing him that she was not the simple, cowering woman she appeared. "Leave your hands from me, and your interests thither, Si—Lord Bernard. Please. There is naught that you—or anyone—can do. And do not call me Joanna!"

"My lady, I—"

"Nay!" Her voice rose even as she pressed her hand against his chest. This movement stilled him, this first time she reached to touch him—though the message of the touch was naught but a rebuff. "Nay, my lord, your interference would serve only to incense him further...and make it all the more difficult for me."

Then, as though realizing where they were, she whirled to look toward the stable and the bailey as if afraid they might have been seen. Fortunately, during the course of their conversation, they'd moved behind a cluster of raspberry bushes and were out of sight of anyone walking toward the stables. "Please, Lord Bernard, if he were to find—"

"Is it Harmon? Is he your husband? Is it he who lays his hands upon you thus?" Bernard reached, gently closing his fingers around her cleft chin, reveling in the warmth of her sun-drenched skin. He looked into her eyes, past the grey-blue color of her irises and into their depths. He saw fear and anxiety, but he did not see repulsion or anger. 'Twas good. She was not afraid of him.

"Aye." Her voice was but a breath, but 'twas enough.

"Then I will rid you of him. And you shall be free to wed with me." His words were soft, steely, and deadly serious.

"You—Lord Bernard, you cannot! Wed with you?" The first part of his threat seemed to disintegrate as she fixated on the latter promise. "Wed with you?" Shock lined her beautiful, heart-shaped face as she looked up at him, hands raised in front of her as if to thrust him away. "Are you mad? I am wed, and—and you know naught of me to say that you will marry me."

Bernard laughed in spite of the unhappy situation. God's bones, she was lovely! And had a spine, she did, under the weight of the fear from her own husband. If he could indeed remove that fear from her eyes, she would make a fine wife…and a fine *chatelaine* for Derkland Castle. "My sweetling, Lady Joanna, I know as much of you as I need know that you are the woman I have waited to marry. My father has groused at me for over the last fortnight, and now that I have found you, I will find a way to please him and marry you at the oncet."

She sank to the ground, not as if in obeisance, but as though her legs could no longer hold her up under the weight of this conversation. Bernard knelt next to her, taking care not to tread upon her skirts; but arranging himself closely enough that he could smell the womanliness of her scent.

"Lord Bernard, you truly know nothing of me. How can you? We've met naught but once.…" She raised her face to his and his breath caught in his throat at the hunger in her eyes…the hunger, he saw, not for him as much as to know that there was aught of herself that he should want.

"I know that you are the most beautiful woman I have ever seen," he told her quietly; then, with a flash of jest, he added, "with the exception of my mother." He thought for a moment, then added, "Nay, you are even more beautiful than she." Her smile came and went, leaving more than a trace of sadness in its wake.

"I have never met my mother, as she perished birthing Ava when I was but two summers."

Bernard closed his fingers over her hand, which rested on the ground, feeling the warmth of her next to the cool moistness of the rich earth. "I know that beyond your lovely face and beautiful form that you are a kind-hearted woman, who would put her own comfort—and safety—at risk for the life of a cat and her litter. I know that you speak well even to serfs such as the lowly stable-boy Leonard…I know that you care for your sister and wished to spare her any angst that might have come her way on the night of her wedding. I know, too, that you are brave enough to stand up to a man when you are not trapped with him by marriage—which means that you are not foolish in your bravery, only prudent. And I know that my heart has been yours from the moment I pinned your thick, heavy braid into your hair last even, and smelled the rosewater you must use, and felt the softness of your skin."

He looked into her eyes—eyes that now held wonder—and said, "That is all I need to know, Joanna."

"My lord….Bernard.…" she breathed, her fingers twisting in his to cling to his hand. "I.…"

He reached to pluck a white gillyflower from a low-growing bush behind her and brought it around to her face. Dropping a kiss onto it, he raised it to brush its many ruffled petals over her cheeks and chin, ending with her lips. "I vow to you, Joanna, on the life of my father and mother—and my own—that I will find a way to free you from the ties by which you are bound. And then, if you will have me, I will wed you and care for you and love you all of our days."

The perfume of the flower touched his nose, mingling with nearby rosemary and Joanna's own erotic scent. It was too much for him to resist—he leaned forward to taste her parted lips.

She trembled under him, and moved naught but for that slight tremor; so he forced himself to barely brush against her mouth, taking care not to drag the bristles of his beard and moustache too harshly over her tender skin. Joanna was sweet and plump and warm, as he'd known she'd be…and she tasted of mint and strawberries—or something like them. Or mayhap 'twas just her. Just Joanna.

When she pulled back, he allowed her to, and took a deep

breath to slow his racing heart. "And now that I know you taste like heaven," he murmured, the intensity of his emotions coming out as a crooked smile, "I am thrice as indebted to my vow."

Knowing they'd tested Fate long enough, and not able to trust that he wouldn't put her to the test again, he pulled to his feet. "I must leave you now, Joanna. But know that you are not alone…nor will you be."

III.

Joanna started when her husband strode purposefully into their chamber. She sat near the window-slit of the room that had been hers before she married and moved with Harmon to Swerthmoor, mending a rent in his garment by the dim light.

"What do you here?" Harmon grated, sliding his sword from the sheath around his waist. He took his time, allowing the steel to scrape slowly and deliberately over its metal casing.

The hair at the back of Joanna's neck rose, prickling, and her breath quickened though she tried not to show it. "I but sew the tear in your tunic, my lord."

He stepped closer, his booted foot ringing solidly on the stone floor and causing her stomach to churn. Joanna clamped her lips together as she continued to sew, her fingers clumsy with tremors as he stood, watching. "Have you spoken with your father betimes?"

"Nay. I—"

"Joanna." His voice, dry and cracked as her throat, lashed into the room. "I want that map." With a sudden movement, and a glint of steel, he moved, and the point of the sword slipped under her chin, resting there flatly.

Joanna swallowed, and felt the weight of the cold steel shift against her throat. "My lord, I thought to speak with him on the morrow—after the melee tournament. He is sure to be in a fine mood with the purses you will win as his champion."

"A poor attempt at flattery will not turn my eyes from your disobedience, Joanna." She hated the way he said her name —the way the sounds came so gutturally from his mouth, twisting it into something mocking and ugly. The point of the sword pricked the soft skin under her chin and she did not move, barely breathing, focusing her thoughts on the leather pouch still hidden in the stable…and the earnestness in Bernard of Derkland's face.

Harmon would not kill her—at the least not until he got the map. But there would likely be pain to come, and she steeled herself for it. She could—she would—endure it.

"Well, my lady? Have you swallowed your tongue?" Something warm trickled down her neck.

"I do not mean disobedience, my lord," she managed to speak without moving her jaws or lips. "I would speak with my father on the right occasion so that he will grant your wish."

Mercifully, the sword tipped away, and he slid it back into its case. Then, untying the sheath from his waist, he flung it onto the bed—all the while his eyes boring heavily into her. "Did you remove that stain from my tunic of last eve?"

"Aye, my lord. 'Tis clean and awaits your attention." She gestured to a trunk near the fireplace, then returned her hands to a clench in her lap.

"I'd as lief have a crossed sword with the whoreson bastard that spilled his ale on't." Harmon sat on a stool near the fire and kicked off his boots.

Joanna obediently moved to kneel in front of him, untying his chausses and unwinding them from his leg. She bit her lip as she tended to the task, keeping her head bowed.

"Bernard of Derkland," sneered Harmon, and Joanna flinched at the name, her heart-speed increasing. "I'll meet him on the lists on the morrow and teach the oaf to have a care near his betters." He stood and Joanna forced herself to raise the tunic over his head, coming too close to his sweaty, stale skin. She turned away quickly to place it on the trunk, but the hand on her arm jerked her to a halt.

"He was the big man in the bridal chamber last evening, Joanna. Know you him?"

She dared not pull from his grasp, and she dared not look him in the eye. Aye, she knew him…he'd haunted her thoughts all the night and day since their meeting in the stable. Joanna concentrated on folding his tunic as she phrased her answer. "Nay, my lord, not until I saw him last even."

He released her and she turned away, her throat dry and her heart thumping madly. She placed the tunic deliberately on the trunk, then, when she had no further choice, she turned back.

"He looked at you, Joanna. He did not watch the bride. He looked at you."

The blood drained from her face, and she swayed slightly. All of her strong focus scattered. "My lord—"

He stood, not so much taller than she, in his hose and tunic; his craggy face stark with the look she knew too well. "You are beautiful, Joanna. Oh, aye—mayhaps too beautiful. An' he shoots too high if he looks to you. But mayhaps you are too beautiful and aught should be done to remove that temptation from his sight."

Acid rose in her throat as all feeling in her limbs disappeared. "My lord—"

"You would not tempt the man, would you, Joanna?"

He stepped toward her.

"Nay." Her voice was a thread wisping through the air.

"He wishes to have the best of me. And you'll not be a part of it."

"My lord Harmon, I—"

"Come here, Joanna." He pulled a long, thin, leather cord from around his hose. "We've time before supper."

Aye, Maris of Langumont was beautiful. Bernard endured three wagging-eyebrow grins from his father before his own ferocious countenance caused Harold to desist. But his father could not resist one last well-placed kick under the table before turning his attention to Maris's father, Lord Merle.

"'Tis the first time you've traveled from Langumont?" Bernard asked Maris as he used his knife to tear the rabbit meat from its bone. He glanced out over the hall, hoping to catch sight of Joanna as he pushed some of the dry, stringy meat to Maris's side of their trencher.

"Aye, at the least, the first time that I do recall," she replied. "Other than to visit Father's other fiefs, I've been nowhere from Langumont. I should like to visit the court—'tis much I've heard about the future queen Eleanor."

"My brother travels with Henry's court, and was there when they wed," Bernard replied. His sharp ear caught a snatch of the conversation between their two fathers—and he tensed at the words "betrothal" and "Christ's Mass." By the rood, his father had best refrain from sealing any contracts without his approval!

"They speak of our betrothal," Maris told him needlessly. She leaned closer, and a pleasing scent came with her—but the floral scent only reminded him of Joanna, and their proximity in the garden. "But 'twill be for naught, for I've told my father I've no wish to wed."

He stopped in the middle of a chew, looked blankly at her, then resumed. "But of course you shall wed if your father wishes it so."

"Nay. He'll not force me. And," she rested her hand with overt familiarity on his arm, "'tis nothing of you, my lord Bernard, truly. You are most kind and polite and easy on the eyes. 'Tis only that I see no reason to bind myself to a man."

Bernard found that he needed a large gulp of ale to digest this stunning piece of information. "Is that so, Lady Maris?" He attempted to keep the incredulity from his voice even as he cast his gaze over the hall of diners yet again.

"I have no need of a husband, as Father has trained me to be chatelaine and also to manage the fiefs as well as any man.

I ride and hunt as well as many of his men-at-arms...not with a sword, of course, but I've my own bow and falcon."

He turned to look into her large, quite serious, hazel eyes and suddenly wished his brother Dirick were there. He would find such a woman a welcome challenge. "But who would manage the accounts?" he asked, refilling her wine and then his own. "And defend the castle from siege?" He could think of naught else to say—for what else should a woman do but marry and breed?

Then he saw her—near the dais where her father sat with the newly-wedded couple. All else faded from his attention as Bernard watched Joanna pace—so very slowly—behind her husband, and take her seat next to him. Her hair and neck were covered by a veil that shimmered with her movements, and her face, so fair and pale, seemed small within its confines.

How would he find a way to free her from her life's lot? Bernard's mouth tightened, his lower lip drawing up under his moustache.

"What is it, my lord?" asked Lady Maris. "Your face became so angry just now."

He looked back at his dinner partner, swiftly gathering his thoughts. "'Twas only that I reminded myself of aught that I'd forgotten. My pardons, my lady, for disturbing you."

She laughed—not daintily, but with true gusto. "Nay, my lord, you did not disturb me. The only distress I felt was for whomever should bring such an expression to your face."

Bernard's countenance did not relax—for Maris's concern was well founded. "Aye, my lady, and well it should." Then, with great effort, he turned his attention to his dinner partner, and, with a reference to the heads of their huddled fathers, commented, "'Tis our lot in life to be harangued into marriage, then, is it not my lady? We each have our duty—as the heirs to our fathers' lands."

Maris nodded slowly. "Aye, 'tis what my father would say—but he would not force me; and I do not intend to find a man whom I will marry." She looked up at him from under her lashes, and again, Bernard was struck by her beauty—if not daunted by her boldness—and added, "So you may rest easy, my lord, that we shall not find ourselves signed, sealed, and betrothed ere this wedding celebration is over."

Bernard opened his mouth, searching for something to say, but, mercifully, his father leaned over to interrupt. "My son handles the lute better than that vagabond over yonder, Lady Maris. Mayhap 'twould be his pleasure to sing for you."

Maris smiled so warmly that Harold blushed and kicked Bernard again. "Lord Harold, what a splendid suggestion. Mayhap you should hail the minstrel hither and he could do so." And then, under her breath, she added only for the ears of Bernard, "An' if you dare compare my eyes to stars, or my hair to the wind, I shall kick you myself under the table!"

Joanna slowly raised her goblet to sip deeply of the wine. It was warm and soothing as it coursed through her limbs, numbing her body and blanketing her mind with its gentle fog.

She forced herself to eat the capon that Harmon tore from the bird between them. He speared it with his knife—he did not permit her to carry her own, as harmless as it would have been—and tore into it with relish.

She hurt.

Marry, she hurt.

But she'd managed to speak with Leonard's sister before supper, who carried the message from the stable boy that her parcel had been moved—with Cleome the cat—into the loft of the stable. If she could remain focused on the possibility of freedom that the leather packet of gold coin might bring, she knew she could survive the rest of the se'ennight at Wyckford Heath.

She'd found Bernard, seated many rows away from the dais, immediately. He'd been looking for her—'twas clear, for she felt the weight of his stare as she followed Harmon to their seats. A smile began to curve her lips, but she stopped it before Harmon could notice.

Bernard had been so gentle, so kind and soothing to her. His face haunted her dreams, along with the memory of his pleasantly-heavy hands—pinning up her braid, covering hers in the garden…and the softness of his mouth touching hers. Warmth and a shiver, inexplicably opposite sensations, traveled through her body—warming her as the wine had not—and she wondered what it would be like to be held in his strong arms, to be safe. To be secure. To be loved.

A covert glance at Harmon told Joanna that he was imbibing less than usual anight—most likely because of the jousting and melee tournament on the morrow. Bernard had somehow attracted the attention—the venomous attention —of her husband. She must warn him to stay away from her, else he might find himself the victim of Harmon's irrational anger—for, even though 'twas customary and expected to use blunted weapons at such celebratory tournaments, men had been injured and even killed in them.

And Joanna could not bear the thought of the gentle, brave Bernard sliced to ribbons.

"Ah…the oaf sings like a lady." Harmon's grating voice, somehow reaching inside her to make her cringe, pulled Joanna's attention from her own musings.

She froze, her hand closing around a crust of bread. It had not taken Joanna more than a few weeks of marriage to Harmon to learn that traps such as these were as common as the tiny pebbles ground into wheat bread. If she looked up, he'd accuse her of casting her eyes upon another man…if she did not respond, he would be angry that she ignored him.

A loud guffaw and the retort, "Aye, he looks like a sot-head who doesn't know the sharp end of a sword from his arse!" caused Joanna to exhale in relief. 'Twas a friend of his, who sat across the table, to whom Harmon spoke.

But when she glanced up, looking toward the singer with

the smooth, mellow voice, her heart nearly stopped beating. It was Bernard.

Somehow, he'd come by a lute, and, even more oddly, he'd moved to the dais, where he stood, leaning against the side of the raised floor, plucking the strings of the lute...and singing.

And watching her.

Joanna ducked her head, turning her attention to the crust she'd mangled, but his image was burned into her memory. And even as his voice reached her ears, clear and deep as the River Wyckford, she saw his dark head and serious eyes.

He sang a common song, one about an oath between a knight and his lady...a vow made over a relic of the True Cross....But Bernard changed the words to sing of a promise made over a gillyflower, in a garden, to a maiden fair.

When she looked up again, her heart swelling hugely, Bernard no longer looked at her. Instead, he smiled upon several ladies who had taken seats near him, and who gazed up at him as though he was the Savior himself. At their urging, he ran his fingers over the strings and began to pluck another ballad from the lute.

Joanna measured her moments carefully: watching him for as long as she dared before Harmon might turn to look at her...and taking care to note every detail about him.

She would carry this memory—the memory of the man who'd been so gentle and kind—when she was gone.

When Harmon excused himself—if standing and walking off with a companion to play at dice could be called excusing himself—Joanna was surprised and pleased to be relieved of his volatile presence.

She stood and slipped among crowded trestle tables, dancers, and jugglers to make her way slowly out of the hall. Every step made her wince, and once, when an overly enthusiastic man-at-arms bumped into her shoulder, she gasped aloud from the pain.

"Does aught ail you, lady?"

Joanna had just reached the hallway that led to a row of chambers when this voice stopped her. She turned to see a young woman, of her age, with dark hair and fine clothing. "Nay, lady. I am merely a bit sore."

"I am Maris of Langumont," said the woman, stepping toward her. Concern lit her eyes. "I do not believe you, I am afraid. You are in some pain. I would try to help you."

Joanna rested her hand against the stone wall as a wave of dizziness washed over her. "I am Joanna of Swerthmoor, daughter of the Lord of Wyckford Heath. You are very kind to have a care for me when you do not know me."

"I have care for anyone who is ill or injured. I am a healer." She offered her arm. "Here, Lady Joanna, walk with me. We shall see what can be done for your pain."

"You are a healer? Nay, you are a lady." Joanna slipped her arm through Maris's, and allowed the taller woman to help her along.

"I am a great heiress, but I am also a healer. Now, tell me as we walk, what causes your pain? Have you had it long?"

Joanna gave a short, bitter laugh. "I've had pain since I wed my husband one year past."

The sound of heavy footsteps echoed in the corridor behind them, coming quickly and purposefully. Joanna started and sprang away from Maris, who looked at her in surprise. "What—"

"Joanna!" The voice was not the one she'd feared to hear, but 'twas familiar to her.

She turned to see Bernard striding toward them, and her heart leaped even as she darted her glance around to see that no one else was there.

"Lady Joanna," Bernard said as he approached. "I wish to have a word with you." He glanced at Maris, who appeared to be watching with very sharp eyes, and added, "If you would excuse us, my lady. I wish to speak with Jo-Lady Joanna." His gaze raked over Joanna, touching her from head to toe as though to assure himself that she was all right.

She raised her face high to look up at him, for her head reached only to the top of his broad chest. "Lord Bernard... I did not know you to be such a fine singer." His eyes were dark, shadowed by the flickering torchlight, and his mouth set in a firm line that echoed the straightness of his neat moustache.

"Many thanks, my lady," he replied, a startled look passing over his face. "But I would wish—"

"Did you not hear Lord Bernard as he sang such beautiful ballads this eve?" Joanna turned casually to Maris. "I trow, there's never been a minstrel with such a rich voice."

"Aye, 'tis so," Maris replied, her gaze moving from one to the other. "Lord Bernard, Lady Joanna is in some pain, and I was just about to—"

"You are hurt? I bethought that the veil was to hide something!" His face darkened further as he tore the flimsy covering from her head, even as Joanna tried to duck aside.

"Mary, Mother of God...." Maris breathed.

Bernard's hand fell to his sword even as he reached gently to touch the tender swelling on the side of her face. "He does not deserve to live...." he ground out. "I'll kill the worm, by God!"

"Bernard, nay!" Joanna grasped his arm, clutching hard ridges of muscle. "Nay, you cannot—do you not be a fool. I am his wife. He can do with me what he will." She looked up at him and saw a frightening rage in his eyes. "I belong to him."

Maris stepped forward, brushing one of Joanna's thick braids back from her temple to look more closely at the bruising all along her face. "He deserves to die, he who would do this. Come, Joanna, I'll tend you in my chamber." When Bernard would speak, she looked up at him, "Nay, Bernard— you cannot attend her. 'Twould not be meet. Your task is to ensure that her husband does not return, looking for her, until midnight at the least. Now go, you."

"'Tis a good thing you do not wish to wed, Lady Maris—for I know of few men who would have a termagent such as you," Bernard muttered.

Joanna drew back, insulted for her new friend and shocked that he would utter such words, but Maris merely laughed. "'Tis my own secret—and now yours—that that is the way I wish it to be. Now make haste!"

Bernard took Joanna's hand, raising it to his lips and brushing his mouth over her palm and the sensitive inside of her wrist. Prickles of warmth skittered up her spine, and she breathed a faint gasp at the unexpected pleasure. A soft tickling of his moustache, then his warm lips pressed one last kiss on the back of her hand before he released it. "Joanna, would that I could protect you now….But I cannot—not yet. I will find a way, my lady. Have a care anight, and I will see you on the morrow." He turned to Maris, giving a faint bow, and added, "My thanks, my lady, for caring for her." He took two steps, stopped, and turned back, holding Joanna's veil. "I shall wear your favor on the lists tomorrow." Then he strode off.

"Come, Joanna." Maris once again slipped her arm through hers.

"'Tis dangerous for Bernard," Joanna said as they paced along the corridor. "Harmon—my husband—bears ill will toward him."

Maris looked at her, faint amusement showing in her face. "It would appear that Bernard can protect himself, Joanna. I am most concerned with you and your fate." The humor faded from her expression. "Here." She stopped in front of a door and opened it for them to enter. She spoke immediately to the young servant within. "Anna, do you sit without the chamber and knock should anyone approach." As her maid hurried to do her bidding, Maris gently pulled Joanna into the chamber and directed her to sit on the bed.

"Now, let us get that gown off. I trow there is more hidden beneath it."

Her bruises were so painful that Joanna was forced to allow Maris to assist her in disrobing, and when the other woman saw the marks and cuts on her back, arms, and legs, she knelt beside her, clasping her hand. Tears filled her eyes as she looked up at Joanna. "How do you bear it?" she asked. "How do you bear it so bravely, so strongly?" A gentle hand smoothed down her back—the first touch Joanna had received on bare skin that was not designed to hurt.

She moved her shoulders in an awkward shrug. "I have no choice. 'Tis my lot." She pressed her hand onto Maris's. "I could hide in my chambers all the day—'tis true—or end my life—or cower and squeak like no more than a mouse. An' there are times when I must try to be invisible, and there are times when the merest noise causes me to jump—for it might be him."

She took a deep breath as Maris rose. "I am most likely damned, for I cannot accept my lot. I know that I must be obedient to my husband—that he owns me, and may do with me what he will…but I cannot accept that."

"And well you should not!" Maris returned to the bed, carrying a thick leather satchel. She flipped it open, and it unrolled, exposing small pouches, packets wrapped in leather and parchment, and other utensils. "God helps those who help themselves, and accepting of such a life is foolish. You will be killed if he continues like this."

Joanna drew in her breath deeply as Maris began to smooth a soothing salve onto her bruised face, and down to the shoulder that had been jolted by the man-at-arms in the hall.

She took some small, dried green leaves and, crumbling them in her hands, sprinkled them over the salve on Joanna's shoulder where Harmon's knife had cut her. "Woad. Dried woad will ease the pain and start the healing. Jesu, no man should be allowed to live after this!"

Joanna laughed bitterly. "Aye. There are many a night when I contemplate ways to send him to his death. But 'twould be almost as much of a sin—more, aye—than what he does to me." She passed a shaking hand over her hair, pushing a thick lock from her face. "But I've dreamed of it."

"You are a better woman than I—for I would have done it after the first moon of enduring such treatment, damnation or nay." Maris pressed a strip of cloth onto the herb-sprinkled salve. "Can your father not help? Can you not flee to him for protection?"

"'Tis my father who gave me to Harmon. He does not care—he says what all men say: that a wife belongs to her husband."

"Another reason I shall never wed," Maris said, dabbing something onto another fresh cut. It stung, but not so much as the leather whipcord had, and Joanna barely flinched.

"You shan't wed?"

"Nay. My father will not force me, and I do not wish to be bound to a man."

Joanna shook her head slowly. "I do not mind being wed—but to a man such as Harmon, 'tis hell. When I leave, I shall have no—" Realizing what she'd said, she bit back her words and froze into silence.

"Leave?"

Joanna said nothing, cursing herself for letting her tongue relax.

"Is Bernard to help you to leave? Do you run off with him?" Maris looked sharply at her.

"Nay, oh nay! I would not allow it of him—or anyone. If Harmon does find me, he shall kill me—and whoever would be with me."

Joanna's pain began to ebb, and her head to clear as she continued to speak. "Harmon does not allow me to leave Swerthmoor, but he could not keep me from coming to my sister's wedding celebration, so I have this chance—this one chance—to run from him. I have been saving gold pieces, waiting for this chance—he does not notice the small amount missing."

"Where will you go?"

"I know of an abbey nearby—as I grew up here—and the sisters will take me in, and hide me. I shall live in a cloister all the rest of my days. If Harmon does not find me, and follow me, I shall be safe. And...." She hesitated.

"Is there more?"

"Aye. My father bears a map of this keep, for there is a tale of great treasure hidden in the warren of secret tunnels beneath it. It is through them I will take my flight so as to get without the walls unseen."

"Do you have the map?"

"Nay. And my husband has demanded that I obtain it from my father." Her lips curved into a slight smile. "I will make a false copy of the map and give it to Harmon—and use the true one for my own purposes."

Maris stopped her work to grin at her. "Clever girl. For even should he attempt to follow you, he will be lost."

"Aye."

They were silent for a moment—Joanna enjoying the touch of a healer and the moment where she need not fear that her peace would be interrupted. Maris worked quickly and precisely, and she was obviously skilled, for the pain was already fading.

When she finished her work, Maris carefully rolled up the leather satchel and walked to a large trunk beside the fireplace. As she turned, she spoke.

"What of Bernard, Joanna? How does he figure into this scheme?"

'Twas a question Joanna had avoided in her own mind, and now she was face to face with it. "I do not know. Any involvement with me will anger Harmon...but Bernard has promised to free me from my husband. In sooth, I do not know how he would—other than to murder him." She looked at Maris, who stood solemnly watching her. "He is an honorable man. He would not do that."

"Do you care for him?"

"Aye." Oh, aye. She could not think of him without a smile

starting to rim her face, and a warmth bubbling within—and a sadness that he'd come into her life so tardily.

She stood, thrusting those thoughts away. "I must take your leave now, Maris. I am so very grateful that we have met—and I thank you for tending to me."

There was an awkward moment before Maris stepped forward to embrace her gingerly—but even so, Joanna drew in her breath at the pain. "Have a care, Joanna. I would sit with you on the morrow to watch the jousting."

"Thank you again. I will find my own way to my chamber." And with that, Joanna slipped out the door and back into her life of hell.

IV.

As it was most often, Bernard's instinct was accurate. He made an early visit to the stables and found Joanna within.

She halted in the act of climbing a ladder into the loft of the stable when he approached, and for the barest moment, a flicker of anxiety crossed her face. But then, she gestured for him to join her as she continued her ascension.

"Good morrow, my lady," Bernard said in a low voice as he stepped onto the thick hay, joining her in the loft. He ducked nearly double to walk toward her, finally sinking into a spot next to her.

"Good morrow, my lord." She glanced briefly at him, then, as though shy in his presence, turned her attention to Cleome—who nestled comfortably in a pile of straw. As he watched, she withdrew a cloth-wrapped parcel, unfolding it to reveal a bit of meat and cheese.

"Are you well?" he asked, scrutinzing her as well as he could in the dim light. "I had to see that Harmon did you no further ill last eve."

"Nay. He returned to the chamber very late, and fell asleep immediately. 'Twas strange, as he had not had much ale to drink at dinner." She fed Cleome from her hand.

Bernard could not keep a satisfied smile from his face. He'd taken care to keep Harmon from returning to the chamber by soundly defeating the man in a very long game of dice. Though Harmon's parting words were an angry threat to meet him on the lists this day, Bernard gave little thought to the warning. "Good."

He reached for her hand, gently taking the remainder of Cleome's food from her fingers, and turning Joanna to face him. "Come hither, my lady. I wish for a token from you before I joust this day."

"But you have my favor," she replied in confusion.

"I speak not of that favor, but of another, sweeter, one." With a gentle tug, he brought her shoulders and face closer to him. "Now, where we cannot be seen, might I take a soft kiss from you, my lady? As though I were going into battle?"

Her lips curved softly, and she ducked her head. "Aye, my lord, though I am not well-practiced in the art of kissing. I would that you should teach me."

Her simple statement caused a great surge of affection and desire to course through him. What other arts would she need tutoring in?

"Joanna…." He fitted his hands around her face, cupping her chin with his palms and curving his fingers about the back of her ears. Her braids rested heavily against his wrists, and her scent filled him, even before he brought his mouth to cover hers. She raised her eyes trustingly, and for the moment, he was taken aback that she—who had been so abused by a man—should so easily come to trust him. He was humbled, for he would never have been able to open himself thus.

Her lips parted as he covered them, and the hint of warm moistness tasted as it had before—of strawberries and freshness. This time, however, Bernard took more than the faint brushing of lips in the garden. He fitted his mouth to hers, nibbling on her lips, delving into her mouth, inhaling the essence of Joanna.

She gave a soft moan that vibrated against his lips, sending a new wave of arousal through him. She lifted her hands from their place in the hay, shifting so that she leaned into him, and brought her fingers to gently touch the curls on his head. His scalp came alive at that unfamiliar touch, tingles shooting down the back of his neck and along his spine. Then, as she kissed him with growing fervor, her hands smoothed down over his ears and to his shoulders, where their heat burned him, but their weight was barely noticeable.

Pulling her to his chest, so that their torsos fit together as they knelt in the straw, he deepened the kiss—fighting to keep from frightening her with his desire, but needing to get his fill. It was the softness, the gentleness, the sweet freshness of her scent that he held and wanted…and through the haze of irrational desire, vowed he would have.

At last, she pulled away, and he opened his eyes to see whether he'd taken too much from her. But the swollen curve of her lips, and the soft light in her eyes told him that, nay, she had been plundered no more than what she herself had desired. When she raised her hand to touch his cheek, smoothing the bristles of hair that grew there, he smiled and her fingers slipped near his mouth. She traced his lips, hidden by the moustache, before he captured her hand for a last kiss in her palm.

"Enough, now, my lady—else I shall not be at my best on the lists this day." With reluctance, he set her away from him and moved himself back so as to be out of easy reach of temptation.

Marry, but she was beautiful-—all plump-lipped and heavy-eyed, with her hair still perfectly braided and coiled in sworls on her head.…He nearly pulled her to him again, but caught himself in time.

"I shall carry that favor in my heart, and this one,"—he pulled a scrap of white from the sleeve of his tunic— "on my lance."

"Oh, Bernard, you had best not. Please, should Harmon see it.…"

"He would recognize this piece of cloth as yours?" he asked, pulling it through his hands. It was soft, as she was, and smelled of her—and well he knew, for he'd slept with it on his pillow the last eve.

"Oh, yes, Bernard. Harmon has the most…discerning eye for such things." She looked at him with such fear in eyes that had been dazed with desire only moments before.

"Then I shall wear this favor near my heart," he told her. With a quick jerk, he had his over tunic off, and then his *sherte*, leaving him bare-chested. She drew in her breath deeply, and Bernard could not help the swell of pride that she should react thus. After all, she had been the victim of a man built less powerfully than he.

She watched him as he wrapped the white linen veil around his solid, well-furred chest, and, as though she could not remain away any longer, moved forward to take the ends of the veil and tie it herself. Then her hands slipped boldly—so boldly for his shy, demure Joanna—up through the thick coarse hair and over the top of his shoulders, sending the same searing heat that came from her gaze.

"You are wondrous," she told him. "And 'tis all the more miraculous that you have the gentleness of a mare about you. With such strength, you could rule the simple life of any-one."

Touched, and shamed that his fellow man should be the cause of such grief, Bernard reached to stroke her face, gently, over the purpling bruise. "One with my strength has no need to prove his power at the expense of a weaker one. Nor should any man need have that urge. I am sorry that you should know other yourself, but, Joanna, I will protect you. I will find a way."

She tipped her face to touch her mouth to his, then drew back before the kiss could deepen. "Aye, Bernard…and God be with you on the lists today—for Harmon does bear you ill. You do not intend to meet him, do you?"

His eyes jolted open in surprise. "But of course I will meet him, Joanna! Knocking the bastard on his arse will be the greatest pleasure for me. Would that I could do more dam-age, but of course, I cannot in such a tournament. But I vow that you'll have naught to worry you on this eve, for Harmon will be in no shape to raise a hand to you."

Sweat trickled down his back, and along the sides of his cheeks, as the noon sun beat down upon him. Bernard shifted the heavy, straight lance in his hand, testing its weight even as he reined back Rock from his eagerness to leap forward.

A roar of approval rose from the crowd that lined both sides of the lists as a lance found its mark on a second pass, dumping an unfortunate jouster onto the dusty ground. The victor raised his lance and galloped along the front of the stands, kicking up more dust and causing a greater shout from the crowd.

"Lord Bernard of Derkland…challenged by Sir Marven de Hanover."

A thrill of anticipation shot through him as Bernard wheeled Rock forward to take their place at one end of the list. As his squire handed him his shield, he glanced briefly at the crowd, in hopes of locating Joanna, but did not place her before the signal to commence was given.

Bernard did not know Sir Marven, and he did not care why the man challenged him—'twas likely for no other reason than the opportunity to gain a greater purse. He looked down the list at his opponent, noting that he was a solid, well-built man who rode a passable mount. Though size was helpful in most competitions, in jousting it was not as important as skill and balance. A large man could easily be unseated by a skilled jouster, regardless of whether the opponent was of his size or nay.

'Twas likely why Harmon had chosen to threaten Bernard thus—the man was not fool enough to believe he could best Bernard in sword play—or even in any combat requiring skill of the mind, he thought dryly—but at the least the man had a chance at unseating him in a joust. Not a large chance, Bernard smirked, but a chance never the less.

He snapped to attention as the signal sounded, and dug his heels into Rock's straining body. The destrier was ready for his first action of the day, and leapt forward, taking one bounding step where the opponent's mount took three. Wind rushed over him, cooling Bernard's sweaty face and neck, as he positioned the lance, aiming it for his opponent's right shoulder. One good hit with the blunted lance—for 'twas not meant to injure, only to unseat—and Sir Marven would tumble to the ground.

The lance lay across his thigh, pinned firmly under his arm and held in place by Bernard's left hand, whilst the other leveled his shield to protect himself. When the lance struck the shield of his opponent, it barely moved, as its aim was true, and Marven fell neatly off his mount and onto the ground.

Bernard turned Rock to ride back again, glancing at the man to assure himself he'd attained no hurts, and then along the line of spectators, still hoping to see Joanna. He was rewarded this time, for he saw her, sitting next to Maris near the middle of the stands. He nodded in the general direction of the crowd, but when he placed his hand over his heart— and the hidden favor that rested beneath his tunic—'twas meant for her.

He galloped back to where his squire—and his father— waited as the next challenge was announced.

"Fine job, son," greeted Harold as his son wheeled up to him. "'Twasn't a sufficient test of your abilities—but 'twas over quickly and simply." Coughing and waving the dust out of his eyes, he looked up with a smirk. "Do you not wear the favor of your lady?"

"Aye, that I do—but 'tis not for your eyes, Father." He handed the lance to his squire, Rowan, and swiped an open hand over his damp curls. "And do you not give me a look with that smugness, for you have no reason to believe your machinations are true."

Harold's thick brows rose up a high forehead. "Oh, aye? And did I not see you with mine own eyes head-to-head with

Lady Maris on the last eve, and did I not see you follow in her steps out of the Hall? You do not fool me with such protestations, as I saw where your eyes led over yonder." He gestured toward the spectator stands, and still the satisfied smile curved his face.

Bernard's response was lost as his name was again announced, coupled with a different challenger. With a smile of pleasure, he kicked Rock, and they bounded off for the lists.

The powerful thrust of his opponent's lance was poorly aimed, but nearly unseated Bernard on the second pass. He held firm in the saddle, taking the brunt of the blunted lance in the shoulder of the arm with which he wielded his own lance. Even through the mail that protected his body, Bernard felt the strength of the man's blow.

On the third pass, the same lance struck the same odd spot on Bernard's shoulder, and he cursed aloud as the pain intensified. His aim was true, though, and he took pleasure in watching his stocky opponent waver, then fall from the saddle just as they passed each other. With a grunt of triumph, Bernard allowed his own lance to his rest on his thighs, and prodded Rock into a canter back to his squire.

Groaning in pain, Bernard slid from the saddle as Rowan leapt to take the shield from him. Harold and his own squire attended him as well. "God's blood—that bastard had poor aim to strike twice in the same wrong place." He tried to rotate his shoulder, but the throbbing heat radiated up his shoulder and along his arm, fading over to his shoulder blade.

"Aye," Harold said. He began to pull Bernard's tunic off his shoulder, but his son jerked his arm away.

"Father, there is no need to play nursemaid to me—especially when there are others watching. The injury is not that severe."

But he had barely spoken those words when his name was called yet again. "*Peste!*" Bernard turned to whistle for his horse, but Rowan had heard the challenge and brought Rock immediately. He pulled himself into the saddle, smothering a wince, and took a new lance offered by Harold's squire.

"Stay in your seat!" Harold called after him as they galloped off.

Swiping the sweat from his face yet again, Bernard eyed his third opponent. It wasn't Harmon—though he'd been expecting to be called to challenge him at any moment. This man again was someone that he did not know—and he appeared very solid and heavy in his saddle. The horse was fine—enough for Bernard to notice in appreciation—though not nearly as perfect as his own Rock.

He'd barely settled the lance in his lap, attempting to keep it from weighting on his injured shoulder until the very last moment, when the signal was given. Rock leapt forward before Bernard even gave him the heel of his boot, and suddenly the wind streamed over his face as they galloped down the list.

Thwack! The impact of his opponent's lance struck Bernard even as his own bounced off the top of the other man's shoulder. The power of his thighs gripping Rock was the only thing that kept him from tumbling onto the ground; and his hands loosened, dropping the lance onto the dusty ground.

A loud exclamation rose from the crowd—mayhap because it was the first time Bernard had missed a hit, or because he'd taken a good one—but he barely heard it through the searing pain that shot down his arm. The other knight's lance had caught him again near the injury he'd sustained in the last challenge, and now agonizing heat caused black spots to dance before his eyes.

Gritting his teeth, Bernard turned Rock and headed back to his side of the list—keeping the dancing mount to a trot to give himself time to catch his breath. Rowan met him there, with a choice of four lances to choose from. Again, taking as much time as he could, Bernard hefted each one in his hand before selecting the first one.

He gave a quick nod to his father's questioning glance,

then, steeling himself for one—mayhaps two—more passes, he kicked Rock into motion. He managed to make it through the next two charges without being unsaddled— though 'twas a close one on the last. He did not manage, however, to unseat the other man—and, instead, took one more hit to his shoulder.

"Who have you angered thus to keep you in the lists?" asked Harold jovially as Bernard returned and dismounted, tossing his shield to Rowan.

Breathing heavily, Bernard nearly discounted the jest, but then realized that without meaning to, his father spoke the truth. 'Twas Harmon's doing, most like. For Bernard knew few of the men here, and none of his challengers thus far. His intent was likely to tire him before meeting him on the lists, and mayhap causing him some injury. "Bastard."

His father looked at him, but Bernard dismissed him with a wave of his hand. "'Tis naught of your concern."

At last, after Bernard was called thrice more, the challenge he'd been waiting for was announced. A fresh wave of anger—and determination—rushed through him as he selected a lance. He'd saved himself as much as possible during the last passes, now knowing Harmon's game.

With a glance toward the stands, Bernard stroked Joanna's veil, feeling its softness clinging to his sweaty torso. If for no other than her, he'd see Harmon face-down onto the ground.

Bernard and Rock settled into their place at one end of the list, the stallion dancing with impatience as though sensing that there was more at stake with this challenge. The signal broke the tension and they leapt forward, galloping toward Harmon at full speed.

Thwump! Bernard nearly screamed aloud as his opponent's lance passed by his shield, driving into his injury, just where his arm and shoulder met. He saw black and heard a chortling laugh as they passed by, his own lance slipping off into nothing and nearly causing him to topple. He could barely breathe, the pain was so intense, and he realized what had happened.

He'd given Harmon too little credit—for the man had selected very skilled jousters to challenge him—not to up-end him from the saddle, but to injure him in a manner that would keep him from his best. All of them had struck the same place—purposely. And now Harmon had chosen to put the finish on him before claiming victory.

Weary, but his teeth clenching hard enough to take his mind from his throbbing shoulder, Bernard chose another lance and, adjusting his shield, turned to face his opponent.

Twice more.

They charged as the signal was given, galloping down the list toward each other at breakneck speed. Bernard felt sweat slicken his hand, but he held fast, determined to knock the bastard onto the ground this time.

He concentrated as Harmon sped toward him, picking out his faint slant in the saddle, looking for an opening—and found it. He leveled the long lance, aiming, forgetting the pain in his shoulder, and just as they met, just as the other halberd brushed his shoulder, he twisted slightly and found his mark. The other lance slipped harmlessly up and over Bernard's shield and the other man teetered in his seat.

Bernard and Rock roared past Harmon, and only the disappointed groan from the crowd told him that his opponent had recovered. He cursed at the luck of the devil, and spun his mount around to choose his last lance.

Breathing heavily, Bernard took little care in selecting the halberd offered by Rowan—he trusted his squire, and meant only to get back to the lists for the final pass. His shoulder's ache had lessened slightly, but when he moved to steady his long halberd, the pain shot down his arm.

Last time.

He sensed the fury and hatred emanating from the other man—waves of it came across the field—and it seemed as though the watchers felt it too, for a near hush fell over them. Only the sound of Rock stamping his feet, and the jingle of mail and bridle, fell on his ears…or mayhap 'twas just that he concentrated so solidly.

The cry to arms bellowed from the announcer, and he kicked Rock forward. They nearly flew through the air, smoothly, as one. The intensity of his pain diminished as he sighted the lance on Harmon's shield, focusing on the place that would dump him from the saddle.

He leaned forward, urging Rock on, holding the lance steady as they barreled toward Harmon. One moment more …he fought the hovering pain as he gripped the lance, steadying it, ready to thrust it forward….

Thump!

Pain crashed over him as he took the brunt of Harmon's own blow in his shoulder, even as his lance connected with the other man's shield. With a howl of rage, Bernard held steady and gave one last thrust as they passed by.

He heard the roar of the crowd dimly through hot, white streaks that shot up his arm and across his shoulder. Gasping for air, he turned Rock around in time to see Harmon struggling to his feet. A faint lift of one side of his mouth was all he could manage as he galloped past the stands and to his father and squire.

Bastard.

V.

Joanna smoothed the crinkling paper, examining the black marks that identified the warren of tunnels beneath Wyckford Heath Hall. Even as a young girl, she'd heard stories of the passages that led out of the keep, but had never been able to find them.

She'd also heard the tales that treasures hidden centuries earlier by the Saxons during the Anglo invasion were still in the tunnels below. Therein lay Harmon's interest in the map—whilst hers rested only in the freedom it would gain her.

She rolled the map and tucked it behind a loose stone near the fireplace; for she hadn't time to make a false sketch for Harmon before he returned from the tournament.

At the thought of the competition, a great rush of warmth surged through her as she recalled the mighty, powerful Bernard—how he rode his steed, and wielded his lance in too many challenges to count. She'd watched him, swelling with pride and nearly crying when he was struck with bone-shattering blows—yet he'd remained in his saddle as Harmon had not.

Maris had rushed to see to his hurts after the last challenge, while Joanna returned to her chamber, grieving the fact that she could not attend him as well. Instead, she relived the gentle moment with him in the stable loft, where they'd come together in a passionate kiss that still caused her heart to race. She might be damned for wanting and kissing another man whilst she was bound to another, but in her heart of hearts, she believed that God—who helped those who helped themselves—would not judge her too harshly. For was not love the greatest gift? And Bernard was the first person in her life to truly show her love.

The door to the chamber flew open and Joanna turned, startled, to see Harmon limp in. His face held no expression as he stared at her. Her middle dropped and she moved to stand by her stool at the fire.

Without relieving her from his gaze, Harmon shoved the door behind him, and it closed with a dull thud that made sweat spring to her temples. Her voice wavered. "May I tend to you—"

"Silence!" His voice lashed across the room.

Joanna swallowed, her heart thumping so hard that she thought it would burst from her chest. Harmon took a step toward her...then another. "Do you gloat at my defeat this day?"

She did not move—even to step away—and replied, "Nay, my lord, I do not—"

"Bitch!" he snarled.

The slap sent her head crashing into the stone wall, and sharp pain radiated along the side of her face. Warm, metallic liquid filled her mouth. A pounding reverberated in her temple where she'd struck the wall.

He stared at her, his harsh breathing rasping in the air between them. "Do you dare to laugh at me? I would show you the error of your ways, Joanna."

Her fingers became ice and the room shifted. "My lord, please—"

"Did I not tell you to be *silent*?"

A fist plowed into her breast, and another into her abdomen. Her breath disappeared and she could not gather enough air to cry out....She sank to the floor, her hand splaying over the rough stone. Her fingers spasmed over the slate as his booted foot smashed into her hip.

"Where is the map?" Her stool crashed onto the floor next to her, splintering in pieces and barely missing her head.

The map. Somehow she dragged herself from the pain to realize that he would not kill her until he had it. Struggling to draw a breath, she whispered, "I do not have it."

"You do not have it?" he screamed, lashing out with his foot.

Joanna tried to roll away, but she found herself trapped between Harmon and the unyielding wall. Fists and feet pummeled her, driving her into a corner from which she had no escape but the warm memories of Bernard.

Bernard endured the excruciating pain inflicted upon him by Maris's direction to Harold and Rowan. His arm had become dislodged from his shoulder with Harmon's last thrust, and it took the strength of the two men to pop it back into place.

That done, he promptly slid into the comfort of blackness even as he heard Maris giving straight direction to Rowan.

When Bernard awoke, it was evening—and well into the evening meal. Rowan, as a good squire should, stayed with him to tend to his needs—but 'twas obvious he was as hungered as Bernard. They went down to find a place at the long trestle tables, Bernard's injured arm strapped to his torso by an adamant Maris.

Joanna was not at dinner—though her evil husband sat near her father, the Lord of Wyckford Heath. Bernard crimped his lips at the thought of Harmon's manipulations this day, and he felt that same penetrating fury he'd experienced earlier emanating from across the loud hall.

Once, Harmon turned to look at him, steadily, for a long moment, and Bernard felt prickles erupt along the back of his neck. There was a self-satisfied glint in the man's eyes, accompanied by dark fury. Though he knew himself to be the stronger and more-skilled fighter, Bernard felt a queasiness curdle in his middle. The man was pure evil.

A sudden burning desire to see Joanna—to hold and kiss her, and to whisk her away from her monstrous husband—caused Bernard to bolt to his feet. Now, whilst Harmon busied himself with dinner…now, mayhap he could chance to find her in her chamber.

Lord Harold, who sat head-to-head with Maris of Langumont's father, looked up and gave his son a knowing smile. Bernard drew his brows together in a glower and gave an angry shake of his head before turning to stalk out of the hall. When would his father give up the chance to meddle in his life?

It did not take much to learn where the chamber of Harmon, Lord of Swerthmore, and his wife, Lady Joanna, boarded. One simple question to the stable boy Leonard, and Bernard found himself hurrying back into the keep and down a dark, torchlit passageway to a chamber on the second floor.

He knocked boldly, caring not that anyone might hear him—wanting only to see the woman who had somehow become everything to him in the last two days.

There was a long pause, and then just as he raised his hand to pound again, the door cracked open…then was flung wide.

"Lady Maris!" Bernard stepped in to find the room warm and sunny with a blazing fire and three candles. "What do you here?"

He did not need to wait for her answer, for in the wake of his words, he saw his Joanna lying on her side in a large bed. She was curled into a ball, her hand fisted under her cheek, her eyes closed and her breathing fast and shallow.

When he saw the cuts on her face and hand, the black and purpling on her face, he swayed and had to clutch at the bedpost as white rage poured through him. "Joanna!" he choked, moving to her side to touch her clammy cheek, to trace gently an angry cut along her fair cheek.

"She is well hurt," Maris told him. "She was beaten nearly to death by Harmon." Even as she spoke, she ground herbs with a small mortar and pestle.

Joanna remained still, only her short puffs of air belying that she yet lived. Bernard felt rage and guilt swell within him as he looked down at her battered body. "She must be taken from him, Lady Maris, and then *I will kill him.*"

How could he have left her to this man's anger? He should have known—*known*—that Harmon, having lost the battle, would take out his fury on Joanna.

'Twas his own fault, Bernard's, that Joanna now lay still as death—for if he'd not angered Harmon so, the bastard would not have been propelled to injure her thus.

"We must take her from here, now."

Maris shook her head regretfully. "Nay, Bernard, 'twould not be best for her to be moved. She has two broken ribs and she is very, very weak. Can you not settle a guard here?"

Bernard snorted. "In the home of the father who wed her to this monster? Aye, I'll do it, but I do not know how long he'll allow it."

"Allow it?" Maris echoed. "When his daughter has been near beaten to the death, her own father will not allow it?"

Bernard shook his head, sick at heart. What could he do to ensure Joanna's safety? With all his being, he desired nothing more than to stalk back to the great hall and plunge a dagger into the throat of Harmon.

Such an action would free Joanna from the man, certainly, but would leave Bernard hanging for murder and Joanna unencumbered to be wed to another man. Much as he had the blood lust to do away with Harmon, Bernard knew he could not also allow Joanna to belong to anyone but him.

He stood, leaned to press a kiss to the cool, still cheek of his beloved, and turned to Maris. "I will fetch my father's men-at-arms and send them here anon. Please have a care for your-self and my beloved. I will find some way to tend to this."

VI.

Through a heavy murkiness, Joanna heard a haze of voices …staccato bursts of anger.

She struggled to open her eyes, but it felt as though her lashes were weighted onto her cheeks. Pain radiated through her body, echoing everywhere so that she could not tell where it began … and where it ended.

Her senses faded, and she slipped into the depths of still-ness, buffered from the pain.

She heard the voices again, and they pulled her from her deepest, safest place. They tugged her relentlessly from the numb cocoon that kept the agony at bay…and as she became more aware, the heaviness of her hurts throbbed and battered her body, even though she lay still.

This time, she managed to pry her eyes open—the only part of her body that moved—to see Harmon holding some-thing in his hand—something flowing, and white. His face was a mask of fury, and even as she watched, he whirled in anger upon another figure in the room—a woman, it appeared—and turned upon her, grabbing her shoulders and tossing her aside.

The other woman screamed, then fell to the floor, silenced. And Harmon rounded upon her, Joanna, in her bed.

"Wake up, you bitch!"

Hands seized her shoulders, and she was jerked up, her

head snapping back as a scream choked in the back of her throat. Red-hot pain stabbed her head, flashing through her body. She could not control the wail that erupted from her abdomen and burst from her mouth.

"What is this? What is this?" he was shrieking. Somehow, through all of the hazy pain, she felt the spittle fly from his mouth, flecking her face. "Whore!" He released her, and she fell back onto the bed, her teeth jarring together.

She struggled to make sense of what he raged about, fighting to focus her eyes on the white cloth that he brandished whilst she prepared herself for the blows and pain yet to come.

"You thought to cuckold me?"

He raged about the room, not yet deigning to take his fury out on her physically…but she knew 'twas only a matter of moments before the blows fell. What was he angry about?

"My squire heard you in the stable—with your lover! He saw you make the whore of yourself—and 'twill be the last time you do!" He leaned forward, menacing, over her. His eyes were wild and yellow in his face, and Joanna nearly fainted as his words penetrated.

His hand closed around her throat, squeezed and released, so that she coughed in agony. She gathered all of her strength, trying to twist away…but in its battered state, her pain-filled body was no match for his iron grip. His fingers closed again, and she reached to claw them away as spots of black light flashed at the corners of her eyes.

Death. 'Twould be welcome—'twould be heaven compared to living her life in this fear.

Bernard.

His face flashed before her as the life began to seep from her body.

And suddenly, Joanna had one last chance. She forced herself to form the single syllable that might save her life.

"Map."

As though 'twere magic, the word, grating even to her ears,

caused Harmon to lessen his grip. She sucked in a huge breath of air, her body shuddering with the effort, and gasped the word again. "Map."

"Where is it? *Where is the map, Joanna?*"

As she'd hoped, greed proved a stronger force to Harmon than anger. She managed to nod her head, barely.

"You have it?" His hands flew to grip her shoulders and she gasped in pain. "Where is it, bitch? Tell me and I might spare your life!"

"Fire…place," she whispered, streaks of agony catching her breath and making the words nearly unbearable.

He was on her in a moment. "You *burned* it?" The rage turned his face into a grey stone mask with burning yellow eyes, and he reached for her with clawed hands.

With all of her effort, she half-rolled away, screaming, "*Nay!*"

He whirled away from her, toward the fireplace, and began to pull on the stones, kicking them, shoving at them. "Is it here?"

Joanna stifled her sobs of pain as she struggled to rise from the bed.

She managed to pull herself up to sit, her head spinning crazily and her mouth dry with pain, when she saw movement out of the corner of her eye. If she'd had any strength, she would have screamed in shock and fear…but when she saw Maris of Langumont pull to her feet from the floor, Joanna's fears subsided.

She watched as Maris took a heavy wooden bowl and, stepping behind Harmon, brought it down with a loud *crack!* onto his head.

He slumped instantly into a heap at the fireplace hearth.

Maris turned to Joanna, staggering slightly as she made her way to the bed. "Come, we must go!"

She slipped an arm around her, and eased her off the bed. Joanna tried to find her feet, but the room spun and she sagged against the taller woman. "Come," Maris puffed, half-dragging her to the door. "Come." 'Twas as though she said the words to keep herself moving.

They made it to the door, and a moan from Harmon nearly caused Joanna to faint. Maris managed to prop Joanna against the wall, and Joanna, for her part, kept her knees from buckling whilst her friend got the heavy door open. They fairly fell into the dark, empty passageway beyond her chamber, and Maris shut the door behind.

Joanna summoned more energy and managed to wrap her arm around Maris's waist and to actually take a step. They paced slowly down the hall until they came to another corridor. A small alcove recessed behind it, and Joanna pulled away toward the dark corner. "Go. You cannot...carry me...." she gasped. "I will stay. Safe."

Maris hesitated, then seeing the wisdom of searching for someone who could carry an ill woman, gave a quick nod and stepped back, looking carefully to see if Joanna would be noticed should Harmon erupt from their chamber. "I'll get my father."

And she was gone.

Bernard raged into the great hall, pushing past revelers and serfs, using his free elbow as a battering ram. His eyes focused on the dais where Joanna's father sat...and where Harmon had also eaten his meal. He saw immediately that Harmon was no longer at his father-by-law's side, and worry for Joanna propelled his feet even faster.

"Lord Wyckford," he bawled, charging up to the high table, caring little that he interrupted a jester at his tricks. "Lord Wyckford, I must speak with you!" He nearly leapt upon the dais, and was at the man's side in one quick stride.

"Who are you to accost me so boldly?" The Lord of Wyckford shot a disdainful glance at Bernard, and buried his face in his goblet.

Bernard restrained the urge to knock the cup from his hand

and instead planted his one free hand on the table next to the man, bringing his face into his. "Your daughter Joanna lies near death in her chamber—"

"What say you?"

"And 'tis the fault of her husband that she has been beaten near to her grave! You must place guards at her door to keep him from further harming her."

Wyckford looked at him and blinked slowly. "Do you not give me orders in my own home," he grunted. "And I cannot interfere betwixt a man and his wife—for 'tis the law of the church that the wife is the chattel of her lord."

Bernard's rage blinded him. "She lies near death, man! She is your *daughter*!" He clenched his fist into the table and splinters pierced the skin under his nails.

Wyckford glanced over Bernard's shoulder and seemed to reconsider. The hall had grown quiet and all appeared to listen for his response. "I shall send guards as you have requested. But I do not relish coming between a husband and his wife…and you, sirrah, should have a care for yourself, else you are accused of worse. Now begone!"

Bernard's teeth creaked as he turned away, clamping his jaw in fury. He would send his own men, damn the man! He spun on his boots, jumped off the dais, and began to push his way out of the hall with the same force as he'd arrived.

The crowd melted away as he stalked through them, his face a set, still mask that likely brought fear to more than one man's heart. In a haze of anger, he started for the quarters of the men-at-arms in search of his own men…then again spun on his heel and started back down a long corridor.

Foolish! Whilst Bernard berated Wyckford and sought his own men, Harmon was nowhere to be found…and with a lump in his throat that threatened to choke him, Bernard had a fear that he knew where Harmon had gone.

He ran down the corridor, through the twisting passageway lit by flickering torches and silent as a tomb. Maris would not be able to stand up to Harmon should he appear…and

Joanna was so weak that one blow could send her to her grave.

His footsteps rang with hollow thuds as he dashed down the corridor and around the corner to the hallway leading to the chamber where Joanna lay. He stamped to a halt when he reached the room and saw that the door was slightly ajar.

A heavy fear settled over him as he prodded the door open with his toe, uncertain of what he would find. The door swayed open, silently, baring the chamber to his gaze. Bernard stepped onto the threshold and saw that the room was in shambles: stools overturned, the bed empty, clothing strewn about, the only light from a sputtering fire.

He started into the dim room, fear clutching him. Joanna was nowhere to be found, nor was Maris....

He did not know what alerted him, but aught caused Bernard to swivel just as something dark and fleeting *whooshed* toward him. Instinct propelled him out of harm's way, and Bernard groped, one-handed, for the dagger that he wore at his waist.

"Whoreson!" Harmon's grating voice reached his ears just as the man made his appearance from behind the door. "You thought to steal my wife from beneath my nose!" He brandished a long sword that gleamed in the flickering firelight. "Bastard—you will learn better from me now!"

Rage and satisfaction surged through Bernard....At last he would have his opportunity. They were well-matched— Harmon with two working arms and a sword, and Bernard with one arm and a dagger. He would relish the opportunity to fight the bastard to his death.

The slice of the sword cut through the air, stirring Bernard's hair, even as he drove a quick thrust of his short dagger at Harmon's shoulder. A squeal of rage told him he'd hit his target even as he whirled from the sword's upswing, narrowly missing being caught by it.

Spittle flecked the corner of Harmon's mouth as he charged toward Bernard. Fury drove his movements, making him careless, and 'twas simple for Bernard to feint aside at the last moment and allow Harmon to lurch past him. When the man turned, Bernard was waiting with his dagger poised and ready to bury in the man's throat—but for a shriek behind him.

Bernard recognized the voice as his beloved...and it distracted him only for an instant...but it was enough for Harmon to bring the flat of his sword down, knocking the dagger from Bernard's hand, sending it clattering to the floor.

Joanna shrieked again, but Bernard, having seen that she stood sagging in the doorway, knew that she was unhurt...and that he could not be distracted again. The sword came down, slicing through the tunic on his good shoulder, and with a roar of pent up rage, Bernard launched himself at Harmon whilst the sword was on that downswing.

His timing was perfect, and the two men fell to the rough stone floor, the sword pinned between them. Bernard was at a disadvantage now, with one arm bound to his side, and Harmon, fueled by crazy rage, drove his knee into Bernard's middle, then with a great shove, pushed him off. Bernard rolled to one side with a grunt, gasping for air, and his head slammed against the stone wall.

He struggled to roll back, but Harmon had already leapt to his feet and retrieved the grip on his sword, trapping Bernard against the wall.

"Prepare to die, bastard." He raised the sword with both hands, and drove it down.

Bernard pushed away from the wall, knocking into Harmon and unbalancing him just as the sword's point slammed into the floor. A scream of rage erupted from Harmon and he slashed the broken tip of the sword down again just as Bernard caught sight of his dagger lying on the floor. Joanna saw it, and staggered forward to kick it toward him.

The sword missed Bernard's throat by a hairsbreadth and, pulse thrumming wildly, he rolled again, closing his fingers over the coolness of his knife.

He became dimly aware of newcomers to the scene, crowding in the doorway, but Bernard was too ensconced in the fight for his life to note who they were. He tightened his grip on the dagger and prepared....

Harmon towered above him, brandishing the sword—all the more deadly now with its jagged edge—and Bernard tensed, ready....

It happened at once. The sword came down, Bernard thrust up, the dagger found its mark, and the sword clattered helplessly to the floor. Harmon screamed and collapsed in a heap next to it.

Bernard jerked to his feet and, bracing himself, stood staring down at the fallen man. He lay unmoving, blood oozing from the wound in his neck, his eyes closed in death.

"Joanna!" Bernard said, never taking his eyes off Harmon, but opening his arm for her. She moved swiftly, nearly falling into his embrace, and she clutched him as they stood staring down at her husband.

A loud clearing of the throat brought Bernard's attention to the audience that had clustered in the doorway.

"Aye, Merle, it appears that our machinations have all been for naught." Bernard's father, Lord Harold, coughed into his hand. "My son has a mind of his own."

"Aye, and my daughter, too," responded Merle of Langumont, tucking said daughter's arm through the crook of his elbow. "Now, let us help Bernard in ridding himself of this vermin."

Joanna and Bernard were wed a fortnight hence.

Joanna's father, Lord Wyckford, presented himself as the outraged father—angry at his former son-by-law's treatment of his daughter...much to Bernard's disgust. He did not argue when Bernard informed him that he would wed Joanna—for Derkland's lands would be a valuable asset to the lands Wyckford already controlled through his own demesne and those of Swerthmore.

Lady Maris stood witness to the wedding, and Bernard's brother Thomas performed the ceremony. Bernard's other brother, Dirick, was absent from the wedding as he still traveled with the king...but Bernard hid some hope that mayhap he would some day meet Lady Maris of Langumont. She would be more than a challenge for his wild, devil-may-care brother.

After Harmon's death, Joanna slept with a security she'd not known for many years. And when she joined Bernard in their wedding bed, she found beauty and love and peace by his side.

The story of the Derkland brothers
continues in Colleen Gleason's

A Whisper of Rosemary

coming February 2001 from Avid Press!

Dirick of Derkland, man of the king, sets off on a mission of revenge after his father's brutal murder. His mind is bent solely on vengeance until he meets the beautiful Maris of Langumont....

Maris of Langumont has vowed never to wed...but her father must do his duty to protect her, and he promises her to Victor D'Arcy—a man who turns her blood cold.

Bon de Savrille rests his eyes upon Maris only once, and decides she must be his. He whisks her away just before her betrothal ceremony, determined to force her into marriage.

When Dirick appears at the castle where Maris is held captive, she believes he is part of the plot....and 'tis nearly his death she causes during her chance to escape.

Win $100 of free books!

Enter the **Journeys of the Heart** Treasure Hunt Contest!

Search through the stories in **Journeys of the Heart** *to find the answers to the questions below....*

Complete the entry form below and mail to Avid Press by August 31, 2001. All correct entries will be entered in a drawing for a $100 Gift Certificate from Waldenbooks!
(see reverse for mailing instructions and complete rules)

Complete the questions below. No purchase necessary to enter.

1. In *Dream Angel,* in which state does the elephant Matthew Grey plow Arthur Macy's field? _____

2. In *Miss Trixie's Fancy-Man*, where is Miss Trixie's Pleasure Palace? _____

3. In *Passion's Legacy*, where did Maria hide Raci?

_____

4. In *The Mystic's Promise*, what was the name of the mountain range where Sebastian's men were camped? _____

5. In *The Gillyflower Promise*, what was Lady Joanna's cat's name? _____

Name: _____ Phone: _____

Address: _____

City:_____State: _____ Zip: _____

Email address: _____

Journeys of the Heart Treasure Hunt Contest Rules

1. Entries must be postmarked by August 31, 2001 to be eligible for the drawing.

2. Only entries with the correct answers will be entered in the drawing.

3. One entry will be selected from the drawing on September 10, 2001, and the winner will received a gift certificate for $100 to be used at any Waldenbooks store.

4. There is no purchase necessary to win.

5. The entry form may be copied or recreated in any reasonable format to include all necessary information to determine if the entry is correct.

6. Entries must be mailed to:

Avid Press, LLC
5470 Red Fox Drive
Brighton, MI 48114-9079

7, Avid Press employees, authors, artists or their immediate families are not eligible to enter the contest.

8. The winner will be posted on the Avid Press website by September 15, 2001. The website is www.avidpress.com.

9. Winner will be notified by phone, mail, or email.